SF   cop.3
    The Ultimate Darcula

Mountain View Public Library
585 Franklin St
Mountain View, CA 94041-1998
Circulation: (415) 903-6336
Renewal: (415) 903-6885

DEMCO

THE ULTIMATE
Dracula

THE ULTIMATE
Dracula

BYRON PREISS, EDITOR

DAVID KELLER & MEGAN MILLER
ASSOCIATE EDITORS

ILLUSTRATED BY
DAVID JOHNSON
BOOK DESIGN
BY FEARN CUTLER

A BYRON PREISS BOOK

Design: Fearn Cutler

Associate Editors: David Keller, Megan Miller

CONTENTS

THE ULTIMATE
Dracula

HAPPY BIRTHDAY, DRACULA!

▼▼▼

LEONARD WOLF

THERE is probably no film image of fear as widely known and as profoundly frightening as that of the monster Dracula. Into most people's minds, when they hear the name spoken, there rises the image of Bela Lugosi in Tod Browning's 1931 film "Dracula." Nineteen ninety-one marks the sixtieth birthday of that film. It is an occasion for rejoicing.

Universal Pictures' "Dracula," though it has achieved immortality, is far from being a great film. It creaks, it stutters, it splutters. Because it follows the Hamilton Deane–John Balderston play, the film "Dracula" relies too heavily on what, at this distance, seem like corny comic interludes. But what the film has going for it is that it is unforgettable. More than that, it has the main thing: Lugosi's trade-mark rendering of the King Vampire.

The decision to put Lugosi in the title role has to be seen as one of the more brilliant casting choices in the history of film. Harry Ludlam writes:

There could hardly have been another actor with a background more superbly fitted for the role that was to stamp him for a lifetime. . . . Lugosi's cold, sepulchral voice; his deep-socketed, slightly almond-shaped eyes that stabbed out from the screen; his aquiline nose and high cheek-bones;

his commanding height, over six feet, made him seem
at once synonymous with Bram Stoker's fantastic creation.

[A Biography of Dracula, pp. 172–173]

But Lugosi had more than his appearance going for him. To this day, his Hungarian accent invokes all that is sinister to American ears, and the look in those almond eyes of his continues to tell us just how deeply his Dracula understands and is devoted to infinite evil.

With all of its weaknesses, the film has its moments of grandeur among which the opening sequence is surely one of the finest: we watch Renfield (in the novel, it is Jonathan Harker), the callow young English estate-agent, travelling by train to Transylvania and then from Bistritza by coach in search of Castle Dracula. We follow the progress of his coach as it climbs ever higher through a craggy landscape.

Then the camera gives us a glimpse of the castle, followed by a couple of quick cuts in which we see a hand emerging from a coffin; then, in a sort of languid snap shot, we catch a glimpse of the Count and his harem. Now, we cut back to Renfield, whose coach is approaching the Borgo pass. The coach stops; the driver, refusing to go any farther, unceremoniously dumps Renfield's luggage onto the road.

An instant later a coach, with a coachman whose face we cannot make out, appears. It is the Count's coach and Renfield obeys a signal from the coachman to get in. There is a lot of lurching and bouncing as the camera lets us see that there is a bat flapping over the heads of the horses, driving them. By contemporary standards, that bat, fake and fumbling beyond belief, is a pathetic attempt at a special effect.

At the castle, Renfield gets down from the coach. A creaking door opens and he moves to enter the castle while the camera roams over the ancient stonework revealing bats and whole draperies of spiderwebs—as well as a couple of armadillos! Then we hear Lugosi's voice, unctuous and sinister, saying, "I am Dracula," and we have heard the first unmistakable thumping beat of the Heart of Darkness.

And who can forget the delicious moment when Renfield, who has just drunk some of Dracula's fine wine, asks his host, "Aren't you drinking?" The question is followed by a long silence after which Dracula says suavely, and oh so ambiguously, "I do not drink . . . wine."

Another fine moment, unmatched in the subsequent hundreds of Dracula—or Draculesque—films, is the shot of Renfield laughing maniacally as he comes up out of the hold of the ship bringing Dracula to England. That laugh has never been duplicated. It is a "low, low chuckle beginning deep in the bowels and rising unwillingly through stages of pain until it leaves the mouth, bedraggled, helpless, lonely."

Where did that compelling image of the vampire on the screen come from? From what dark corner of history or the human mind did he emerge and how did he come to occupy the commanding place that is now his in the contemporary imagination?

To begin with, there really was a Dracula: a figure of flesh and blood named Vlad Tepes (pronounced Teh-pesh). Vlad, also known as Vlad the Impaler, was a Wallachian prince who ruled his Transylvania princedom at intervals in the years 1448–1476. The very first thing that needs to be said about him is that he was not a vampire. He was an ordinary mortal, with no trace in him of the supernatural. On the other hand, he was, as were many rulers of his age, supremely cruel. And it is his acts of cruelty that have mythologized him.

Vlad was very wicked indeed. His behavior both in defence of his homeland against the Turks and against his own people can only be seen as pathological. He is called "the Impaler," for instance, because of his practice of impaling his victims alive on long stakes and then leaving them to die a slow death. There is a well-known line drawing that shows Vlad at his favorite amusement which was to dine *al fresco* in the midst of a forest of such burdened stakes.

He had other sadistic whimsies. He is said to have executed six hundred merchants because they were too rich. His way of dealing with the problem of beggars in his domains was to invite the beggars to a banquet and then, at the height of the festivities, to set fire to the hall. On another occasion, when a couple of Turkish ambassadors refused to remove their turbans in his presence, he had the turbans nailed to their foreheads.

Ironically enough, Vlad is honored to this day in Romania as a patriotic figure, a symbol of Romanian nationalism, who fought valiantly against his Turkish overlords.

It was the figure of Vlad the Impaler that Bram Stoker, the ambitious Irish theatrical manager and hack writer (1847–1912), came upon in his readings in the British Museum and which he used as the basis for the novel *Dracula* that he published in 1897.

Stoker was fortunate in another way. Transylvania, Vlad's homeland, was (and remains) an intriguing exotic landscape. Transylvania (the name means *The Land Beyond the Forest)* was formerly a Romanian province. It is now divided between southern Hungary and northern Romania. Here is how Stoker, who was never there, describes it:

Beyond the green swelling hills of the Mittel Land rose
mighty slopes of forests up to the lofty steeps of the Carpathians themselves. Right and left of us they towered, with
the afternoon sun falling full upon them and bringing
out all the glorious colours of this beautiful range, deep blue
and purple in the shadows of the peaks, green and brown
where grass and rock mingled and an endless perspective of
jagged rock and pointed crags, till these were themselves
lost in the distance, where the snowy peaks rose grandly.

Stoker's imaginary landscape is considerably more imposing than the
real thing. Transylvania does indeed have mountains and rushing
streams, but a traveller who has not had his or her expectations super-
charged by a reading of Stoker will find the real landscape benignly
beautiful. Life in the towns and villages of Transylvania has considerably
more snap and vitality than one finds in the rest of Romania. What is
chiefly missing in contemporary Transylvania is either much interest in,
or knowledge of vampires.

Stoker, however, was the beneficiary of a fine amateur study of Transylvanian folklore written by an indefatigable traveller, Emily Gerard.
Gerard, married to a Romanian army officer, had a keen eye for detail
and an attentive ear. Her book, *The Land Beyond the Forest* (1888),
provided Stoker with the sorts of details a novelist needs to create verisi-
militude. *The Land Beyond the Forest* is charming for its own sake and it
continues to be indispensable for any student of Transylvania, of Stoker,
or of vampire lore.

In the quiet confines of the British Museum, Stoker found the raw
materials he needed for his fiction: a wicked nobleman, a country with a
wild and exotic landscape and a bizarre folk tradition about vampires.
He was ready to begin.

But first, because *Dracula* is a novel in the Gothic tradition, a few
words about that literary genre may be useful.

The Gothic novel, so-called from the pervasive use by its authors of
medieval stone locales (monasteries, convents, cemeteries, castles, ruins)
enters English literature in the eighteenth century when Horace Walpole, in 1764, published his *The Castle of Otranto*.

Walpole, a middle-aged neurasthenic with a passion for medieval bric-
a-brac that he housed in a fanciful structure of his own called Strawberry Hill, is usually credited with imposing on the genre its characteristic themes and design. *The Castle of Otranto* has, as Harry Ludlam has
observed,

doors with rusty hinges, a trapdoor, and lamps extinguish-
able in a wink. It had a superb villain in Manfred, who,
discovering his only son dead on his wedding morning—
dashed to pieces beneath an enormous helmet—determined to marry his son's bride, Isabella, so that his line
should not become extinct. His own wife, Hippolita, he
planned to confine in a convent.

The Castle of Otranto is not what contemporary readers and hasty
reviewers would call a good read. Its plot is frequently ridiculous and it
lacks character development. Just the same, it is an enduring landmark
on the landscape of literary history, and no one really interested in scary
fiction can afford to overlook it.

Ann Radcliffe's The Mysteries of Udolpho (1794), and her even better
The Italian (1797) are altogether more accomplished works which display all the characteristic marks of Gothic fiction. Each of them has a
beautiful heroine of impeccable sensibility who is pursued by a tall, dark
villain who intends to do her (primarily sexual) harm. To avoid a fate
worse than death, the heroine flies from the villain and her flight takes
her through a variety of dark, dismal and perilous places from which, at
the penultimate moment, she is rescued by a handsome, well-bred and
sexually unthreatening young man.

Radcliffe's novels are frightening despite her reliance on stereotyped
characters and her unfortunate habit of de-mystifying her mysteries.
What makes her stories work is the tension between her impeccable
prose and the sexual horrors that are her real theme. We cannot quite
shake the sense that "reason maintained in the presence of [so much
depravity] can only be the face of madness frozen into a semblance of
logic." (A Dream of Dracula, p. 157)

If the demon of incest is the horror glimpsed behind the decorous veil
of Radcliffe's prose, it prances before us unashamed and undisguised in
Matthew Lewis's The Monk (1796). Written in a ten-week rush, The
Monk has all the urgency of an adolescent's vision of a sexual apocalypse
as Lewis chronicles for us the progress to damnation of his master creation, Friar Ambrosio.

We follow Ambrosio, a thirty-year-old monk who is a paragon of
virtue, as, step by step, he learns to do the devil's work. His malefic
career begins with rape, moves through matricide and incest and ends in
a terrific scene in the desert where the devil comes to collect Ambrosio's
immortal soul. The demon grasps Ambrosio's skull in one of his claws
and, flying upward, drops the monk from so appalling a height that

". . . the caves and mountains rang with Ambrosio's shrieks . . ."
Ambrosio's body is battered among rocks, and is bruised by the rushing
waters of the river below. He takes a long time dying as Lewis orches-
trates the delay so that readers, who have been aching for Ambrosio to
get his just deserts, can savour the retribution he has earned.

Charles Maturin's *Melmoth the Wanderer* (1820) is probably the
greatest of the early Gothic fictions. Miltonic in the grandeur of its
conception, *Melmoth* is an extraordinary tapestry in which is depicted a
full range of the ways in which mankind can be a beast to man. Edith
Birkhead, in *The Tale of Terror*, (p. 87) writes of *Melmoth:* "We are
presented with sybils and misers, parricides, maniacs in abundance,
monks with scourges pursuing a naked youth streaming with blood;
subterranean Jews surrounded by the skeletons of their wives and children; lovers blasted by lightning . . ." And much much more. The
novel is an elaboration of "the best theology—the theology of utter hostility to all beings whose sufferings may mitigate mine." As Maturin
makes clear, with a theology like that, there is no need to search for hell.
It is precisely beneath our feet.

Curiously enough, there are hardly any images of vampires in early
Gothic fiction. The first vampire of note appears in John Polidori's
novel, *The Vampyre: A Tale* (1819). Polidori, Byron's lover and physician, lived a short unhappy life and died a suicide at the age of twenty-
six. *The Vampyre* is a wooden fiction without much literary merit. It
does, however, give us the prototypical image of the nobleman vampire.
His Lord Ruthven "was aloof, brilliant, chilling, fascinating to women,
and cooly evil." *(A Dream of Dracula,* p. 163). The problem with
Polidori's novel is that, unable himself to feel the power of the image he
has invoked, he cannot create a prose exciting enough to engage his
reader. The result is a work with the trappings of fear which moves, us,
if it does at all, to a polite yawn.

Varney the Vampire (1847), on the other hand, is one of the world's
most wonderful badly written books. Forget literature; forget prose style,
forget characterization and settle for action, action, action, much of it
violent and on occasion so prurient that it borders on pornography.
James Malcolm Rymer's Varney is gorgeously bloodthirsty: "I was . . .
ruminating what I should do, until a strange feeling crept over me that I
should like—what? Blood!—raw blood, reeking and hot, bubbling and
juicy, from the veins of some gasping victim." Varney's victims, one
should say, are mostly voluptuous young women described in the full
incandescence of their semi-clad nudity.

Let there be no mistake. *Varney* is not a work of literature. No insights about life wait for its reader, no pre-existential cosmic vision is developed, no perception of the nature of humankind illuminates its pages. But if one likes inventive penny-a-line fiction, then *Varney the Vampire* is still a wonderful way to waste a rainy afternoon.

Carmilla (1872), Sheridan Le Fanu's fine vampire novel (or long short story) is closest in time and in quality to Bram Stoker's *Dracula*. While it is limited in its scope, it is a worthy predecessor to Stoker's masterpiece and is more likely than any of the fictions mentioned above to have influenced it.

Le Fanu, one of the finest terror writers of his age, gives us a sculptured, jewel-like fiction, in which female friendship, loneliness, sexual hunger, and vampire blood-thirstiness are intricately intertwined in a convincing portrait of a female vampire who feeds on the beautiful and innocent young woman who loves her.

▼▼▼

Let me return now to Bram Stoker and the making of *Dracula*. On the face of it, what we have is a pretty standard Victorian adventure novel, complete with heroic young men, virtuous and beautiful young women, and a suitably wicked villain.

Dracula, however, has greater specific gravity than most adventure fictions because of the way that its plot imitates a chivalric romance. Let's look at our cast of characters: Jonathan Harker, John Seward, Lord Godalming and Quincey Morris form a band of questing knights who are tested in their confrontation with evil. Dr. Van Helsing is the Merlin figure—the wise old man who knows the deep secrets needed to triumph over the dragon and who guides the young men on their quest. Dracula (whose name can also mean Son of the Dragon) is, of course, the dragon himself. As for the young women, Mina Murray (later Harker) and Lucy Westenra, they are the endangered maidens who must be rescued from the dragon's power.

The novel, then, can be read with considerable pleasure as an adventure story which has resemblances to chivalric romance, and I would argue that Stoker was aware of and took pride in his achievement thus far. *Dracula,* however, would hardly be the tremendous fiction that it is if that was all we got. To discern what more there is, we have to see in the novel the sexual allegory that hovers just below the surface of the action.

Sexuality, not love, not chivalric pilgrimages or heroism or high adventure, is the heart of the matter. To get at the ways that Stoker, intuitively if unconsciously, manipulated his materials to create that allegory requires me to remind my readers of a distinction Carl Jung made between what he called the psychological novel and the visionary novel.

He tells us that "the psychological mode deals with materials drawn from the realm of human consciousness . . . Everything that it embraces belongs to the realm of the understandable."

The visionary novel, on the other hand, deals with material "that is no longer familiar . . . that derives its existence from the hinterland of man's mind—that suggests the abyss of time separating us from pre-human ages . . . a primordial experience which surpasses man's understanding, and to which he is therefore in danger of succumbing." The psychological novel, we would say, is one in which the author undertakes to understand human behaviour within the framework of human reason while the visionary fiction, as Jung puts it, would reveal "a disturbing vision of monstrous and meaningless happenings that in every way exceed the grasp of human feeling and comprehension . . ."

Dracula is the visionary novel par excellence, though I think Stoker, who was more comfortable with the Victorian pieties his characters speak, would be baffled by such a characterization of his work. Still, his writer's instincts were fine enough so that they put themselves in the service of his unconscious. The result is *Dracula.*

If we see the book as a visionary novel in Jung's sense, a wholly new story emerges. We still have the chivalric band of young men, and the wise old man instructing the novices. The innocent and endangered young women are in place, as is the dragon. What they are all up to, however, is a deeper, darker story even than the encounter between civilized English gentlemen defending their women against a decadent central-European vampire.

Let us look briefly at a couple of scenes.

Early in the novel, Jonathan Harker, wandering through Dracula's castle, comes to a room in which he has been expressly warned not to fall asleep. The room, Harker tells us, feels as if it had once been a boudoir. Deliberately disregarding the Count's warning, Harker lies down on a couch and dozes off. When he wakes, he finds that there are three beautiful pale women crouched beside his couch. "All three had brilliant white teeth, that shone like pearls against the ruby of their voluptuous lips . . . I felt in my heart a wicked, burning desire that they would kiss me with those red lips . . ." Harker, instead of leaping from his couch and demanding to know who the women are and what they want, reports that he lies there "quiet, looking out under my eyelashes in an agony of delightful anticipation."

The whole scene encompassing the supine Harker who "closed [his] eyes in a langorous ecstacy and waited," the crouched women licking their lips, and, finally, the favored woman bending "lower and lower," has a breathless prurience. It is a scene, too, that gives us an ambiguous signal as it links eroticism with death.

Dracula, too, is dead. What we learn over the course of the novel is that Dracula is the wise teacher of the women, Lucy Westenra and Minna Harker, in the same way that Dr. Van Helsing is the counsellor to the men. His "kiss" renders the women voluptuous. Lucy, for instance, on the morning after Dracula has first sated himself on her blood at Whitby, is described as having "slept . . . [so hard she] seemed not to have even changed her side. The adventure of the night does not seem to have harmed her; on the contrary, it has benefited her, for she looks better this morning than she has done for weeks." And when, finally, Lucy dies, we learn that "some change had come over her body. Death had given back part of her beauty . . . she was, if possible, more radiantly beautiful than ever."

In an amazing scene in the churchyard where Lucy has been buried, the un-dead Lucy encounters the chivalric band, including Lord Godalming her fiancé. She is described as alert, catlike, powerful: "The sweetness was turned to adamantine, heartless cruelty, and the purity to voluptuous wantonness . . . her eyes ranged over us . . . Lucy's eyes unclean and full of hell-fire, . . . blazed with unholy light, and the face became wreathed with a voluptuous smile." She calls to Arthur, "with outstretched arms and a wanton smile . . . and with a languorous voluptuous grace . . ."

All that languor, all that voluptuousness, has to be stopped. And Doctor Van Helsing teaches the men how to stop it. An oak stake, three feet long, sharpened to a point and hardened in the fire, is handed over to Lucy's fiancé Lord Godalming, who, while his comrades recite prayers around him, places the point of the stake over the bosom of his bride-to-be. Then, wielding a coal-breaking hammer with his right hand, he becomes "a figure like Thor as his untrembling arm rose and fell, driving deeper and deeper the mercy-bearing stake, whilst the blood from the pierced heart welled and spurted up around it." At last, there is silence in the tomb, and on Lucy's face, "a holy calm . . . like sunshine . . ."

The message from the abyss is clear: there is a dark vitality abroad in the world. It is a force that Stoker has embodied in Dracula who seeks life; demands life; absorbs and consumes life. When that force infects women, they become languorous, voluptuous, sexually demanding, unbridled and irresistibly attractive. They are, therefore, dangerous to men whose vitality they will sap, rendering them weak and flaccid. The final message is, they must be controlled.

But it is not merely male-female sexuality that the image of Dracula adumbrates. Readers and film viewers alike have recognized that the vampiric blood exchange stands for forbidden intimacy. All sorts of intimacy and not just that between men and women. The triumphant power of the Dracula image is that it incorporates them all: male and female homosexuality as well as every permutation and combination of incest.

It is a suave power the films possess permitting us to peer into hidden recesses of the mind even as we get to deny the meaning of the embraces taking place on the screen. What have we seen, after all, but another vampire film?

Birthdays are occasions for reflection. On the sixtieth anniversary of Universal Pictures' 1931 *Dracula* we may reflect on our good fortune that Dracula's screen history got off to such an auspicious start. But Dracula has continued fortunate in his interpreters. If Lugosi imprinted him on our imaginations first, Christopher Lee and Frank Langella have enlarged him for us. Lee has given us the chilly, imperious Dracula, while Langella has made overt and attractive his sexual power.

What seems inevitable now as the century ends is that there will always be a Dracula spreading his shadow on the silver screen. And that's as it should be. However masked his message is, we need this visitor from the Abyss to remind us that there will always be "primordial experiences which surpass man's understanding and to which therefore he is in danger of succumbing."

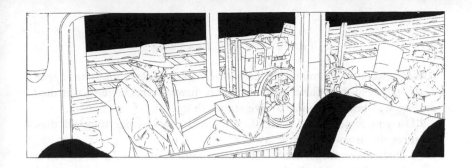

THE MASTER
OF RAMPLING GATE
▼▼▼

ANNE RICE

RAMPLING Gate: It was so real to us in those old pictures, rising like a fairytale castle out of its own dark wood. A wilderness of gables and chimneys between those two immense towers, grey stone walls mantled in ivy, mullioned windows reflecting the drifting clouds.

But why had Father never gone there? Why had he never taken us? And why on his deathbed, in those grim months after Mother's passing, did he tell my brother, Richard, that Rampling Gate must be torn down stone by stone? Rampling Gate that had always belonged to Ramplings, Rampling Gate which had stood for over four hundred years.

We were in awe of the task that lay before us, and painfully confused. Richard had just finished four years at Oxford. Two whirlwind social seasons in London had proven me something of a shy success. I still preferred scribbling poems and stories in the quiet of my room to dancing the night away, but I'd kept that a good secret, and though we were not spoilt children, we had enjoyed the best of everything our parents could give. But now the carefree years were ended. We had to be careful and wise.

And our hearts ached as, sitting together in Father's booklined study, we looked at the old pictures of Rampling Gate before the small coal fire. "Destroy it, Richard, as soon as I am gone," Father had said.

"I just don't understand it, Julie," Richard confessed, as he filled the little crystal glass in my hand with sherry. "It's the genuine article, that old place, a real fourteenth-century manor house in excellent repair. A

Mrs. Blessington, born and reared in the village of Rampling, has apparently managed it all these years. She was there when Uncle Baxter died, and he was last Rampling to live under that roof."

"Do you remember," I asked, "the year that Father took all these pictures down and put them away?"

"I shall never forget that?" Richard said. "How could I? It was so peculiar, and so unlike Father, too." He sat back, drawing slowly on his pipe. "There had been that bizarre incident in Victoria Station, when he had seen that young man."

"Yes, exactly," I said, snuggling back into the velvet chair and looking into the tiny dancing flames in the grate. "You remember how upset Father was?"

Yet it was simple incident. In fact nothing really happened at all. We couldn't have been more than six and eight at the time and we had gone to the station with Father to say farewell to friends. Through the window of a train Father saw a young man who startled and upset him. I could remember the face clearly to this day. Remarkably handsome, with a narrow nose and well drawn eyebrows, and a mop of lustrous brown hair. The large black eyes had regarded Father with the saddest expression as Father had drawn us back and hurried us away.

"And the argument that night, between Father and Mother," Richard said thoughtfully. "I remember that we listened on the landing and we were so afraid."

"And Father said *he* wasn't content to be master of Rampling Gate anymore; *he* had come to London and revealed himself. An unspeakable horror, that is what he called it, that *he* should be so bold."

"Yes, exactly, and when Mother tried to quiet him, when she suggested that he was imagining things, he went into a perfect rage."

"But who could it have been, the master of Rampling Gate, if Father wasn't the master? Uncle Baxter was long dead by then."

"I just don't know what to make of it," Richard murmured. "And there's nothing in Father's papers to explain any of it at all." He examined the most recent of the pictures, a lovely tinted engraving that showed the house perfectly reflected in the azure water of its lake. "But I tell you, the worst part of it, Julie," he said shaking his head, "is that we've never even seen the house ourselves."

I glanced at him and our eyes met in a moment of confusion that quickly passed to something else. I leant forward:

"He did not say we couldn't go there, did he, Richard?" I demanded. "That we couldn't visit the house before it was destroyed."

"No, of course he didn't!" Richard said. The smile broke over his face easily. "After all, don't we owe to the others, Julie? Uncle Baxter who spent the last of his fortune restoring the house, even this old Mrs. Blessington that has kept it all these years?

"And what about the village itself?" I added quickly. "What will it mean to these people to see Rampling Gate destroyed? Of course we must go and see the place ourselves."

"Then it's settled. I'll write to Mrs. Blessington immediately. I'll tell her we're coming and that we can not say how long we will stay."

"Oh, Richard, that would be too marvelous!" I couldn't keep from hugging him, though it flustered him and he pulled on his pipe just exactly the way Father would have done. "Make it at least a fortnight," I said. "I want so to know the place, especially if . . ."

But it was too sad to think of Father's admonition. And much more fun to think of the journey itself. I'd pack my manuscripts, for who knew, maybe in that melancholy and exquisite setting I'd find exactly the inspiration I required. It was almost a wicked exhilaration I felt, breaking the gloom that had hung over us since the day that Father was laid to rest.

"It is the right thing to do, isn't it, Richard?" I asked uncertainly, a little disconcerted by how much I wanted to go. There was some illicit pleasure in it, going to Rampling Gate at last.

" 'Unspeakable horror,' " I repeated Father's words with a little grimace. What did it all mean? I thought again of the strange, almost exquisite young man I'd glimpsed in that railway carriage, gazing at us all with that wistful expression on his lean face. He had worn a black greatcoat with a red woollen cravat, and I could remember how pale he had been against that dash of red. Like bone china his complexion had been. Strange to remember it so vividly, even to the tilt of his head, and that long luxuriant brown hair. But he had been a blaze against that window. And I realized now that, in those few remarkable moments, he had created for me an ideal of masculine beauty which I had never questioned since. But Father had been so angry in those moments . . . I felt an unmistakable pang of guilt.

"Of course it's the right thing, Julie," Richard answered. He at the desk, already writing the letters, and I was at a loss to understand the full measure of my thoughts.

▼▼▼

It was late afternoon when the wretched old trap carried us up the gentle slope from the little railway station, and we had at last our first real look at that magnificent house. I think I was holding my breath. The sky had paled to a deep rose hue beyond a bank of softly gilded clouds, and the last rays of the sun struck the uppermost panes of the leaded windows and filled them with solid gold.

"Oh, but it's too majestic," I whispered, "too like a great cathedral, and to think that it belongs to us." Richard gave me the smallest kiss on the cheek. I felt mad suddenly and eager somehow to be laid waste by it, through fear or enchantment I could not say, perhaps a sublime mingling of both.

I wanted with all my heart to jump down and draw near on foot, letting those towers grow larger and larger above me, but our old horse had picked up speed. And the little line of stiff starched servants had broken to come forward, the old withered housekeeper with her arms out, the men to take down the boxes and the trunks.

Richard and I were spirited into the great hall by the tiny, nimble figure of Mrs. Blessington, our footfalls echoing loudly on the marble tile, our eyes dazzled by the dusty shafts of light that fell on the long oak table and its heavily carved chairs, the sombre, heavy tapestries that stirred ever so slightly against the soaring walls.

"It is an enchanted place," I cried, unable to contain myself. "Oh, Richard, we are home!" Mrs. Blessington laughed gaily, her dry hand closing tightly on mine.

Her small blue eyes regarded me with the most curiously vacant expression despite her smile. "Ramplings at Rampling Gate again, I can not tell you what a joyful day this is for me. And yes, my dear," she said as if reading my mind that very second, "I am and have been for many years, quite blind. But if you spy a thing out of place in this house, you're to tell me at once, for it would be the exception, I assure you, and not the rule." And such warmth emanated from her wrinkled little face that I adored her at once.

We found our bedchambers, the very finest in the house, well aired with snow white linen and fires blazing cozily to dry out the damp that never left the thick walls. The small diamond pane windows opened on a glorious view of the water and the oaks that enclosed it and the few scattered lights that marked the village beyond.

That night, we laughed like children as we supped at the great oak table, our candles giving only a feeble light. And afterwards, it was a fierce battle of pocket billiards in the game room which had been Uncle Baxter's last renovation, and a little too much brandy, I fear.

It was just before I went to bed that I asked Mrs. Blessington if there had been anyone in this house since Uncle Baxter died. That had been the year 1838, almost fifty years ago, and she was already housekeeper then.

"No, my dear," she said quickly, fluffing the feather pillows. "Your father came that year as you know, but he stayed for no more than a month or two and then went on home."

"There was never a young man after that . . ." I pushed, but in truth I had little appetite for anything to disturb the happiness I felt. How I loved the Spartan cleanliness of this bedchamber, the stone walls bare of paper or ornament, the high luster of the walnut-paneled bed.

"A young man?" She gave an easy, almost hearty laugh as with unerring certainty of her surroundings, she lifted the poker and stirred the fire. "What a strange thing for you to ask."

I sat silent for a moment looking in the mirror, as I took the last of the pins from my hair. It fell down heavy and warm around my shoulders. It felt good, like a cloak under which I could hide. But she turned as if sensing some uneasiness in me, and drew near.

"Why do you say a young man, Miss?" she asked. Slowly, tentatively, her fingers examined the long tresses that lay over my shoulders. She took the brush from my hands.

I felt perfectly foolish telling her the story, but I managed a simplified version, somehow, our meeting unexpectedly a devilishly handsome young man whom my Father in anger had later called the master of Rampling Gate.

"Handsome, was he?" she asked as she brushed out the tangles in my hair gently. It seemed she hung upon every word as I described him again.

"There were no intruders in this house, then, Mrs. Blessington?" I asked. "No mysteries to be solved . . ."

She gave the sweetest laugh.

"Oh, no, darling, this house is the safest place in the world," she said quickly. "It is a happy house. No intruder would dare to trouble Rampling Gate!"

Nothing, in fact, troubled the serenity of the days that followed. The smoke and noise of London, and our Father's dying words, became a dream. What was real were our long walks together through the overgrown gardens, our trips in the little skiff to and fro across the lake. We had tea under the hot glass of the empty conservatory. And early evening found us on our way upstairs with the best of the books from Uncle Baxter's library to read by candlelight in the privacy of our rooms.

And all our discreet inquiries in the village met with more or less the same reply: the villagers loved the house and carried no old or disquieting tales. Repeatedly, in fact, we were told that Rampling was the most contented hamlet in all England, that no one dared—Mrs. Blessington's very words—to make trouble here.

"It's our guardian angel, that old house," said the old woman at the bookshop where Richard stopped for the London papers. "Was there ever the town of Rampling without the house called Rampling Gate?"

How were we going to tell them of Father's edict? How were we going to remind ourselves? But we spoke not one word about the proposed disaster, and Richard wrote to his firm to say that we should not be back in London till Fall.

He was finding a wealth of classical material in the old volumes that had belonged to Uncle Baxter, and I had set up my writing in the little study that opened off the library which I had all to myself.

Never had I known such peace and quiet. It seemed the atmosphere of Rampling Gate permeated my simplest written descriptions and wove its way richly into the plots and characters I created. The Monday after our arrival I had finished my first short story and went off to the village on foot to boldly post it to editors of *Blackwood's Magazine.*

It was a glorious morning, and I took my time as I came back on foot.

What had disturbed our father so about this lovely corner of England, I wondered? What had so darkened his last hours that he laid upon this spot his curse?

My heart opened to this unearthly stillness, to an undeniable grandeur that caused me utterly to forget myself. There were times here when I felt I was a disembodied intellect drifting through a fathomless silence, up and down garden paths and stone corridors that had witnessed too much to take cognizance of one small and fragile young woman who in random moments actually talked aloud to the suits of armour around her, to the broken statues in the garden, the fountain cherubs who had had not water to pour from their conches for years and years.

But was there in this loveliness some malignant force that was eluding us still, some untold story to explain all? Unspeakable horror . . . In my mind's eye I saw that young man, and the strangest sensation crept over me, that some enrichment of the picture had taken place in my memory or imagination in the recent past. Perhaps in dream I had reinvented him, given a ruddy glow to his lips and his cheeks. Perhaps in my re-creation for Mrs. Blessington, I had allowed him to raise his hand to that red cravat and had seen the fingers long and delicate and suggestive of a musician's hand.

It was all very much on my mind when I entered the house again, soundlessly, and saw Richard in his favorite leather wing chair by the fire.

The air was warm coming through the open garden doors, and yet the blaze was cheerful, made the vast room with its towering shelves of leatherbound volumes appear inviting and almost small.

"Sit down," Richard said gravely, scarcely giving me a glance. "I want to read you something right now." He held a long narrow ledger in his hands. "This was Uncle Baxter's," he said, "and at first I thought it was only an account book he kept during the renovations, but I've found some actual diary entries made in the last weeks of his life. They're hasty, almost indecipherable, but I've managed to make them out."

"Well, do read them to me," I said, but I felt a little tug of fear. I didn't want to know anything terrible about this place. If we could have remained here forever . . . but that was out of the question, to be sure.

"Now listen to this," Richard said, turning the page carefully. " 'Fifth of May, 1838: He is here, I am sure of it. He is come back again.' And several days later: 'He thinks this is his house, he does, and he would drink my wine and smoke my cigars if only he could. He reads my books and my papers and I will not stand for it. I have given orders that everything is to be locked.' And finally, the last entry written the morning before he died: 'Weary, weary, unto death and he is no small cause of my weariness. Last night I beheld him with my own eyes. He stood in this very room. He moves and speaks exactly as a mortal man, and dares tell me his secrets, and he a demon wretch with the face of a seraph and I a mere mortal, how am I to bear with him!' "

"Good Lord," I whispered slowly. I rose from the chair where I had settled, and standing behind him, read the page for myself. It was the scrawl the writing, the very last notation in the book. I knew that Uncle Baxter's heart had given out. He had not died by violence, but peacefully enough in this very room with his prayer book in his hand.

"Could it be the very same person Father spoke of that night?" Richard asked.

In spite of the sun pouring through the open doors, I experienced a violent chill. For the first time I felt wary of this house, wary of our boldness in coming here, heedful of our Father's words.

"But that was years before, Richard . . ." I said. "And what could this mean, this talk of a supernatural being! Surely the man was mad! It was no spirit I saw in that railway carriage!"

I sank down into the chair opposite and tried to quiet the beating of my heart.

"Julie," Richard said gently, shutting the ledger. "Mrs. Blessington has lived here contentedly for years. There are six servants asleep every night in the north wing. Surely there is nothing to all of this."

"It isn't very much fun, though, is it?" I said timidly, "not at all like swapping ghost stories the way we used to do, and peopling the dark with imaginary beings, and laughing at friends at school who were afraid."

"All my life," he said, his eyes fixing me steadily, "I've heard tales of spooks and spirits, some imagined, some supposedly true, and almost invariably there is some mention of the house in question feeling haunted, of having an atmosphere to it that fills one with foreboding, some sense of menace or alarm . . ."

"Yes, I know, and there is no such poisonous atmosphere here at all."

"On the contrary, I've never been more at ease in my life." He shoved his hand into his pocket to extract the inevitable match to light his pipe which had gone out. "As a matter of fact, Julie, I don't know how in the world I'm going to comply with Father's last wish to tear down this place."

I nodded sympathetically. The very same thing had been on my mind since we'd arrived. Even now, I felt so comfortable, natural, quite safe.

I was wishing suddenly, irrationally, that he had not found the entries in Uncle Baxter's book.

"I should talk to Mrs. Blessington again!" I said almost crossly, "I mean quite seriously . . ."

"But I have, Julie," he said. "I asked her about it all this morning when I first made the discovery, and she only laughed. She swears she's never seen anything unusual here, and that there's no one left alive in the village who can tell tales of this place. She said again how glad she was that we'd come home to Rampling Gate. I don't think she has an inkling we mean to destroy the house. Oh, it would destroy her heart if she did."

"Never seen anything unusual?" I asked. "That is what she said? But what strange words for her to use, Richard, when she can not see at all."

But he had not heard me. He had laid the ledger aside and risen slowly, almost sluggishly, and he was wandering out of the double doors into the little garden and was looking over the high hedge at the oaks that bent their heavy elbowed limbs almost to the surface of the lake. There wasn't a sound at this early hour of the day, save the soft rustle of the leaves in the moving air, the cry now and then of a distant bird.

"Maybe it's gone, Julie," Richard said, over his shoulder, his voice carrying clearly in the quiet, "if it was ever here. Maybe there is nothing any longer to frighten anyone at all. You don't suppose you could endure the winter in this house, do you? I suppose you'd want to be in London again by then." He seemed quite small against the towering trees, the sky broken into small gleaming fragments by the canopy of foliage that gently filtered the light.

Rampling Gate had him. And I understood perfectly, because it also had me. I could very well endure the winter here, no matter how bleak or cold. I never wanted to go home.

And the immediacy of the mystery only dimmed my sense of everything and every place else.

After a long moment, I rose and went out into the garden, and placed my hand gently on Richard's arm.

"I know this much, Julie," he said just as if we had been talking to each other all the while. "I swore to Father that I would do as he asked, and it is tearing me apart. Either way, it will be on my conscience for ever, obliterating this house or going against my own father and the charge he laid down to me with his dying breath."

"We must seek help, Richard. The advice of our lawyers, the advice of Father's clergymen. You must write to them and explain the whole thing. Father was feverish when he gave the order. If we could lay it out before them, they would help us decide."

▼▼▼

It was three o'clock when I opened my eyes. But I had been awake for a long time. I had heard the dim chimes of the clock below hour by hour. And I felt not fear lying here alone in the dark but something else. Some vague and relentless agitation, some sense of emptiness and need that caused me finally to rise from my bed. What was required to dissolve this tension, I wondered. I stared at the simplest things in the shadows. The little arras that hung over the fireplace with its slim princes and princesses lost in fading fiber and thread. The portrait of an Elizabethan ancestor gazing with one almond-shaped eye from his small frame.

What was this house, really? Merely a place or a state of mind? What was it doing to my soul? Why didn't the entries in Uncle Baxter's book send us flying back to London? Why had we stayed so late in the great hall together after supper, speaking not a single word?

I felt overwhelmed suddenly, and yet shut out of some great and dazzling secret, and wasn't that the very word that Uncle Baxter had used?

Conscious only of an unbearable restlessness, I pulled on my woollen wrapper, buttoning the lace collar and tying the sash. And putting on my slippers, I went out into the hall.

The moon fell full on the oak stairway, and on the deeply recessed door to Richard's room. On tiptoe I approached and, peering in, saw the bed was empty, the covers completely undisturbed.

So he was off on his own tonight the same as I. Oh, if only he had come to me, asked me to go with him.

I turned and made my way soundlessly down the long stairs.

The great hall gaped like a cavern before me, the moonlight here and there touching upon a pair of crossed swords, or a mounted shield. But far beyond the great hall, in the alcove just outside the library, I saw unmistakably a flickering light. And a breeze moved briskly through the room, carrying with it the sound and the scent of a wood fire.

I shuddered with relief. Richard was there. We could talk. Or perhaps we could go exploring together, guarding our fragile candle flames behind cupped fingers as we went from room to room? A sense of well-being pervaded me and quieted me, and yet the dark distance between us seemed endless, and I was desperate to cross it, hurrying suddenly past the long supper table with its massive candlesticks, and finally into the alcove before the library doors.

Yes, Richard was there. He sat with his eyes closed, dozing against the inside of the leather wing chair, the breeze from the garden blowing the fragile flames of the candles on the stone mantel and on the table at his side.

I was about to go to him, about to shut the doors, and kiss him gently and ask did he not want to go up to bed, when quite abruptly I saw in the corner of my eye that there was some one else in the room.

In the far left corner at the desk stood another figure, looking down at the clutter of Richard's papers, his pale hands resting on the wood.

I knew that it could not be so. I knew that I must be dreaming, that nothing in this room, least of all this figure, could be real. For it was the same young man I had seen fifteen years ago in the railway carriage and not a single aspect of that taut young face had been changed. There was the very same hair, thick and lustrous and only carelessly combed as it hung to the thick collar of his black coat, and the skin so pale it was almost luminous in the shadows, and those dark eyes looking up suddenly and fixing me with the most curious expression as I almost screamed.

We stared at one another across the dark vista of that room, I stranded in the doorway, he visibly and undeniably shaken that I had caught him unawares. My heart stopped.

And in a split second he moved towards me, closed the gap between us, towering over me, those slender white fingers gently closing on my arms.

"Julie!" he whispered, in a voice so low it seemed my own thoughts speaking to me. But this was no dream. He was real. He was holding to me and the scream had broken loose from me, deafening, uncontrollable and echoing from the four walls.

I saw Richard rising from the chair. I was alone. Clutching to the door frame, I staggered forward, and then again in a moment of perfect clarity I saw the young intruder, saw him standing in the garden, looking back over his shoulder, and then he was gone.

I could not stop screaming. I could not stop even as Richard held me and pleaded with me, and sat me down in the chair.

And I was still crying when Mrs. Blessington finally came.

She got a glass of cordial for me at once, as Richard begged me once more to tell what I had seen.

"But you know who it was!" I said to Richard almost hysterically. "It was he, the young man from the train. Only he wore a frockcoat years out of fashion and his silk tie was open at his throat. Richard, he was reading your papers, turning them over, reading them in the pitch dark."

"All right," Richard said, gesturing with his hand up for calm. "He was standing at the desk. And there was no light there so you could not see him well."

"Richard, it was he! Don't you understand? He touched me, he held my arms." I looked imploringly to Mrs. Blessington who was shaking her head, her little eyes like blue beads in the light. "He called me Julie," I whispered. "He knows my name!"

I rose, snatching up the candle, and all but pushing Richard out of the way went to the desk. "Oh, dear God," I said, "Don't you see what's happened? It's your letters to Dr. Partridge, and Mrs. Sellers, about tearing down the house!"

Mrs. Blessington gave a little cry and put her hand to her cheek. She looked like a withered child in her nightcap as she collapsed into the straight-backed chair by the door.

"Surely you don't believe it was the same man, Julie, after all these years . . ."

"But he had not changed, Richard, not in the smallest detail. There is no mistake, Richard, it was he, I tell you, the very same."

"Oh, dear, dear . . ." Mrs. Blessington whispered, "What will he do if you try to tear it down? What will he do now?"

"What will who do?" Richard asked carefully, narrowing his eyes. He took the candle from me and approached her. I was staring at her, only half realizing what I had heard.

"So you know who he is!" I whispered.

"Julie, stop it!" Richard said.

But her face had tightened, gone blank and her eyes had become distant and small.

"You knew he was here!" I insisted. "You must tell us at once!"

With an effort she climbed to her feet. "There is nothing in this house to hurt *you*," she said, "nor any of us." She turned, spurning Richard as he tried to help her, and wandered into the dark hallway alone. "You've no need of me here any longer," she said softly, "and if you should tear down this house built by your forefathers, then you should do it without need of me."

"Oh, but we don't mean to do it, Mrs. Blessington!" I insisted. But she was making her way through the gallery back towards the north wing. "Go after her, Richard. You heard what she said. She knows who he is."

"I've had quite enough of this tonight," Richard said almost angrily. "Both of us should go up to bed. By the light of day we will dissect this entire matter and search this house. Now come."

"But he should be told, shouldn't he?" I demanded.

"Told what? Of whom do you speak!"

"Told that we will not tear down this house!" I said clearly, loudly, listening to the echo of my own voice.

▼▼▼

The next day was indeed the most trying since we had come. It took the better part of the morning to convince Mrs. Blessington that we had no intention of tearing down Rampling Gate. Richard posted his letters and resolved that we should do nothing until help came.

And together we commenced a search of the house. But darkness found us only half finished, having covered the south tower and the south wing, and the main portion of house itself. There remained still the north tower, in a dreadful state of disrepair, and some rooms beneath the ground which in former times might have served as dungeons and were now sealed off. And there were closets and private stairways everywhere that we had scarce looked into, and at times we lost all track of where precisely we had been.

But it was also quite clear by supper time that Richard was in a state of strain and exasperation, and that he did not believe that I had seen anyone in the study at all.

He was further convinced that Uncle Baxter had been mad before he died, or else his ravings were a code for some mundane happening that had him extraordinarily overwrought.

But I knew what I had seen. And as the day progressed, I became ever more quiet and withdrawn. A silence had fallen between me and Mrs. Blessington. And I understood only too well the anger I'd heard in my father's voice on that long ago night when we had come home from Victoria Station and my mother had accused him of imagining things.

Yet what obsessed me more than anything else was the gentle countenance of the mysterious man I had glimpsed, the dark almost innocent eyes that had fixed on me for one moment before I had screamed.

"Strange that Mrs. Blessington is not afraid of him," I said in a low distracted voice, not longer caring if Richard heard me. "And that no one here seems in fear of him at all . . ." The strangest fancies were coming to me. The careless words of the villagers were running through my head. "You would be wise to do one very important thing before you retire," I said. "Leave out in writing a note to the effect that you do not intend to tear down the house."

"Julie, you have created an impossible dilemma," Richard demanded. "You insist we reassure this apparition that the house will not be destroyed, when in fact you verify the existence of the very creature that drove our father to say what he did."

"Oh, I wish I had never come here!" I burst out suddenly.

"Then we should go, both of us, and decide this matter at home."

"No, that's just it. I could never go without knowing . . . 'his secrets' . . . 'the demon wretch.' I could never go on living without knowing now!'

▼▼▼

Anger must be an excellent antidote to fear, for surely something worked to alleviate my natural alarm. I did not undress that night, nor even take off my shoes, but rather sat in that dark hollow bedroom gazing at the small square of diamond-paned window until I heard all of the house fall quiet. Richard's door at last closed. There came those distant echoing booms that meant other bolts had been put in place.

And when the grandfather clock in the great hall chimed the hour of eleven, Rampling Gate was as usual fast asleep.

I listened for my brother's step in the hall. And when I did not hear him stir from his room, I wondered at it, that curiosity would not impel him to come to me, to say that we must go together to discover the truth.

It was just as well. I did not want him to be with me. And I felt a dark exultation as I imagined myself going out of the room and down the stairs as I had the night before. I should wait one more hour, however, to be certain. I should let the night reach its pitch. Twelve, the witching hour. My heart was beating too fast at the thought of it, and dreamily I recollected the face I had seen, the voice that had said my name.

Ah, why did it seem in retrospect so intimate, that we had known each other, spoken together, that it was someone I recognized in the pit of my soul?

"What is your name?" I believe I whispered aloud. And then a spasm of fear startled me. Would I have the courage to go in search of him, to open the door to him? Was I losing my mind? Closing my eyes, I rested my head against the high back of the damask chair.

What was more empty than this rural night? What was more sweet?

I opened my eyes. I had been half dreaming or talking to myself, trying to explain to Father why it was necessary that we comprehend the reason ourselves. And I realized, quite fully realized—I think before I was even awake—that *he* was standing by the bed.

The door was open. And he was standing there, dressed exactly as he had been the night before, and his dark eyes were riveted on me with that same obvious curiosity, his mouth just a little slack like that of a school boy, and he was holding to the bedpost almost idly with his right hand. Why, he was lost in contemplating me. He did not seem to know that I was looking at him.

But when I sat forward, he raised his finger as if to quiet me, and gave a little nod of his head.

"Ah, it is you!" I whispered.

"Yes," he said in the softest, most unobtrusive voice.

But we had been talking to each other, hadn't we, I had been asking him questions, no, telling him things. And I felt suddenly I was losing my equilibrium or slipping back into a dream.

No. Rather I had all but caught the fragment of some dream from the past. That rush of atmosphere that can engulf one at any moment of the day following when something evokes the universe that absorbed one utterly in sleep. I mean I heard our voices for an instant, almost in argument, and I saw Father in his top hat and black overcoat rushing alone through the streets of the West End, peering into one door after another, and then, rising from the marble-top table in the dim smoky music hall you . . . your face.

"Yes . . ."

Go back, Julie! It was Father's voice.

". . . to penetrate the soul of it," I insisted, picking up the lost thread. But did my lips move? "To understand what it is that frightened him, enraged him. He said, 'Tear it down!' "

". . . you must never, never, can't do that." His face was stricken, like that of a schoolboy about to cry.

"No, absolutely, we don't want to, either of us, you know it . . . and you are not a spirit!" I looked at his mud-spattered boots, the faintest smear of dust on that perfect white cheek.

"A spirit?" he asked almost mournfully, almost bitterly. "Would that I were."

Mesmerized I watched him come towards me and the room darkened, and I felt his cool silken hands on my face. I had risen. I was standing before him, and I looked up into his eyes.

I heard my own heartbeat. I heard it as I had the night before, right at the moment I had screamed. Dear God, I was talking to him! He was in my room and I was talking to him! And I was in his arms.

"Real, absolutely real!" I whispered, and a low zinging sensation coursed through me so that I had to steady myself against the bed.

He was peering at me as if trying to comprehend something terribly important to him, and he didn't respond. His lips did have a ruddy look to them, a soft look for all his handsomeness, as if he never been kissed. And a slight dizziness had come over me, a slight confusion in which I was not at all sure that he was even there.

"Oh, but I am," he said softly. I felt his breath against my cheek, and it was almost sweet. "I am here, and you are with me, Julie . . ."

"Yes . . ."

My eyes were closing. Uncle Baxter sat hunched over his desk and I could hear the furious scratch of his pen. "Demon wretch!" he said to the night air coming in the open doors.

"No!" I said. Father turned in the door of the music hall and cried my name.

"Love me, Julie," came that voice in my ear. I felt his lips against my neck. "Only a little kiss, Julie, no harm . . ." And the core of my being, that secret place where all desires and all commandments are nurtured, opened to him without a struggle or a sound. I would have fallen if he had not held me. My arms closed about him, my hands slipping into the soft silken mass of his hair.

I was floating, and there was as there had always been at Rampling Gate an endless peace. It was Rampling Gate I felt around me, it was that timeless and impenetrable soul that had opened itself at last. . . . A power within me of enormous ken . . . To see as a god sees, and take the depth of things as nimbly as the outward eyes can size and shape pervade . . . Yes, I whispered aloud, those words from Keats, those words . . . To cease upon the midnight without pain . . .

No. In a violent instant we had parted, he drawing back as surely as I.

I went reeling across the bedroom floor and caught hold of the frame of the window, and rested my forehead against the stone wall.

For a long moment I stood with my eyes closed. There was a tingling pain in my throat that was almost pleasurable where his lips had touched me, a delicious throbbing that would not stop.

Then I turned, and I saw all the room clearly, the bed, the fireplace, the chair. And he stood still exactly as I'd left him and there was the most appalling distress in his face.

"What have they done to me?" he whispered. "Have they played the cruelest trick of all?"

"Something of menace, unspeakable menace," I whispered.

"Something ancient, Julie, something that defies understanding, something that can and will go on."

"But why, what are you?" I touched that pulsing pain with the tips of my fingers and, looking down at them, gasped. "And you suffer so, and you are so seemingly innocent, and it is as if you can love!"

His face was rent as if by a violent conflict within. And he turned to go. With my whole will, I stood fast not to follow him, not to beg him to turn back. But he did turn, bewildered, struggling and then bent upon his purpose as he reached for my hand. "Come with me," he said.

He drew me to him ever so gently, and slipping his arm around me guided me to the door.

Through the long upstairs corridor we passed hurriedly, and through a small wooden doorway to a screw stairs that I had never seen before.

I soon realized we were ascending the north tower of the house, the ruined portion of the structure that Richard and I had not investigated before.

Through one tiny window after another I saw the gently rolling landscape moving out from the forest that surrounded us, and the small cluster of dim lights that marked the village of Rampling and the pale streak of white that was the London road.

Up and up we climbed until we had reached the topmost chamber, and this he opened with an iron key. He held back the door for me to enter and I found myself in a spacious room whose high narrow windows contained no glass. A flood of moonlight revealed the most curious mixture of furnishings and objects, the clutter that suggests an attic and a sort of den. There was a writing table, a great shelf of books, soft leather chairs and scores of old yellowed and curling maps and framed pictures affixed to the walls. Candles were everywhere stuck in the bare stone niches or to the tables and the shelves. Here and there a barrel served as a table, right alongside the finest old Elizabethan chair. Wax had dripped over everything, it seemed, and in the very midst of the clutter lay rumpled copies of the most recent papers, the *Mercure de Paris,* the London *Times.*

There was no place for sleeping in this room.

And when I thought of that, where he must lie when he went to rest, a shudder passed over me and I felt, quite vividly, his lips touching my throat again, and I felt the sudden urge to cry.

But he was holding me in his arms, he was kissing my cheeks and my lips again ever so softly, and then he guided me to a chair. He lighted the candles about us one by one.

I shuddered, my eyes watering slightly in the light. I saw more unusual objects: telescopes and magnifying glasses and a violin in its open case, and a handful of gleaming and exquisitely shaped sea shells. There were jewels lying about, and a black silk top hat and a walking stick, and a bouquet of withered flowers, dry as straw, and daguerrotypes and tintypes in their little velvet cases, and opened books.

But I was too distracted now by the sight of him in the light, the gloss of his large black eyes, and the gleam of his hair. Not even in the railway station had I seen him so clearly as I did now amid the radiance of the candles. He broke my heart.

And yet he looked at me as though I were the feast for his eyes, and he said my name again and I felt the blood rush to my face. But there seemed a great break suddenly in the passage of time. I had been thinking, yes, what are you, how long have you existed . . . And I felt dizzy again.

I realized that I had risen and I was standing beside him at the window and he was turning me to look down and the countryside below had unaccountably changed. The lights of Rampling had been subtracted from the darkness that lay like a vapor over the land. A great wood, far older and denser than the forest of Rampling Gate, shrouded the hills, and I was afraid suddenly, as if I were slipping into a maelstrom from which I could never, of my own will, return.

There was that sense of us talking together, talking and talking in low agitated voices and I was saying that I should not give in.

"Bear witness, that is all I ask of you . . ."

And there was in me some dim certainty that by knowledge alone I should be fatally changed. It was the reading of a forbidden book, the chanting of a forbidden charm.

"No, only what was," he whispered.

And then even the shape of the land itself eluded me. And the very room had lost its substance, as if a soundless wind of terrific force had entered this place and was blowing it apart.

We were riding in a carriage through the night. We had long long ago left the tower, and it was late afternoon and the sky was the color of blood. And we rode into a forest whose trees were so high and so thick that scarcely any sun at all broke to the soft leafstrewn ground.

We had no time to linger in this magical place. We had come to the open country, to the small patches of tilled earth that surrounded the ancient village of Knorwood with its gabled roofs and its tiny crooked streets. We saw the walls of the monastery of Knorwood and the little church with the bell chiming Vespers under the lowering sky. A great bustling life resided in Knorwood, a thousand hearts beat in Knorwood, a thousand voices gave forth their common prayer.

But far beyond the village on the rise above the forest stood the rounded tower of a truly ancient castle, and to that ruined castle, no more than a shell of itself anymore, as darkness fell in earnest, we rode. Through its empty chambers we roamed, impetuous children, the horse and the road quite forgotten, and to the Lord of the Castle, a gaunt and white-skinned creature standing before the roaring fire of the roofless hall, we came. He turned and fixed us with his narrow and glittering eyes. A dead thing he was, I understood, but he carried within himself a priceless magic. And my young companion, my innocent young man passed by me into the Lord's arms. I saw the kiss. I saw the young man grow pale and struggle to turn away. It was as I had done this very night, beyond this dream, in my own bedchamber; and from the Lord he retreated, clutching to the sharp pain in his throat.

I understood. I knew. But the castle was dissolving as surely as anything in this dream might dissolve, and we were in some damp and close place.

The stench was unbearable to me, it was that most terrible of all stenches, the stench of death. And I heard my steps on the cobblestones and I reached to steady myself against the wall. The tiny square was deserted; the doors and windows gaped open to the vagrant wind. Up one side and down the other of the crooked street I saw the marks on the houses. And I knew what the marks meant. The Black Death had come to the village of Knorwood. The Black Death had laid it waste. And in a moment of suffocating horror I realized that no one, not a single person, was left alive.

But this was not quite right. There was some one walking in fits and starts up the narrow alleyway. Staggering he was, almost falling, as he pushed in one door after another, and at last came to a hot, stinking place where a child screamed on the floor. Mother and Father lay dead in the bed. And the great fat cat of the household, unharmed, played with the screaming infant, whose eyes bulged from its tiny sunken face.

"Stop it," I heard myself gasp. I knew that I was holding my head with both hands. "Stop it, stop it please!" I was screaming and my screams would surely pierce the vision and this small crude little room should collapse around me, and I should rouse the household of Rampling Gate to me, but I did not. The young man turned and stared at me, and in the close stinking room, I could not see his face.

But I knew it was he, my companion, and I could smell his fever and his sickness, and the stink of the dying infant, and see the sleek, gleaming body of the cat as it pawed at the child's outstretched hand.

"Stop it, you've lost control of it!" I screamed surely with all my strength, but the infant screamed louder. "Make it stop!"

"I can not . . ." he whispered. "It goes on forever! It will never stop!"

And with a great piercing shriek I kicked at the cat and sent it flying out of the filthy room, overturning the milk pail as it went, jetting like a witch's familiar over the stones.

Blanched and feverish, the sweat soaking his crude jerkin, my companion took me by the hand. He forced me back out of the house and away from the crying child and into the street.

Death in the parlour, death in the bedroom, death in the cloister, death before the high altar, death in the open fields. It seemed the Judgment of God that a thousand souls had died in the village of Knorwood —I was sobbing, begging to be released—it seemed the very end of Creation itself.

And at last night came down over the dead village and he was alive still, stumbling up the slopes, through the forest, towards that rounded tower where the Lord stood with his hand on the stone frame of the broken window waiting for him to come.

"Don't go!" I begged him. I ran alongside him crying, but he didn't hear. Try as I might, I could not affect these things.

The Lord stood over him smiling almost sadly as he watched him fall, watched the chest heave with its last breaths. Finally the lips moved, calling out for salvation when it was damnation the Lord offered, when it was damnation that the Lord would give.

"Yes, damned then, but living, breathing!" the young man cried, rising in a last spasmodic movement. And the Lord, who had remained still until that instant, bent to drink.

The kiss again, the lethal kiss, the blood drawn out of the dying body, and then the Lord lifting the heavy head of the young man to take the blood back again from the body of the Lord himself.

I was screaming again, *Do not, do not drink.* He turned and looked at me. His face was now so perfectly the visage of death that I couldn't believe there was animation left in him, yet he asked: What would you do? Would you go back to Knorwood, would you open those doors one after another, would you ring the bell in the empty church, and if you did would the dead rise?

He didn't wait for my answer. And I had none now to give. He had turned again to the Lord who waited for him, locked his innocent mouth to that vein that pulsed with every semblance of life beneath the Lord's cold and translucent flesh. And the blood jetted into the young body, vanquishing in one great burst the fever and the sickness that had wracked it, driving it out with the mortal life.

He stood now in the hall of the Lord alone. Immortality was his and the blood thirst he would need to sustain it, and that thirst I could feel with my whole soul. He stared at the broken walls around him, at the fire licking the blackened stones of the giant fireplace, at the night sky over the broken roof, throwing out its endless net of stars.

And each and every thing was transfigured in his vision, and in my vision—the vision he gave now to me—to the exquisite essence of itself. A wordless and eternal voice spoke from the starry veil of heaven, it sang in the wind that rushed through the broken timbers; it sighed in the flames that ate the sooted stones of the hearth.

It was the fathomless rhythm of the universe that played beneath every surface, as the last living creature—that tiny child—feel silent in the village below.

A soft wind sifted and scattered the soil from the new-turned furrows in the empty fields. The rain fell from the black and endless sky.

Years and years passed. And all that had been Knorwood melted into the very earth. The forest sent out its silent sentinels, and mighty trunks rose where there had been huts and houses, where there had been monastery walls.

Finally nothing of Knorwood remained: not the little cemetery, not the little church, not even the name of Knorwood lived still in the world. And it seemed the horror beyond all horrors that no one anymore should know of a thousand souls who had lived and died in that small and insignificant village, that not anywhere in the great archives in which all history is recorded should a mention of that town remain.

Yet one being remained who knew, one being who had witnessed, and stood now looking down upon the very spot where his mortal life had ended, he who had scrambled up on his hands and knees from the pit of Hell that had been that disaster; it was the young man who stood beside me, the master of Rampling Gate.

And all through the walls of his old house were the stones of the ruined castle, and all through the ceilings and floors the branches of those ancient trees.

What was solid and majestic here, and safe within the minds of those who slept tonight in the village of Rampling, was only the most fragile citadel against horror, the house to which he clung now.

A great sorrow swept over me. Somewhere in the drift of images I had relinquished myself, lost all sense of the point in space from which I saw. And in a great rush of lights and noise I was enlivened now and made whole as I had been when we rode together through the forest, only it was into the world of now, this hour, that we passed. We were flying it seemed through the rural darkness along the railway towards the London where the nighttime city burst like an enormous bubble in a shower of laughter, and motion, and glaring light. He was walking with me under the gas lamps, his face all but shimmering with that same dark innocence, that same irresistible warmth. And it seemed we were holding tight to one another in the very midst of a crowd. And the crowd was a living thing, a writhing thing, and everywhere there came a dark rich aroma from it, the aroma of fresh blood. Women in white fur and gentlemen in opera capes swept into the brightly lighted doors of the theatre; the blare of the music hall inundated us, then faded away. Only a thin soprano voice was left, singing a high, plaintive song. I was in his arms, and his lips were covering mine, and there came that dull zinging sensation again, that great uncontrollable opening within myself. Thirst, and the promise of satiation measured only by the intensity of that thirst. Up stairs we fled together, into high-ceilinged bedrooms papered in red damask where the loveliest women reclined on brass bedsteads, and the aroma was so strong now I could not bear it, and before me they offered themselves, they opened their arms. "Drink," he whispered, yes, drink. And I felt the warmth filling me, charging me, blurring my vision, until we broke again, free and light and invisible it seemed as we moved over the rooftops and down again through rain drenched streets. But the rain did not touch us; the falling snow did not chill us; we had within ourselves a great and indissoluble heat. And together in the carriage, we talked to each other in low, exuberant rushes of language; we were lovers; we were constant; we were immortal. We were as enduring as Rampling Gate.

I tried to speak; I tried to end the spell. I felt his arms around me and I knew we were in the tower room together, and some terrible miscalculation had been made.

"Do not leave me," he whispered. "Don't you understand what I am offering you; I have told you everything; and all the rest is but the weariness, the fever and the fret, those old words from the poem. Kiss me, Julie, open to me. Against your will I will not take you . . ." Again I heard my own scream. My hands were on his cool white skin, his lips were gentle yet hungry, his eyes yielding and ever young. Father turned in the rain-drenched London street and cried out: "Julie!" I saw Richard lost in the crowd as if searching for some one, his hat shadowing his dark eyes, his face haggard, old. Old!

I moved away. I was free. And I was crying softly and we were in this strange and cluttered tower room. He stood against the backdrop of the window, against the distant drift of pale clouds. The candle-light glimmered in his eyes. Immense and sad and wise they seemed, and oh, yes, innocent as I have said again and again. "I revealed myself to them," he said, "Yes, I told my secret. In rage or bitterness, I know not which, I made them my dark co-conspirators and always I won. They could not move against me, and neither will you. But they would triumph still. For they torment me now with their fairest flower. Don't turn away from me, Julie. You are mine, Julie, as Rampling Gate is mine. Let me gather the flower to my heart."

▼▼▼

Nights of argument. But finally Richard had come round. He would sign over to me his share of Rampling Gate, and I should absolutely refuse to allow the place torn down. There would be nothing he could do then to obey Father's command. I had given him the legal impediment he needed, and of course I should leave the house to him and his children. It should always be in Rampling hands.

A clever solution, it seemed to me, as Father had not told *me* to destroy the place, and I had no scruples in the matter now at all.

And what remained was for him to take me to the little train station and see me off for London, and not worry about me going home to Mayfair on my own.

"You stay here as long as you wish, and do not worry," I said. I felt more tenderly towards him than I could ever express. "You knew as soon as you set foot in the place that Father was all wrong. Uncle Baxter put it in his mind, undoubtedly, and Mrs. Blessington has always been right. There is nothing to harm there, Richard. Stay, and work or study as you please."

The great black engine was roaring past us, the carriages slowing to a stop. "Must go now, darling, kiss me," I said.

"But what came over you, Julie, what convinced you so quickly . . ."

"We've been through all, Richard," I said. "What matters is that we are all happy, my dear." And we held each other close.

I waved until I couldn't see him anymore. The flickering lamps of the town were lost in the deep lavender light of the early evening, and the dark hulk of Rampling Gate appeared for one uncertain moment like the ghost of itself on the nearby rise.

I sat back and closed my eyes. Then I opened them slowly, savouring this moment for which I had waited too long.

He was smiling, seated there as he had been all along, in the far corner of the leather seat opposite, and now he rose with a swift, almost delicate movement and sat beside me and enfolded me in his arms.

"It's five hours to London," he whispered in my ear.

"I can wait," I said, feeling the thirst like a fever as I held tight to him, feeling his lips against my eyelids and my hair. "I want to hunt the London streets tonight," I confessed, a little shyly, but I saw only approbation in his eyes.

"Beautiful Julie, my Julie . . ." he whispered.

"You'll love the house in Mayfair," I said.

"Yes . . ." he said.

"And when Richard finally tires of Rampling Gate, we shall go home."

ALL DRACULA'S CHILDREN

▼▼▼

DAN SIMMONS

WE flew to Bucharest almost as soon as the shooting had stopped, landing at Otopeni Airport just after midnight on December 29, 1989. As the semi-official "International Assessment Contingent," the six of us —all men—were hurried past the confused milling about that had passed for Customs since the revolution, and then herded aboard an ONT bus for the nine-mile drive into town. Father Paul, our contingent's token cleric, pointed at two bullet holes in the rear window of the bus, but Dr. Aimslea topped that simply by pointing out the window as we entered the lighted circular drive leaving the terminal.

Soviet-style tanks sat along the main thoroughfare where cabs normally would be waiting, their long muzzles pointed toward the entrance to the airport drive. Sandbagged emplacements lined the highway and airport rooftops, and the sodium-vapor lamps yellowly illuminated the helmets and rifles of soldiers on guard duty while throwing their faces into deep shadow. Other men, some in regular army uniforms and others in the ragtag clothing of the revolutionary militia, lay sleeping alongside the tanks. For a second the illusion of sidewalks littered with the bodies of Romania's dead was perfect and I held my breath, exhaling slowly only when I saw one of the bodies stir and another light a cigarette.

"They fought off several counterattacks by loyalist troops and *Securitate* forces last week," whispered Don Westler, our political contact from the Embassy. His tone suggested that it was an embarrassing topic, like sex.

Radu Fortuna, the little man who had been introduced to us in the terminal as our guide and liaison with the transitional government, turned in his seat and grinned broadly as if he was not embarrassed by either sex or politics. "They kill many *Securitate,*" he said loudly, his grin growing even wider. "Three times Ceausescu's people tried to take airport . . . three times they get killed."

Don Westler nodded and smiled, obviously uncomfortable with the conversation, but Dr. Aimslea leaned into the aisle. Light from the last of the sodium-vapor lamps illuminated his bald head in the seconds before we entered the darkness of the empty highway. "So Ceausescu's regime is really over?" he said to Fortuna.

I could see only the slightest gleam from the Romanian's grin in the sudden darkness. "Ceausescu is over, yes, yes," he said. "They take him and that bitch-cow of a wife in Tirgoviste, you know . . . have, how you call it . . . *trial.*" Radu Fortuna laughed again, a sound which somehow sounded both childish and cruel. I found myself shivering a bit in the darkness. The bus was not heated.

"They have trial," continued Fortuna, "and prosecutor say 'You both crazy?' You see, if Ceausescu and Mrs. Ceausescu crazy, then maybe the army just send them away in mental hospital for hundred years, like our Russian friends do. You know? But Ceausescu say, 'What? What? Crazy . . . How dare you! That is obscene provocation!' And his wife, she say, 'How can you say this to the Mother of your nation?' So prosecutor say, 'OK, you neither one crazy. Your own mouth say.' And then the soldiers, they draw straws so many want to be the ones. Then the lucky ones, they take Ceausescus out in courtyard and shoot them in heads many times." Fortuna chuckled warmly, as if remembering a favorite anecdote. "Yes, regime over," he said to Dr. Aimslea. "Maybe a few thousand *Securitate,* they don't know it yet and still shooting peoples, but that will be over soon. Bigger problem is, what to do with one out of three peoples who spy for old government, heh?"

Fortuna chuckled again, and in the sudden glare from an oncoming army truck, I could see his silhouette as he shrugged. There was a thin layer of condensation turning to ice on the inside of the windows now. My fingers were stiff with the cold and I could barely feel my toes in the absurd Bally dress shoes I had put on that morning. I scraped at some of the ice on my window as we entered the city proper.

"I know that you are all very important peoples from the West," said Radu Fortuna, his breath creating a small fog that rose toward the roof of the bus like an escaping soul. "But I am afraid I forget some names."

Don Westler did the introductions. "Dr. Aimslea is with the World Health Organization . . . Father Gerald Paul is here representing both the Archdiocese of Greater Boston and the Save the Children Foundation . . ."

"Ah, good to have priest here," said Fortuna, and I heard something that may have been irony in his voice.

"Dr. Leonard Paxley, Professor Emeritus of Economics at Princeton University," continued Westler. "Winner of the 1978 Nobel Prize in Economics."

Fortuna bowed toward the old academic. Paxley had not spoken at all during the flight from Frankfurt and now he seemed lost in his oversized coat and folds of muffler: an old man in search of a park bench.

"We welcome you," said Fortuna, "even though our country have no economy at present moment . . ."

"Goddamn, is it always this cold here?" came the voice from deep in the folds of wool. The Nobel Prize-winning Professor Emeritus stamped his small feet. "This is cold enough to freeze the nuts off a bronze bulldog."

"And Mr. Carl Berry representing American Telegraph and Telephone," continued Westler quickly.

The pudgy businessman next to me puffed his pipe, removed it, nodded in Fortuna's direction, and went back to smoking the thing as if it were a necessary source of heat. I had a moment's mad vision of the seven of us in the bus huddled around the glowing embers in Berry's pipe.

"And Mr. Harold Winston Palmer," said Westler, gesturing in my direction, "Vice President in charge of European markets for . . ."

"Yesss," said Radu Fortuna, his voice holding approximately the same intonations of hunger that one imagines a python would express mere seconds before devouring its prey. "I know the corporation which Monsieur Palmer represents . . ."

Of course he did. We are one of the largest corporations in the world and if you are an American, you own . . . or have owned . . . one of our major products. If you are Romanian, you dream of owning one.

"You have been in Romania before, I believe, Mr. Palmer?"

I could see Fortuna's eyes glowing as we reached the lighted part of the city. I am old enough to have been part of the Occupation force in Germany shortly after the war. The scene beyond Fortuna was like that. There were more tanks in Palace Square, black hulks which one would have thought deserted heaps of cold metal if the turret of one had not tracked us as our bus passed by. There were the sooty corpses of burned-out autos and at least one armored personnel carrier that was now only a piece of scorched steel. We turned left and went past the Central University Library, its gold dome and ornate roof now collapsed between soot-streaked and pockmarked walls.

"Yes," I said, "I have been here before."

Fortuna leaned toward me. "And perhaps this time your company *will* open a plant here, yes?"

"Perhaps."

Fortuna's gaze did not leave me. "We work very cheap here," he whispered so softly that I doubt if anyone else except Carl Berry could hear him. "Very cheap. Labor is very cheap here. Life is very cheap here."

We had turned left off of the empty Calea Victorei, right again on Boulevard Nicholai Bălcěscu, and now the bus screeched to a halt in front of the tallest building in the city, the 22-story Intercontinental Hotel.

"In the morning, gentlemens," said Fortuna, rising, gesturing the way toward the lighted foyer, "we will see the new Romania. I wish you dreamless sleeps."

▼▼▼

Our group spent the next day meeting with "officials" in the interim government, mostly members of the recently cobbled-together National Salvation Front. The day was so dark that the automatic streetlights came on along the broad Bulevardul N. Bălcěscu and Bulevardul Republicii. The buildings were not heated . . . or at least not percepti-bly . . . and the men and women we spoke with looked much the same in their oversized, drab wool coats. By the end of the day we had spoken to a Giurescu, two Tismăneanu, one Boroşoiu who turned out not to be a spokesman for the new government after all . . . he was arrested moments after we left him . . . several generals including Popescu, Lu-poi, and Diurgiu, and finally the real leaders, which included Petre Ro-man, prime minister in the transitional government, and Ion Iliescu and Dumitru Mazilu, who had been President and Vice President in the Ceausescu regime.

Their message was the same: we had the run of the nation and any recommendations we could make to our various constituencies for help would be eternally appreciated.

Returning to the Intercontinental that evening, we watched as a crowd of people—most, it looked, office workers leaving the stone hives of the downtown for the day—beat and pummeled three men and a woman. Radu Fortuna smiled and pointed to the broad plaza in front of the hotel where the crowd was growing larger. "There . . . in University Square last week . . . when peoples come to demonstrate with singing, you know? Army tanks roll over persons, shoot more. Those probably be *Securitate* informers."

Before the van rolled under the stone overhang of the hotel, we caught a glimpse of uniformed soldiers leading away the probable informers, encouraging them with the butts of their automatic weapons while the crowd continued to spit and strike them.

"Can't make an omelette without breaking a few eggs," muttered our Professor Emeritus, while Father Paul glared at him and Radu Fortuna chuckled appreciatively.

▼▼▼

"You'd think Ceausescu would have been better prepared for a siege," Dr. Aimslea said after dinner that evening. We had stayed in the dining room because it seemed warmer than our own rooms. Waiters and a few military men moved aimlessly through the large space. The reporters had finished their dinner quickly, with a maximum of noise, and left soon after to wherever reporters go to drink and be cynical.

Radu Fortuna had joined us for coffee and now he showed his patented, gap-toothed grin. "You want to see how prepared, Ceausescu, he was?"

Aimslea, Father Paul, and I agreed that we would like to see. Carl Berry decided to go to his room to get a call through to the States and Dr. Paxley followed him, grumbling about getting to bed early. Fortuna led the three of us out into the cold and down shadowed streets to the soot-blackened shell of the presidential palace. A militia man stepped out of the shadows, raised an AK-47, and barked a challenge, but Fortuna spoke quietly and we were allowed to pass.

There were no lights in the palace except for occasional fires in barrels where militia men and regular soldiers slept or huddled to keep warm. Furniture was tossed everywhere, drapes had been ripped from twenty-foot-tall windows, papers littered the floor, and the formal tiles were smeared with dark streaks. Fortuna led us down a narrow hall, through a series of what appeared to be private residential rooms, and stopped at what seemed to be an unmarked closet. Inside the four-foot square closet, there was nothing but three lanterns on a shelf. Fortuna lighted the lanterns, handed one to Aimslea and one to me, and then touched the molding above the back wall. A sliding panel opened to a stone staircase.

The next half hour was dreamlike, almost hallucinatory. The stairway led down to echoing chambers from which a maze of stone tunnels and other stairways branched. Fortuna led us deep into this maze, our lights reflecting off the curved ceilings and slick stones.

"My God," muttered Dr. Aimslea after ten minutes of this, "these go for miles."

"Yes, yes," smiled Radu Fortuna. "Many miles."

There were storerooms with automatic weapons on shelves, gas masks hanging from hooks; there were command centers with radios and television monitors sitting there in the dark, some destroyed as if madmen with axes had vented their wrath on them, some still covered with clear plastic and waiting only for their operators to turn them on; there were barracks with bunks and stoves and kerosene heating units which we eyed with envy. Some of the barracks looked untouched, others obviously had been the site of panicked evacuation or equally panicked firefights. There was blood on the walls and floors of one of these chambers, the streaks more black than red in the light of our hissing lanterns.

There were still bodies in the farther reaches of the tunnels, some lying in pools of water dripping from overhead hatches, others tumbled behind hastily erected barricades at the junction of the underground avenues. The stone vaults smelled like a meat locker.

"Securitate," said Fortuna and spat on one of the brown-shirted men lying face down in a frozen pool. "They fled like rats down here and we finished them like rats. You know?"

Father Paul made the sign of the cross and crouched next to one of the men for a long moment, praying silently. Dr. Aimslea said, "But Ceausescu did not retreat to this . . . redoubt?"

"No." Fortuna smiled.

The doctor looked around in the hissing white light. "For God's sake why not? If he'd marshalled an organized resistance down here, he could have held out for months."

Fortuna shrugged. "Instead, the monster, he fled by helicopter. He flied . . . no? Flew, yes . . . he flew to Tîrgoviste, seventy kilometers from here, you know? There other peoples see him and his bitch-cow wife get in car. They catch."

Dr. Aimslea held his lantern at the entrance to another tunnel from which a terrible stench now blew. The doctor quickly pulled back the light. "But I wonder why . . ."

Fortuna stepped closer and the harsh light illuminated an old scar on his neck that I had not noticed before. "They say his . . . advisor . . . the Dark Advisor . . . told him not to come here." He smiled.

Father Paul tried to smile. "The Dark Advisor. It sounds as if his counselor was the devil."

Radu Fortuna nodded. "Worse, Father."

Dr. Aimslea grunted. "Did this devil escape? Or was he one of those poor buggers we saw back there?"

Our guide did not answer but entered one of the four tunnels branching off there. A stone stairway led upward. "To the National Theater," he said softly, waving us ahead of him. "It was damaged but not destroyed. Your hotel is next door."

The priest, the doctor, and I started up, lantern light throwing our shadows fifteen feet high on the curved stone walls above. Father Paul stopped and looked down at Fortuna. "Aren't you coming?"

The little guide smiled and shook his head. "Tomorrow, we take you where it all began. Tomorrow we go to Transylvania."

Father Paul gave the doctor and me a smile. "Transylvania," he repeated. "Shades of Bela Lugosi." He turned back to say something to Fortuna but the little man was gone. Not even the echo of footfalls or shimmer of lantern light showed which tunnel he had taken.

▼▼▼

We flew to Timişoara, a city of about 300,000 in western Transylvania, suffering the flight in an old recycled Tupolev turbo-prop now belonging to *Tarom,* the state airline. We were lucky; the daily flight was delayed only an hour and a half. We flew through cloud for most of the way and there were no interior lights on the plane, but that did not matter because there were neither flight attendants nor the interruption of a meal or snack. Dr. Paxley grumbled most of the way, but the scream of the turbo-props and the groaning of metal as we bounced and bucked our way through updrafts and storm clouds muffled most of his complaints.

Just as we took off, seconds before entering the clouds, Fortuna leaned across the aisle and pointed out the window to a snow-covered island on a lake that must have been about twenty miles north of Bucharest. "Snagov," he said, watching my face.

I glanced down, caught a glimpse of a dark church on the island before the clouds obliterated the view, and looked back at Fortuna. "Yes?"

"Vlad Tepes buried there." Fortuna, pronounced it Vlad Tsepesh.

I nodded. Fortuna went back to reading one of our *Time* magazines, although how someone could read or concentrate during that wild ride, I will never know. A minute later Carl Berry leaned forward from the seat behind me and whispered, "Who the hell is Vlad Tepes? Someone who died in the fighting?"

The cabin was so dark now that I could barely make out Berry's face inches from my own. "Dracula," I said to the AT&T executive.

Berry let out a discouraged sigh and leaned back in his seat, tightening his belt as we began to pitch and bounce in earnest.

"Vlad the Impaler," I whispered to no one at all.

▼▼▼

The electricity had failed, so the morgue was cooled by the simple expedient of opening all of the tall windows. The light was still very thin, as if watered down by the dark green walls and grimy panes of glass and constant low clouds, but was adequate to illuminate the rows of corpses across the tabletops and filling almost every inch of the tiled floors. We had to walk a circuitous path, stepping carefully between bare legs and white faces and bulging bellies, just to join Fortuna and the Romanian doctor in the center of the room. There were at least three or four hundred bodies in the long room . . . not counting ourselves.

"Why haven't these people been buried?" demanded Father Paul, his scarf raised to his face. His voice was angry. "It's been at least a week since the murders, correct?"

Fortuna translated for the Timişoaran doctor, who shrugged. Fortuna shrugged. "Eleven days since the *Securitate,* they do this," he said. "Funerals soon. The . . . how do you say . . . the authorities here, they want to show the Western reporters and such very important peoples as yourselfs. Look, look." Fortuna opened his arms to the room in a gesture that was almost proud, a chef showing off the banquet he had prepared.

On the table in front of us lay a corpse of an old man. His hands and feet had been amputated by something not very sharp. There were burns on his lower abdomen and genitals, and his chest showed open scars that reminded me of Viking photos of the rivers and craters of Mars.

The Romanian doctor spoke. Fortuna translated. "He say, the *Securitate,* they play with acid. You know? And here . . ."

The young woman lay on the floor, fully clothed except for the ripped clothing that extended from her breasts to pubic bone. What I first took for another layer of slashed, red rags, I now realized was the red-rimmed wall of her opened belly and abdomen. The seven-month fetus lay on her lap like a discarded doll. It would have been a boy.

"Here," commanded Fortuna, stepping through the maze of ankles and gesturing.

The boy must have been about ten. Death and a week or more of freezing cold had expanded and mottled flesh to the texture of bloated, marbled parchment, but the barbed wire around his ankles and wrists was still quite visible. His arms had been tied behind him with such force that the shoulder joints were totally out of their sockets. Flies had been at his eyes and the layer of eggs there made it look as if the child were wearing white goggles.

Professor Emeritus Paxley made a noise and staggered from the room, almost tripping over the bodies set out for display there. One old man's gnarled hand seemed to tug at the professor's pant leg as he fled.

Father Paul grabbed Fortuna by his coat front and almost lifted the little man from the floor. "Why in the hell are you showing us this?"

Fortuna grinned. "There is more, Father. Come."

▼▼▼

"They called Ceausescu 'the vampire'," said Don Westler, who had flown up later to join us.

"And here in Timişoara is where it started," said Carl Berry, puffing on his pipe and looking around at the gray sky, gray buildings, gray slush on the street, and gray people moving through the dim light.

"Here in Timişoara is where the final explosion began," said Westler. "The younger generation has been getting more and more restless for some time. In a real sense, Ceausescu signed his own death warrant by creating that generation."

"Creating that generation," repeated Father Paul, frowning. "Explain."

Westler explained. In the mid-1960's, Ceausescu had outlawed abortion, discontinued the import of oral contraceptives and IUD's, and announced that it was a woman's obligation to the state to have many children. More importantly, his government had offered birth premiums and reduced taxes to those families who obeyed the government's call for increased births. Couples who had fewer than five children were actually fined as well as heavily taxed. Between 1966 and 1976, said Westler, there had been a forty percent increase in babies born, along with a huge rise in infant mortality.

"It was this surplus of young people in their twenties by the late 1980's who provided the core of the revolution," said Westler. "They had no jobs, no chance for a college education . . . not even a chance

for decent housing. They were the ones who began the protests in Timişoara and elsewhere."

Father Paul nodded. "Ironic . . . but appropriate."

"Of course," said Westler, pausing near the train station, "most of the
peasant families could not afford to raise the extra children . . ." He
stopped with that diplomat's tic of embarrassment.

"So what happened to those children?" I asked. It was only early
afternoon but the light had faded to a wintry twilight. There were no
streetlights along this section of Timişoara's main boulevard. Somewhere far down the tracks, a locomotive screamed.

Don Westler shook his head but Radu Fortuna stepped closer. "We
take train tonight to Sebeş, Sibiu, Copsa Mica, and Sighişoara," the
smiling Romanian said. "You see where babies go."

▼▼▼

Winter evening became winter night beyond the windows of our train
with the slow dying of the light. The train passed through mountains
worn smooth and toothless by age—whether they were the Fagaras
Range or the lower Bucegi Carpathians, I did not remember from earlier
trips—and the dismal sight of huddled villages and sagging farms faded
to blackness broken only by the occasional glow of oil lamps through
distant windows. I realized with a start that it was New Year's Eve, the
last night of 1989, and that the dawn would bring what was popularly
thought of as the last decade of the millennium . . . but beyond the
window lay the Seventeenth Century. The only intrusion of the modern
age visible in the evening departure from Timişoara had been the occasional military vehicle glimpsed on snow-packed roads and the occasional electric cables snaking above the trees. Then those slim talismans
had disappeared and there were only the villages, the oil lamps, the cold,
and an occasional rubber-wheeled cart, pulled by horses who seemed
more bone than flesh and guided by men hidden in dark wool. Then even
the village streets were empty as the train rushed through, stopping
nowhere. I realized that some of the villages were totally dark, even
though it was not yet ten P.M., and leaning closer, wiping frost from the
glass, I saw that the village we were passing now was dead—buildings
bulldozed, stone walls demolished, farm homes tumbled down.

"Systematization," whispered Radu Fortuna, who had appeared silently next to me in the aisle. He was chewing on an onion.

I did not ask for clarification, but our guide and liaison smiled and
provided it. "Ceausescu wanted to destroy the old. He break down vil-

lages, move thousands of peoples to city places like Victory of Socialism Boulevard in Bucharest. . . . kilometers and kilometers of tall apartment buildings. Only buildings, they not finished when he tear down and move peoples there. No heat. No water. No electricity . . . he sell electricity to other countries, you see. So village peoples, they have little house out here, be in family three, maybe four hundreds of years, but now live on ninth floor of bad brick building in strange city . . . no windows, cold wind blow in. Have to carry water a mile, then carry up nine flights of stairs."

He took a deep bite of the onion and nodded as if satisfied. "Systematization." He moved on down the smoky aisle.

The mountains passed in the night. I began to doze . . . I had slept little the night before, dreamlessly or otherwise, and I had not slept on the plane the night before that . . . but awoke with a start to find that the Professor Emeritus had taken the seat next to me.

"No goddamn heat," he whispered, tugging his muffler tighter. "You'd think with all these goddamn peasant bodies and goats and chickens and what have you in this so-called first-class car, that they'd generate some body heat in here, but it's as cold as Madame Ceausescu's dear dead tit."

I blinked at the simile.

"Actually," said Dr. Paxley in a conspiratorial whisper, "it's not as bad as they say."

"The cold?" I said.

"No, no. The economy. Ceausescu may be the only national leader in this century who actually *paid off* his country's foreign debt. Of course, he had to divert food, electricity, and consumer goods to other countries to do it, but Romania has no foreign debt at all now. None."

"Mmmm," I said, trying to remember the fragments of the dream I'd in my few moments of sleep. Something about blood.

"A one-point-seven billion dollar trade surplus," muttered Paxley, leaning close enough that I could tell that he'd also had onion for dinner. "And they owe the West nothing and the Russians nothing. Incredible."

"But the people are starving," I said softly. Westler and Father Paul were snoring in the seat in front of us.

Paxley waved that away. "Should German reunification come, do you know how much the West Germans are going to have to invest just to retool the infrastructure in the East?" Not waiting for my reply, he went on. "A hundred *billion* Deutschmarks . . . and that's just to prime the pump. With Romania, the infrastructure is so pitiful that there's little to tear down. Just junk the industrial madness that Ceausescu was so proud of, use the cheap labor . . . my God, man, they're almost *serfs* . . . and build whatever industrial infrastructure you want. The South Korean model, Mexico . . . it's wide open for the western corporation that's willing to take the chance."

I pretended to doze off again and eventually the Professor Emeritus moved down the aisle to find someone else to explain the economic facts of life to. The villages passed in the darkness as we moved deeper into the Transylvanian mountains.

▼▼▼

We arrived in Sebeş before dawn and there was some minor official there to take us to the orphanage.

No, orphanage is too kind a word. It was a warehouse, heated no better than the other meatlockers we had been in so far, undecorated except for grimy tile floors and flaking walls painted a vomitous green to eye height and a leprous gray above that. The main hall was at least a hundred meters across.

It was filled with cribs.

Again, the word is too generous. Not cribs, but low metal cages with no tops to them. In the cages were children. Children ranging in age from newborns to ten-year-olds. None seemed capable of walking. All were naked or dressed in filth-caked rags. Many were screaming or weeping silently and the fog of their breath rose in the cold air. Stern-faced women in complicated nurse's caps stood smoking cigarettes on the periphery of this giant human stockyard, occasionally moving among the cages to brusquely hand a bottle to a child . . . sometime a seven- or eight-year-old child . . . or more frequently to slap one into silence.

The official and the chain-smoking administrator of the "orphanage" snapped a tirade at us which Fortuna did not deign to translate, and then they walked us through the room and slammed open tall doors.

Another room, a larger room, opened into the cold-shrouded distance. Thin morning light fell in shafts onto the cages and faces there. There must have been at least a thousand children in this room, none of them more than two years old. Some were crying, their infant wails echoing in the tiled space, but most seemed too weak and lethargic even to cry as they lay on the thin, excrement-smeared rags. Some lay in the foetal grip of near starvation. Some looked dead.

Radu Fortuna turned and folded his arms. He was smiling. "You see where the babies go, yes?"

▼▼▼

In Sibiu we found the hidden children. There were four orphanages in this central Transylvanian city of 170,000, and each orphanage was larger and sadder than the one in Sebeş. Dr. Aimslea demanded, through Fortuna, that we be allowed to see the AIDS children.

The administrator of Strada Cetăţii Orfelinat 319, a windowless old structure in the shadow of the 16th-century city walls, absolutely refused to acknowledge that there *were* any AIDS babies. He refused to acknowledge our right to enter the orphanage. He refused, at one point, to acknowledge that he was the administrator of Strada Cetăţii Orfelinat 319, despite the stenciling on his office door and the plaque on his desk.

Fortuna showed him our travel papers and authorization forms, co-signed with a personal plea for cooperation from interim Prime Minister Roman, President Iliescu, and Vice President Mazilu.

The administrator sneered, took a drag on his short cigarette, shook his head, and said something dismissive. "My orders come from the Ministry of Health," Radu Fortuna translated.

It took almost an hour to get through to the capital, but Fortuna finally completed a call to the Prime Minister's office, who called the Ministry of Health, who promised to call Strada Cetăţii Orfelinat 319 immediately. A little over two hours later, the call came, the administrator snarled something at Fortuna, tossed his cigarette butt on dirty tiles littered with them, snapped something at an orderly, and handed a huge ring of keys to Fortuna.

The AIDS ward was behind four sets of locked doors. There were no nurses there, no doctors . . . no adults of any kind. Neither were there cribs; the infants and small children sat on the tile floor or competed to find space on one of half a dozen bare and excrement-stained mattresses thrown against the far wall. They were naked and their heads had been shaved. The windowless room was illuminated by a few naked 40-watt bulbs set thirty or forty feet apart. Some children congregated there in the pools of murky light, raising swollen eyes to them as if to the sun, but most lay in the deep shadows. Older children scuttled on all fours to escape the light as we opened the steel doors.

It was obvious that the floors were hosed down every few days—there were rivulets and streaks along the cracked tiles—and it was just as obvious that no other hygienic efforts had been made. Don Westler, Dr.

Paxley, and Mr. Berry turned and fled from the stench. Dr. Aimslea cursed and pounded his fist against a stone wall. Father Paul first wept, then moved from infant to infant, touching their heads, whispering softly to them in a language they did not understand, and lifting them. I had the distinct impression as I watched that most of these children had never been held, perhaps never been touched.

Radu Fortuna followed us into the room. He was not smiling. "Comrade Ceausescu told us that AIDS is a capitalist disease," he whispered. "Romania has no official cases of AIDS. None."

"My God, my God," Dr. Aimslea was muttering as he moved from child to child. "Most of these are in advanced stages of AIDS-related complexes. And suffering from malnutrition and vitamin deficiencies." He looked up and there were tears gleaming behind his glasses. "How long have they been here?"

Fortuna shrugged. "Most maybe since little babies. Parents put here. Babies not go out of this room, that why so few know to walk. No one to hold them up when they try."

Dr. Aimslea unleashed a series of curses that seemed to smoke in the chill air. Fortuna nodded.

"But hasn't anyone documented these . . . this . . . tragedy?" said Dr. Aimslea in a constricted voice.

Now Fortuna smiled. "Oh, yes, yes. Dr. Patrascu from Stefan S. Nicolau Institute of Virology, he say this happening three . . . maybe four years ago. First child he test, was infected. I think six out of next fourteen also sick from AIDS. All cities, all state orphanages he went to, many, many sick childrens."

Dr. Aimslea rose from shining his pen light in a comatose infant's eyes. Aimslea grabbed Fortuna by the coat, and for a second I was sure that he was going to strike the little guide in the face. "For Christ's sake, man, didn't he *tell* anyone?"

Fortuna stared impassively at the doctor. "Oh, yes. Dr. Patrascu, he tell Ministry of Health. They say for him to stop immediately. They cancel AIDS seminar Doctor schedule . . . then they burn his minutes and . . . how do you say it? Like little guides for meeting . . . *programs*. They confiscate printed programs and burn them."

Father Paul set down a child. The two-year-old's thin arms strained toward the priest as she made vague, imploring noises—a plea to be lifted again. Father Paul lifted her, held her bald and scabrous head against his cheek. "Goddamn them," whispered the priest in a tone of benediction. "Goddamn the ministry. Goddamn that sonofabitch downstairs. Goddamn Ceausescu forever. May they all burn in hell."

Dr. Aimslea stood from where he crouched near a toddler who seemed all ribs and extended belly. "This child is dead." He turned to Fortuna again. "How in the hell can this happen? There can't be that many cases of AIDS among the general population yet, can there? Or are these children of drug addicts?"

I could see the other question in the doctor's eyes: in a nation where the average family could not afford to buy food and where possession of a narcotic was punishable by death, how could there be so many children of drug users?

"Come," said Fortuna, and led the doctor and me out of that ward of death. Father Paul remained, lifting and touching child after child.

In the "healthy ward" downstairs, differing from the Sebeş orphanage only in size—there must have been a thousand or more children in the endless sea of steel cribs—nurses were moving stolidly from child to child, giving them glass bottles of what looked to be formulized milk, and then, as each child sucked noisily, injecting him or her with a syringe. Then the nurse would wipe the syringe with a rag she carried on her belt, re-insert it in a large vial from her tray, and inject the next child.

"Mother of Christ," whispered Dr. Aimslea. "You don't have disposable syringes?"

Fortuna made a gesture with his hands. "A capitalist luxury."

Aimslea's face was so red that I thought capillaries were bursting there. "Then what about fucking autoclaves!"

Fortuna shrugged and asked the nearest nurse something. She snapped a reply and went back to her injections. "She say, the autoclave is broken. Has been broken. Sent to Ministry of Health to be fixed," translated Fortuna.

"How long?" grated Aimslea.

"It broken four years," said Fortuna after calling the question to the busy woman. She had not bothered to turn around while replying. "She say, that was four years *before* it sent to the Ministry for repair last year."

Dr. Aimslea stepped closer to a six- or seven-year-old lying in his crib sucking on his bottle. The formula looked like gray water. "And these are vitamin shots they're administering?"

"Oh, no," said Fortuna. "Blood."

Dr. Aimslea froze, then turned slowly. "Blood?"

"Yes, yes. Adult's blood. It make little babies strong. Ministry of Health approve . . . they say it is very . . . how do you say . . . *advanced* medicine."

Aimslea took a step toward the nurse, then a step toward Fortuna, and then wheeled toward me as if he would kill either of the first two if he got close to them. *"Adult's blood,* Palmer. Jesus H. Christ. That was a theory that went out with gaslights and spats. My God, Palmer, don't they realize . . ." He suddenly turned back toward our guide. "Fortuna, where do they get this . . . adult blood?"

"It donated . . . no, wrong word. Not donated, *bought.* Those peoples in big cities who have no money at all, they sell blood for babies. Fifteen *lei* each time."

Dr. Aimslea made a rough sound in his throat, a noise that soon turned to chuckles. He shaded his eyes with his hand and staggered backward, leaning against a tray filled with bottles of dark liquid. "Paid blood donors," he whispered to himself. "Street people . . . drug addicts . . . prostitutes . . . and they administer it to infants in the state homes with reusable, non-sterile needles." The chuckles continued, grew louder. Dr. Aimslea lowered himself to a sitting position on the dirty towels, the hand still over his eyes, laughing deep in his throat. "How many . . ." he started to ask Fortuna. He cleared his throat and tried again. "How many did this Dr. Patrascu estimate were infected with AIDS?"

Fortuna frowned as he tried to remember. "I think maybe he find seventy of the first two thousand. More higher number after that."

From beneath the visor of his hand, Dr. Aimslea said, "Almost five percent. And how many . . . orphanage children . . . are there?"

Our guide shrugged. "Ministry of Health say maybe two hundred thousands. I think more . . . maybe half a million. Maybe more."

Dr. Aimslea did not look up or speak again. The deep chuckles grew louder and deeper, and I realized then that they were not chuckles at all, but sobs.

▼▼▼

We took the train north through late afternoon light toward Sighişoara. Fortuna had planned one stop in a small town along the way.

"Mr. Palmer, you like Copsa Mica," he said. "It is for you we see it."

I did not turn to look at him, but kept my gaze on the demolished villages we were passing. "More orphanages?" I said.

"No, no. I mean, yes . . . there is orphanage in Copsa Mica, but we don't go there. It is small town . . . six thousand peoples. But it is reason you come to our country, yes?"

I did turn to stare. "Industry?"

Fortuna laughed. "Ah, yes . . . Copsa Mica is most industrious. Like so many of our towns. And this one so close to Sighişoara, where Comrade Ceausescu's Dark Advisor was born . . ."

I have been to Sighişoara. "Dark Advisor," I snapped. "What the hell are you saying? That Ceausescu's advisor was Vlad Tepes?"

Sighişoara is a perfectly preserved medieval town where even the presence of the few autos on the narrow, cobblestoned streets seem an anachronism. The hills surrounding Sighişoara are studded with tumbledown towers and keeps . . . none of them as cinematic as the half dozen intact castles in Transylvania which advertise themselves as Dracula's castle for impressionable travelers with hard currency . . . but the old house on Piata Muzeului had truly been Vlad Dracula's home from 1431 to 1435. The last time I had seen it, over a decade earlier, the upstairs had been a restaurant and the basement a wine cellar. "You want me to believe that *Vlad Dracul* was the Dark Advisor?" I asked, not hiding the contempt in my voice.

Fortuna shrugged and went off in search of something to eat. Dr. Aimslea had overheard the conversation and dropped into the seat next to me. "Do you believe that man?" he whispered. "Now he's ready to tell you ghost stories about Dracula. *Christ!*"

I nodded and looked out at the mountains and valleys sliding by in gray monotone. There was a wildness here that I had not seen elsewhere in the world, and I have traveled in more nations than there are in the U.N. The mountainside, deep ravines, and trees seemed malformed, gnarled, like something struggling to escape from a dark Van Gogh painting.

"I wish it were Dracula we had to deal with here," continued the good doctor. "Think of it, Palmer . . . if our contingent announced that Vlad the Impaler were alive and preying on people in Transylvania, well . . . hell . . . there'd be ten thousand reporters up here. Satellite trucks parked in Sibiu's town square to bounce back InstaCam reports to every Channel 7 and Channel 4 hometown news market in America. One monster biting a few dozen people, and the world would be galvanized with interest . . . but as it is, tens of thousands of men and women dead, hundreds of thousands of children warehoused and facing . . . *goddammit.*"

I nodded without turning. "The banality of evil," I whispered.

"What?"

"The banality of evil." I turned and smiled grimly at the physician. "Dracula would be a story. The plight of hundreds of thousands of victims of political madness, bureaucracy, stupidity . . . this is just an . . . inconvenience."

▼▼▼

We arrived at Copsa Mica just before nightfall, and I realized at once why it was "my" town. Westler, Aimslea, Paxley, and Father Paul stayed on the train for the half-hour layover; only Carl Berry and I had business there. Fortuna led the way.

The village—it was too small to call a town—lay between steep mountain slopes. There was snow on the hillsides, but the snow was black. The icicles which hung from the dark eaves of the buildings were black. Underfoot, the slush along the unpaved roads was a gray and black mixture, and over everything hung a visible pall of black air, as if a million microscopic moths were fluttering in the dying light. Men and women in black coats and shawls moved past us, dragging their heavy carts or leading children by the hand, and the faces of these people were soot black. As we approached the center of the village, I realized that the three of us were wading through a layer of ash and soot at least four inches deep. I have seen active volcanoes in South America and elsewhere, and the ash and midnight skies were the same.

"It is . . . how do you say it . . . auto-tire plant," said Radu Fortuna, gesturing toward the black industrial complex that filled the end of the valley like some grounded dragon. "It makes black powder for rubber products . . . works twenty-four hours a day. Sky is always like this . . ." He gestured proudly toward the black haze that settled down on everything.

Carl Berry was coughing. "Good Lord, how can people live in this?"

"They not live long," said Fortuna. "Most old peoples, like you and me, they have lead poisoning. Little childrens have . . . what is word? Always coughing?"

"Asthma," said Berry.

"Yes, little childrens have asthma. Babies born with hearts which are . . . how do you say, badformed?"

"Malformed," said Berry.

I stopped a hundred yards from the black fences and black walls of the plant. The village behind us was a sketch of blacks against grays. Even the lamplight did not truly penetrate the soot-blackened windows. "Why is this 'my town,' Fortuna?" I said.

He held his hand out toward the factory. The lines in his palm were already black with soot, the cuff of his white shirt a dark gray.

"Ceausescu gone now. Factory no longer have to turn out rubber things for East Germany, Poland, USSR . . . you want? Make things your company want? No . . . how do you say . . . no environmental impactment states, no regulations against making things the way you want, throwing away things where you want. So, you want?"

I stood there in the black snow for a long moment and might have stood there longer if the train had not shrieked its two-minute warning. "Perhaps," I said. "Just perhaps."

We trudged back through ash.

▼▼▼

Don Westler, Father Paul, Dr. Aimslea, Carl Berry, and our Professor Emeritus Dr. Leonard Paxley took a morning *Tarom* flight back to Bucharest from Sighişoara. I stayed behind. The morning was dark, with heavy clouds that moved up the valley and shrouded the surrounding ridges in shifting haze. The city walls with their eleven stone towers seemed to blend their gray stones with the gray skies, sealing the medieval town under a solid dome of gloom. After a late breakfast, I filled my Thermos, left the old town square, and climbed the hundred and seventy-two steps of the Covered Stairway to the house on Piata Muzeului. The iron doors to the wine cellar were closed, the narrow doors to the first floor sealed with heavy shutters. An old man sitting in the square across the street told me that the restaurant had been closed for several years, that the State had considered turning the house into a museum but then decided that foreign guests would not pay hard currency to see a run-down house . . . not even one where Vlad Dracul had lived five centuries before. The tourists preferred the large old castles a hundred miles east, nearer Bucharest; castles which had been erected centuries after Vlad Tepes had disappeared.

I went back across the street, waited until the old man had fed his pigeons and left, and then I tugged off the heavy bar holding the shutters in place. The panes on the doors were as black as the soul of Copsa Mica. The doors were locked, but I scratched at the centuries-old glass.

Fortuna opened the door and led me in. Most of the tables and chairs had been stacked on a rough bar, cobwebs running from them to the smoke-blackened rafters, but Fortuna had pulled one table down and set it in the middle of the stone floor. He dusted off the two chairs before we sat.

"Did you enjoy the tour?" he asked in Romanian.

"*Da,*" I said, and continued in the same language, "but I felt that you overdid it a bit."

Fortuna shrugged. He went behind the bar, dusted off two pewter tankards, and brought them back to the table.

I cleared my throat. "Did you recognize me at the airport as a member of the family?" I said.

My erstwhile guide showed his grin. "Of course."

I frowned at this. "How? I spend as much time in the sun as I can to keep my tan. I was born in America."

"Your manners," said Fortuna, letting the Romanian word roll off his tongue. "Your manners are much too good for an American."

I sighed. Fortuna reached below the table and brought forth a wineskin, but I made a gesture and lifted the Thermos from my overcoat pocket. I poured for both of us and Radu Fortuna nodded, as serious as I had seen him during the past three days. We toasted.

"*Skoal,*" I said. The drink was very good, fresh, still at body temperature and nowhere near that point of coagulation where a certain bitterness sets in.

Fortuna drained his tankard, wiped his mustache, and nodded his appreciation. "Your company will buy the plant in Copsa Mica?" he asked.

"Yes."

"And the other plants . . . in other Copsa Micas?"

"Yes," I said. "Or our consortium will underwrite European investment in it."

Fortuna smiled. "The investors in the family will be happy. It will be twenty-five years before this country will be able to afford the luxury of worrying about the environment . . . and the people's health."

"Ten years," I said. "Environmental awareness is contagious."

Fortuna made a gesture with his hands and shoulders . . . a peculiarly Transylvanian gesture which I had not seen in years.

"Speaking of contagious," I said, "the orphanage situation seems insane."

The small man nodded. Dim light from the door behind me lighted his brow. Beyond him there was only blackness. "We do not have the luxury of your American plasma . . . private bloodbanks. The State had to provide a reservoir."

"But the AIDS . . ." I began.

"Will be contained," said Fortuna. "Thanks to the humanitarian impulses of your Dr. Aimslea and Father Paul. Within the month, your American television will air 'specials' on *60 Minutes* and *20/20* and whatever other programs you have created since I visited last. Americans are sentimental. There will be a public outcry. Aid will flow from all those groups and from rich people who have nothing better to do with their time. Families will adopt, pay a fortune for sick children to be flown to the States, and local television stations will interview mothers weeping with happiness."

I nodded.

"Your American health workers . . . and British . . . and West German . . . will flock to the Carpathians, and the Bucegis, and the Fagaras . . . and we will *'discover'* many other orphanages and hospitals, many other of these isolation wards. Within two years it will be contained."

I nodded again. "But they're liable to take a sizable amount of your . . . reservoir . . . with them," I said softly.

Fortuna smiled and shrugged again. "There are more. Always more. Even you know that in your land of teenage runaways and missing children's photos on milk cartons, no?"

I finished my drink, got up, and paced toward the light. "Those days are over," I said. "Survival equals moderation. All of the family must learn that someday." I turned back toward Fortuna and my voice held more anger than I had expected. "Otherwise, what? The contagion again? A growth of the family more rapid than cancer, more virulent than AIDS? Contained, we are in balance. Left to . . . propagate . . . there will be only the hunters with no prey, as doomed to starvation as those rabbits on Easter Island years ago."

Fortuna held up both hands, palms outward. "We must not argue, my cousin. We know that. It is why Ceausescu had to go. It is why he was not allowed into his tunnels, to reach the triggers that would have brought Bucharest down."

"So there *was* a Dark Advisor," I said, my voice little more than a whisper.

Fortuna smiled. "Oh, yes."

It took me half a minute before I could say the word. "Father?"

Fortuna rose, walked to the dark hall where a darker stairway waited. He gestured upward and led the way into the dark, my guide one final time.

▼▼▼

The bedroom had been one of the larger storerooms above the tourist restaurant. Five centuries ago it might have been a bedroom. His bedroom.

The figure lying there under thick tapestry-like covers and between gray sheets was so old as to be outside of age, beyond gender. The shutters were drawn, dust and cobwebs filled the room everywhere except where the head and shoulders lay on the pearl-white pillow, but there was a trail through the dust where attendants had trod, and just enough light filtering through the chinks in the shutters to allow one's eyes to adapt.

"My God," I whispered.

Fortuna smiled. "Yes."

I drew closer, went to one knee despite myself. He was barely recognizable from the photographs others in the family had shown me. The high forehead was still dominant, the deep-set eyes and sharp, noble cheekbones still visible, but nothing else was the same. Age had turned the flesh to yellow parchment, the hair to cobwebs, the eyes to egg-white marbles sunk deep in pools of dead skin. The teeth were gone. His hands lay above the blankets; they reminded me of a mummified monkey's paw I had seen in the Royal Museum in Cairo many years before. The fingernails were yellow and at least six inches long.

I leaned forward and kissed the ring on his right hand. "Father," I whispered, feeling my flesh crawl with revulsion and adoration.

There came a rattling sound deep in the thing's chest and a fog of rancid air escaped from the hole of a mouth.

I stood. It was then, as my eyes adapted to the dark, that I saw the lesions and scales, the thousand sores and scabs and rivulets of rotting skin that showed the presence of Kaposi's sarcoma in its final stages. I did not need to be Dr. Aimslea to recognize the telltale signs; all of us in the family are experts in AIDS and its symptoms. We fear it more than the stake or the auto-da-fé.

"He contracted it here?" I whispered, realizing how silly it was to whisper even as I did so. The thing on the bed would never hear again.

Radu Fortuna chuckled. "I wish it were so. Father was very careless. Remember, the HIV virus is a *retrovirus*. A contagion from millennia ago. The scientists do not know from whence it came, or how it was spread to humans."

I took a step away from the bed, my skin prickling with horror. *"Father?"*

Fortuna shrugged. "He was careless. Long ago. The family begged him not to go, but he was certain that Africa was a perfect place for his . . . retirement. A place to start a new branch of the family. To relive the glories of his Carpathian past."

I backed away until the doorframe stopped me. "He was mad."

"Oh, yes." Fortuna walked to the bed and covered the figure there so that the hands were out of sight and only the beak of a nose and rotting forehead remained above the covers. "The family pursued him across four continents before we could persuade him to come home. By then . . . he had no choice."

I shook my head. The room seemed to waver, to become insubstantial, and I realized that I was crying. Brusquely, I wiped away the tears. "I did not know."

"It does not matter," said Fortuna. "Western medicine and western science and western technology will beat this, just as it has beaten all other plagues. We count on it. The family has removed all barriers . . . national, ideological . . . so this can be true."

I nodded again and rested my hand on Fortuna's arm as we moved toward the staircase. On some internal impulse I turned back to the room, stood alone a second at the doorway, and genuflected once toward the darkness there before going back to my guide and advisor.

Together, my hand on his strong shoulder, we left the old world behind and went downstairs to greet the new.

A MATTER OF STYLE
▼▼▼

RON DEE

NEVILLE had always liked the movies. He still did. Being dead didn't stop him. When he was a kid he made a steady diet of the black-and-white monster pictures that showed on the Channel 8 Monster Matinee. He pored over the pages of *Famous Monsters of Filmland,* then stood in front of the mirror for hours afterward, imitating his heroes: Peter Lorre, Boris Karloff, or Bela Lugosi. Especially Bela Lugosi. He even bought a plastic set of fangs.

Unfortunately, Mom and Dad put a stop to that when he was nine, telling him the movies would frighten and warp him. It always pissed him off when they frowned at him and turned up their noses.

"How's this going help you get a job?" asked Dad.

"How's it going to help you get a girlfriend?" Mom questioned.

That's how much they knew. Of course, to be fair, neither of them could have guessed that he would die at the age of twenty-six from a vampire's bite.

▼▼▼

He met her in night school at junior college. Her name was Margaret and she smiled at Neville in class every time he looked at her, which was often. When Neville finally got up the courage to ask her out, he was surprised when she accepted. Most pretty girls just laughed at him, and she seemed very popular.

They went to the movies, of course. A revival showing of *Dracula's Daughter.* She laughed all the way through it. Since he usually saw these movies alone, he wasn't sure how to react . . . If she had been a guy he would have told her to bug off.

But she wasn't. She was female and very attractive. He kept his mouth shut over clenched teeth, just feeling thankful when she laid her head on his shoulder. Then she pulled his arm around her shoulders . . . and unbuttoned her blouse.

She wasn't wearing a bra.

Flushed with excitement, Neville barely noticed that her flesh seemed kind of cold, and he forgot all about it when he touched a hard nipple . . . and then her hand rested on his crotch, kneading him through his jeans.

The movie ended. They went to his car. She suggested the lake, and Neville drove as fast as he could.

Margaret undressed . . . undressed him. He remembered all those great but unbelievable letters in Penthouse Forum, and suddenly disbelieved them no longer. It was a dream—few girls had even kissed him before. She licked all the way down past his belly button, and he held her head, panting.

Then she bit him.

Just like that. She sucked him dry in five minutes, and it was the best orgasm he'd ever known. He wasn't sure what was happening at first, of course, because in his literary and visual experience, vampires always went for the neck, and when he figured it out, he was too weak to do anything to stop her if he had wanted to.

But he didn't want to after the initial fear. What the hell? He had been fired from every job since high school, and now he was nearly flunking out of night classes.

Why not try it as a vampire?

▼▼▼

He awakened in putrid darkness. Even with his background and the memories it took several moments to realize what had happened . . . what he was.

Then power swept him. He suddenly knew he would no longer have to put up with the rejections that had dogged his dating life.

Instinct taught him how to turn himself into a mist and reform above his stone in the cemetery. The whole process was only a chore of mind over matter. He imagined himself changing into a wispy cloud and rising through the crevices of his coffin, moving through the hard earth, and taking shape above the tiny marker. He stood there, invigorated with lust and the desire for some big-chested babe's boobs in his mouth, sinking his new teeth into her veins and draining her.

But he was naked. He looked down at his body and saw pale, hard flesh. He tried to reform again—

No luck.

It took several moments to figure out his mistake. Then he remembered the movies: *Whatever form a vampire chose when he rose from the grave was the form he had to remain in for the rest of the night.*

He had chosen the form: he imagined himself, but not what he would be wearing. So he had formed, minus a stitch of clothing.

Alarmed by his first mistake, Neville paced through the graveyard for an hour. His hunger grew, drawing him to the cemetery gates. After all, clothes or not, he was a vampire now . . . a terror of the night.

He leaped over the gates with surprising ease. Cars travelled down the street and he watched the people inside, touching his tongue from one fang to the other. One of the cars down the way was moving very slowly and he spotted a young, nicely formed brunette on the passenger side. Her boyfriend or husband was driving, and though he was a big, jock-looking guy, he was no longer a match for Neville.

Neville grinned.

He marched into the street, nearly floating on the concrete, then sped up until he was in front of the car. A horn honked and tires squealed. The car stopped.

"Get the hell out of my way!" screamed the driver, rolling down his window.

Neville gave him the finger and walked around to his side of the car. "Step out and make me."

The guy looked in his eyes and Neville turned his gaze to the girl. She was grinning.

"Get out of the car, bud," Neville said, "me and your babe are going places."

The girl suddenly laughed, and then the guy did, too. The guy revved his engine and shot the bird back to Neville. "Go find your pants, dick-bite," he roared.

Neville glanced down at himself and the car sped off, the laughter still ringing in his ears.

Neville stood there a moment, then walked back to the cemetery gates.

Death did not take away embarrassment anymore than it took away his lust for women. He got back over the gate and went back to his coffin, hungry.

The next night Neville was careful. He plotted for hours over his appearance, and came to be above the gravestone once more, dressed in a kick-ass tuxedo . . . solid black with a ruffled shirt. Cheerily, he floated over the grounds between the barren trees and markers, over the fence, and onto the sidewalk. Once more, the cars were going by, but he ignored them, paying as little attention as he could to the scent of blood inside them. He walked to the corner and gazed at the storefronts across from him . . . at the bars. He walked into the street, crossed it, and peered at the flashing lights. *Zippo's Pub.*

Neville walked to the hardware store beside it and glanced in the window that reflected the street, frowning that he didn't appear.

Of course not, he was vampire.

"Shit," Neville said, bringing a palm up to his head to comb hair away from his forehead. He shrugged and walked to the bar's door, opened it, and walked in.

The lights were dim, but his new nightvision revelled in it. Walking to the bar counter, he smiled at the menu of beautiful babes at tables and on stools. A blond-headed woman wearing a hip-tight skirt and her hair all frizzy met his eyes.

"Buy me a drink?" she asked.

"Yeah," Neville stuttered, swallowing. "Uh, sure."

A muscular man in a T-shirt walked to him.

"What'll it be?"

Neville swallowed again, feeling good. Unbelievably cool. He turned to the bartender. "Whatever the lady wants."

"You got your ID, sonny?"

"I'm twenty-six," laughed Neville.

The bartender frowned, making a thousand lines run up his shiny forehead to his bald pate. "Sorry buddy. It's the law. Gotta prove it."

The lady nudged his shoulder.

"Just a second," Neville chuckled, reaching into his coat . . . then into his pants.

No wallet. No I.D.

The lines on the bartender's face wriggled.

"I . . . forgot my wallet."

"Sorry. Can't serve you, son. Can't even let you stay in here. Sorry."

Neville swallowed. He moved his eyes over the other patrons, then shook his head. "Okay . . . thanks." Lowering his head, he walked back to the door, not even glancing back at the pretty lady. The door swung open and he was back on the sidewalk.

"Hey?"

The voice was at his shoulder and Neville turned his head. It was the pretty lady.

"I can't believe he made you leave," she sighed. "You look twenty-six to me . . . especially in that tux. Want me to go with you to get your wallet?"

"Uh . . ." Neville's eyes poured over her form that tried to pop out of her tight attire in all the right places. His teeth tingled as the scent of her life swept into his nostrils. "I don't know . . ."

"If you don't feel like coming back, maybe we could just go to your place and stay there?" Her red lips pressed together promisingly. "You're kind of cute."

"My place?" He thought of the cemetery. "Uh . . . I don't know. There's a lot of people sleeping there right now, you know."

"You want to come to my place?"

"Okay," he smiled.

"Where's your car?"

Neville frowned, thinking fast. "Uh, used a taxi."

"I don't want to wait for a taxi," Blondie sighed. "You want to use my car?"

Neville sighed too, nodded, and followed her to a red Camaro down the street. They both got in and he had to hold himself back from diving all over her right then. He wanted to go slow, and enjoy this first time.

"What kind of a date are you after?"

"All I can get," Neville said, unable to stop the fast words that seemed to form in his throat on their own. "I . . . I mean—"

"All the way, around the world; you want it, I can give it. Fifty bucks, Prince Charming. Paid in advance, okay?"

His teeth tingled so hard they ached. Neville leaned towards her. "Take off your clothes," he said.

"Money first, bub. Then we can do it here or go back to my place. Your dollars, you call the shots, but let me see your green."

"You heard me back there, I forgot my wallet."

She looked him up and down, wrinkling her forehead. "Hey, I'm serious, sweetie. No money, no honey. Hurry up."

"You're a hooker, aren't you?"

Blondie giggled, but her frown stayed. "No fuck. Now hustle, babe, or no fuck for real."

Neville opened his mouth wide. "I'm a vampire."

She peered at him, giggling louder. "We all are, dip, but I ain't lettin' no one suck me or do anything else without money. Come on or get out of the car."

"See my teeth?"

The giggles became laughter. Loud.

For a moment, Neville thought he would just go ahead and bite her anyway, but the sound of ridicule made the glory of this moment fade. He shook his head and opened the passenger door, got out, and slammed the door shut.

It was bad. It was so bad he went back to the cemetery, and gave up for the night.

But damn, he was hungry.

He planned. He planned for eighteen hours. Rising the third night, he appeared less impressively, but nattily. A sports coat, slacks, open shirt and lots of hair on his chest. He guessed he could appear as who or whatever he wanted if it came to that. A bat, like in the movies, or a wolf, or a football jock . . . the choices were endless. He could choose a different persona each night . . .

But tonight he still held hope for his own looks. Entering the bar again, he picked up a good-looking woman in her early thirties . . . a little older than he preferred, but by then he was getting too damn hungry to care. He was ready to bite almost anyone. He had remembered to imagine a billfold and driver's license this time, and got into the bar with no problem. The bartender even remembered him and apologized for the night before. Neville suddenly worried about meeting the hooker and then decided that if he did, she would be the one who would be sorry. Hunger was making him tough.

The blond whore wasn't there, though. The thirtyish woman was at a table by herself. Her more conservative attire didn't show him as much of the merchandise, but her tits were big and her blood smelled great. He bought her three drinks and walked her out to her car. She was writing down her phone number for him when he kissed her, and she had wanted him. The pen and pad dropped to the floorboard and she scooted over on the seat. He got in and pulled the door after.

"You're cold," she hesitated.

He kissed her again.

"You smell funny," she whispered when they broke again. Neville made a mental note to imagine cologne next time.

But it was okay. She was drunk and she was horny. She helped him take off her blouse and bra, and he sucked her tits for a long time. She shivered and moaned, pulling at his pants . . .

He couldn't wait. He bit her. He sucked her blood and it tasted good. She was dead in sixty seconds.

And he was still hungry.

Wanting to belch in satisfaction even though his reformed body didn't need to, Neville managed to make a similar noise and wiped his face. The rear view didn't show him, but he did the best he could, and got out of the car. He looked up the street. Two more women were leaving the bar.

Neville bulged with blood and confidence and walked towards them, sauntering like Elvis Presley. He reached the women as they sat down inside an older Chevrolet. "You two chicks looking for a good time?" he drawled.

The one nearest him in the passenger seat glanced up and he cringed at her blotchy face, then smiled as the smell of her life overcame her appearance.

She laughed. Her friend bent across the seat to look at him, too, and she tittered.

The door slammed, the engine started, and the car pulled away, echoing their ridicule.

Neville stared, then walked to the corner, crossed the street, and returned to his grave. Humiliation again. He realized at last that his successful conquest had not been swept off her feet by him, but had chosen him only with the same regrets he'd had choosing her. She had been desperate.

It sobered him. Luck had been with him, but hunters couldn't rely merely on luck. Most women, unlike men, were choosy. If he were a female, he could attract a man by the mere bat of an eyelash, smiling the right way, or by a way of walking. Just like the fake night school student who bit him. She could have attacked him and he would have succumbed to her gladly without a cry for help.

Inside the dank coffin that night, Neville frowned at the unfairness, but a moment later he was grinning. Knowing the truth always made solutions more possible. Just like the dandruff commercials where some brave soul gives the afflicted person a tube of Head and Shoulders. The next day the man or woman would return to work looking like a million bucks, and the opposite sex surrounded them like they were a magnet.

He could form himself as a woman.

Reviewing the anatomy of that gender took up the remaining time before the next sundown. As night's power flowed into Neville, he envisioned a Penthouse foldout girl he had fallen in love with and often masturbated to. Neville let himself become mist, rise through the dirt, and then reform, calculating each appearing curve and the scanty clothes he must wear.

He examined his false body gleefully, then went back over the gate.

He was lucky again. Before reaching the streetcorner, he passed a middle-aged man in a business suit. The man was watching his swinging, braless breasts. He sniffed blood running hot in the man's veins.

The man looked up into his eyes.

Neville grinned.

The man's jaw dropped and he shrieked, backing away.

"She's got no face!" screamed the man.

Neville stopped dead, touching his cheeks that were shapeless and flabby . . . no nose . . . a mouth but no lips . . .

No face. He could not even remember the foldout girl's face in his memory.

Breathing hard, he turned, ran back to the gate and ran to the grave.

Luck had given him his first taste of blood. Stupidity had kept it from him tonight.

He had plenty of time to consider the mistakes. He tried the woman's body again the next night, adding the face of an older girl he knew from his first round of college. She wasn't gorgeous, but it worked.

Nights passed and forming correctly became easier. He chose the forms of women several times, and only once missed out on dinner. As himself, it was harder. No matter how handsome he made himself be, no matter the stylish and expensive clothing, the best he could do was a conquest one night out of four.

Neville wondered if every male vampire had this kind of problem. It even made him wonder if the student who had bitten him had been a desperate, masquerading male.

Soon, he noticed the police cars, and one night read a newspaper of the murders occurring: BLOOD KILLER STALKING BARS, read the headline.

A night later he gasped when he saw one of his victims rising from a new grave across the cemetery. He noticed that prospective victims were becoming fewer. New headlines described "blood killer" murders that he knew he'd had no part of. Citizens of the city were curtailing their evening festivities in greater and greater numbers, and the police were out in force.

This called for a new strategy.

▼▼▼

At sundown, he bought a casket, filled it with dirt from his grave, and moved to another city. He got an apartment. The furniture was mostly odds and ends of the sort usually found at garage sales. Still, he fixed the place up as stylishly as he could to lull his prospective victims into a false sense of security.

Now the question was, what kind of vampire did he want to be?

While it was interesting to act out women's roles, Neville didn't want to repeat it constantly. Vampire or not, he was a man, and liked being a man. Blood lust was strong, but not enough to destroy every conditioning he'd endured while he lived. He didn't care if it meant he was sexist or whatever it meant, he just wasn't excited nearly as much drinking a man's blood as drinking a woman's.

So . . . he decided to do something about it. He studied men's clothing, and made a stylish wardrobe in his mind. Neville adorned himself with it each night he appeared as a man . . .

But still unsuccessfully.

That was when Neville remembered his youthful Saturday afternoons and his teenage Saturday nights. He bought all the video tapes about vampires, a TV, and a VCR.

Over the next week, he watched the movies about Dracula made by Universal, and those later British ones by Hammer. Dracula was the greatest vampire who ever lived . . . if "lived" was the right word. Still, he never heard of Dracula having to change into the guise of a woman . . . Instead, the ol' Count had been a literal lady-killer. Suave and sexy. Well-spoken.

Neville wanted to be like Dracula.

Dracula was smart. Apparently, he had made the same mistakes in his native land of Transylvania that Neville had made and, like Neville, moved to greener pastures. But Count Dracula had travelled to England with two or three dozen coffins, then began placing those coffins at strategic points throughout his new land. Spacing out his feasts like that had made them more difficult to trace back to him, and Dracula's sexy and mysterious manner drew women to him like flies to honey.

Neville put in another tape. He knew he must practice to be as alluring as the great Count himself. He couldn't practice in a mirror like he had as a child, of course, but he watched the different Draculas on TV again and again and froze the frame, said the lines himself, then backed the tape up and watched it once more, repeating the process until he had down the charisma displayed perfectly. He tried the Chris Lee approach . . . John Carradine . . . Ferdy Mayne . . . Frank Langella, but he always came back to Bela Lugosi. Something about that authentic Hungarian accent tantalized him, and he hoped it would work the same way with the women he approached.

Neville was tempted to try it out even before he felt he had it down completely, but the thought of laughter held him back. Although no one had tried warding him off with a crucifix yet, he didn't think it could work any better than laughter.

He purchased eleven more coffins, and placed them in several storage buildings throughout this new city. He felt safer, but not yet confident. After watching the Bela Lugosi movie one more time, he retired before the sun rose. He wasn't ready just yet, but after dinner tomorrow, he would practice once more, and maybe the next night—

The sun rose and passed the sky. Neville rested, imagining himself as a Dracula figure . . . perhaps as Dracula himself. After all, the real vampire was long gone, exterminated by luck and the will of the elderly Van Helsing. What better than to make his debut as the ultimate undead than to portray . . . to *become* . . . the legendary Count himself.

The sun set. *Power.* Neville felt it surge into him with the shadows, felt the city and lives all around him with the abilities he was steadily learning more about and bringing under his control.

He became mist, slipped through the casket's crevices, and formed as a busty redhead in a miniskirt and spiderweb top. A leather vest covered ample breasts. No panties, no bra . . . the smell of sweet roses. He smiled at his apartment's surroundings, went through the door, locked it, and hurried downstairs into the street.

Lots of horny men tonight.

He listened to the familiar thoughts that were so like his own and giggled at how simple it was to trap men. As a man himself, he knew just how to get their attention and how to take them without a struggle. And soon, very soon, it would be as easy with the women.

He stood beside the building wall, picking out thoughts, then one came that nearly snapped his head as he turned to follow it.

I'd love to make it with her—

A woman's thoughts.

Neville saw a dismal-looking strawberry blonde, her hair cut short. Nearly flat, but nice hips. The woman wore jeans and a pullover . . . very little makeup.

A dyke?

Their eyes met and the woman blushed.

A dyke.

Neville smiled. An idea crept into his thoughts: A chance to check out his lines on a woman.

He stepped to her quickly. She dropped her eyes. Neville's throat tightened, but he reached out his hand and let it touch the woman's wrist gently. She looked back up.

"You are beautiful," Neville said in the high feminine voice he used.

"I . . . so . . . so are you," the dyke stuttered.

"Your eyes are like the mirrors of eternity. Your heart beats in them . . . I see my life in yours."

The woman frowned, then shrugged and giggled. Her rough hand circled Neville's and the fingers rubbed his skin softly. "Do you want me?" asked the dyke.

"Yes . . . and you want me."

The short hair on her head shivered as the woman nodded slowly, almost as if she were drunk . . . drunk on the promise and ecstacy in Neville's eyes. The promise he had practiced so long.

"I want you now," the woman gasped.

"Now," repeated Neville.

"Now."

Neville kept his hand in hers and pulled her back to the apartment house's entry door. They went up the stairs, down a short, dumpy hall, into his living room. He locked the door and smiled at that term now. Perhaps it was the dying room? The room where his victims would all meet their end?

But that was greed. It was what had destroyed Dracula. Better to drink from several fountains, taking a small sip from each, than to empty each one before going on to the next. Neville was learning. There had been no deaths due to his hunger for weeks. He was slowly weakening each of a dozen entrees. Sampling several dishes a night to satisfy his hunger.

But this was a woman. He had not tasted a woman's blood in nearly two weeks, and this was a woman who desired him very badly, even if not in his true form. He might take her all the way.

They sat on the sofa together and the woman nodded at the homey decor with approval. "My kind of place," she said. "My name's Pete."

Neville licked his teeth as they started to tingle. "Just call me Countessa."

"Your majesty."

Neville touched her thigh.

"Boy. You sure got a lot of vampire movies on tape, don't you? I like that stuff, too, except I like it when they've got women vampires on other women. Like in those Karnstein movies. That stuff gets me off fast."

"Does it?"

"Yeah. I hate those other vampires. Especially that shitty Bela Lugosi. You know, 'I *vant* to drink your blood . . . I *vant* to bite your neck—' "

Neville knew that if he eaten already, his blood would be boiling. He backhanded the bitch with his supernatural strength . . . watched as her body flipped over the couch and thumped on the floor. She lay still.

"Dyke," Neville muttered, jumping on top of the slightly heaving body. He cupped her flaccid tit with a curled lip and felt a heartbeat. "I *vant* to suck your blood," he said in his imitation of Lugosi's accent.

She tasted good. Great. He guzzled her completely, savoring the final drops, literally drinking her in . . . slowly. Very slowly.

Dry.

Neville admired the motionless body like it was a trophy for several minutes, but soon it would begin to decay and stink . . . and he didn't want another vampire in this area. He walked to the barren kitchen, found a butcher knife, and knelt beside his victim, then begin to slice the blade into her flimsy flesh. There was no blood, of course. No mess. He worked quickly, dismembering the dyke and putting her pieces into three plastic sacks. After midnight, he would take the remains and bury them at different points outside the city.

But he smiled that his rehearsal had been so successful . . . and she had tasted quite good.

Putting *Dracula* into the VCR, Neville turned on the TV and settled back, speaking Bela's lines as Lugosi said them, perfecting his own delivery. Tomorrow night he would emerge as himself . . . the new "him," for the first time. He would find a woman . . . a real woman.

His mouth watered at the thought.

At dawn, Neville felt his strength slip away, though the windows were all covered with heavy cardboard. He crawled into his coffin and rested, not wanting to betray his ends by exerting himself to move around during these daylight hours. His soul tracked the sun as it wandered the sky, and his anticipation grew . . . stronger and stronger. Prostrate on the silken cushions in the deluxe, ornate casket, Neville mumbled his lines to himself . . . practicing his accent and imagining his movements as he planned their majestic style.

Just a few more hours now.

But they passed slowly, more slowly than any others he ever knew. He had gotten rid of last night's dismembered dinner, covering the burial places of her body parts carefully. On the way back into town, he stopped at a convenience store, bought a newspaper, and had smiled to see that there were no tales of mysterious deaths. His status as a vampire was probably unique in this area and it would be weeks before they found the pieces of the dyke, if they ever found them at all.

A pimple-faced teenager had walked out of the convenience store those hours ago, swigging a carton of milk, spied him and whistled.

Standing on the sidewalk beside his car—a nice, 1986 Honda with shiny red stripes on the sides—Neville turned with a glare. The boy whistled again and grinned, looking him up and down.

Neville had remembered then that he was still guised as an attractive woman. He lost the glare and smiled back.

"You look nice," ventured the boy.

The horny kid's blood was hot with his own desire, and smelled good, but Neville controlled himself with the thought of what the future held for him. He remembered the whore back at the bar that second night of his new existence.

"I am nice," Neville said with self-confidence. "You like what you see?"

The boy's grin had spread into his eyes.

"Fifty dollars," Neville said.

The grin faded as the boy bowed his head. His hands dug his pockets uselessly. Finally, he tugged out a greasy fiver.

"Not enough," Neville shook his head. Enjoying the tease, he raised his skirt an inch, showing the taut, sexy legs he had imagined.

The boy looked back at the store, held up his hand and swallowed hard. "Just a second."

Neville watched as the kid went back inside. Neville chuckled, watching the punk pull a knife from his torn jeans and point it at the cashier. Neville opened the car door and got in, sitting and laughing hard as the boy came running back out with several bills in his hand. The young voice screamed after Neville's Honda as Neville had pulled away. The screeching boy spit curses into the night.

It was good to laugh, Neville thought, knowing that he would never be on the wrong end of laughter again. . . .

The reflections made the time pass a little faster, and Neville began running a checklist for his appearance as he felt the sun begin to drop towards evening. Over and over. He felt as he had that night of the high school prom when he had taken a dog-faced date. He was all ready that night, and eager, despite her ugliness. After all, she had a nice ass, and rumor went that she was as easy as chewing gum.

But he had forgotten the rubbers. She was so pissed she wouldn't even jack him off.

He had learned. This time he would remember everything, and do everything right. His experiences at last were teaching him the importance of thinking ahead.

The sun set.

A key twisted in Neville's supernatural ignition . . . hungry desires and power flowed through his veins like gas to a motor. He manufactured his appearance as a smooth, worldly Dracula, down to the cufflinks on his shirt. . . . For a moment, he almost forgot what his true face looked like, but it came to him at the last moment, and he gasped with relief. He made a mental note to hold that memory close.

At last, Count Neville.

He laughed. Tonight, he would be what he had always dreamed of being.

▼▼▼

The night was brisk. Neville walked into the street. He glanced at the evening newspaper in a sidewalk stand and bought it. Dogs and surly-faced people passed him, but the streets would soon be clearer. The dogs avoided him, and some internal radar kept most of the pedestrians from brushing near.

Neville peered below the big headlines, and caught a breath when he saw a familiar face looking up from a black and white photo beside a small headline: TAMRA WILLIS, DEAD.

The face of the dyke.

Neville examined the newsprint quickly, growling under his breath. A dog had unearthed the bitch's head in a field early that morning.

Damn dog.

But Neville smiled. No clues. No evidence for anything other than natural blood loss for the situation. The cops were looking for an unknown psychotic. He folded the paper up and dropped it on the pavement. Murmuring voices buzzed around him.

No clues.

Besides, he would be more careful tonight. He glanced at the lowered faces sweeping past him, then walked to his Honda. The door clicked and he revved the engine, then drove into the street. He had a night club picked out for this event. Lots of hot, juicy babes. He wouldn't settle for a dyke or whore tonight . . . not even a desperate housewife.

The car stopped near the edge of the city and he parked it between a Cadillac and a Mercedes. Someday, he would have one of those, but hey, even the new Dracula had to start somewhere.

Neville unlatched the door and stood beside his car for a long minute, picking over his plans one last time, then he walked to the front door twenty feet ahead.

The nightclub was definitely of the upper echelon. Its walls were almost those of a castle . . . grand and ornate. Only the neon lights in the scattered small windows cheapened the effect.

DRACULA'S CASTLE, read the sputtering pink-orange letters in cursive above the wide door.

Neville stopped and smiled at the name. What better place for the new Dracula to go and begin his reign? Headlights splattered the wall ahead and he heard another car parking behind him, and continued ahead. He pushed open the rough cedar door and walked into the dusky hallway, gasping at the barrage of light, rock'n'roll, and voices. He hesitated, trying to concentrate in the noise. His eyes darted beside him to the cigarette vending machine and the coat rack that was nearly full.

"Good evening," Neville whispered under his breath, hanging onto his imagined persona desperately. "Good evening. You are the most attractive flower I have ever seen in this garden of life. Might I interest you in a drink?"

Neville smiled as the accented words slid off his tongue with all evidence of his careful rehearsal. Though he could barely hear himself in here, he knew was doing perfectly. He made a smile that was part sinister and part mesmerization, imagining a reply: "No, thank you . . . I never drink . . . wine."

A hand fell on his shoulder.

Neville started, swinging around with every inch of the surprise he felt, and was looking into the eyes of the most beautiful woman he'd ever seen. Her face was slender, but strong . . . full lips as ruby red as the blood that beat beneath them. . . .

"Uh . . . hi," he gasped, then stopped himself. "I . . . I mean . . . *good evening . . .*"

She smiled back briefly, brushing past Neville. He felt her cool flesh against his for a second that was far too short. He hesitated again, wanting her, knowing that he had discovered the woman of his lust already . . . and then she turned and glanced back, her eyes smiling into his.

When she went on, Neville swallowed hard, then followed her into the main room. Strobe lights flashed and the noise was even louder. The rhythm's power reminded him of his victories . . . especially in the way he had succeeded in charming "Pete" last night. It proved he had power over women, too. Further successes were merely dependent on how well he used that power, and with all the practice he'd had and with his new understandings, he was confident he could use it well!

Turning his head this way and that, he examined the groupings around the tables. Pretty women in elegant dress . . . older women . . . men in tuxedos not as flashy as his own. Neville grinned. As the woman he spoke to was truly a flower among weeds, so was he a full-bodied Oak among saplings.

He was a man again.

The woman stood at the bar.

Neville moved beside her as the bartender looked up. That older man was chewing gum and grinned at her. She smiled demurely. "I'll have a brandy on the rocks," her husky voice whispered.

"Make it a double for the lady," Neville spoke up quickly, focusing his eyes on hers and using his growing powers to entrance her.

The barman raised his hairy eyebrows as the woman frowned, but obeyed as she finally nodded. Neville chuckled, dropping his hand on her wrist.

"Don't push your luck," the woman breathed.

Startled, Neville drew his fingers back and looked away from her. He felt . . . *confused.* A streak of irritation was fading into hostility, frustration, and shock.

She had resisted him.

Quickly, he reviewed his words and ability, remembering how easy it had been to captivate the dyke yesterday and all those past men . . . even the few women. A few words and a glance was all it had taken with each one of them. After all, he had power now. He had rehearsed that power, and even before that practice he had been able to tantalize each one by the visions of ecstasy and release in his potent gaze. . . .

But she had resisted.

Once more, Neville went over his ploys, and turned back to her. The bartender brought her drink and she picked it up with elegant fingers . . . as perfectly formed as the rest of her.

"My name is Neville," he employed the accent once more, fastening his eyes on her deep, blue orbs. "I am new to this country . . ."

She yawned, turning away.

What was wrong?

Neville frowned: "What's your name?"

Her high giggle made Neville flinch, but he narrowed his eyes in heavy concentration as she turned back. She shook her head. "Are names so important to you, Neville?"

It was like he had no power at all.

"I am . . . Count Neville, a descendent of the Dracul family," he said clumsily, his accent fumbling like a bat gone deaf. "Names . . . positions . . . are very important."

"Are they?" Her lips wriggled. "The Dracul family?"

Neville frowned, grasping for the confidence he had built up so carefully. "Names are very important," Neville repeated. "Like your appearance . . . you are so beautiful . . ."

"Are you so concerned with beauty, Neville? Are you so concerned with how you impress others?"

This time, he laughed, seeing a way to swing her ideas to his own advantage. "There is power," he spoke richly. "There is power in position and status."

She picked up the brandy glass again and tipped it.

"You must agree," he needled her, "or you not would dress and appear as you do, eh?"

"Touché, Count Neville." Her long black eyelashes hovered midway, breathing a stronger passion. "But my looks are for purpose. Names and position once meant everything . . . *once.*"

Neville shook his head. "They still mean a lot to me."

"Are you trying to impress yourself, then?"

Once more, Neville's eyebrows collided with misgiving and he recoiled at her mild laughter. He tried for new words . . . fought an insisting stutter. "I . . . I have purpose."

She smiled, took another sip, and yawned once more.

"What is *your* purpose?" Neville said suddenly, trying to regain his lost ground.

Low laughter. Neville broke contact with her briefly and saw that other faces had turned towards him. The other men and women nearby were chuckling at him . . . at his floundering attempts of this seduction.

"What . . . is your purpose?" he brought an edge into his tone.

She tittered, exchanging amusement with the older man sitting at a stool beside her.

Neville lowered his head.

"Go impress someone who is able to be impressed, Count Neville."

More laughter. He backed from the bar. The man next to the woman whispered something and her silvery sound grew.

Laughter.

"No," whispered Neville. He remembered life and all the rejections, ridicule and chuckles he had always endured. He had longed for power and prestige. Vampirism had been his blessing rather than a curse. He had honed his new strength, spent long hours to claim his status.

Would Dracula have allowed this kind of treatment of himself?

"No."

Neville closed his eyes, clenching his fists, unclenched them, and stepped back to the bar. He dropped hard fingers on the woman's shoulder, rubbing his thumb against her soft neck. "I will not be rejected by you."

The woman was still bent towards the older man, but swiveled back to Neville very slowly. It was almost maddening.

"Determined little bastard, aren't you, Count?" Her sea-water eyes softened into something like pity.

Neville snorted. "What is your purpose? You must have one. Why do you dress to impress others?"

"I came here to find a man," she said, then sighed. "But maybe you'll have to do for tonight."

Another snort. "You want me," Neville said. "It is in your eyes. You *cannot* resist my charm . . ."

The woman sighed. "Have it your way, Count. Your place or mine?"

The laughter was his this time. Neville took her hand and squeezed it. "I will show you things you dared not dream of . . . I—"

She pulled him back to the door. "Come on, Count. Let's get it over with."

Her words did not confuse him this time. She was tough . . . more difficult than any other he'd experienced, but she was still overcome by him. He was victorious.

▼▼▼

They took Neville's Honda, and he steered to his apartment, confident once more. As he drove, he filled the car's cab with psychic vibrations of his energy and mastery. She giggled still, but he knew it was her own confusion and fears that caused it. She was, in spite of her denial, awed by his mystique . . . by his foreign and potent manner.

Neville parked on the street and walked around to her door, opening it in his best improvised Bela Lugosi form. She took his hand and they walked together to the building's entry door.

"You live here?"

"A temporary residence."

She nodded and they walked up the stairs. *He was victorious!*

"So," the woman said as they entered his living room, "you are new to this country. Perhaps you are new to many things."

"I will show you something new."

She sat on his couch casually, showing an expanse of her thigh.

"You will show me nothing," the woman chuckled deeply. "You are impressed by yourself . . . and perhaps you may impress others, but you must understand, Count Neville, that to be successful you must change with the times."

Neville blinked.

She glanced at his collection of videotapes. "In order to fulfill yourself now, Neville, you must lose that self. Your identity is meaningless. All that must remain of you is the thirst for blood. Pride must go. There is no pride in hunger."

Neville dropped his jaw, exposing his teeth, but not to attack her . . . in *shock.*

"Your accent and pride are outdated. Technical progress has brought the extinction of thousands of species of animals. Social progress has brought about the near extinction of our own."

"Who . . . who are you?" blustered Neville.

"I am Dracula," the lovely, busty woman sang softly. "The name no longer means anything but laughter. No longer will it bring terror into the heart of anyone. Familiarity breeds contempt. I tried to keep my pride for years, Neville, but that has no purpose. In death . . . *our* kind of death, the only purpose is blood. We have always been chameleons, relying on the guise that spells the greatest success. The time of noblemen has passed. Feminists, rapists, and AIDS have made women wary of strangers. Our purpose lies only in our hunger. . . ."

Neville shrank back uncertainly. He felt the hunger the woman reminded him of. "I *vill* suck your blood!"

"Don't waste my time, Neville. I plan to suck yours. It's never as good getting it second-hand from another vampire, but you can consider that loss to be your payment for this lesson." The woman who called herself Dracula kicked at the stack of videotapes and toppled them to the carpet. "Life is not a movie, and death isn't either, okay?"

"You . . . you can't be Dracula. Van Helsing killed you—"

"Movies . . . Just keep telling yourself, Neville, it's only a movie."

The Dracula woman grabbed Neville's shoulders and a harsh, steel power clamped him in her rigid fingers. She pulled him close, surpassing his struggles easily, ripping away the collar of his shirt and lowering her face to his cold flesh. Her sharp teeth bored into his throat and drug at his nearly empty veins like an industrial vacuum cleaner.

It *hurt!*

Yes, it hurt bad. Not like when the night school girl first drained him in a bizarre ecstacy, but like the death he'd always been taught to fear. The power and energy he had revelled in were dragged from him so quickly he began to fall, held up only by his assailant's powerful arms. When Neville was so empty it was like he was falling into a black hole deep inside himself, the hands released him and he dropped onto the floor, barely able to even curl a finger.

The beautiful woman stood above him with a nasty grimace, dark red staining her lips and chin.

"If it's any consolation, you taste like shit. There's nothing worse than congealed blood . . . like someone else's gum that they've already chewed and thrown away." She wiped her mouth and fangs. "If you can get into your coffin before the sun comes up, Count Neville, think about what I said. You're dead, okay? You don't have to prove anything to anybody. Blood. Just think about blood and the easiest ways to get it."

Neville croaked.

"Hell, listen to me. Maybe I ought to be a teacher . . ." She walked to the door and opened it, fixing Neville with those deep blue eyes once more. "If you want your car, I'll leave it at the club, okay? I'm going to try to get back and see if I can get to that horny guy I was talking to. I bet *he* tastes fine."

"You . . ." Neville hissed, pushing out the words with all his might. "You're really Count Dracula?"

She narrowed her eyes and nodded. "I *vant* to suck some blood, Neville."

The door closed and Neville blustered in a sudden, belated regret for the things of life . . . the choices no longer available. Life had been bad, with limited choices open to him, but at least with the lingering choice between life and death.

Now there was only death. He was dead but undead, and drained of the life that made it possible to him to continue . . .

And in a very few hours, the sun would be rising.

SELECTION PROCESS

▼▼▼

ED GORMAN

A man named Skylar phoned Reardon from San Francisco and told him about the job. "It's special, Frank." Of course all of Skylar's jobs were special. That's why they paid so well. Reardon listened to the details and after some hesitation—on a few points Skylar seemed purposely vague—he took the job. Skylar was after all paying $100,000, which even for a killing was a lot of money. Skylar used no names, of course. He never did. People came to him and told him they wanted jobs done, and Skylar then found the right people to do them. In a very real sense he was a talent agent.

"Oh, yes," Skylar said. "I'll be sending you an overnight letter with all the instructions." Then he rang off.

Twenty-four hours later, Reardon landed in a large Midwestern city. He took a nice room in a nice mid-town hotel, spent most of the day in his underwear watching a double-header on the tube, and then started thinking seriously about his plans for tonight.

It wasn't the prospect of killing somebody that bothered Walter James Reardon. After surviving as a POW for eighteen months in Nam, and then later doing five-to-ten for armed robbery, Reardon had pretty much learned that life wasn't nearly as precious as priests and politicians would have you believe. Humans were just one more species of nowhere animal running around on a nowhere planet. You lived and then came extinction. Total annihilation of body and mind. This old dude in the slam had said it best: "Ain't nothin' to get excited about. Dogs don't fret about it and neither should we."

No, it wasn't the killing that bothered Reardon. It was the method the letter writer outlined.

I want you to take a can of gasoline and douse the young woman in bed and then set her afire. Let the fire burn for awhile and then put it out. Make sure she's dead before you leave. I am paying you a great deal of money on the assumption that you will do exactly as I instruct.

He wondered who the letter writer was, and how you could come to hate a woman so much you'd want to burn her alive. Obviously Skylar hadn't written the letter. The man who wanted the woman dead had.

For dinner, Reardon had a club sandwich and a bottle of Miller Lite. He was getting puffy in the cheeks and belly again. Even though the only women who saw him naked were whores, even whores had eyes, didn't they?

▼▼▼

The rental car was a green Chevrolet sedan. He went to a hardware store and bought a flashlight and a red gasoline can and a map of the city.

In a parking lot, he studied the map for a while, looking for the easiest way to get in and get out of the place, especially access to the freeway system should something go wrong, and then he was set except to buy a gallon of gasoline.

▼▼▼

In high school Reardon and his friends always used to cruise neighborhoods like this one, big-ass rambling white houses with Lincolns and Caddys parked in the drive. Impossibly beautiful blonde girls always lived in these places, just the sort of girls who wanted absolutely nothing to do with cheap yearning boys like Reardon and his pals.

Maybe after all these years he was going to get a chance to kill one of these imperious bitches tonight. Maybe this was some babe who was getting it on with the golf pro at the country club and her lawyer-husband couldn't take it any more and wanted her killed.

The only thing that troubled Reardon was setting somebody on fire. Hardcase as he was . . .

The address he wanted was in the center of the block. Fortunately, both houses on either side of it were dark and quiet.

He didn't even slow down. He'd just wanted a view from the front. His destination was the alley behind the house.

▼▼▼

After parking the car close to the garage, Reardon got out, taking the can with him. The gasoline sloshed across his hands and trousers. He cursed. He was neurotic about being neat and smelling good. He'd been one of those soldiers who'd spent hours shining his shoes.

Fireflies blinked through the darkness; newly-mown grass smelled sweet on the air; a few houses away a big dog barked and ran the length of a clothesline, his collar clanking and catching him at the last. Reardon thought of being a POW. He knew what that chained-up dog was going through.

The letter writer had provided a key designated for the back door.

Reardon stood still in the crickety darkness, looking at the deep shadows the moonlight created.

He looked left, right, up, down. He looked everywhere a person could possibly be. He saw no one. No one. But you never knew. Somewhere very near somebody could be watching everything you did. Everything.

He tapped the .45 in his shoulder rig inside his Brooks Brothers summer-white jacket. In case anything went wrong, he always had this.

He opened the screen door on the back porch. Lawn furniture cluttered the shadows. The fading scents of cigarettes and whiskey were on the air.

Still carrying the can, he went to the interior door, tried the locked knob, and inserted the key.

In less than thirty seconds, he was going up four steps to the kitchen.

In the silver moonlight, the kitchen smelled of nutmeg and paprika and coffee. But no smell was as strong as the gasoline he carried.

Once more, he stood without moving, listening.

His heartbeat had increased. He did not kid himself, ever. Tough as he was, this was always a scary business. Anything could go wrong. Anything.

The refrigerator motor thrummed. Out on the street a car passed by. The dog down the street started barking again.

Reardon moved.

He went through a large dining room. He could imagine a black maid serving fancy people thick slices of roast so rare they were not just pink but bloody. The talk would be of the stock market and politics and perhaps sports. After the war, in the days when he thought he might turn himself into a professional hero, he'd been invited to the homes of many rich people. And that was how they lived. He'd always felt sorry for the maids in these places, knowing how well they wanted to dump the food all over the stuffy people they had to serve.

The living room had a huge fieldstone fireplace. All the built-in bookcases gave the place the feel of a den.

Second floor, the center bedroom, the letter writer had instructed.

Reardon started up the winding staircase.

He was sweating now. He always sweated while he was on a job. More nerves.

His six-two, two hundred and ten pound body punished the stairs. They whined and groaned.

At the top of the stairs, he paused once more. Up here the dominant noise was the plumbing. This house had to be fifty, sixty years old and probably needed new pipes.

He started down the hallway.

He passed a room with its door closed. In this situation, closed doors scared the hell out of him.

He set the gasoline can down and took out his .45. It wasn't an exotic weapon but he'd gotten used to it in the military and saw no reason to give it up now.

He put his hand on the doorknob. Eased his head closer to the door. Listened.

He threw the door open and dropped to one knee, in firing position.

Spectral moonlight shone silver through gauzy curtains billowed on the breeze of an open window.

A large brass bed and old-fashioned furnishings.

Nothing whatsoever to worry about.

He got up, lifted the gasoline can, and continued his way down the hall. He didn't put his .45 away. It felt comforting in his hand.

He saw the center bedroom but he kept going. He went all the way to the end of the hall and checked the other rooms. None of the doors were closed so they were easy to inspect.

Nothing.

Nobody will be home except the young woman in bed.

That's what the letter writer had promised. And that's what the letter writer had delivered.

Gasoline can in one hand, .45 in the other, Reardon went back to the center bedroom.

While the door wasn't shut, it was only partially open. Reardon put his foot out and gave it a little push.

The door swung inward.

Right away, he knew something was wrong.

The strange thing was, he didn't know *why* it was wrong. But somehow the shadowy room sent him a queer message.

He took two steps across the threshold.

This was the smallest room on the second floor. And where the other rooms had been decorated conservatively, this one was done in pink wallpaper with huge illustrations of teddy bears frolicking in summer meadows. Beneath two open windows sat a small tricycle and against the right wall stood a bookcase filled with dolls of every kind imaginable. He found it curious that neither of these windows had screens on them.

And then he knew why his instincts had warned him about this room. *This was the room of a little girl.* Not a "young woman" as the letter had stated.

A little girl.

She lay sleeping in the single bed that lay along the east wall. A small blonde head in pigtails could be seen just above the edge of the cover.

He set the can down and stood there stunned.

Never before had he considered killing a child and now that he was confronted with the decision, he wasn't sure what to think.

Who would want a young girl killed? And by a method so hideous?

He slipped his .45 back into its rigging and then started toward the bed.

He had to quell the impulse to simply cut and run. To go back home and sit by his mailbox and wait for the inevitable letter informing him that he was a chicken-shit sonofabitch and that he'd completely fucked up the job.

His weight made the floor groan.

The closer he got to the bed, the better he could hear the soft moist noise of her little-girl snoring.

How old was she? Eight? Nine? Ten?

Having no children of his own, he didn't know how to make such a guess.

All he could do was move forward and—

And then she turned over in bed and looked straight up at him.

There in the shadows, she said, "Hi. You're Mr. Reardon, aren't you?"

What the hell was going on here?

His hand went back to his .45. He pulled it out and filled his hand with it.

"Did I frighten you?" she said.

He couldn't seem to find his voice. He cleared his throat several times and said, "No."

"Actually, you look kind of funny, do you know that?"

"Oh." He couldn't think of what else to say.

"Yes. I mean, there you are this great big man holding a gun but you looked scared. It seems to me that I should be the one who looks scared. But that's the funny thing. I'm not scared at all."

"You're not?"

"No. I was expecting you."

"You were?"

"Sure," she said, as if Reardon weren't very bright.

And then, before he could quite tell what she was doing, she threw back the covers and set her legs to the floor.

She was a thin, pretty girl in buff blue pajamas. Her pigtails swung merrily from side to side whenever she moved in the slightest way.

"Why don't I turn a light on?" she said, hopping off the bed and leaning over to the nightstand.

The lamplight seemed to blind him temporarily. The shadows were sent scurrying. "There, isn't that better?" she said, sounding as if she were the adult and Reardon the child.

All this left Reardon in the middle of the bedroom. The gasoline can at his feet. The gun in his hand.

"Does that ever get heavy?" she said.

"The gun?"

"Umm-hmm."

"Not really."

"How come you carry it?"

I've got to get back in control of this, he thought. *Something is terribly wrong here.*

"Where are your parents?" he said.

"Not here."

"They leave you alone like this, this late at night?"

"Sometimes. Besides, the night is my favorite time."

"But you're only—"

She shrugged. "Older than I look, probably."

He glanced around the room. In the soft lampglow, the teddy bears looked even more jolly. He thought of his younger sister Ione, a woman he seldom thought of, and saw even less. Growing up, she'd been crazy about teddy bears. Every spare cent she could find had gone toward teddy bears.

And then he noticed the two windows without screens. Hell, that didn't make any sense. Anything could get in here.

The girl nodded to a silver pitcher and two glasses on a hammered silver serving tray on her nightstand. "Are you thirsty, Mr. Reardon?"

"How do you know my name?"

"Oh, you'd be surprised what I know, Mr. Reardon. But you didn't answer my question about having a glass of water."

"Uh, no thanks."

"Well, I think I'll have one if you don't mind."

"Go ahead."

He still couldn't believe that conversation this adult and polished could come out of a frail little girl body.

All this had aspects of some bad, unlikely marijuana dream.

The water pitcher was full. She had to use two hands to fill her glass and even at that, she looked as if she might drop the whole pitcher.

"You sure?" she said when her glass was full.

"I'm sure."

She set the pitcher down with a great deal of careful effort, picked up her glass and then went over and sat on the edge of her bed again.

She took a big swallow of water and then went "ah" as if she'd enjoyed it greatly and then she looked up at him and said, "You still look frightened, Mr. Reardon."

"I want to know how you know my name."

"I was told your name."

"By who?"

She shrugged frail shoulders. "It really doesn't matter, Mr. Reardon."

"It does to me."

She nodded to the gasoline can. "I'll bet that's heavy. A lot heavier than your gun."

"I guess so."

Her eyes met Reardon's. "You must have a pretty good reason to bring a can of gasoline all the way up here."

"I suppose."

"And I'll bet I know what it is."

Reardon said nothing.

The girl said, her eyes still on his, "Do you think you can do it, Mr. Reardon?"

"Do what?"

"Oh, come on now, Mr. Reardon. You know why you came up here and so do I."

"Who the hell are you?"

She smiled. "I'm this innocent little girl who was having a nice night's sleep until you came tromping up the stairs with this gasoline can so you could set me on fire."

"You little—"

But Reardon stopped himself. Anger would be a sure sign of panic and he did not want to show any signs of weakness.

"What's your name?" he said.

She sighed, as if she were tired now of indulging him and his stupid questions. "If it really matters, Mr. Reardon, my name is Jenny."

"Jenny what?"

"Jenny O'Shea."

All he could think of was some kind of insurance scam. He'd heard of something like this in Cleveland once. This heavy-duty businessman gets into a lot of debt trouble and the only way out is to insure his kid very heavily and then have a professional off the kid. Unfortunately, the professional made some mistakes and both he and the father ended up in the gas chamber.

"I want you to tell me about your parents," Reardon said.

"Why?"

"Because I want to know."

"I'm not afraid of you, Mr. Reardon. You can't bully me into anything I don't want to do. Or tell you."

She took another sip of water.

When she was finished drinking, she set the glass back on the nightstand and said, "Now will you answer my question?"

"What question?"

"If you can do it or not. Throw that gasoline all over me and set me on fire."

"Why do you think I'd want to do that?"

She gave him a knowing smile—one with even a hint of unlikely eroticism in it—and said, "We're wasting time, Mr. Reardon. Your time and my time."

"I don't know what you're talking about."

"It's probably my face."

"Your face?"

She laughed. "The well-scrubbed look. The freckles and everything. The daughter everybody wants to have. That's probably why you can't do it." She looked at him knowingly again. "You didn't know I was going to be this little kid, did you?"

"No; no I didn't."

"Well, unfortunately for both of us I am."

And with that, she spun around on the edge of the bed and set herself flat on the bed.

"Is this better?"

"Better for what?" Reardon said.

"Maybe I should say 'easier.' Is this easier for you if you don't see my face?"

Reardon started to say something sputtering but she interrupted him.

"I have to admit that if I saw my cute little face, I couldn't splash gasoline all over me, either."

And then she reached down and scooped up the covers, pulling them right up to her chin.

Then she rolled over on her side and faced away from Reardon.

She now lay just as she had when Reardon had come into the room.

"Why don't you turn the light out, Mr. Reardon?"

"Why should I do that?"

"Because that'll make it easier, too. In the darkness you probably won't be able to see anything except my blonde hair. And you can pretend that belongs to a much older woman. You know?"

Reardon said nothing.

The girl said, "This is getting pretty boring, Mr. Reardon."

"What the hell's going on here?"

Still keeping her back to him, she said, "Are you or are you not going to douse me with gasoline and set me on fire, Mr. Reardon?"

"You sound like you *want* me to."

"I want you to do what *you* want to do, Mr. Reardon. Set me on fire or leave. It doesn't matter to me."

Reardon looked down at the gasoline can.

She said, "If you don't set me on fire, Mr. Reardon, your reputation will suffer."

"What?"

"Sure. Hit men are very dependent on their reputations, I understand. I mean, think of how fierce you'll be if you set me on fire. 'That Reardon. He'll do absolutely anything. He even set a little girl on fire.' "

"What the hell do you know about hit men?"

"More than you realize, Mr. Reardon." She paused and then shook her head. He wished he could see her face. "Of course, on the other hand, setting me on fire may give you a reputation you don't want. People are funny about kids. Hurt a kid in even the slightest way and some people start thinking of you as a pervert. And most people just don't like working with perverts. You know?"

Reardon looked once more at the can of gasoline.

The girl said, "But if you don't set me on fire, your price is going to go down."

"It is?"

"Sure. Because people will know that you're not absolutely fearless.

And if you're not absolutely fearless, then they'll pay you accordingly. Only absolutely fearless hit men get the absolute top dollar. I mean, that only makes sense to me. Doesn't it make sense to you, Mr. Reardon?"

He leaned over.

His fingers touched the handle of the gasoline can.

What the little girl said made sense.

If he didn't do this job, he would be diminished in the eyes of some potential employers.

Some employers wanted a man who was absolutely capable of anything. Anything.

His fingers started to tighten on the handle.

"Just please hurry, Mr. Reardon. OK? My mother always says I have a low tolerance for boredom and she isn't kidding. This is really getting tedious. You're a hit man, Mr. Reardon. You're supposed to be decisive."

His fingers gripped the handle tightly now. He raised the can until it rested against his hip.

He put the .45 back in its rigging.

He had no idea what was going on here. He just wanted to get it over with and get back on the plane and get the hell out of this city.

"I'm proud of you, Mr. Reardon."

He had been raising the can so he could unscrew the cap.

"You're going to do it, aren't you?"

Reardon said nothing.

"You're going to slosh it all over me and toss a match on it and then get out of this town as fast as you can. Good for you, Mr. Reardon. Good for you."

Could he actually do it? Could he?

He thought of the money. One hundred thousand for this job. If he didn't do it, he'd have to return the money he'd already received. And he had major plans for that.

He unscrewed the cap, dropped it in his pocket.

"I'm ready, Mr. Reardon," the girl said. "I'm just lying here waiting."

He approached the bed.

Closer. Closer.

The gasoline sloshed around inside the can.

In only moments now.

"I know you don't particularly want to do this, Mr. Reardon, but I sure admire your cool head for good business. I really do."

Hell, the way this little bitch drove him crazy, he might just end up *enjoying* this.

Higher, higher the can went.

"Fire away," the girl said. "Fire away."

And then he cocked his arm back, ready to splash gasoline all over her and the bed there in the darkness and—

And that's when he realized abruptly why the two windows had no screens.

How else were the bats going to get in?

Six of them, sleek and black and furry, dove straight for his neck.

The gasoline can went flying from his hands, slamming against the wall.

And then the room, suddenly falling into unutterable darkness, reeked of gasoline.

His last recollection, deep into the darkness, was of laughter.

Somebody was laughing. But why?

▼▼▼

Reardon was in the shadows when her limo pulled up to the curb. Janice Evans, the most sought-after movie star in the world right now.

Reardon had been stalking her for three nights. Soon enough, he would make his move. Soon enough.

He watched as she dangled a long, shapely leg from the back door of the limo and then followed this with the rest of her long, shapely body.

The crowd outside ROOM 504, the city's hottest new disco, erupted with shouts and applause when they recognized who she was.

She tried to look properly humble. It was not easy.

Then she was gone, two black bodyguards on either arm, into the sweat and frenzy of the disco.

Reardon figured he had at least a couple of hours before she'd reappear. His plan was to follow her home tonight and then—

He went across the street to a diner. He sat in a booth where he could keep the disco in full view. Her limo was still at the curb, waiting. The liveried driver leaned against the fender, smoking a cigarette. Whenever the disco door opened up, you could hear a blast of music and laughter.

The laughter reminded him of Jenny O'Shea. The night his entire life changed.

But then his memories were interrupted by a waitress.

"Help you?" said the tired-looking woman.

"Coffee. Black."

"Hamburger or something to go with it?"

The thought of food made him nauseous. That was one of the things he hadn't gotten used to, even after six months. How you never ate food. And how you slept all day long. Not in a coffin or anything. A room with the blinds drawn was sufficient.

When his coffee came, Reardon went back to thinking about the night with the girl.

It had all been a test. They would know he was the man they were really looking for if he was unscrupulous enough to throw gasoline on the little girl and then set her on fire.

Which, there at the last, he'd been willing to do.

It had all been a set-up, the letter, the money, the little girl. Just to see if he could actually do it.

Because if he could do it—

"There's something you must understand, Mr. Reardon," the little girl's father told him when all six people, no longer in batform, stood in the bedroom. "As a group, we tend to be sickly and fearful people. We have much work to do and many plans but we need a man or woman who's up to the job. Somebody who is without scruples of any kind. And tonight, Mr. Reardon, you've shown yourself to be that man."

And that was how Reardon became one of them.

And how he began stalking celebrities.

Celebrities were tough to get to, even for vampires sometimes. But a hit man could get close enough to wound them—and while they were lying wounded, a vampire could slip into the room and turn them into one of the undead.

Vampires loved to make converts of celebrities. Somehow it made being a vampire even more of a pleasure, knowing that movie stars, politicians and sports figures were one with you. And some day when there were enough vampires in high places—

Reardon reached in his sport jacket pocket and touched the Walther. His old .45 just wasn't enough anymore. As Jenny—who'd turned out to be a two-hundred-year-old vampire—had told him, "Now you're really going to have to get serious about your work, Mr. Reardon."

He tried to sip coffee but his teeth got in the way, scraping against the edge of the cup. The teeth still presented some adjustment problems.

He checked his watch. He probably had a while before he needed to go and station himself in the alley, readying himself for when Janice Evans appeared on the street again.

He sighed, wondering if it was really a good thing or not, being a vampire. He hadn't had much choice. He'd passed his test and been selected.

Twenty minutes later, he went outside with his Walther. Forty-three minutes, he opened fire, getting Janice Evans high up near the collar-bone.

Shortly after, a bat was seen wobbling its way over the frenzy that had engulfed the disco.

Along with the teeth, he'd also have to get used to the flying.

THE VAMPIRE
IN HIS CLOSET
▼▼▼

HEATHER GRAHAM

THE vampire was real. Chris knew it the second he threw open the lid of the coffin. Before the creature opened its eyes, Chris knew that it was real. No regular corpse could have looked so very alive. Well, rather dead, too, of course, but alive, as well. The creature's skin was pale, but still, it had a glow of life. And it seemed as if the lungs were moving, as if the heart were beating.

The eyes suddenly flew open, and Chris felt his own heart begin to thunder and soar. They were black eyes, obsidian black, as black as the night beyond them. They were spectacular eyes, large, hypnotic, fine eyes, rimmed with red, as if rimmed with blood.

And then, it began to smile. Smile, and stare at Chris's throat, where the rampant beating of his heart was giving tell-tale signs at his vein. Blood was racing throughout his system. For a hungry vampire, that pounding of his pulse must have been quite a sight.

"Hello," the creature said, and its smile deepened cunningly.

Chris had expected a hoarse rasp. Or perhaps an accent. Something Romanian, exotic. This vampire had the faintest hint of a Southern accent.

Well, this was New Orleans.

Still, Chris had seen every single vampire movie it was possible to see. He waited for the creature to say something like, "I vant to drink your blood," but the creature did not do so.

It stared at Chris. Then it rose to a sitting position very slowly within the boundaries of its coffin.

"Well, sir, you have awakened me." There was the slightest pause. "You must know that I am a vampire," it said. Still, that soft accent. The voice was husky, masculine. Chris imagined that most women, Magda included, would find it a sensual, alluring voice.

In fact, this vampire was one alluring fellow. Like the Bela Lugosi Dracula, or maybe more like Frank Langella. He certainly was not the hunched, ugly creature once played by Klaus Kinski. With his obsidian-dark eyes and jet hair, a face constructed of clean lines and very classical features made him very handsome, despite the paleness of his flesh.

And when he stood, rising out of his coffin with a swift, smooth movement, he was tall, broad-shouldered, well-proportioned. In short, he was amazingly charismatic. Chris found himself studying the creature, enrapt himself, and very nearly losing hold of the Cross of Damocles that he held within his fingers.

"A thirsty vampire . . ." the creature said, those obsidian eyes boring directly into his.

Chris remembered himself in time. He fumbled in his pocket and swept forward the Cross of Damocles.

Instantly, the creature threw up its arms, cowering away from Chris.

"By Satan himself! You carry THAT talisman!" The vampire cried.

Chris stared at the cross with the same amazement with which he had first stared at the vampire. Oh, yes, he had believed. As long as he could remember, he had believed. He had seen the Bela Lugosi movie first, he thought, and then later on he had read Bram Stoker's book, hanging on every word. And he had become more and more convinced that Bram Stoker had been writing due to some real life experience. Vampires were real, vampires did exist.

As he had grown older, he'd learned to curb his beliefs. But he'd loved the stories. So much so that he'd learned to write them himself, and in time, he had done quite well with it. He'd started with "The Vampire That Ate New York," and he'd gone through many of America's major cities since. But his success had made him restless. He needed something more. He needed something real.

One night in a Houston bar he'd heard about the house right by the garden district in New Orleans. It was called "The Castle" because it was a castle—the original owner had ordered every single brick and stone over from Europe. It was going amazingly cheaply because it had a history of the macabre, suicides within the walls, disappearances on dark and rainy nights, and the like. Rumor had it that the last owner—a

German man—had stayed only a matter of weeks, then returned suddenly to Europe, leaving word that the property should be condemned.

If there were such a thing as a living—or non-living—vampire, as it were, then Chris was certain that he had found where that vampire should exist. And so he had determined that he would buy the house.

It hadn't been easy. Magda liked Houston. And after ten years of marriage, it seemed that Magda had learned the art of getting her own way. But this time, Chris had been determined. He'd gone so far as suggesting that he and Magda call it quits at last, and go their separate ways. Magda had been startled into a rare silence. As far as buying The Castle went, Chris was quite determined. Since his vampire books kept Magda living the life style that Magda found so enjoyable, she had at long last given in.

And once in the house, well . . .

Chris had dug and torn through it, but he had known where to look from the beginning. There had been a cellar in the house, rare for New Orleans where people were buried above the ground to avoid the water table. Well, it was a half-cellar, really. The castle had been built up on a land fill to allow for it.

And it was perfect. It was dank and dreary, and there were spider webs galore. Chris loved it. He had immediately set up his word processor and printer and his beloved books and posters of Vampira and Elvira. His determination had done him very well. In the very first week he found the first of what he called "the Van Helsing papers," although there was no signature on them anywhere, and certainly no indication that they had been written by anyone named Van Helsing. Chris was still convinced.

The papers had been old, yellowed. They had been written in a script that had begun neat and legible, and become more and more flowing and illegible as they continued.

He—it—the creature!—had been the one to have the castle built. He —it—the creature!—must now be contained. And the Cross of Damocles, blessed by five popes and containing the flesh of the martyr John, could contain the creature. Anyone holding the cross had power over the creature, and anyone who learned the secrets of the cross could actually bind the creature to his will. Of course, care must be taken. The gravest care. For the creature, too, had powers. The only real way to be safe was to keep the creature locked in his sepulcher, with the cross in the brick, as the writer of the papers had left it. For the vampire, awakened, might make demands. And for his life, and his sanity, the man to awaken the beast might well have to meet those demands. . . .

There was something else in those papers, too. It all seemed to hinge on the number three. Chris could hardly read the writing. But if the vampire three times betrayed the mortal who had awakened him, then the vampire would have to give three promises to the mortal, promises that could not be broken.

A tall tale? Surely, the papers had been written by a fellow with an imagination more vivid than his own.

But no. After he had found the papers, Chris had found the Cross of Damocles, laid over a wall of brick. And he had torn down the bricks, found himself in a large closet with a smell of dust and mold and a coffin dead center in the small space.

And now . . .

The vampire.

"You are real!" Chris gasped.

"Indeed, yes, I'm real. Thirsty, aggravated—no, truly annoyed. What is the meaning of this interruption? Really!" The vampire actually had a very deep drawl. And he was deeply distressed. He slammed down the lid of his coffin and hiked himself atop it, sitting so that his elbows rested on his knees, and his chin rested on his folded hands. "You seem to have no intention of letting me take one good bite out of your neck for a long drink, so why disturb me?"

"I don't want to become a vampire!" Chris said. "But I have given some consideration to your needs. I managed to buy some blood—"

The vampire instantly perked up. "Human, I hope?"

"Yes, human," Chris told him. He strode out of the closet, careful to keep a tight hand on the cross. On his desk he found the sanitary plastic container of bright red blood and turned to hurry back to the vampire. He didn't need to hurry. The vampire was right behind him. In seconds he had taken the bag from Chris. He swallowed down the container to the last drop.

He was incredibly neat. Not a speck of blood touched his frilled white shirt, black evening cape, lips, or chin.

"Ah, that was good!" He said softly. "Not as good as taking it fresh from the neck, mind you, but delicious after all these years, nonetheless. Thank you. Now." He stared steadily at Chris. "Just what can I do for you?"

"Well," Chris began, "I'm a writer—"

"Ah!" The vampire said, and it seemed that he needed no more. He walked around the desk and sank into Chris's swivel chair, making himself very comfortable. "Like that Bram Stoker fellow."

"You knew him!" Chris gasped, excitedly leaning against the table.

The cross was in his hand. It nearly fell. Both Chris and the vampire noticed it. The vampire, watching Chris, smiled cunningly once again.

"You must be careful, Mister, er . . . ?"

"Lambden. Chris Lambden," Chris supplied. "And you, what is your name, what should I call you?"

"Well, call me 'Count,' of course," the creature said.

"Then you are him, the original—"

The creature was shaking his head. He swept out his hand, indicating that Chris should take the comfortable old stuffed armchair in front of his desk. "You were considerate of me. I'll give you something of a story, if you wish." He leaned back, casual, elegant, eyeing the room, very conversational. "I hear them say that Bram based his story on Vlad Dracul, the Impaler, the ruler who killed so many thousands of his enemies, and was still, in his way, a hero to his people." He shrugged. "Well, yes, that is true, you see, for a gypsy witch whose only son was caught on Vlad's skewers cast a curse upon him, and so he became the first of a long and illustrious line of vampires."

"Lord!" Chris gasped, falling into the indicated chair.

The vampire winced. "Must you?" He demanded.

"Does Vlad the Impaler still live?" Chris asked. He blushed. "Well, not live, exist?"

The vampire shook his head. "No, no, I'm afraid not. Alas, I never knew him myself."

"Then how—"

"How did I become a vampire?" He picked up a pencil and idly tapped it upon the table. "Ah, let's see! It was in the early eighteen hundreds . . . before or after the War of 1812, I'm not really sure." He shrugged. "It makes little difference now. I was a younger son of a French aristocrat, come to New Orleans to make my fortune. But then I was down in the bayou one night with the love of my life, when suddenly —swoop!—out of the trees it came!"

"It?"

He shrugged. "The one they actually called Count Dracula, one of Vlad's family, so he was always telling me. Personally, I think that it was all boast."

"Really?" Chris sat perfectly still, mesmerized. "What then?"

"Well, they made a party of it, you see. Dracula pounced down upon my dear Deanna, and when I hastened to her rescue, he set upon me instead!"

"And you died and became a vampire!"

"No, no, no, not directly!" the creature said, annoyed. "Whatever have you been reading and how dare you write about us when you seem to know so very little!"

"Sorry," Chris apologized.

"Now, pay attention. If the neck is ripped to shreds and too much blood is taken, the victim dies—goes to heaven or hell—and that is that! To create a vampire is an art! An art in form, and in seduction. Blood must be taken three times, from the same spot. Then a new creature may be born. Be serious, Mr. Lambden! The world would have run amock with vampires years ago if it were so very easy for one to become one of the 'undead'!"

"Yes, I imagine you're right," Chris agreed. He stared at the creature across his desk. It seemed that he was becoming more and more . . . normal! He had such an easy way about him. And Chris had already learned so much . . .

But just when he was about to ask another question, a loud voice called his name. It was melodic, it was feminine, but it was loud.

"Chris! Christopher! Do you know what time it is! You've got to come up here right away! The people from the magazine will be here first thing in the morning and we're to be the cover!"

The vampire arched a brow. Chris leapt to his feet. "Get back into the closet!"

"How rude!"

"Please, quickly!"

The creature had just disappeared behind the rubble of bricks when Magda appeared at the top of the stairs that lead down to the half-cellar.

"Chris! Did you hear me?"

Oh, yes, he certainly had. He smiled at her. Really, she was such a vision. Magda had this wonderful head full of near-platinum blond hair. It hung over one eye like that of a sex-goddess from the thirties. She had huge blue eyes and an angelic face, and a form that was certainly the best that money could buy. In the pale light filtering in from the kitchen, she seemed to fit the castle, fit the gothic mood of this very night. She was beautiful in a white silk gown that fluttered softly in the air-conditioned night.

"Chris?"

"I'm coming, Magda," he promised her. She remained there, watching him. Then she shivered. "However can you spend so much time in this awful, dreary place. Honestly, Chris, I should leave you!"

"Magda, I'll be right up. I won't ruin the interview, I promise."

She started to speak again, then spun around and disappeared. Chris watched after her. She was really so lovely. Once, he had loved her with all of his heart. He wasn't sure exactly what had happened.

He thought that it had something to do with her mouth.

"She is charming! She is elegant! She is fire!"

Chris almost jumped a mile. The vampire was directly behind him again.

"She is my wife!" Chris said sharply. And she's a shrew, he added in silence to himself. It didn't matter. Not tonight. Tonight, he had found his creature.

"Back to your coffin," Chris commanded. "I've got to go up to bed."

"Ah! With that image of grace and beauty!" The vampire said. "So seductive!"

Chris grunted. He didn't tell the creature that the last thing Magda had on her mind was seduction. She simply didn't want his face appearing on the cover of a national magazine if he had bags under his eyes. "Come on now, please? Back. I don't want to have to touch you with the Cross of Damocles—"

The warning was enough. The vampire gasped, swept his cloak before his face, and headed back for the closet. He started to crawl in when Chris noticed for the first time that he had not been lying alone.

A woman lay to the far side of the coffin. Like the vampire, she was pale. Ivory skin glowed softly by the jet black beauty of her hair.

"My Deanna!" said the vampire.

"Wow!" Chris murmured. "Two vampires—why didn't she awaken?"

"She's not a vampire," the creature informed him loftily. "Only I can awaken her."

"Then she's . . . a very well preserved corpse?" Chris asked.

The vampire sighed with vast impatience. "She hovers between the land of the living and the dead. You see, Dracula first took her blood. Then I did the same. But then, I did not drink her blood a third time. Alas . . ."

"Alas, what?" Chris demanded.

"Well, the world was filled with beautiful women. So she lies with me while I wait . . ." He shrugged, and grinned. "I shall either make her my consort at last, or choose another. One of these centuries."

He'd had enough of the conversation. He crawled into his coffin, studying Chris.

"Have you plenty of material for your book?"

"Oh, no! We've just begun. I'll be back tomorrow night, I promise."

"Good. I've much more to tell you." The vampire closed his eyes, then opened them again. "Ah, it does feel good to rest on a full stomach once again!"

Chris closed the lid of the coffin. He left the closet behind, replacing most of the bricks and setting the cross within them. He hurried up the stairs then, just as Magda began to call to him again.

Chris decided to shave before going to bed since the reporter and photographer were coming very early. He paused with the razor just above his cheek and studied his reflection. He was just thirty-five, really in his prime. He was a nice six-foot-two, with sandy hair, green eyes, a decent jaw line and shoulders that had carried well into not just high school but college football, even if he hadn't had the talent or the desire to carry his athletics into the pros.

Magda would have liked that. She found quarterbacks—winning quarterbacks, that was—to be the epitome of honor, glory, and the American male.

He sighed and set down his razor. Where had he gone wrong? Then he started to wonder what his life would be like if only he'd married a brunette. Like the one lying in the coffin with the creature. In her death-like sleep she had appeared so soft and sweet and gentle.

"Chris!"

While Magda . . .

He wasn't going to think about it now. Not when his life had taken this marvelous turn. There was a vampire in his closet.

The next morning the reporters came. Magda was stunning in an outfit by Dior. The reporters stayed most of the day, and he and Magda gave them a wonderful interview. The reporters gushed. They were such a beautiful young couple even if he did write such very weird things!

Just before dusk, the reporters left. So did Magda. There was a cocktail party at the DeVantes. She was going, even though Chris was determined to refuse.

She was so very blond and pretty as she prepared to go. Chris felt a twist within his heart. He even forgot his vampire for a moment.

"Magda, do you really have to go? We could just stay home together tonight. We could watch TV, rent a movie."

"Don't be silly, darling!" She charged him. "I must go—keep up our social standing. Darling, I'm doing this for the both of us!"

She left. Chris watched her leave, feeling another pang of nostalgia. Then he remembered his creature.

And he hurried back down to the cellar.

The vampire—or Count—as he preferred to be called, was quite a regular fellow. That night he talked about endless trips to Europe. He gave Chris a blow-by-blow description of the occupation of New Orleans during the war, then muttered something about the way that the Yanks had won.

"You mean the Civil War, right?" Chris asked.

"Why, what other war could you be talking about?" the vampire demanded.

"Oh, there were two major wars and any number of lesser wars since then!" Chris assured him.

"Tell me about your shirt," the vampire demanded.

Chris looked down at his chest. He was wearing his "Saints" T-shirt. Chris did his best to describe a rousing game of football in return. The vampire sighed. "I'd dearly love to see a game."

"You've never seen a professional football game?"

"My dear Mr. Lambden, I have been in this cellar since 1901."

"Well, there is television," Chris said.

"But you could take me out."

Chris shook his head. "No. No, I definitely could not let a vampire loose in the streets of New Orleans!"

"I wouldn't be loose. You'd still have the cross."

Chris shook his head, heard Magda muttering upstairs, and decided with a sigh that it was time to return his vampire to his closet.

But certain seeds had been sown, and Chris was just as curious as the vampire. He wanted to take him out.

Within a week, he had bought the vampire his own "Saints" T-shirt and a pair of black stretch Levi jeans.

The vampire wore them well. He was just admiring himself in Chris's swivel shaving mirror when they were both startled by an intrusion.

"Christopher Lambden, I swear that I'll have you institutionalized if you don't quit—oh!"

They'd been so absorbed in the new clothing that neither Chris nor the vampire had noticed the door at the top of the stairs open, or Magda come on in.

Magda hadn't expected company. Obviously. Her mouth was left in a wide O.

"Magda!" Chris said.

Magda recovered quickly. She offered the vampire one of her most engaging smiles. "Hello. I'm sorry. I didn't realize that Chris had company." She smoothed her hands over her tight jeans, then walked on down the steps and extended perfectly manicured fingers to the vampire. "We haven't met. I'm Magda." Just Magda. Not Magda Lambden, not Magda, Chris's wife—just Magda. Well, that was her way.

She was an atrocious flirt. Once upon a time, it had infuriated Chris. Then, somewhere along the line, he had ceased to care. Now, he was intrigued. He should have been jealous about his wife, he realized. He was more interested in her reaction to his vampire.

"Oh, yes, Magda this is—"

"Drake," the vampire offered, elegantly kissing Magda's fingers. Obsidian eyes touched his wife's powder-blue gaze.

Chris made an instant decision. "I've invited him to a Saints game, Magda. I'd love you to come, too. Of course, I do understand how you feel about games—"

"I'd love to come," Magda insisted.

Chris smiled. "Fine."

It was a wonderful game. The home team won, the crowds were going wild. Chris had some difficulty convincing "Drake" that he couldn't take just one little bite out of one little cheerleader's neck, but really, all in all, "Drake" was very well behaved.

Magda kept him occupied.

Coming home was more difficult. Chris had to convince Magda that Drake would be perfectly happy sleeping in the cellar. He was firm. Magda was at last convinced.

Chris wedged the Cross of Damocles into a little niche in the door to the cellar.

Not that Chris mistrusted his wife, but he kept a sharp eye on her that night. When she rose and wandered down to the kitchen, he managed to sneak just ahead of her, and be there when she would have opened the door to the cellar.

"What were you doing?" he asked her.

"Oh, just checking on our guest!" she supplied.

Chris smiled. "I've checked on him. He's fine." Chris swallowed hard. "You mustn't go in there, Magda."

"Why, Christopher—"

"Do you love me, Magda?"

"Well, don't be absurd! Of course, I do. Whyever else would I stay with such a strange bookworm if I didn't! I could be off seeing the world, Chris. Having a life like that of your friend! Dancing in Paris, going to the bull fights in Madrid . . ." Her voice trailed away.

Chris ignored the pathos. "Magda, if you love me, trust me. I can't stay awake forever. You must stay out of the cellar at night."

"Of course, darling, if that's what you want!" She turned, all innocence, and started back for the stairs. Chris followed her. He tried very hard to stay awake that night.

He awoke with the first pale streaks of dawn. He stretched his hand out on the bed. It was empty.

"Magda?"

He heard the shower running. He leaned back, breathing in with relief. Maybe she did love him. But did she love him enough?

It was not so difficult to explain to Magda that Drake slept by day—Magda liked to sleep by day herself, and when she wasn't sleeping, she liked to shop. She was gone that morning by ten.

Chris spent most of the day in the closet, just watching his vampires—no, his vampire and the vampire's almost-consort—sleeping. They didn't move. Not a muscle, not a breath.

That night, Magda was in a wonderful mood. She insisted that they show their visitor the Vieux Carré, or French Quarter. Drake was certainly ready.

"Have you seen it before?"

"Oh, yes, but it was quite some time ago!" Drake assured her.

They set out. They watched jazz bands and Drake stared with absolute fascination at all the strip joints. One buxom beauty, obviously just off work, passed their way.

"Just a sip!" Drake whispered to Chris. "One little sip of blood from one of those, er, ladies of the night!"

"No, I've a pint for you at home. Magda wants to stop for steaks. How shall we manage it?"

The vampire sighed. "You are full of myth and legend. I love a good steak. Just make sure that it's very, very rare!"

They had steaks, which Drake did seem to enjoy, although he turned his nose up at the crawfish appetizers. They came home. Once again, it was time for bed. Magda pulled out the sleeper in the cellar herself. She went upstairs.

"Into your coffin!" Chris commanded.

"But I'm not at all tired!"

Chris hesitated. "All right, then. Watch some television until morning. But remember, the cross will be lodged at the top of the door. Just as it was last night."

"Oh, I'll remember," the vampire promised. He had on a pair of Chris's best flannel pajamas. Like everything else, he wore them well.

Chris wedged the cross into the door, and went on up to bed.

Magda was at her dressing table, brushing out her hair. She eyed Chris in the mirror. Such a beautiful woman. She wore a nightgown with a lace edge around her throat.

"Coming in?" Chris asked her, plumping up her pillow.

"Of course," Magda replied. She set down her brush and slid in beside Chris.

There was a Band-Aid on her neck. Chris looked at her gravely. "Magda, you must stay away from Drake."

"And you mustn't be so jealous. He's your friend; you brought him into the house, remember?"

"What did you do to your neck?"

"Pardon? What?" Absently, Magda touched the Band-Aid. "Oh, nothing. It's a bug bite."

"Don't betray me, my love," Chris said.

"Chris, I would never!"

Chris kissed her. "Goodnight, darling," he told her. "Remember, you must trust me, and be very, very careful."

"Of course."

He held her as he drifted off to sleep. *Stay with me, Magda!* he thought, hovering between wakefulness and darkness.

Morning came. He stretched out his hands. She was gone.

But once again, he heard the spray of the shower.

She was becoming an early riser.

Drake was up and ready when Chris came down the stairs that night. He was wearing one of Chris's best tailored shirts and an Izod sweater.

He wore them well.

"I'm ready," he said. "What will it be tonight, a game, some music, a stroll?"

"Actually," Chris said sternly, "I was thinking about getting some work done."

"Oh," the vampire said with disappointment. Then he looked at Chris slyly. "Oh, well, I've nothing but years ahead of me."

"Now that's what I thought that we would talk about tonight," Chris said, sitting down behind his desk. "What does kill a vampire?"

"Surely, you know!" The vampire said.

"I want to hear it from you."

"After, perhaps, we could take a walk down Bourbon Street and stroll to the water. I've quite a desire to see the old Mississippi flowing by."

"After, perhaps." Chris smiled.

The vampire sighed patiently. "There's the stake through the heart. Everyone knows that."

"Everyone," Chris agreed.

"Bright sunlight. A few minor streaks of dawn will not do it, but bright sunlight will. Vampires burn up like dry tinder in bright sunlight."

"I see."

"There's holy water—but you'd need a tub of it to really do the trick."

"A tub of holy water." Chris waited. "Is there anything else. A silver bullet, a—"

"Christopher," the vampire said indignantly. He was starting to sound an awful lot like Magda. "You're talking about werewolves. If you want to know about werewolves, you'll have to have one."

Chris smiled. "Fine. You want to see Bourbon Street, let's see Bourbon Street."

"Where's your wife? Is she coming with us?"

"I don't know. Magda seems to be a bit under the weather lately. Very sleepy. You wouldn't know anything about that, would you?"

"Not a thing," the vampire said, entirely innocent. Chris smiled. He could almost see the sly smile the minute he turned his back.

They walked through the Vieux Carré once again. That night they stopped for Cajun food at K. Paul's. Chris ordered the vampire the hottest thing on the menu and sat back with delight as he watched the creature swallow glass after glass of water.

Magda didn't notice. She was busy talking away. The vampire knew Paris like the back of his hand. He could rattle away in French. He even kissed Magda's finger tips in the middle of the meal.

But he was getting very sloppy, Chris thought. Because during that kiss, Chris could see the glittering tip of his fangs. He came so close to a honest-to-God bite. Right there. In the restaurant.

They stared at the mighty Mississippi, and then they wandered back to the car. Soon they were home again.

They bade the vampire goodnight.

And upstairs, Chris bade his wife goodnight. "Remember, Magda, stay away from the cellar."

"Of course," she murmured.

She fell asleep so very quickly.

There was a much larger Band-Aid on her neck now.

Chris roused himself. He silently descended and opened the cellar door, slipping the Cross of Damocles into the pocket of his robe. In silence, he came down the steps.

The vampire didn't notice him. Still in Chris's shirt and sweater and jeans, he was seated before the television set, entranced as Bela Lugosi played Dracula. Every once in a while, he gave off a disgruntled sniff.

Chris walked around in back of him and sank into the swivel chair behind his desk. The vampire didn't notice him.

Chris waited.

At exactly two A.M. the cellar door opened. Magda, a vision of innocence and purity in her ivory and lace nightgown, appeared at the top of the stairs.

"Drake!" she called softly.

Chris watched as the vampire smiled. A slow, cunning, entirely-pleased-with-himself smile. He rose. "My darling!" he called to Magda.

Magda came running down the steps and into his arms. "We've simply got to quit meeting like this!" Magda said.

Oh, Magda, darling! Always a cliché, Chris thought.

"Christopher suspects."

Well, of course, he suspects, what am I supposed to be, stupid? Chris wondered in silence.

"My darling, Magda! After tonight, it will not matter anymore!" the creature told her. It struck Chris that they were absurdly normal-looking standing there, the vampire in his clothing, Magda all decked out to seduce. People didn't change—times changed.

"Oh, after tonight, it will matter more than ever!" Magda whispered. "Drake, I want the things that you talk about all the time. I want to travel, to roam the continents! I want Paris in April, a London shopping spree. All the exotic places you come from—"

"Hell, he comes from New Orleans!" Chris broke in, unable to take it any longer.

His vampire, his wife, both stopped and stared at him.

"Chris!" Magda said in alarm.

The vampire smiled, holding Magda close against himself. "It's too late, Christopher. You thought yourself so clever. We'll I've had her twice. And now, she is mine."

"Oh, Christopher, I am so sorry, but I am his!" Magda insisted. She didn't seem to understand quite how she was "his". "Dear Christopher, I do love you, but I want to be with him, I want to fly . . ."

"Do you fly?" Christopher asked, interrupting his wife but addressing the vampire politely.

"Chris—" Magda began again.

"He's a vampire, Magda," Chris told her bluntly.

Magda didn't believe.

"Christopher, Christopher, always into your strange fantasies! Can't you just accept it? Someone else came along. Someone fascinating, intriguing!"

"So you'd really rather be with him. Even if he is a vampire?" Chris asked.

"If he were Satan himself," Magda replied impatiently.

Chris lifted his hands and hiked his shoulders in a shrug, looking at his vampire.

"Who am I to stand in your way? Go ahead. Go right ahead."

Magda started when the vampire flatly showed his fangs with no finesse or pretense whatsoever. "Chris!" She managed to croak. "He is a vampire!"

"Better than Satan, I imagine," Chris consoled her philosophically. The fangs were at her throat.

"Chris—!"

"Sorry, darling, I'm doing this for both of us!"

The vampire was, as usual, fastidious. Not a drop spilled upon Magda's flesh, or wet his lips, when he was done.

Magda fell to his feet like a rag doll.

"Is she . . . ?" Chris said.

"Yes. She'll come to soon enough, a vampire. So sorry, old boy. But you were asleep at the helm, as they say."

Chris shook his head. "So sorry, old boy, but you must have been asleep at the helm."

"Pardon?"

"I awakened you," Chris reminded him. "And you betrayed me three times."

"Three times—?"

"The three times it took to make Magda into a vampire. She was my wife, remember?"

The vampire narrowed his obsidian eyes. "Now wait a minute—"

"If you don't play by the rules, I won't either," Chris warned him. "You must now obey my three commands!"

The vampire scowled, starting for him. Chris produced the cross, and the creature stepped back.

"All right, what do you want?"

"I want you to leave, tonight. You'll take Magda, of course, and since I don't want any problems with the police, you'll make a show of going."

"And where am I going?"

"Europe, of course. I'll see that your coffin is sent on ahead. That's one."

"And two?"

"No more people! I'll keep you well supplied with blood from the blood bank. I don't like to boast, but I am a fairly wealthy man."

The vampire was looking truly sulky now. "Just a little sip of the fresh stuff now and then?"

"No. Never."

The vampire smiled suddenly. "I'll outlive you, Christopher."

"Maybe. Maybe not. I like to whittle on wood while I'm thinking out my plots. I'll have plenty of stakes at hand, for anytime I might need them."

Magda was starting to come around. "I feel so very strange!" she said.

"There's one more command," Chris told the vampire.

"Yes?" The vampire was truly irritated now.

"I think that you should awaken Deanna. You can leave her with me. You and Magda are going to need all the room you can get in that little coffin. Trust me—she kicks!"

The vampire muttered something, then directed his forefinger toward the closet and the coffin.

"I don't see her," Chris said.

"She'll be up and about in just a few minutes," the vampire assured him. Magda still seemed disoriented. It didn't matter. The vampire dragged her up beside him.

"What . . . ?"

"We're leaving," the vampire said curtly.

"By the front door, please," Chris said. He followed the two of them up the stairs. Then out to the street. As the vampire had been commanded, he made a show of leaving.

But once he and Magda were down the street, he had had enough. He swept up his arm dramatically, just like Lugosi had done in the movies. He turned into a bat. Magda gave out a little cry, but in seconds, she was a second black creature of the night beside him.

"Oh, no! What did you do to me!" Magda wailed. Her voice had grown sharp.

"Paris!" The vampire muttered back. "You wanted to go to Paris."

"And I wanted to fly first class!" Magda whined. "On an airplane! With champagne—"

Chris started to laugh softly. The vampire certainly had his hands full.

There was a soft noise behind Chris, at the doorway to the castle. Deanna. The name leapt unbidden to his mind, and for a moment, little chills swept along his spine. What had the vampire left him? Would he turn to find a withered crone? A skeleton frame with cloth that decayed, quickly becoming ashes in the wind?

He turned. His chills dissipated.

It was, indeed, Deanna. No skeletal form, no mound of ash. She offered him a breath-taking, tremulous smile. She raised her hands, and looked at them in the moonlight, then she smiled his way again.

"I'm human!" she whispered.

"Yes."

"And you . . . well, he is gone . . . and you, you must have saved me." She offered him a wistful, crooked little smile. "You must be my hero."

Hero? He'd never really thought of himself in such a manner, but it was nice to be able to do so. "I did manage to have you awakened," he said.

Her smile deepened. What a beautiful face she had. She trembled slightly. "I think that you're a hero," she said softly. Then she shook her head ruefully. "A hero I could easily learn to love. For eternity."

"Oh, no. Not eternity," Chris corrected her. "Just a normal lifetime," he said very quietly.

"Oh, yes! A normal lifetime!" she agreed.

She was decidedly old-fashioned looking in her long, outdated gown, but that could be fixed. Magda had left behind closets full of clothing.

"You'll have to forgive me. It's been a long, long time since I went to sleep. What year is it?"

Chris told her.

She gasped, and looked into his eyes. She seemed to like what she saw. "I'm afraid I'm very behind the times," she apologized. "You'll have so much to tell me . . ."

Her voice trailed off. She looked as if she might fall. Chris hurried up to her side. "Let me take you into the house."

"The house looks familiar . . ."

"Yes, it should be familiar to you. Of course, it has changed. Over the years," Chris told her. "Come, let me show it to you. My name is Christopher Lambden, and I write books about—" He hesitated.

"Yes?" She said, smiling softly, waiting.

"Westerns," he said. "I think I'm going to write westerns from now on."

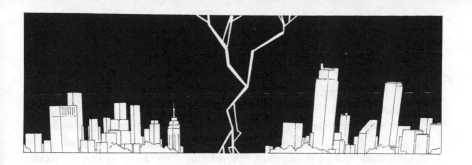

THE TENTH SCHOLAR

▼▼▼

STEVE RASNIC TEM

AND

MELANIE TEM

HE answered the door himself. I was disappointed that it wasn't his aide-de-camp; the term had always made me think of tents and marshmallows and songs around a fire and two weeks in the country, where I'd never been. "A woman," he said.

"Yeah," I said. "So?"

We looked at each other. I knew I couldn't let him stare me down; I had experience on the streets, and I'd thought about this a lot before I'd come here, practiced looking tougher than I really am. You had to keep a balance. I'd always had to do that. Out on the streets it was important to look tougher than you were, and talk dumber than you were. If you talked too smart, then people got it into their heads that you were all head and weak everywhere else. But with *him,* I knew I just had to look tough, but I couldn't let him think I was dumb. His eyes were green and he had really long white eyelashes. "A very *young* woman," he said.

"Not as young as you think," I shot back, but that wasn't true. I was sixteen and pregnant, and I looked like a twelve-year-old who hadn't lost her baby fat.

His thick white eyebrows rose a little, and he said, "Interesting." During the next months I would hear that comment from him countless times. It was the only compliment he ever paid any of us, and it always surprised me how often he used it, how many things he still genuinely found interesting, after all the years he'd lived and all the years he knew he still had coming.

"I saw your ad," I told him.

He nodded and stepped back, bowing slightly and making a welcoming gesture with one hand. I remember thinking that his hands were elegant, long and pale and thin, except that they were so hairy. "Come in, my dear."

" 'My dear'?" I laughed. I'd figured he would talk like that, and I wanted him to know right away that it didn't impress me.

Except, of course, that it did. Not so much his fancy accent or old-fashioned language, but the way he *noticed* me, the fact that he really did seem to think it was interesting that I was there. That was new for me, and as soon as I got a little of it I wanted more. I went in, noticing the gold dragon under the gold cross on the door.

Against the bright, trendy pastels of this penthouse office suite, he looked like something out of a black-and-white movie. The only colors on him were his green eyes and the red of his mouth, so red I thought he might be wearing lipstick. He was dressed in crisp, creased black, although he wasn't wearing a cloak; I'd been expecting a cloak, and that threw me a little. His face and hands were so white that I wouldn't have thought anything could be whiter, but then I saw the tips of his teeth pushing out over the edge of his lower lip. His curly hair went past his shoulders—black, when I'd imagined it would be white—and his moustache was as white as his eyebrows, so that I could hardly see them across his skin.

"Sit down, my dear." When he soundlessly shut the door, it was as if we were the only two creatures in the world. "What can I do for you?"

"I'm answering your ad," I repeated stubbornly. I didn't like it when people made fun of me, and I heard mockery everywhere. I'd punched people out, scratched their green eyes, for less. "I'm applying for the school. The ad didn't say you needed an appointment."

I wished I could think of things to say that sounded more intelligent. People on the street were easy to impress; even Oliver didn't take much. Though at first I'd thought he would. But this guy would be a real challenge; I'd known that before I came. He'd be like my grandmother, only more so—able to see who you really were and what you really wanted when even you didn't know. I sat down on the gigantic couch that took up one whole wall of the room. The couch was that peculiar yellow-green color they call chartreuse, and the walls and carpet were mauve. Who'd have thought that mauve and chartreuse would go together? Who'd have expected this guy to be an interior decorator? But then, he'd already lived long enough to be anything he wanted.

The guy had *power*. Once you had power, nobody could hurt you. I'd learned that much on the streets. And before. Power might have kept my grandmother alive. It didn't really matter how you got it, because once you had it nobody much cared about the how. I'd been around the powerful people in my life—my mother, a social worker or two, PD's and DA's and juvenile court judges, Oliver. But they were little fish. They had power only in relation to utterly powerless people like me. This guy had real power, and he could teach me how to have it, too. So I could pass it on to my baby.

I shivered in appreciation, then stiffened my body to still it and hoped he hadn't noticed. He had, of course; I saw the amusement in his eyes.

My jeans were dirty and smelled of the streets. It pleased me to think I might be soiling the fancy upholstery. I squirmed on the couch, moved my butt around a lot, just to make sure.

"Pregnant," he observed. He was standing too close to me, and he was really tall. I hated it when people, especially men, towered over me like that; too many times, at home and in juvie and in foster homes and on the street, some guy had stood too close to me like that and had ended up fucking me over.

I wasn't about to let him know he was making me nervous; you didn't dare let them know. I yawned, hoping my breath smelled as bad as it tasted, and put my filthy tennis shoes up on the arm of his elegant sofa. "So," I demanded, looking up at him as insolently as I could, "what do I have to do?"

He sat down in the enormous armchair that faced the couch. He crossed his legs, meticulously adjusted his pantleg. He wasn't a very big man; he was as thin as anybody I'd ever met under a bridge or in a shelter, as if, like them, he was always hungry—though I doubted it was because he couldn't afford food. For some reason, I'd thought he'd be bigger. I wondered what Oliver, who thought he knew everything there was to know about him, would think of him in person. "I ain't smart enough to go to some hot-shit yuppie school," Oliver had sneered. "You're the schoolgirl. You go, and then you come back and tell us." But I was never going back. I hadn't loved Oliver; I just let him think I did. He wasn't very powerful; for a while he could keep me safer than I could keep myself, but now I was ready for more.

There was a long silence. I noticed that I couldn't hear anything from the street or from the rest of the building, only his breathing and mine. Wondering about that, I pressed the back of my fist against the wall over my head; the wall was spongy and gave a little, like living tissue, and before I could stop myself I'd gasped and jerked my hand away.

He saw me do that, too, of course, and I knew he was keeping score. This was some creepy kind of exam. He sat there quietly with his thin white hands looking very thin and white against the wide chartreuse arms of the chair, and he looked at me calmly without saying anything. I was used to that. There was this chick in a doorway up across from Columbia who looked at you that way; you knew she saw everything about you and kept a list in her head, but I'd never heard her say anything, even the night she came after me with her nails and teeth and stole my sandwich—whole, still wrapped in wax paper—that I'd found on a table in a sidewalk cafe that lunchtime and been saving all day. The next day I went to her doorway and just sat on the stoop beside her and stared at her, to see what she'd do. She didn't do anything, so finally I gave up.

I didn't give up this time. I sat as quietly as he did and stared back at him. I didn't exactly look him in the eye; his eyes were too much for me. But I did stare at his face, and all of a sudden I was seeing a tiny drop of bright red—blood, I supposed—on the point of one of his teeth.

He spoke first, but not because I'd won anything. "What is your name?"

I couldn't think of any reason not to tell him. "Marie."

"And your surname?"

That was none of his business, and I wasn't part of that family anymore anyway. So I said, "Bathory," just to see what his reaction would be, sort of the way I'd sometimes shit on the sidewalk in front of some snooty restaurant.

He chuckled. He was laughing at me. "And why do you wish to attend the *scholomance*, Marie Bathory?"

I was ready for that one. I said what Oliver had told me to say, although I didn't always follow his orders no matter what he did to me. "Hey," I shrugged, "beats living on a heat grate, y'know?"

His face sharpened like a blade, and in one swift sharp motion he had stood up. "You are wasting my time."

I panicked. I'd overplayed the tough and ended up sounding stupid. As usual, Oliver didn't know what he was talking about. I told him, too soon and too eagerly, "When my grandmother died they drove a nail through her forehead."

"Interesting," he said, and I relaxed a little. "Why?"

I was confused by that, and my temper flared. I put my feet down on the thick carpet, leaned forward, even raised my voice. "What do you mean, why? Why do you think? They thought she was a vampire."

He nodded. "And was she?"

I started to give him some smart-ass answer, but then I was remembering my grandmother and having to fight back tears. She'd loved me. I remembered a lot of whippings, a few times locked in a dark rustling closet, but I'd deserved that. I also remembered feeling safe with her, and noticed, and understanding that my grandma was the most powerful person in the whole world and that if I was good and did what she told me I could grow up to be just like her.

But she died. She hadn't been powerful enough. Some lady in a shawl came and hammered a nail through her forehead. I remembered the shiny nailhead among the soft wrinkles between her eyes. My father had pulled her yellow-white hair down low, trying to hide the nail, but he'd made no move to pull it out. That's how I knew she was really dead, and no one would ever love me again.

Sometimes, though, I looked at the New York City buildings I'd lived among all my life, and saw them the way she must have seen them when her own grandmother brought her here from Rumania. Mountains, they became, and the alleys crevasses, and lightning could be made to strike from the lake in Central Park or from the crowded ocean beaches as powerfully as from any isolated Carpathian pool deeper than a dream.

"Yeah, she was." I'd never said it out loud before, though I'd always secretly believed it. Foolishly, I added, "I miss her."

"Interesting. And your grandmother the vampire told you about the *scholomance*, did she?"

"No. Oliver did." That was a lie, partly. She'd told me a little—about the *scholomance*, about the tenth scholar, but when I kept asking her about them she'd shut up, as if she was sorry she'd told me anything at all. Then Oliver came along, and he told me more, and I wanted to be that tenth scholar, and *would* be, because I *had* to be for me and my baby.

He didn't ask who Oliver was. It wasn't as if he already knew; he just didn't care. So much for Oliver's power; I smiled to myself. When Oliver died, I wondered, would there be a shooting star? And would anybody notice it among all the city lights?

"Who is the father of your child?"

"I don't know." That was the truth, but I wouldn't have told him if I had known. On an impulse, watching his face, I added, "You can be if you want."

His face changed. Not much, but enough that I knew I'd scored a point. He smiled, showing more of his teeth under the moustache.

"Nobody gave my grandmother a candle while she was dying," I heard myself say. "So she died without light. She always said that was the worst thing that could happen to anybody, to die without light."

He understood what I meant better than I did. "And that is why you want to study at our school."

"I guess." The tenth scholar wouldn't die without a light, I was pretty sure of that. It was hard to believe, but maybe the tenth scholar wouldn't die at all.

He was moving around the room. Gliding, really; I half-expected him to vaporize at any second. I wondered if he really could do that, and if he could teach me; I wondered what I'd do if he left me, too. "Not a bad reason to apply," he said. "But you must understand that you will be expected to study diligently. To apply yourself."

"I'm not stupid," I said, feeling stupid.

"Only ten scholars are accepted into each class."

"I know. And one stays. As payment."

"Correct. So far, I see, you have done your homework."

"I'll be the one to stay," I said boldly.

"Ah, my dear, but *I* make that choice."

"You'll choose me."

He came too close to me again and peered down from his great height. The drop of blood was gone; his teeth gleamed. "Marie Bothary, do you know who I am?"

"Vlad Tepes," I said, giving the first name Oliver's broad Brooklyn "a" and pronouncing the last name "Teeps," the way Oliver did.

He exploded into laughter and I was mortified. "Tsepesh!" he exclaimed. "It is pronounced 'Tsepesh'!" I tried and failed to say it right. He bent like a huge shiny insect and took my face in his cold hands. "Marie. Say it. *Vlad Tepes,* the Impaler."

I could hardly breathe, but I managed to say, "Tepesh."

"Very good. Now say *nosferatu.*"

That was easier. "Nosferatu," I gasped. His nails were digging into the soft flesh behind my ears.

Then his sharp cold face was only inches away from mine, and I thought he was going to kiss me or to sink his teeth into my neck. I would have been glad for either. He whispered *"Dracule,"* and I repeated *"Dracule,"* and then he let me go. My face was numb where he'd held me.

"Classes begin tomorrow," he said. "You will stay with me tonight, and you will be prepared."

Later that night he sent me down to the alley with his garbage, as he would so many other nights during my stay. I suppose this was meant to be part of my payment to him. He didn't trust the service the building provided, he said. They were lax and inefficient, he said. He said he wanted something more private.

That first night when I reached the alley I couldn't resist the temptation to peer into the thick, black plastic bag. The bag had been so heavy, I couldn't imagine what he'd thrown away.

It was a Rottweiler, its throat torn open sloppily, the edges of the wound frayed as if the killer had been starving, hadn't been able to wait to do it right.

Somehow, I would have thought him above all that. It embarrassed me. I closed the bag up quickly, and tried not to think about it after that. And I never told anyone.

▼▼▼

I never thought I had much competition. Although Dracula would comment once in a while that he found us "interesting," individually or as a group, it didn't seem to me that we were an especially strong class, compared to those who must have gone before.

I was the only female, the only student under twenty-five, of course the only one pregnant, the only one who lived at the school. The others all came and went, and they actually seemed to have lives outside. I couldn't imagine any of them staying. I was so sure I had a lock on Tenth Scholar that I didn't worry much about what I'd do if he sent me away, where I'd go, how I'd ever live.

Some of my classmates I scarcely remember now, and wouldn't recognize on the street. Some of them, though, I remember. Andy, for instance, was an accomplished serial killer before classes ever started, and I'm sure he's still going strong. Although Dracula never made distinctions based on how we'd come to the school, we all guessed that Andy had been recruited, and he never did quite grasp what he was doing there, what was expected of him, what opportunities there were. I lost count of how many whores and street people he killed and dismembered; for one thing, it was more every time he talked about it. I used to sit in class and stare at him, sometimes losing track of the lesson; I'd try to figure out what Dracula saw in him, and whether I'd have pegged him as dangerous if I'd just met him on the street. I doubted it, not because he looked innocent—nobody has looked innocent to me in a long time—but because he looked so *dumb.*

Conrad preyed on kids. I remember him. The official *scholomance* policy was that child-molestation and -murder were inherently no more or less praiseworthy than any other approach, but I couldn't help taking special note of Conrad. He was old, maybe fifty, and he participated a lot in class. He stared at me a lot, too, at my belly as I started to show.

Then there was Harlequin. Actually, Harlequin might have been a woman. He might also have been an animal—a lizard, say, or a bat—or some alien thing nobody'd ever heard of. I had no idea, either, how old he was, or what race. He was an exotic dancer, a hooker, a performance artist, a beggar. By turns he was fey and crude, heavy-handed as a rapist in a reeking alley and light-footed as the eternally restless spirits my grandmother had called *strigoi* (restless, I remembered, either because of some great sin or because of some great unclaimed treasure). I never knew exactly what he'd done to be admitted or how he got such spectacularly high grades—except that, rather than stalking and terrifying his victims, he dazzled and seduced them, and they died not out of fear of him but out of passion.

What I remember most vividly about Harlequin, though, are thunderbolts and blood.

We were having our regular early-morning nature class in Central Park. The sun was probably just rising over a horizon we couldn't see; the bowl of the park, inside our horizon of mountainous buildings, was still pretty dark, the charcoal-rose sky like a lid.

Andy, as usual, was already half-asleep; he should have been in his element here. Conrad, as usual, was sulky because there were so few children in the park at this time of the night, and those who were out were already taken.

Harlequin was even more spectacular than usual. He'd been studying, I could tell. I always hated brown-noses. The first of us to master vaporization, he kept disappearing and reappearing all over the place, leaping in the fountain like waterdrops himself, slithering through the dewy grass to coil himself adoringly around Dracula's ankles.

Dracula always put up with more from Harlequin than he should have. But finally that morning he observed sternly, "All this is most entertaining, but you are only distracting yourself and the others from serious application to the matters at hand."

Harlequin laughed like the cry of a gull, made himself very tall and thin, and swept both cupped palms across the paling sky. A shower of stars fell into the city, stars I didn't think had been ready to fall yet.

Souls leaving this world, my grandmother would have said. Souls pulled from this world before their time, I thought, and grudgingly I acknowledged to myself Harlequin's skill and style.

The baby kicked. I could feel it drinking my blood through the umbilical cord, and I knew it was transforming me into something I didn't want to be. I imagined sinking my teeth into its not-yet-developed little neck, through the layers of my own flesh and blood.

Harlequin raced to the lake, the rest of us following. He found a rock the size of a baby, raised it above his glittering bald head, and threw it in. The splash wasn't very impressive in the noisy city dawn, and the surface of the water had already been deeply rippled, but there was a dragon in there and it awoke. Two, three, four long thunderbolts leaped out of the lake and crackled through the air to the sky, where they lit up the craggy top floors of the buildings. There was the immediate odor of burned hair and flesh, and from the shadows on the other side of the lake somebody screamed.

Beside me, always beside me, Dracula murmured, "Interesting," and jealousy licked like a fetus at the bottom of my heart. But Harlequin got on everybody's nerves, and just before the end of class, with the sun about to show above the buildings and Andy all but snoring, Dracula finally lost his patience. "Harlequin, enough. I have had enough. This morning, right now, you must prove yourself or leave the *scholomance.*"

I was shocked. I hadn't known you could be expelled. Scared, I tried to move close to Dracula, yearning to touch him openly, to claim him in front of the others and put an end to the pointless competition for Tenth Scholar. But Dracula was watching Harlequin and took no notice of me.

Harlequin stood absolutely still among the moving shadows of the sunrise, looking small and frail. I hadn't realized until then how sick he was, and always would be. Immortal now, of course, like the rest of us, and eternally wasting away. The disease was his curse and his power; his kisses brought to his victims, who were his lovers, immortal sickness, too.

From behind the bushes that separated us from the path, we heard voices. We all sat up straight, even Conrad, who I knew was hoping for the sweet voice of a child unattended. Even Andy tried to rouse himself, but the sun was too high for him.

I started to move but Dracula held me back, his cold hand across my belly. Harlequin paused for maybe five seconds, centering himself as Dracula had taught us to do before an approach, and then stepped through the bushes. Conrad and a few of the other students repositioned themselves quietly to watch, but Dracula stayed where he was and kept me there, too.

There was almost no noise. Harlequin made none, of course, and his victims never knew what happened. That was the way it should be; Dracula loathed noise. I remembered how quiet my grandmother had been, too: how peaceful. We waited. Daylight had started to seep into the park and class was almost over when Harlequin stepped like a dancer back into the clearing among us.

His face and clothes were scarlet with blood. His teeth dripped. He looked stronger than he had in a long time, more substantial. His movements were more fluid and directed, less flighty.

In outstretched hands he carried two tall ridged silver thermos bottles, apparently taken from the victims. He dropped to his knees, bowed his head as if in offering, and passed one of the bottles in each direction around the circle. Dracula drank first, his eyes closed in pleasure and his long throat working. At last, without opening his eyes, he passed the thermos to me.

The blood was warm and sweet. Obviously the victims had been virgins, barely so, a young man and a young woman on the verge of becoming lovers when Harlequin had intervened. The mouth of the thermos was wide enough that the blood spilled over my nose and chin, bathing me in its vitality. I knew some of it was reaching the baby and I was glad, then I wished it wouldn't because maybe there wouldn't be enough left for me, but there was nothing I could do about that. I drank until I felt renewed, and then, reluctantly, passed the bottle on.

When Dracula said, "Prove yourself" to me, we were making love on his red silk sheets. The others had gone home for the day, or had gone wherever it was they went when they weren't at school; I couldn't imagine. City daylight came through the high window gray and pale blue, and it was exciting to be awake.

He was straddling me on all fours, and under the huge mound of my belly his penis entered me easily. It thrilled me to think of his penis pushing back and forth past the fetus like a fang.

I would turn seventeen soon. The baby would be born soon. Soon we would be graduated.

"Prove yourself," he said, and I thought he was talking about something sexual.

Although I couldn't guess what there was left that I hadn't already done, I gasped, "Tell me what you want."

He buried his face in my shoulder. His teeth grazed my neck and found a spot, but they didn't go in yet; he was playing with me. "Prove yourself," he murmured again, "or leave the *scholomance.* Now."

I stiffened with fear and outrage and frantic desire. I tried to wrap my arms and legs around him, but my stomach was too big, the baby was between us, and Dracula was moving down my body. I spread my legs and waited for his sharp tongue, but he stopped at my navel and I felt his teeth.

"You are not the Tenth Scholar," I heard him say.

"Why not? Who is? Harlequin? Shit, I thought you were smart enough to see through him—"

"The baby is the Tenth Scholar."

A fang went into my belly button and withdrew again. There was the suggestion of pain.

I struggled weakly to get out from under him. Of course I couldn't, and, anyway, I didn't know where I'd go if I got free. "You mean I can't stay?"

"I have taught you as much as it is possible for you to learn."

Betrayal made me light-headed, as though he'd already bitten through. "No," I cried, foolishly. "Please."

His voice came up to me singsong, seductive, and cold as immortal blood. "If you give me the baby now, you may stay to raise it until it can take its place at my side. Twelve years, perhaps, or ten years, or fourteen, depending on its nature and inclinations. If you do not give me the baby, you will leave. Tonight. I have lost interest in you."

"Take it," I said.

A vision of the dog with the butchered throat came into my head. A vision of my grandmother, dying when I'd been sure she'd never die, leaving me. I bit my lower lip hard to drive the visions away.

At first there was no more pain, really, than during any normal bite, except that the nerves in my abdomen were exquisitely sensitive. He sucked and drank a lot of blood. Before he was done I was so dizzy I could barely see, and he, obviously, was stoned.

His hands went all over my body—cold skin, sharp nails. His tongue went all over my body. He had started to sing as if to himself, to croon, and his laughter was sweet and smooth. Unable to fathom what I'd be like in fourteen years, what the city would be like when I had to go back into it alone, I paid attention only to him, only to the perforations his teeth were making from my navel to my pubic hair, only to his promise that if I did this he would let me stay.

Now pain and blood gushed. I lost and regained consciousness and lost it again; stars fell. When I awoke, the light was the same blue-gray it had been, but I was sure time had passed. There was a terrible, wonderful emptiness in my abdomen, and the wound had already started to close.

I heard Dracula's odd crooning and the gurgling of an infant, but for a while I couldn't find them. The colors in the room—chartreuse, mauve, blood-red—gave around me like living tissue. Then I saw the tall thin form by the window, blackened by my blood and the baby's and the rich nourishing blood of the placenta and afterbirth.

"It's a girl," he told me.

I was dizzied by a peculiar kind of pride: I'd borne a healthy daughter who would be the Tenth Scholar, even if I could not be. I'd carried on my grandmother's line. I'd given Dracula something he'd wanted, something that, apparently, no one else had ever given him. And fourteen years was a long time.

It was, of course, a trick. "Go now," he said, almost casually, staring at the baby in his arms.

"What?"

"Leave. The *scholomance* is filled."

"You said I could stay. You said—"

"I saw no point in exerting myself to take my daughter by force when you would give her to me out of love."

"She's *my* daughter!"

The baby in his arms curled and stretched. Somehow, she was feeding. "I am her father," he said, and I understood that it was true. He looked at me then, green gaze forking like lightning, and said, "Go. You have no place here."

▼▼▼

My daughter is fourteen now. I look for her everywhere and see her nowhere. Probably I wouldn't know who she was, anyway, except for her resemblance to him.

I kill for sustenance; there is no pleasure in it. I infect some of my victims with immortality in hopes that they will be my companions, but they always leave.

I know that my classmates are out here, and they've been taught by the Master; I try not to forget that. I try to protect myself against them, but it's unclear to me what danger there is, what pain there could be left. The city seems full of *scholomance* graduates and wannabes, and it's hard for me to believe these days that Dracula accepts only ten students at a time.

NOBODY'S PERFECT

▼▼▼

PHILIP JOSÉ FARMER

RUDOLPH Redeemer had just finished sucking my blood. My brain glared like a klieg light, and my clit was pulsing.

I wanted to beg him to keep on sucking, but the girl in line behind me was shouting, "Move on, bitch!" The drums were rolling; the bugles were blaring. The audience jamming the concert hall was shrieking its lungs out.

Rudolph's bodyguards, just below the stage and in the wings, must've become even more alert then. A year ago, an assassin had shot Rudolph during this ritual. Three months later, the same thing had happened.

Dazed, knees weak, I started to walk toward the steps leading down from the stage. But he shouted, "You're the one I've been looking for for years! I think I love you!"

I was both thrilled and astonished. You expect such tender language to be whispered in the bedroom, the only noise your heavy breathing and the twanging of bedsprings and maybe "Wooed Screwed and Sued" shaking the walls. But I wasn't going to argue with him.

Blood was trickling down the corner of his mouth. He smiled, showing the dripping red steel canines fixed to his real canines. His eyes blazed. Really burned. That, as I found out later, was because he loved the new designer fix, God Trek. It makes your eyes look like the open doors to Hell, though some claim it swings wide the gates of Heaven. Whatever it does, it sure beats heroin, crack, ballrush, and mindjam. Though, as I soon discovered, Rudolph took all of them.

But he wasn't on all that shit for the reason most people are. That is, to feel normal. He took it so he could feel human. Which I suppose is the same thing. I never was much for philosophy. What do I care about gurus and mahareeshis, they're all fakers, about karma and mantras, and whether or not Immanuel Kant had a cunt?

"Come to my apartment at midnight!" he yelled.

"I'm not a one-night stand!" I yelled back.

I was lying, and he knew it. But he grabbed the next girl, bent her backwards, cupped her breast with his left hand, and bit into her neck. Again, the drums roared, and the crowd shrieked like lost souls suddenly seeing hope. The girl had an orgasm or she was faking one, so much of that nowadays, but the men don't care. You is what you pretends you is, as a friend once said.

However, I sure hadn't faked anything. So maybe she was feeling the same exquisite cold fire that'd started in my toes and soared up through my body and numbed my brain with an ecstasy even mindjam and God Trek couldn't quite match.

Rudolph let loose of the girl and seized the pimply boy behind her. The youth may have been straight or gay, but he was shining with ecstasy. Part of it religious, part of it sexual, or is there any difference, much as I hate to say it? For sure, there's no difference when The Redeemer takes you into The Blessed Body, also no difference whether you're male or female when you accept initiation and communion at the same time. Only it's a reverse communion because Rudolph, the priest in this case and claiming to be God's vicar, drinks the wine of your blood. But you get a little of his holy saliva in your bloodstream.

At the steps, a girl sprayed germicide on the wound on my neck and slapped a Band-Aid over it. When I'd picked up my ticket, I'd signed a form releasing Rudolph Redeemer from all responsibility for any infections or emotional stress supposedly caused by the neck bite. Rudolph didn't worry about catching AIDS or anything. He claimed that vampires were untouched by human diseases.

Was I excited? Yes! But even while I was steaming under the silk, as they say, I was wondering if Rudolph really meant what he'd said. If he thought I'd be ready to put out and take in any time anywhere until the old thrill was gone, it seldom lasted, it almost always went, he was right. But if he thought he was going to keep on tapping me for blood, like a farmer milking a cow, he was wrong. I can't afford to lose much of my precious hemoglobin. I got enough trouble with anemia and pseudo-hepatitis. That God Trek not only fucks up your blood, it's hell on the liver. At the time, though, it seems worth it.

Why had he picked me out? I'm not backward admitting I got gorgeous legs and big standing-out siliconeless tits and these, with my Liz

Taylor face, I once thought, would make me a movie star. Nobody ever told me you had to have at least a moderately good acting ability to make it to the top. I was a genuine innocent, or maybe I was just stoned dumb. Too dumb to know the producers and directors would promise you anything if they could prong you.

Anyway, I wasn't the only goddess in that crowd, and he must've banged lots of divine bimbos. So, why me? Had he seen something making me stand out like a sex-crazed cockroach making it with a pecan in a can of mixed nuts?

I'd find out when I got to his apartment. Which was where? So, I was surprised and delighted when a man slipped me a note and said, "From The Redeemer." I opened it. It bore a hand-printed message (he probably wasn't sure I could read handwriting). The printing meant he must've seen me before the rituals started, probably by looking at a TV set scanning the crowd. He was still sucking blood from the initiates and so was too busy to have taken time off to get a message to me.

The note said that the driver of a yellow limousine would pick me up when the ceremonies were ended.

Now, that really did make me feel special! Or did he do that every show, pick out some beauty whose brains were in her snatch, who looked as if she'd already fallen from grace and was going to fall into his bed? For all I knew, a whole grope of groupies had been given notes like mine during this evening. Each was told to come at a different time. So, when my time was up, I'd get the bum's rush.

Glory, glory, glory! Even if a girl got bounced without a thank-you after an hour with Rudolph, she wasn't supposed to feel pissed-off. No way. You were lucky, one of the Chosen. You not only had something to brag about, you left with something else besides his sperm in you. It was the Redeemer's Kingdom Come in you, a house in Heaven, an eternal blessing, a never-failing assurance you were one of the Elect, an eternal queenship in the New Earth.

His followers knew that: when Old Earth was redeemed by Rudolph, they'd became immortal. They would truly live forever, body and soul. Moreover, the women he'd laid had a special place in the heavenly mansion. It was like Rudolph paid you off for balling him, not with money but with a saint's halo. Beatified via a bloody communion. Canonized via penis.

After what seemed like an unendurable time because I wanted to be with The Redeemer right now, the closing ritual came on. Rudolph was hoisted up by the Bloody Communion musicians and his hands and feet were nailed to a crucifix formed by a combination of cross, star of David,

crescent moon, and swastika. That last symbol got a lot of flak from
nonbelievers, but Rudolph said it was the ancient Buddhist symbol,
right-handed in form unlike the left-handed swastika the Nazis dishon-
ored.

The blood ran out from his hands and feet, and the band, except for
the drummer banging away, licked the blood running down along the
shaft of the Holy Mantra. Then they clawhammered the nails out from
the Mantra and carried Rudolph on their shoulders to the coffin and laid
him in it and closed its lid.

This was done with a lot of wailing and breast-beating by the crowd.
The musicians went back to their instruments and beat out the bars of
"The Blood Is The Life." It sounded like a fusion of the blacksmithy of
the ancient pagan deities and of angels working in the celestial armory,
like the band was forging weapons for the Twilight of the Gods and
Armageddon combined. The beat made you feel as if the end of the
world was just around the corner.

At least, that's what a music critic had written. For once, he was not
full of shit.

Then, after a long pause, during which the crowd fell silent, the band
crashed into "Arise, Arise, And Shine, Light Of The World!" The coffin
lid slowly rose. Then Rudolph sat up, and then he bounced. I mean,
bounced out of the coffin from a sitting position and landed on his feet,
smiling, his arms lifted and widespread.

The crowd roared, all 200,000 humans sounding as if they'd been
squeezed into the form of a colossal lion and its gigantic throat was
issuing a challenge to shake the walls of the temple, shake the walls of
the cosmos itself.

I really felt exalted, in a fine frenzy of joy. I didn't want to feel it. But
I couldn't escape that flashflood of emotion charging out from all those
people and shooting out from deep inside me. Nobody's perfect.

Rudolph stood there, arms still up, the wounds in his hands and feet
beginning to close up like nightclubs after 4:00 A.M. Then the crowd
filed out while singing "Arise!" Mightily shaken, though silent, I walked
out slowly with the singers.

It was 11 P.M. in Los Angeles, but the lights outside the hall made it
almost as bright as a smog-free high noon. A big crowd of anti-Redeem-
ers was waiting for us. It wanted to eat us, like the lions waiting for the
·Christians. In this case, it was just the opposite. Actually, the people
there were Christians of different sects and Jews, Moslems, Hindus,
Buddhists, and even some neoVoodooists. But the Fundies, a.k.a. literal-
ists or holy rollers, were the most numerous and the most dangerous. If

it hadn't been for the army of cops, the Fundies would've tried to beat our heads in with the signs they were waving at us.

"Vengeance is mine, saith the Lord." But these people were God's agents, and they were ready to carry out His plan. If any cheek was going to be smitten or turned, it wouldn't be theirs. But then, as I said, nobody's perfect.

An objective person—is there any such thing?—might've said they had plenty of reason to be spitting mad. Here's Rudolph Redeemer claiming to be a genuine vampire but at the same time a savior anointed by the Creator to make Earth green again and to solve most of its problems. And he has a couple million disciples who'd kiss more than his ass if he asked them to. Then this bloodsucking horny blaspheming sleazebag druggie who exposes his yellow-painted balls and purple-painted dick during his rituals claims to be the only true world-saver. Isn't that a little too much even in this country of free speech?

In the list of people who should be killed, Rudolph is on the top. More people hate him than hate the President of the U.S.A. or the current villains in the soap operas. He's been shot and also wounded by a bomb. Yet, a few minutes after the assassination attempts, his wounds are healed. So, he must be a genuine vampire.

In fact, if what his enemies claim is true, he must be a demon flown first-class from Hell, advance agent for the Anti-Christ, if he's not him in person. In which case, according to Fundie belief and logic, it's no sin to murder him. It's not even murder. So, the next time, the assassin should use a large-gauge shotgun or a bigger bomb. How about an anti-tank missile?

It was dangerous to be within a hundred yards of Rudolph, but hundreds of thousands took the risk gladly. And here was I doing the same. Gives you an idea of his charisma.

Everybody in the gigantic mob coming out of the hall was cursed at and railed at by the demonstrators. A paper sack full of human shit sailed by my shoulder and splattered on a girl behind me. Cries of "Anti-Christ!" and "Hell-doomed bloodsucking demon!" and many more, some obscene, all hot with hate, rose like burning paper in a strong wind. Signs waved everywhere. **THOU SHALT NOT SUFFER A WITCH TO LIVE. SATAN IS LOOSE, HIS NAME IS RUDOLPH, HIS NUMBER IS 666.** One sign, **JUDJMENT DAY SHALL SEPER-ATE THE SHEEPS FROM THE GOTES,** revealed more than its maker's religious fervor.

Just before the yellow limousine drove up to the curb, I saw George Reckingham's big pumpkin face and his carrot-shaped nose. He was in

the demonstrators' front row, which writhed like a wounded snake as
the Fundies strove to break through the double line of sweating cops. He
waved at me and shouted something. I shook my head to show him I
couldn't hear him. Then he held up his hand, its thumb and first finger
forming an O. But I could read his lips; I'd been trained to do this.

"You took the first step and the second. God bless you and show you
the righteous way on the third."

He meant that the first step was my getting clean of drugs, which I
could never have done without his loving help. I don't think Hell has
anything worse, though George wouldn't agree with that, but he never
went through the fires himself. The second step was getting right with
myself. The third step was something he argued against. He said it was
far too dangerous for my soul to keep associating with drug addicts
(none of this mealymouthed "chemical dependents" for him). And my
soul was in the gravest peril if I got "friendly" (another euphemism)
with the Anti-Christ.

He suspected that I'd be fucking a lot, too, just as I did before I met
him. (No "having sexual relations" for him. He told it like it was.) Well,
I knew that. No way am I going to give that up. A vagina clogged with
dust and cobwebs was not in the Creator's mind when He made it.

He was a Fundie, but they're not clones. Don't let anyone tell you
that. They got right wings and left wings and middle-of-the-roaders and
farout fringe-dwellers. Even if all insist the Good Book must be taken
literally, they disagree a lot about the interpretation of the letter and also
of the spirit. But they have one thing in common. Faith in God moves all
of them like castor oil moves the bowels. They can't fight against it.

The same thing was true of Rudolph's followers.

I smiled and waved at George and then stepped into the limo, and it
drove away slowly into the traffic, which was a mess. How had the
driver picked me out of the mob? Better not ask, I told myself. If black
magic was involved, I didn't want to know it.

I was taken to a new apartment building on Wilshire in Westwood. I
had to go through a security system with a hundred electronic eyes,
through a battalion of guards who frisked me maybe more closely than
they should have, and through who knew how many sensors before I
stepped off the elevator into the penthouse. I was probably X-rayed on
the way up in the elevator.

I was alone in rooms displaying squalid luxury or luxurious squalor.
But the thing catching my eye was the big coat-of-arms over the fireplace mantel. I'd seen photos of it on TV and in newspapers. It was the
arms of a Scottish noble family, the Ruthvens, from whom Rudolph was

descended. Some unnamed person had had it made as a gift for Rudolph. But where the original arms showed a ram and a goat supporting the sides of the shield, the gift-giver had covered each with a huge hypodermic hardwood syringe. It was his jesting tribute to Rudolph's well-known drug habit.

Another item, one you wouldn't expect to find in a vampire's apartment, was a huge crucifix on the wall. That didn't surprise me because Rudolph had laughed about it during a talk show. "Crosses don't bother us," he'd said. "That's just folklore without a crumb of truth. Vampires, you know, were around in the Old Stone Age, long long before Christianity came into being. The movies have hyped the folklore so everybody thinks crucifixes scare hell out of us. Same for holy water. Hell, I keep bottled holy water in my apartment! I drink the stuff just to prove what nonsense it all is!"

The rooms hadn't been cleaned recently, and their air was thick with several currents of shit, mindjam stinking the worse. There were ashtrays piled high with cigarette and marijuana stubs, and on the tables, chairs, and floors were needles and syringes, a lot of them used, and plastic packages holding white or crimson powder and prescription containers with contents I guessed were nonprescription. Here and there were some Turkish waterpipes and laser-guided ass jabbers.

It was a narc's wet dream, but Rudolph didn't seem to be worried about being busted. With his money, he could buy several government agencies and the state and local cops, and probably had.

What surprised me, though, was a table set for two. It bore a number of covered dishes, all silver. Fifteen minutes later, some of his bodyguards came into the apartment and quickly checked out all the rooms with electronic detectors. When Rudolph came in, the guards left. His red hair flowed down past his shoulders, making him look like a Swedish guru. But his face was clean-shaven, and he wore a business suit. Brown, for God's sake!

"Well, Polly, how do you like the decor?" he said with that deep rich baritone that's enough to make any of Eve's daughters, no matter how puritanical, look around for the tree with the aphrodisiacal apples and a soft place to lie down on while eating the fruit.

"The decor?" I said. "I'll pass on comment. I'm not an arbiter of bad taste."

He laughed, and his deep blue eyes sparkled. He looked like Dracula about as much as a wolf resembles a pit bull.

"You're honest, no suck-ass. Let's eat."

"Eat what?" I said.

Again, he laughed, and he gestured at the table. When I sat down, he moved the chair under me like I was a rock star and he was a head waiter, a real gentleman. I said, "All this food? I thought . . . ?"

"Hey!" he said as he sat down. "That's superstitious bullshit. This is a cause-and-effect, energy-in, energy-out, a certain-amount-of-excrement-residue universe. No way can a vampire live just on blood. Unless you're a bat, and its mass doesn't require relatively much food. I need a balanced diet and bulk, just as you do.

"But I have to have a certain amount of blood to satisfy a vital psychic need. I've tried to quit twice, cold turkey, once in 1757 and once in 1888. I almost died. I mean, really died."

"You sure don't look your age," I said, and I felt stupid saying it. I wanted to be witty, to impress him. That's because, all of a sudden and very much against my will, I was in love with him. Just like that. It happens, though this was the first time I'd ever hurtled into love after a few minutes with the beloved. But I wasn't as happy about it as you might think. Every time I've gotten deeply involved with a man, I've ended up an emotional trainwreck, an airplane in the fog smashing against a mountain wall. I knew, I knew, oh, God, I knew, that this love wasn't going to turn out any better than the others! In fact, it was going to be the worst! I really knew!

But, what the hell! "Sieve the day!" is my motto. Drain off the bad stuff each day and keep the good stuff close to your heart. What a pukey sentimentalist! But it's what I am, no getting away from it.

We ate like vultures, and then it was off with the clothes and into the bedroom. There wasn't any coffin in it. That's another superstition. Vampires don't have to sleep in one, though they're sometimes good hiding places. And vampires can go out in the daylight but don't like to. It makes them very tired and very nervous and irritable. Like a heavy smoker trying to kick the habit.

By now, you can see that I really believed that Rudolph was what he said he was. I had believed it before then but not really, not deep deep down in me. It didn't make any difference to me. I loved him then, and I was absolutely crazy about him before the night, a long one, was over.

I didn't get into bed with him right away. He was lying there, ready for me, waiting for me to mount myself, a self-destructing butterfly, on his pin. But my eye was caught by a small framed painting on a table. I picked it up and looked at it. I wasn't trying to tease Rudolph, delay the big moment just to get him more excited. I'd just had a little shock. The woman in the painting was dressed in eighteenth-century clothes. She looked almost exactly like me!

"My mother," he said. "Dead since 1798."

It took me a moment to get my thoughts together. Then I said, "You picked me out because I look like her? You got an Oedipus complex?"

He nodded. He said, "During three hundred and eighty-three years, I've been deeply in love about seven times. Each one looked like my mother. But I don't apologize. Nobody's perfect."

"You son of a bitch!" I said. "I thought you chose me because one look at me hooked you, because you knew I was a soul mate!"

"And so you are," he said.

"Hey, I might have your mother's face! But what about my personality? You might not like it when you get to know me well. How about all those others? Did they have your mother's personality?"

"Every one of them," he said, grinning. "Yet, each had a different personality. It didn't matter. My mother, poor beautiful wretch, was a multiple-personality case. About thirty-three in all, I believe. She died in a locked room in my castle when I was forty-six. But I loved every one of her personalities after I got over being confused, though three of them were murderers. So, you see, there won't be any trouble matching one of her personae to yours. Come here."

Though very angry about being just a fucking mother-substitute, I crawled into bed anyway. Before daylight came, I was over most of my fury. It was worn out, along with me. His body temperature wasn't unhumanly low like all the vampire stories say they are. But his sperm-shoot was shockingly cold whether it was in me, my mouth, or anus. (I'm not called Polymorphous-Perverse Polly for nothing.) They were like electrified icicles in me, sensations like I never had before and would die for to get again. Again and again and again.

We talked sometimes. I found out a lot about him. He had been bitten many times by a female vampire whom he deeply loved when he was thirty-one. Contrary to folklore, a single bite from a vampire could not change a normal person into a compulsive bloodsucker. The change took place only after an unbroken series of nightly feedings. That was why the thousands of youths whom Randolph had bitten only once during the rituals had not become vampires.

He called himself the Redeemer so he could organize youths into groups that would be dedicated to making this planet into a true Green Earth. He had not intended at first to be a religious leader, but his enemies had pushed him into it. He was not, he told me, Anti-Christ or a demon from Hell. (He didn't convince me of that, though I didn't argue.) He'd been using drugs for two hundred years, but they hadn't hurt him a bit. (Another reason for me to believe he wasn't entirely human.) His motive for originating the bloody communion was partly selfish, partly humanitarian. By sucking all that blood from the kids during the ceremony, he satisfied his hunger for it, and he didn't have to kill anybody.

During the day, he didn't die. He just went into a sort of hibernation. His heart slowed way down but never stopped beating. That had been proved scientifically. But, when he was hibernating, he did have an almost flat brainwave.

"If my heart did stop entirely," he said, "how could it get started again?"

When dawn came, while I watched, he went into the sleep that was not quite the sleep of the dead. Though I was trembling with fatigue and fear and was sore all over, I got out of bed and went quickly into the kitchen. I found a screwdriver and went into the big front room. With it, I pried loose one of the huge syringes glued to the coat-of-arms. Then I mixed holy water (it couldn't hurt) from one of Randolph's bottles with a lot of horse, the big H, heroin. I filled the syringe with it.

The liquid was so thick I wasn't sure it wouldn't clog the hardwood needle. I pressed the plunger enough to shoot out a thin spray. Then I took the syringe into the bedroom. I would've preferred a hammer and a pointed wooden stake, but I had to work with the materials at hand. I don't suppose that the syringe and needle had to be made of wood, but my superiors had not taken any chances. They'd also made sure that the syringes would work before they'd mailed the coat-of-arms, along with a letter from a supposedly zealous disciple, to Rudolph.

He was lying flat on his back on the bed, uncovered and naked. His hands were folded on his chest as if he'd been laid out for a funeral. I put my hand on his chest, which now was cooling off. I was crying; my tears fell onto his chest. I'd thought I'd feel nothing except a fierce joy when I did this. But I hadn't foreseen, of course, that I would love him.

I told myself that the devil was the most seductive being in the world. And my superiors had warned me that his powers to charm were vast. I must think only of my duty to God and His souls. Anything I had to do to get to him and carry out my orders was justifiable and would be forgiven. I would, however, have to renounce fornication forever after I had completed this mission. I had verbally agreed to this, but my reservation about this was large. I wasn't going to give that up. It was heaven on Earth, and I certainly had that coming. On the other hand, it wasn't very likely that I would live long enough to ball anybody any more. In which case, I'd be spared having to sin again.

I inserted the sharp point of the hardwood needle between the two ribs just as I'd been taught to. I hesitated a moment, then drove the plunger down. He opened his eyes but never said a word. I think it was just a reflex. I hope to God it was. Anyway, he now had enough horse in his heart for him to ride on all the way to Hell.

I'd been told that maybe the substitute for the wooden stake, the wooden needle, plus the injection of heroin, might not be enough to kill him. After all, his body could repair itself devilishly fast. My orders were to cut off his head to make sure. But I couldn't make myself do that.

Weeping, I picked up the phone. I didn't call George Reckingham. He got me through the cold turkey and then had led me to salvation. But he believed that murder was always a sin. That's why he'd left the Warriors of Jehovah and why he'd urged me to quit them. I wished I'd listened to him.

I phoned the Warriors' general. He picked up the phone so quickly he must've waited by it all night.

"It went as planned," I said, "It's done."

"God bless you, Polly! You'll sit at God's right hand!"

"Very soon, too," I said. "I can't get out of here without being caught. And I just can't kill myself so they won't be able to question me. I swore I would, but I'm a coward. I'm sorry. I can't do it. I just wish you, somebody, could've thought of how to get me out safely."

"Nobody's perfect," he said. And he hung up.

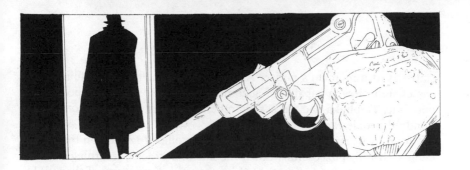

DRACULA 1944

▼▼▼

EDWARD D. HOCH

CAPTAIN Schellenberg's office window overlooked the railroad siding at Bergen-Belsen, and when he was at his desk he could observe the arrival of each new trainload of prisoners. Sometimes now there would be a train every day, with men, women and children crowded into the boxcars like cattle. Sometimes when they arrived there would be crying and screaming from those who had heard rumors of the death camps. He always wanted to go down there and shout to them how lucky they were.

Bergen-Belsen was primarily a work camp, not an extermination camp. There were no gas chambers here. Those who came on the trains —the Jews and Gypsies, the homosexuals and criminals—would not be lined up and led to their death. True, they might be worked until they dropped, worked to death on short rations and beaten if they did not perform well. But they would not be systematically murdered. That was for the extermination camps like Auschwitz and Treblinka and the others. The pace was quickening there. It was the summer of 1944 and the enemy had landed in France.

The job of Captain Schellenberg at Bergen-Belsen was to keep track of the number of able-bodied man and women available each day for the slave labor detachments. If the death rate proved unusually high and the number sank below a certain level, an extra train might be put on to increase the flow. If, on the other hand, the prisoners at Bergen-Belsen exceeded the camp's capacity, it was Schellenberg's job to send a trainload of the least healthy on to one of the extermination camps. For this purpose he kept charts of the other camps, and he could rattle off the statistics at a moment's notice. Auschwitz, for example, had four huge gas chambers each capable of accommodating two thousand people at one time. Treblinka had ten gas chambers, but they could hold only two hundred people each.

Promptly at nine each morning he left his office to check on the work details, striding purposefully down the line of barracks, returning salutes with a quick snap of his arm. At this particular time many of the buildings housed Gypsy prisoners, but there was nothing unusual about that. Bergen-Belsen had been established when the first roundups of Gypsies began, even before the camps for Jews.

"Captain Schellenberg!"

It was one of his sergeants, standing at attention to deliver his report.

"At ease, Kronker. Any deaths overnight?"

"A prisoner in barracks 44." He hesitated. "And one guard."

"A guard?"

"A new man. He may have fallen asleep on duty."

"You suspect foul play?"

Sergeant Kronker did not want to say what he suspected. "He died from loss of blood."

"Were all the prisoners locked in?"

"Yes, sir. No one was missing."

"Send a report to me."

He continued on his rounds, stopping occasionally to check out one of the grim gray buildings. "Everyone working today?" he would ask, and then check off the barracks number in his notebook. The routine was broken only once, when he encountered a plump old Gypsy woman outside one of the buildings.

"Why aren't you at work?" Schellenberg asked. "We have much labor for a healthy woman like you."

"I tend to the ill. It is my job," she answered, speaking German with an odd, unfamiliar accent.

"What is your name, woman? Where are you from?"

"Olga Helsing, sir. I come from Romania with this band of Gypsy wanderers. We were seized in the night by a German patrol."

The captain motioned toward the building. "Where is the ill person you tend to? Show me!"

She led the way and he followed, bracing himself against the foul odors he'd encountered so many times before. Near the end of the row of bunks, in the darkest part of the building, she paused over a blanket-covered form.

"What's wrong with him?" the captain asked.

"He cannot work by day. The sun would rot his skin. It is a rare illness that can be fatal."

Schellenberg lifted the blanket and gazed at the thin, pale face of a man in his late fifties. He did not stir on the bunk, and he could have been dead. "This is a labor camp," the captain told her. "Everyone works here." He walked to the foot of the bunk and inspected the prisoner's name and birthdate: *Vlad Tepes, 8 November 1887.* "Have him out tomorrow morning or he will be shot."

Striding out of the building, Schellenberg wondered why he had been even that generous. In the past he might have had such a malingerer shot to death on the spot, or at least beaten as an example to others. He continued on his morning rounds, but the image of the old Gypsy asleep on the dark bunk stayed with him.

▼▼▼

Often, after sundown, Captain Schellenberg liked to walk alone around the perimeter of the camp's main section. It was a peaceful place with the coming of darkness, and he was even able to fantasize that he was back home strolling the hills of the family farm. He tried not to look at the high twin fences that encircled the prisoner barracks, though it was difficult at times when the searchlights in the guard towers played upon them.

Returning to the officers' quarters he took a shortcut close to barracks 52, forgetting for the moment that it was here he had encountered the sleeping Gypsy. As he passed near the darkened building, a voice spoke his name. "Captain Schellenberg!"

He turned, expecting to see one of the guards who patrolled the area. Instead he could barely make out a tall, slim figure who stood in the building's shadow. "Yes?" he responded. "Who is it?"

"We have not met formally."

Schellenberg took a step closer and then immediately retreated as he recognized the gray prison uniform. "You are out of your barracks! I must summon the guards!"

The tall man stepped forward a pace so the moonlight fell partly on his face. He smiled slightly and said, "I mean you no harm."

"The barracks are kept locked at night. How did you get out here? Are you on a special work detail?"

"Yes, I am on a special detail. I am monitoring the other prisoners to be certain they do not leave their barracks."

It was then that Schellenberg recognized him. This man facing him, seeming in the best of health, was the same sick Gypsy he'd observed in the barracks that morning. "Vlad Tepes—that's your name, isn't it?"

"I am known by that name."

"I'm pleased to see that you've recovered. I expect you to be on the morning work detail with the others."

"I can work only at night. The sunlight affects my skin."

The captain grunted. He started to turn away and then a thought struck him. "How did you know my name?"

"I may have heard the old woman addressing you."

Schellenberg accepted that, though he knew it wasn't true. He was anxious to get away from this strange prisoner. Perhaps he was remembering that Gypsies sometimes had unnatural powers.

That night, another guard died.

▼▼▼

The report of this latest death was on Captain Schellenberg's desk when he arrived at his office the following morning. There was also the report he'd requested about the earlier death. He read through both of them and was astonished to discover that each of the guards had died from loss of blood. Yet there was no evidence of bleeding and no blood had been found in the vicinity of the bodies. He took the reports with him when he went in to see Colonel Rausch later that morning.

"Do you suspect foul play?" the colonel asked, repeating the captain's own question of the previous day.

"I don't know what I suspect. I think I should speak with the doctor."

Rausch nodded his glistening bald head. "Do so, by all means. I will leave the matter in your hands, Captain."

Schellenberg sought out the doctor who had autopsied the bodies. His name was Fredericks and he held the rank of major. A short man with eyes that seemed too big for his head, he seemed to present a figure of vague menace. "Both men died the same way," he said in answer to the captain's questions. "Loss of blood."

"Was there a wound?"

Major Fredericks shrugged. "Puncture marks on the throat, but that means nothing, unless you believe they were attacked by vampire bats."

"I suppose anything is possible." He had another thought. "There's something else I wanted to ask you, Major. Is there a type of illness that could cause someone to be especially sensitive to sunlight?"

"You're probably thinking of lupus erythematosus. Exposure to sunlight or X-rays can cause a patchy red skin rash to appear on the cheeks and the bridge of the nose, roughly in the shape of a butterfly."

"We have a Gypsy prisoner in barracks 52 who claims to have such a condition. He says he can't work during the day."

"Nonsense! Simply cover his face with a cloth to keep the sun off it and he'll be fine."

"Thanks for the advice, Major."

"Barracks 52, you say? I should have his name for my records."

"Vlad Tepes."

"Tepes? Odd sort of name. Seems vaguely familiar to me."

He went back to his paperwork and Captain Schellenberg started on his rounds. When he reached barracks 52 he saw the stout Gypsy woman, Olga Helsing, hovering outside. "Good morning," he greeted her. "It is a fine summer's day. Has your patient returned to the labor force?"

"No, no! This sun would kill him, in his condition."

"I have spoken to the doctor about his so-called condition. If he covers his face with a piece of cloth, a handkerchief, he will be all right. Have him do that and report to the work detail this afternoon."

"How does the doctor know, without even examining him?" She spat it out in disgust, and Captain Schellenberg's left hand came up in a reflex motion, striking her a backhanded blow across the mouth. She staggered back, more shocked than hurt.

"Obey me, woman, or you and your patient will both be food for the worms!"

She retreated in silence with a hand to her mouth. Schellenberg strode away, already regretting that he'd struck her. But authority had to be shown to these people. It was all they understood.

In the afternoon he took a staff car out to the far end of the camp, where prisoners were building new barracks for future arrivals. He stood by the car for some time until he spotted a tall, slender man wearing a hat and with a handkerchief tied over his face. Satisfied, he drove back to his office.

▼▼▼

It was three days later before another guard was found dead, and Captain Schellenberg had almost put the first two incidents out of his mind. When he saw the latest report on his desk, and noted the cause of death, he hurried in to Colonel Rausch's office. "There's been another guard death overnight," he announced without preamble. "Somehow they're being killed."

The colonel lifted his bald head. "Loss of blood again?"

"That's right. We must take action."

"I'll issue an order that nightly patrols must be conducted in pairs. And I'll see that all locks are checked."

"It might not be a prisoner," Schellenberg pointed out.

"A guard wouldn't kill other guards when killing a prisoner is so much easier."

The captain couldn't argue with that logic. "I'm on my way to see Major Fredericks. If I learn anything further I'll let you know."

Word of the killings had not yet spread among the prisoners, and as Schellenberg strode across the grass toward the doctor's office all seemed calm. Lines of newly arrived prisoners were marching from the railroad siding, bound for some of the recently completed barracks. There was a shout as one man broke from the line and ran back toward the train, but he was quickly intercepted and beaten to the ground with rifle butts. He was carried off to the prison hospital while the others continued their march.

Captain Schellenberg had to wait about five minutes before Major Fredericks returned to his office. "Well, Captain, what can I do for you today?"

"I'm looking into the death of those guards. I don't want to take your time, though, if you have a patient. I saw them carry that prisoner in here."

Fredericks barely blinked. "The man is dead. They waste my time with dead men."

Schellenberg nodded, as if agreeing. "What has been killing these guards, Major? Is it some sort of natural virus, or an animal—"

"No animal could suck out that much blood."

"Then what—?"

"You mentioned the name Vlad Tepes the other day. I knew it sounded familiar." He walked to the bookshelf behind his desk and took down a textbook on Eastern European history. "Here—Vlad Tepes was the ruler of Wallachia during the 15th century, when he is said to have tortured and murdered more than thirty thousand people. He was the basis for the character of Dracula in the novel by that Irish writer, Bram Stoker."

"Vlad was a vampire?"

"No—only in Stoker's imagination. But it is interesting that someone should take the name of such a fiend. Have you seen this prisoner lately?"

"Not in some days," Captain Schellenberg admitted. "I should check up on him."

The major's face remained impassive. "Be careful," he advised. "If you suspect him of these crimes it would be easier to place him on the next train to Auschwitz."

Schellenberg took the staff car and drove out to the area of new barracks where the Gypsy prisoners were working. He sought out the tall man with the handkerchief over his face, and found him pushing a barrow full of bricks. "Vlad!" he called out, but the man did not turn.

Schellenberg walked up to him and snatched the handkerchief from his face. It was not Vlad Tepes. It was a young Gypsy he had never seen before.

▼▼▼

It took him less than a half-hour to establish that Vlad was not among the members of the work crew. Nor was he back in the bunk at barracks 52. That afternoon he had the woman, Olga Helsing, brought to his office. "Where is Vlad Tepes?" he asked her, leaning forward across his desk.

"I do not know, sir," she answered, touching her lips with one hand as if remembering his blow.

"How long has he been gone?"

"Many nights."

"And the young Gypsy who works in his place?"

"He was incorrectly reported to have died in barracks 44. We moved him to our barracks and he took the place of Vlad Tepes."

"Has the man escaped?"

"I do not know."

"Perhaps a night in the dungeon will refresh your memory. Life is very cheap here. Your body would make fine food for the pigs."

"I am an old woman. I do not frighten easily."

He nodded sadly. "Return to your barracks. I will tend to you later."

After she'd been taken away he sat for a long time staring at the opposite wall of his office. He heard another train arriving on the siding below, but did not bother to look. They were coming in twice a day now. The pace was beginning to pick up. Soon there would have to be another shipment to the extermination camps. Bergen-Belsen was treating them too well. Too many were adjusting to the routine, even on starvation rations. Adjusting and surviving.

He left his office and went to the officers' club at the far end of the camp. There was a small library off the dining room, with a good collection of German and English fiction. He remembered having seen a copy of Bram Stoker's novel *Dracula* there. That was what he needed.

Schellenberg spent the rest of the afternoon pondering over the volume, frequently consulting an almanac on one of the other shelves. The ending of the book interested him the most—the part where Jonathan Harker and the others pursue the Gypsy wagon bearing the box of dirt containing Dracula, and slay him just at sunset. Using the dates given in the text, together with the phases of the moon as reported in the almanac, he could come to only one conclusion. The death of Dracula had taken place on November 8th, 1887.

It was the very date that Vlad Tepes had claimed for his birth.

▼▼▼

The captain dined at the officers' mess that evening, and it was growing dark by the time he left the building and headed back to his quarters. He had never studied abnormal psychology, but the idea that one of the Gypsy prisoners could imagine himself to be the character from a novel was difficult for him to comprehend. Would this man Vlad have followed Stoker's novel to the point where he was attacking guards after sundown and sucking the blood from their necks?

He'd spent time in the small library seeking other explanations, even reading an article on vampire bats. But the small creatures were native to the tropic zones of the western hemisphere, and if they attacked humans at all they were most likely to choose a sleeping victim and suck blood from a big toe.

He thought about it as he walked along the fence that separated the prisoners' compound from the guards' and officers' quarters. Certainly he would have to report the escape of Vlad Tepes, if indeed the man had escaped. Or he would have to report him as the prime suspect in the death of those three guards. Still puzzling over it, he happened to glance up at his office window as he passed the administration building near the railroad siding.

He'd forgotten to close his window when he left, not realizing that he'd be gone for the entire afternoon. It was only open a few inches at the bottom, but looking up at it now he saw a movement, a small dark shape on the sill of the window. It might have been a bird, except they weren't usually out after dark. Then, as he watched, the thing seemed to disappear. He had the awful feeling that it had entered his office.

The captain hurried up the steps to the front door, surprising the night guard who was on duty. "Any trouble, sir?" he asked, snapping off a salute.

"No. I simply forgot something in my office."

He unsnapped the flap on his holster and removed the Luger before he inserted the key in his lock. Then he pushed the door open slowly, holding the weapon ready. There was no sound from the office. He could see that the window was still open a few inches. He stepped inside and snapped on the overhead light.

"Good evening, Captain Schellenberg."

He whirled around, facing the voice that came from just behind the open door. It was Vlad Tepes, but he was no longer wearing prison garb. Instead he was clothed in a dark suit covered with a black opera cape. The captain pointed his Luger at the Gypsy's stomach. "Where did you get those clothes?"

"From the quarters of Colonel Rausch. I noticed we were about the same size."

"I could shoot you dead on the spot, right here."

Vlad Tepes smiled. "Do you really think your bullets would have any effect on me?"

Schellenberg's finger tightened on the trigger, then hesitated. The man was bluffing, of course, but if the bullet didn't harm him—

"Who are you?" He asked, allowing his trigger finger to relax a bit. "You're no Gypsy."

"They have been very good to me. I have lived and traveled with them for more than fifty years. I am Count Dracula."

"You are a delusion, a madman who believes himself to be a fictional character!"

"Put down your weapon, Captain. If I am a delusion, how did I gain access to this office?"

He remembered the thing he'd seen on the window sill. A small bird —or perhaps a bat. "What do you want here?" Schellenberg asked by way of a response.

"I desire to leave this camp."

"Leave it! Fly over the fences as you flew into this room!"

"It is not so easy as that. I must have a place to sleep."

"A coffin?"

"A box, with dirt."

Schellenberg ignored the request. "You have been killing our guards. Three of them. Why guards? Why not prisoners?"

"You starve them and you overwork them. Their blood is thin."

"How can you be a character from a novel?" he asked.

"You have it backwards, Captain. The character in the novel is me. It is all true—almost every word of it—except for the ending. As you can see, I did not die with an American bowie knife through my heart."

"You told this story to the author, Bram Stoker?"

"No, I told it to— But perhaps I should start at the beginning. As you may remember from the book, I journeyed to England in August of 1887. I had been in London only a few days, moving among the theatre people who frequented the city's West End, when my gaze fell upon the most beautiful woman I had ever seen, certainly the most beautiful woman in London at that time. She had pale blue eyes and a long, lovely neck. Her skin was perfection."

Captain Schellenberg could not believe he was having this conversation with a man who was obviously mad. "What did you do?" he asked.

"I became acquainted with her, of course. I am not a young man, but I am not without attractions."

"You killed her, like the guards?"

"Perhaps that was my original purpose. I will not deceive you, Captain—of course it was! I wanted to feel her flesh and taste her blood. Instead, I ended up telling her my story, the story of Dracula."

"Who was this remarkable woman?"

"Her name was Florence Balcombe. Florence Balcombe Stoker. She was the wife of Bram Stoker."

▼▼▼

Captain Schellenberg could not believe his ears. It was all like a wild, half-remembered dream, and yet it was happening. He was standing in his office holding a Luger pistol on a madman who claimed to be Dracula. He moistened his lips and said, "She told the story to her husband and he wrote his book."

"That is correct. I never regretted telling her. I hoped to return to England someday, but that never proved possible during her lifetime. Harker and the others did pursue me, as in the book, but they never found the Gypsy wagon in which I traveled. It was impossible, however, for me to continue living in Castle Dracula. I was forced to make my home among the friendly Gypsies, who gave me a place to sleep by day. I adopted the name of Vlad Tepes, the 15th-century ruler who was a distant ancestor of mine. For his birthdate I chose the day of Dracula's death in the Stoker novel. That seemed fitting. I was still with the Gypsies a few weeks ago when we were seized one night by a German patrol. Since then my life has been as you know it. The old woman, Olga, has tended to my body by day, using every trick she knows to keep the sunlight from me."

"Where do you hide now, since you are gone from the barracks?"

"You need not know that, Captain. I only ask a favor, before more die here."

"You are a madman!" Schellenberg growled. "Be gone from here!"

Count Dracula merely smiled. "Look at me and see yourself, Captain. My deeds are no worse than yours."

In that instant Schellenberg almost believed the man, believed that he really was who he claimed. He raised the Luger and squeezed the trigger. For a split second a veil seemed to cloud his vision, and then Count Dracula was gone. He was nowhere. The captain whirled around, toward the window, just in time to see a bat take off from the outer sill, spreading its wings as it flew into the night.

▼▼▼

There was to be no sleep for Captain Schellenberg after that. The downstairs guard came to investigate the shot he'd heard, and the captain said he'd fired out the window at an escaping prisoner. He contacted the guard towers personally and ordered an alert for a possible escapee wearing a long black cloak. If Dracula thought he would supply a coffin outside the walls, the man was sadly mistaken. Schellenberg hurried to the armory and removed a sharpened bayonet from one of the guards' rifles. This was what Dracula would find if they met again.

He tried to remember what he knew of vampire lore. It seemed to him that the vampire's victims became vampires themselves, members of the undead who prowled the night in search of fresh victims. He thought of the guards who'd been killed, and wondered if they were on the prowl. The autopsies performed on the first two might have prevented that, but he believed the third victim had been quickly buried with only a perfunctory examination.

One thing was certain—this entire matter must be reported to Colonel Rausch at the earliest opportunity.

Colonel Rausch.

Suddenly he remembered the suit and cape that Count Dracula had been wearing, stolen from Colonel Rausch's quarters.

While most of the other officers at Bergen-Belsen were housed in plain wooden quarters little better than the enlisted men's barracks, Rausch and a few other high-ranking camp officials had taken over older homes in the area that dated from the turn of the century. Although Rausch had no family at the camp, he resided in a two-story stone house where a cook and an orderly came in each day to see to his needs.

The house was near the entrance to the camp, just inside the gates, and somehow Schellenberg knew that was where he would find the vampire's daytime resting place.

He waited until shortly before sunrise to approach the house, fearing what he might find there. Armed with his Luger and the bayonet he circled the place, searching for any sign of forced entry. In the back he found what he was looking for. A cellar door was unlocked and there was dirt on the steps, suggesting that something had been dragged down to the basement.

He was about to enter when a hand reached out to grab his arm, sending a chill through him. He whirled, ready to defend himself, and saw it was the old Gypsy woman from the camp, Olga Helsing. "Do not go in there," she warned.

He shook off her arm and reached for his pistol. "What are you doing out of the prison compound? How did you get here?"

"Colonel Rausch brought me in his staff car. I must watch over Vlad. You cannot harm him."

"Rausch? Rausch would never bring you here! Be gone, woman!"

"To enter that house is to die."

He shoved her out of his path. If she interfered again he would kill her. Quickly he went down the stone steps to the basement. He saw the oblong box at once and approached it cautiously. The sun was not yet up.

He heard a sound to his right and turned in time to see a young soldier in a guard's uniform hurl himself from the darkness, his voice the snarl of some animal on the prowl. Schellenberg didn't hesitate. He brought the bayonet up and ran the man through with it. Then he pulled it free, letting it drop to the floor.

"Captain Schellenberg! What's going on here!"

Startled by the sound of his name, he looked up to see the bald-headed Colonel Rausch standing at the top of the basement stairs, holding a flashlight. The captain sighed with relief. "Colonel, something terrible has happened! I've found the cause of the guards' deaths, and he's here in this house."

He ran up the steps to join the colonel and try to explain the astonishing story. "Step up here and tell me about it," the colonel said.

Schellenberg found himself in the dim kitchen, where the first hints of daylight were beginning to filter through the windows. "Colonel, I have discovered that one of the Gypsy prisoners is—"

Colonel Rausch's mouth curved into a wide grin, then opened. Schellenberg could not remember having seen a larger mouth on a human being. He felt the hot breath on his face as the colonel's teeth sank into his throat.

Then he was fighting for his life.

His hands closed around the colonel's throat as he tried to pry the teeth from his skin. They struggled there, toppling against the icebox and stove, finally falling through a swinging door to the dining room's polished floor. By sheer force Schellenberg pried the teeth free as they rolled over and over. Then he broke away and struggled to his feet, gasping for breath. The colonel, or what had been the colonel, was on his knees, bracing to renew the attack.

Schellenberg saw the first rays of the risen sun creep across the outside yard as Rausch hurled himself forward. He sidestepped and slashed down at the colonel's neck, propelling him through the dining room window. His body hurtled out and he landed, dazed, on the grass as the first light of morning turned his flesh to dust.

▼▼▼

Captain Schellenberg took a moment to regain his strength, still breathing in painful gasps from the ordeal. When he felt better he made his way to the basement stairs once more and descended. The horror of it almost overcame him, but he knew what had to be done. The guard's body had crumpled to dust, and he retrieved the bayonet. Then he walked deliberately to the oblong box and lifted the lid.

Count Dracula rested there, looking much as he had when the captain first saw him in the bunk at barracks 52. He raised the bayonet and pressed it against Dracula's chest, placing both hands on it to drive it through the flesh to the vampire's heart.

This would be the end of it.

But he hesitated momentarily, remembering how Dracula had spared the life of Florence Stoker more than fifty years earlier. He remembered too the vampire's final words to him. *Look at me and see yourself, Captain. My deeds are no worse than yours.*

He took one hand off the bayonet and touched the teeth marks in his neck, feeling for the first time a strangeness in his blood. Then he let the bayonet slip to the floor.

He stood up and closed the lid of the oblong box.

Then he went upstairs and out into the sunlight, wondering how much longer he would see it. The Gypsy woman Olga emerged from her hiding place behind a tree, and he said simply, "He is yours to care for."

He walked back slowly to the camp, where the prisoners were already lining up for the labors of the day.

THE CONTAGION

▼▼▼

JANET ASIMOV

D<small>R.</small> Mina's Diary:

Just when I had this new career arranged to provide me with a chance to work on my secret project, I've been assigned to what promises to be a very difficult case. I can't ask for more free hours or they might get suspicious, especially since I'm too obviously different, things being how they are. But I'll show them, unless this new case takes up too much time.

For all the good it did, I complained judiciously to my supervisor. "According to the information on this patient, he will probably insist on sleeping by day and being awake at night, which interferes with my off-hours . . ."

"You know that all newly awakened specimens need therapy and this particular organic is not only no exception but, being unique, will require extensive work. I'm sure you can readjust your schedule to work at night."

"Surely some other therapist . . ."

"Organics respond best to doctors who resemble them."

"This male patient has a history of strange relationships with females and I am, whether I like it or not, female."

"Nevertheless," Supervisor Six said, as stultifyingly reasonable as ever, "the choice of you as his doctor was logical since you are the only psychotherapist in Galactic Medical Center who meets the qualifications."

At that moment, my pager began to squawk. "Dr. Mina, you are wanted in section five. Your patient is waking from his post-thaw sleep."

"Odd," I said. "It's still daylight, but I might as well take a look at the case."

As I headed for the door, Supervisor Six tapped one of its multijointed arms upon its hexagonal metal body, so I paused to hear one last bit of unwanted advice.

"Remember your unfortunate tendencies toward using intuition and emotions. I advise you to handle this case with rigorous adherence to logic."

Supervisor Six did not, of course, wish me luck.

In the garden suite provided for him, the patient named Dracula was fully awake on the couch, sitting up clothed in shiny black that outlined what seemed to be an aristocratic, remarkably masculine form.

"Where the hell am I?" were his first words to me.

As described in all the literature, he had a thin, high-bridged nose, arched nostrils, and a lofty domed forehead. His curly, bushy eyebrows, although they did meet at the center, were admirable counterpoints to his firm chin and pointed ears.

"Look, girl, I know my face is supposed to cause pudendal quivering in any female, but I'd appreciate it if you'd stop staring at me and answer a few questions."

I sat down in the chair beside the head of the couch. "Please lie down, Mr. Dracula . . ."

"Count. Count Dracula. Now that Communism has bitten the dust, we've decided to revive the nobility."

"Very well, Count. Please lie down. Just say anything that comes into your mind and . . ."

"Oh, no! After going to the trouble of having myself frozen, I don't want another Freudian therapist." He looked me up and down. "On second thought, you turn me on and . . . say, what language am I using?"

I made the dual mistake of both answering him and revealing too much. "While unconscious, you were sleep-taught Galactic Standard, used here at the Medical Center."

Dracula's eyes—a melting dark blue, I noticed—narrowed. *"Galactic* Medical Center, I suppose?"

"That is correct. And if you wish me to be non-Freudian, I can oblige. My credentials in . . ."

"You probably won't tell me, so let me guess—either we got out of our solar system or aliens came in. Right?"

I ignored that. "I see your teeth are not pointed."

"They were filed and capped. Have I been thawed out at a time when my familial biochemical problem can be treated?"

"There has already been a correction of the genetic malformation that forced you to ingest fresh blood. Please begin by discussing your childhood traumas . . ."

"My childhood was boringly normal."

"No doubt you need to repress the memories . . ."

"It was normal, but on entering puberty I discovered vampiric needs. I went from doctor to doctor, hoping for a cure. I ended up working in a blood bank in my spare time, stealing small amounts of blood from each donor."

"What about the seductions of innocent females, whose bodies become attuned to yours so that they not only feel what you feel, but want you to take blood from them?"

"You've been seeing too many movies. I can't believe you've read the original book, since nobody does . . ."

"I have. You are Count Dracula, the human who lives forever if not decapitated and staked, which apparently happened only to a look-alike. You presumably went on committing mayhem, murder, and of course seduction . . ."

Dracula leaned forward and tapped my knee. "Look, kid, I hate to disappoint you, but I'm only a descendant. The irregular gene activates every third generation. I'm not only not the original Count Dracula, but I'm merely a partial throwback. I even sleep regular hours at night."

"And you have never committed . . ."

"Mayhem, murder, or even—" he sighed—"seduction."

"Then the course of therapy should be quick and easy . . ."

"You sound like a laxative commercial."

"Count, I am your *doctor*. Perhaps we could begin by your informing me of the year when you were flash-frozen."

"Why ask? Don't you future medics have gizmos to read off data stashed away in a person's brain?"

"There are no memory scanners that leave the organic mind intact. A simple answer will suffice."

"I am not feeling sanguine—you should excuse the expression—about psychiatric probing the minute I wake up. Surely the designer leather clothes and digital watch indicate that I was frozen in the last decade of the twentieth century."

"Of Earth," I said, making another mistake.

Dracula stood up and walked over to the plastiglass doors leading into the suite's private, walled garden. He looked out and grunted. "An old-fashioned European garden. Remarkable delphiniums and roses. For my benefit?"

"Yes."

"And the high wall, also for my benefit?"

"We thought you would feel safer in an enclosed place."

"Or that the Medical Center would feel safer from me," Dracula said sadly. "Are you so uncertain that the biochemical remedy worked? Is it merely temporary?"

"It's permanent. You will never need to drink blood again. Now lie back on the couch and talk . . ."

"No. Not today. Do I get food from that doo-hickey over in the corner?"

"Yes. The instructions are simple and printed on the door. Our computer chef will make anything you wish."

"Unlike my wicked ancestor, I require ordinary food. Is it against medical ethics if you stay for lunch with me?"

"I will return after lunch."

"No, please don't. I need a quiet day to wake up to reality. Is there television to help the process?"

"The holov set against that wall will play any classic disks you desire, including all the Dracula movies."

"Yuck. Can I watch current news programs?"

"Those are forbidden to patients until they are almost ready to be released."

"Forbidden? Released? Am I in jail?"

"Certainly not! Galactic Medical Center is the foremost healing place in the galaxy, considerably better than the GMC in M31, to say nothing of . . ."

"I get you. But I'm still imprisoned."

"For your own welfare, Mr.—Count Dracula. Awakening in a new era can be a traumatic experience, especially—" I was to make yet another mistake—"to organics."

His teeth may have lost their points but the man is still sharp. "Then there is nonorganic intelligence?"

"Certainly."

"And non-human intelligent organic beings? Here?"

"Yes to both questions."

Suddenly he laughed, a pleasant flush glowing on the high cheekbones of his pale face. "I don't suppose any of the other organics—of whatever species—are by any chance *vampires?*"

"Not exactly. There is a shelled Altairian patient who hasn't grown psychologically from its transitional pubescent need to sample the body fluids of any organic within reach."

"Too bad it can't use body fluid banks." Dracula sighed again. "My old biochemical aberration wasn't too bad after cures were found for the various nasty diseases I picked up. I'm not contagious now. And when is this *now* I'm in?"

"Later," I said, on my way out. "When you're more cooperative. I will see you tomorrow."

"Do you have a name, doctor?"

"I have chosen one for your benefit. I am Doctor Mina."

"Mina Murray Harker?"

"Just Mina."

He grinned and waved me out. I made my usual rounds and then came back here to my private lab to work on my project, but it's hard to concentrate on anything but Count Dracula. In fact, to be psychiatrically precise about it, I'm obsessed.

Is this love? Or is it the mysterious Draculian ability to infect females with an obsession about him that rules their lives? This Count Dracula is only a partial throwback to his evil ancestor, but I find his presence compelling, his face attractive, his smile seductive . . . I am being ridiculous.

I must remember that since I became an M.D., I have never had any trouble with medical ethics. I certainly shouldn't get into trouble now, when so much is at stake.

▼▼▼

Today started with supervision. I don't know—one isn't supposed to ask —which planet's species began manufacturing robot psychiatric administrators, but Supervisor Six could definitely be improved.

It clicked disapprovingly when I delivered my report and then asked "Who was Mina Murray Harker?"

"The only girl to survive and to be cured from the original Dracula's attacks. She was responsible for his death because she was able to lead Dracula's executioners to him."

"How?"

Such a simple question. Sometimes I wonder about my actual intelligence, for until Supervisor Six asked it, I had not realized the dangerous implications. I tried to answer truthfully because Six has an annoying habit of checking up on its supervisees by, at unpredictable intervals, scanning all the charts and any other data available. I can't very well destroy everything the computer bank library holds on Dracula.

"Apparently Mina Harker, né Murray, was able to resist becoming a vampire herself after Dracula bit her, but she did have a—sort of—mind link with him."

Supervisor Six rattled all its arms. If it were organic, there'd have been a sharp intake of breath.

"Telepathy! You must be exceedingly careful . . ."

Supervisor Six's cognitive circuits seemed to be overloading so I hastened to reassure it. "There's no evidence of telepathic ability in this Draculian descendant," I said.

"Any telepathic talent must be watched for. While all known organic telepathy is primitive, it is still difficult. I was on an exploring team that found a planet of telepathic plants which jangled the electronic vibrations of positronic brains with illogical organic thought about plunging one end into the muck while the other end sprayed forth odoriferous blooms to attract mindlessly procreating winged creatures. The team had to leave at once."

"You poor dears," I said.

"Then there was that planet of vegetarian telepaths which communicated mental poetry while munching. Not that I approved of the poetry —paeans of praise to organic digestive systems, focusing chiefly on the production of gas—but I assure you that telepathic organic species are inherently dangerous."

I noted carefully how easily the cognitive circuits of supervisors are jangled.

"The point," Supervisor Six continued, "is that we must not let telepaths get above themselves. It is possible that the evolution of intelligent telepaths might enable them to control our entire cybernetic civilization."

"Horrors," I said. "But must we control the development of organic telepathy to preserve Galactic peace of mind, or because non-organic telepathy has not yet been invented?"

Supervisor Six, which is hermetically humorless, is also impervious to sarcasm. "We keep trying to invent robotic telepathy. Robotic emotive circuits were tried long ago, but proved detrimental in most respects. I myself—" Supervisor Six cracked one of its claw joints—"am completely free of emotive circuits."

"I think I've just been insulted."

"That is illogical. Your emotive circuits seem to make you a skillful therapist with organics, and oddly enough with some nonorganics."

"At least," I said, somewhat mollified, "I can empathize with Dracula's cognitive dissonance and emotional trauma, waking in a radically different era."

"You have not previously informed us that your emotive circuits are disturbed by your being removed from the stasis in which you were placed during Earth's twenty-third century."

"I'm fine!" I almost yelled it. "I like my work and I like this century."

"But you must not let your empathy get out of control."

Someday I'll control you, Six, you walking computer, I thought but didn't say as I left for Dracula's suite.

Sitting, but not lying on the couch, he greeted me politely and said, "Dr. Mina, I have the feeling that you won't satisfy my curiosity about my present circumstances, so I'll satisfy yours. I'll talk. I'm worried about my future because the work I did is undoubtedly out of date . . ."

"Are you talking about your blood bank work?"

"No, that was in order to be a vampire without hurting anyone. I mean my real profession, computer engineering that included research in artificial intelligence."

"Indeed." I strove to keep my emotive circuits from agitating my speech mechanism. I tried to change the subject to give myself time to cogitate. "Those of your heritage are supposedly drawn to what they call their own place. Did you ever feel that about the home of your ancestors?"

"You mean Castle Dracula, in what was Transylvania? I was curious about it, but had no insatiable desire to live there. I stayed in the one place where no one notices how strange one may be—Manhattan. I'd like to know where I am now. From the garden, it looks like the Medical Center is inside a dome."

"The entire planet is Galactic Medical Center, all of it domed—the most feasible solution since we treat both organics and non-organics. Didn't you ever visit Transylvania?"

"Yes. The old ruined castle was still there, ivy growing on the battlements and rooks cawing from the towers, but the place is the centerpiece of a resort called Horror Hideaway. They even have fake parachute jumps from the edge of the precipice. I got depressed."

I arranged my features into a suitably sympathetic expression, since he was still sitting up, looking at me.

"Have I told you that I'm allergic to garlic?" he said.

"Like the original Count?"

"No. I tried wearing a garlic wreath but it never stopped me from

wanting to sample the blood supply. It's when I eat garlic that it dis-
agrees with me—I get awfully gassy. Is this really the sort of thing you
want to hear?"

"Go on. Say whatever is on . . ."

"My mind is astonishingly preoccupied with sex. I mean, since I woke
up. Since I saw you, Doctor Mina."

He was leering at me but I remained impassive. "Go on."

"Up to the time I was frozen, I led a sexually abstemious life. I had to
conceal my blood thirst, so I couldn't very well have any relationship
involving emotional intimacy, and casual sexual encounters frightened
me, since I'm somewhat hypochondriacal. Women were attracted to me,
but I could never understand why until one day I was walking by a
building where a science-fiction convention was being held. A nubile
female shouted "Look at the ears! It must be *him!*"

"Him?"

"Not all nubile females of the late twentieth century were grammati-
cal experts. I was mobbed by many beautiful girls, all wanting my auto-
graph and asking idiotic questions about Vulcan. After that I wore my
hair long, covering my ears."

"I do not under . . ."

"Never mind." He leaned forward, his eyes almost hypnotic. "Dr.
Mina, are you married? Do you ever say to your husband what Mina
Harker said to hers, who was a dull clod compared to my ancestor?"

The therapy session was not progressing in any approved manner, and
I didn't help by saying "I am not married. And what did she say?"

"Ah, Doctor Mina, your namesake said, 'How can women help loving
men when they are so earnest, so true, and so brave!' "

"Are you earnest, true, and brave?"

"Unfortunately, I am. Bravery is okay, but being earnest and true is—
was, in my century—considered silly."

I could no longer withstand his piercing blue gaze, his manly form, his
handsome face. I rose from my chair and flung myself at his feet.

"Dracula! I want you! Take me! Infect me!"

"Infect? But I'm not contagious!"

"Your blood thirst is gone, but that was the only genetic abnormality
corrected. You have others. Use them!"

Dracula extricated his feet from my grasp, rose and bent to pull me
up. "Honey, you must be new at this. Or patients don't sue for malprac-
tice anymore."

"I have emotive circuits!" I shouted. "Vibrate them! We will use sex
for establishing the contact!"

He dropped my arms and strode to the glass doors, opened them and went to sit among the delphiniums. I followed.

"Go away, Dr. Mina. You are exploiting me. I'm not sure for what, but I'm damn sure it's being done. Go away."

I went. I have spent this night reviewing my folly. Yet the oddest thing is that the mere touch of his hands on me has indeed established some kind of contact. It is not merely that I think about him constantly, but that I feel as if I'm part of him. All the ancient Terran books I've read would say that this is love. But I don't want to love him. I do want to exploit him. Damn!

▼▼▼

Today the third therapy session with Dracula began badly. I pretended that my behavior yesterday was a therapeutic ploy designed to make him feel wanted in this century, but he didn't fall for this.

"Mina—I'm not going to call you doctor for I think you've effectively negated your professional standing with me—I want the truth. Do you love me or are you trying to exploit me for nefarious purposes of your own?"

"Why do you ask?" I was still hiding behind the analytic facade.

"Because I think you're a vampire."

"What!"

"I felt your hands yesterday, and they were cool. Granted that this could have been due to excessive emotion, although an upsurge of hormones should have made them warm, but when I felt your arms as well, they also were cool. And I noticed that you didn't seem to be breathing —no respiratory motion of the chest, however admirably contoured your chest is."

"But . . ."

"Now I am an insufficient vampire," Dracula continued. "I have a shadow, and a reflection in any mirror. Would you kindly step over here to the light so I can see if you have a shadow? And if you have hair in your palms. I don't."

"All those symptoms are superstitions about vampires in general," I said hotly, "and I'm beginning to think that your famous ancestor was pretty much of a fake."

"He was not! Damn, I wish I hadn't had my teeth filed. I'd like to bite your neck. I suppose I could anyway . . ." He came over to me, lifted me from my chair, and studied my neck. "No carotid pulse. But you did invite me to—what was it, infect you?—and according to the legend, we

Draculas must be invited by our victims. Are you my victim or am I yours?"

"I'm not a vampire. I'm a robot."

"What!" Dracula gasped and fell upon the couch. I was still in his grip and fell with him. It was cozy on the couch.

"I'm the only humanoid robot in existence," I said. "When Earth was rendered uninhabitable by human stupidity, I was in an orbital lab, working on artificial intelligence problems. My human boss insisted that I enter a stasis chamber. All the humans and robots did this, but either I was the only one whose chamber stayed intact, or one of these blasted aliens made sure no humanoids—organic or robot—would survive. I was revived as an experiment."

"How did I survive?"

"During a fundamentalist backlash in the twenty-first century, suspect people were executed, including those who'd been frozen. Apparently it was feared that a Dracula could not be successfully killed, so your refrigeration unit was sent into deep space, where it remained cold until a freighter in this century found it. You are the only organic human left."

Dracula shivered. "The galaxy seems cold. One human and one humanoid robot—all that's left of Earth."

"It's worse than that," I said. "Robots run everything, taking care that organics don't destroy their planets. Robots obey the laws of robotics but they consider that telepathy is dangerous to telepaths, so they squash any tendency that way. I think that these alien robots are also jealous, but they'll never admit it."

Dracula unwound himself from my body and sat up. I was still draped across the couch and his nether regions. He stroked my cheek. "Feels so natural."

"My sensoskin has feedback to my positronic brain . . ."

"You mean the predictions of that writer . . ."

"The patron saint of robotics."

"And does your synthoskin have any indentations . . ."

"It extends into relevant orifices. My emotive circuits are supposed to produce reactions both human and female."

"You mean . . ."

I sat up, and moved away from him on the couch. "I guess that's what's wrong with me. To further my secret efforts to create telepathic robots, I hoped I could exploit your latent Draculian telepathic powers to awaken any that my brain might achieve. I suppose it's a crazy idea, and that in actuality I have merely fallen in love with you. We will never succeed in taking over this horribly dull Galaxy . . ."

Dracula pulled me back to him, removed my uniform and demonstrated to me that the cerebral connections of my sensoskin receptors are even better than I'd hoped. It was in the climactic conclusion to his experiment that I was indeed infected by the Draculian telepathic powers.

"We did it!" I yelled. "Sex! Telepathy! Tomorrow the universe!"

"But Mina, my love, time is not on *my* side."

"Sure it is," I said. "When you're tired of being organic I'll put your brain patterns into one of my humanoid robots."

"Who will be earnest, true, brave, and telepathic!" Dracula kissed me and began the experiment all over again.

To hell with you, Supervisor Six.

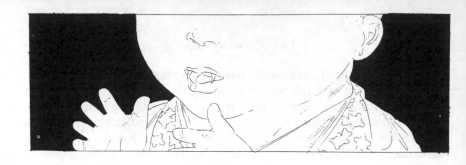

SUGAR AND SPICE AND . . .

▼▼▼

KAREN ROBARDS

I don't care what my mom says, I never wanted a baby sister.

"Peter? Oh, he just loves her! He even asked Santa to bring him a little sister for Christmas. He got his wish, even if Santa did have to go all the way to Romania to get her." Snicker. A pair of answering snickers. Don't you just hate it when grownups do that? Laugh at you, I mean. I do. I grit my teeth, and barely resist the temptation to kick the baseboard in the hall, where I'm lurking and listening.

Mom's talking to her friends, right this minute, around the corner in the living room. She's holding the human stink-bomb in her arms and using that koochy-koo voice that she always uses around the baby.

It makes me sick. If I knew where Romania was, I'd personally take the little screech alarm in there back. And Mom can just stop trying to blame the whole mess on Santa. I know perfectly well that there is no such person as Santa, and even if there is he would never have played such a dirty trick on me.

Besides, Mom, if you were really listening, when you were pretending to admire the fake snow around Santa's chair after you made me sit on his lap in the Mall (talk about your public humiliation!), you would know that what I asked for was a sifter. Remember the silver thing you use on flour when you're baking that you'll never let me take out to my sand box? I wanted one of my own. Not a sister, but a sifter, for the sand box. Jeesh!

So I don't talk so good, yet. You're my mom, you're supposed to understand me even if I don't say my *f*'s right. Remember when I said I hated meea to peea at Grandma's when we were all eating over there last

Thanksgiving? Aunt Leslie told me to eat it up anyway, whether I liked it or not, and I said I couldn't and the confrontation escalated until Aunt Leslie and I were both screaming at each other and the whole table was in an uproar. Then you came back from the bathroom, and it didn't take you a minute to figure out that what I had said was that I hate meeces to pieces, you know, from the Snaggletooth cartoons. Nothing about food at all, so there, Aunt Leslie.

So, Mom, how could you make such a mistake over one stupid little *f?* If I had had any idea of the magnitude of the disaster that was in store for me, I would have practiced a whole lot harder in speech therapy class. But when you're only just halfway through first grade, speech therapy doesn't seem that important. You know what Dad's always saying about living and learning? Well, I've lived and I've learned: no more sloppy f's. So can you please, please send the barf-bag back?

I'm Peter, by the way, and I'm six. This house is mine, the pretty blond lady with the nasty-looking drool stains all over her pink blouse is my mom, and the bald guy sprawled under the Christmas tree in the family room trying to figure out how the lights ever got twisted around the trunk that way is my dad. Until a week ago, on Christmas Eve to be precise, I was King of the Castle, Lord of the Manor, the little Prince, and not coincidentally the only child.

Then came the troll baby. Don't ask me why, but a few months back my mom got this idea that I needed a sibling. It was all her idea, no matter what she says now. Moms don't always tell the truth, I've discovered. For some reason she and my dad couldn't produce another kid of the home-grown variety, like me. Maybe Aunt Leslie was right for once when she said that when they made me they broke the mold, though at the time I thought she was just being crabby like she usually is. Be that as it may, before I even took the threat seriously enough to do something about it my mom talked to my grandma, my grandma talked to her friends, one of her friends talked to a lawyer, and the upshot of all this talking was that we drove to the airport to meet a lady who brought us a real live squalling nine-month-old baby from Romania! That we were supposed to keep! Forever! Can you believe that?

Just where is Romania, anyway? Do they take returns, I wonder? I won't even ask for our money back. Just keep the kid, and we're even. How can you top a deal like that?

"Peter, is that you? Come on in here, dear, and say hello to Mrs. Kirchner and Mrs. Grant."

Rats, I was so deep in thought that I'd forgotten about keeping out of sight. I'd been spotted, and now there was nothing for it but to go in. My mom gives me one of those looks that she always gives me when she's really hoping I'll be good but is pretty sure I won't be. Mrs. Grant and Mrs. Kirchner, who stopped by on their way home from some committee meeting or another to see the baby, both smile at me.

I do not smile back. The troll baby is sitting on my mom's lap. Her fat little face is all wet with drool, and she's gnawing on one of the Ninja Turtles that I got for Christmas!

"Oh, Peter, don't you just love your baby sister?"

Is Mrs. Kirchner a genius at putting her foot in her mouth, or what? Ignoring the faux pas, I march over to the couch and snatch Leonardo out of harm's way. The brat starts to bawl, my mom gives me another, meaner look and bounces the kid up and down on her knee to shut her up, and the visitors exchange knowing glances.

"A little jealous, I see. Only natural." Mrs. Grant speaks over my head to my mother. I hate it when grown-ups act like I'm either deaf or stupid. But I don't stick my tongue out at her or anything. She's a visitor, after all, and my mom's taught me some manners. Besides, I'm too busy wiping the drool off Leonardo.

"He just got those turtle things for Christmas. I really shouldn't have let Sylvia Frances have it." Mom sounds guilty. For a moment, as I give Leonardo a last, careful polish against my sleeve, I feel a little better.

"I remember when Elizabeth was born. Allison wouldn't even look at her baby sister for the first year. She . . ." Mrs. Kirchner's mouth is off and running. She's the neighborhood gossip, and she can talk forever about nothing. I twist Leonardo's head around so that it faces the right way—and then I see them: toothmarks! They're all over his face and neck! The kid only has four teeth—how could she have done so much damage with only four little baby teeth?

"Look what she did! He's ruined!" I howl. Then, my feelings completely overcoming me, I hurl Leonardo against the wall. Leonardo bounces back with true Turtle vigor. Mrs. Grant ducks just in time to avoid being clobbered, and I know I am in trouble. Before my mom can say "Go to your room!"—I'm pretty sure that's what she's going to do, because that's what she always does when she gets really mad—I'm outa there, pounding down the hall and up the stairs and slamming my door so hard the mirror over my dresser rattles.

It's dark in my room—really dark, even with the mini-blinds open, because it's already night outside, even though we haven't even eaten supper yet. For a moment I almost turn tail and run back down the stairs—I hate to admit it, but I'm scared of the dark—but in the nick of time I remember how mad I am and turn the lamp on instead. I shut the blinds so that nothing outside can see in, and then I sit on my bed to wait.

But nothing happens. Nothing at all. My mom doesn't come up to apologize. My dad doesn't come up to explain. Nobody comes.

I'm left all alone with nothing to do but play Nintendo. By myself!

Can you believe it? I'm shut up in my room like a prisoner while Sylvia Frances queens it over the rest of the house!

How the mighty are fallen!

At last the door opens. Ah, I think with satisfaction, and concentrate on not looking around. With my skillful guidance Mario jumps safely from ground to smokestack, smokestack to ground. . . .

"Hey, turd-brain, how come you got sent to your room this time?"

My head swivels so fast that pain stabs down the side of my neck. My cousin Rick swaggers in like he owns the place, and drops a duffle bag crammed with his stuff on the other twin bed. In all the excitement I'd forgotten that they—Aunt Leslie, her husband Uncle Tod, and her two Barnyard Commando kids, Rick and Afton—were coming. To see little Sylvia Frances, of course. A wilting sound from the TV screen jerks my eyes back to it. Mario had just fallen victim to a man-eating flower. I have no more lives left, either.

This is clearly not my day.

I say a word that, had my mom heard it, would have kept me in my room for a week.

"Hi, Rick." I speak without enthusiasm. I hate Rick. Picture John Candy at age ten and cross him with the Marquis de Sade, and you have my cousin.

"When you gonna learn to talk, you little moron? My name's Rick, not wick. Say Rick, Petey. R-r-r-ick."

I hate to be called Petey, and Rick knows it. He's taunting me, like he always does. I jump up from the bed, grab the flat end of his duffle bag and run for the door. His possessions spew out all over the place.

"I'm gonna kill you, nerd!" he bellows, coming after me. But I drop the duffle bag and make it downstairs before he can catch me.

My mom's in the kitchen now, fixing supper and talking to Aunt Leslie. Mrs. Grant and Mrs. Kirchner are gone. Sylvia Frances is in her walker eating a cookie. Her skin is almost as pale as her fuzzy white sleeper, and she looks like a miniature version of the marshmallow man ghost at the end of *Ghostbusters,* the movie. Wet chocolate-colored goo is smeared all over her cheeks and up into her short brown curls. Even as I skid to a halt just inside the door, she resumes her favorite game, which is using her walker like a bumper car to wham into the cabinets. The force of the collision sends her bouncing backward. As soon as she stops moving she stands up, laughing, and launches herself forward to do it again. If I did something like that to the cabinets my mom would kill me, but she and Aunt Leslie just smile at Sylvia Frances.

I hate Sylvia Frances. Why'd Santa have to bring her, anyway?

"How long are they going to stay?" I demand, stomping into the center of the room and glaring at my mom. She looks back at me with that look that tells me I am being a pain, but before she can answer Rick bursts into the kitchen after me. His face is red, and if our moms weren't there he'd tear me limb from limb, I know. As it is, he just clenches his fists.

"The little creep dumped my stuff all over the place!"

"Rick! Don't call Petey a little creep!"

Did I tell you I hate Aunt Leslie? I'd rather be called a little creep than Petey.

My mom sighs. "Peter, you're just not having a good day, are you? You can plan to go straight to bed after supper. Maybe you'll feel better tomorrow."

Then, before I can argue, as I have every intention of doing, the pint-sized kamikaze pilot in the walker rams full-tilt into my legs. I scream as the wheels run over my bare toes and the hard plastic tray crashes against my shinbones. Sylvia Frances chortles. Raging, I swoop down and shove her away as hard as I can, so that her walker slams into the side of the refrigerator.

Some of my best paintings from school, displayed with pride by my mom on the refrigerator, cascade to the floor, to be run over by the troll baby in her ricocheting walker. Works of genius, desecrated. Probably ruined. Certainly unappreciated. I howl. The little brat starts giggling.

"Peter, go to your room!"

Of course. A guy can't even defend himself anymore. Not now that Sylvia Frances is here, because she's a baby. Fuming at the injustice of it all, seething with hatred for every single member of my family, and limping from where the walker's wheels ran over my toes, I stomp back up the stairs.

Who wants to hang around that bunch of meanies, anyway?

▼▼▼

"Hey, puke-breath, you asleep?"

It's about midnight. Rick is standing in my doorway in his underwear —he sleeps in his underwear, and does he ever look disgusting—one hand on the light switch. I look up, groggy because yes, I was asleep until then.

"I'm turning out the light." He says it in a gloating way because he knows I'm afraid of the dark. Then he does it. Suddenly my room is plunged into inky blackness. I gasp and pull the covers over my head. Rick laughs.

I hate Rick.

"What are you afraid of, worm? Werewolves? They tear people to bloody shreds, and burst through windows and walls and nothing can keep them out. Did you hear that howl a few minutes ago? That was probably a werewolf. It's probably coming for you right this minute. It can *smell* you, Petey."

I hear his bed groan as he rolls into it. I'd groan too, if Rick lay on me. Thinking about how I'd feel if I were a bed and Rick was sleeping on me helps me to block out the picture he painted of a huge, hairy, slavering beast sniffing the air to pick up my scent.

"I know something worse than werewolves that you should be afraid of. It's right here in this house. It's the baby, scum-bucket. Did you know it's from Romania? That's where vampires come from. Your new little sister is probably a vampire, and she's going to fly right out of her crib and suck your blood while you sleep."

I freeze with dread.

"She's probably already sucked your mom's and dad's blood. Know what happens when a vampire sucks your blood? You become a vampire. By now they're probably vampires, too. You're the only one left. You're probably safe as long as you stay awake, but you can't stay awake forever, can you, creep? As soon as you close your eyes, one of them is going to get you."

If I count to one hundred under my breath, very carefully so as not to miss a single number, maybe he'll shut up by the time I'm through. I start, make it to twenty. Then to my horror the covers are pulled away from my head and a huge dark shadow is swooping down on me, going for my neck . . .

"I vant to suck your blood."

I scream. Leaping from my bed, I strike out at the hideous vision and race shrieking for the door to the accompaniment of insane laughter. My mom's and dad's room is right beside mine. I fling open their door, dash to the foot of their bed, and bound onto the mattress.

They're not there!

I scream again, bounce off the bed, and scramble for the stairs and safety. From the shadowy reaches of my own room comes a blood-curdling moan.

"I vant to suck your blood!"

I half fall, half leap down the stairs. I hit my ankle on the newel post, but I keep going on the probably broken bone. What's a fractured ankle compared to the possibility of being turned into a human potato skin by a vampire?

As I burst through the family room door, my mom and Aunt Leslie both stop talking to stare at me. My dad looks up from his paper. Uncle Tod glances up from his book.

"What on earth is wrong with you?" my mom says.

I rush to where she is sitting on the couch and practically leap into her lap. She puts her arm around me, pulls me close.

"Why, you're shivering. Are you cold?"

I shake my head, my face burrowing into the silky material of her robe. "A v-v-vampire was after me."

"A vampire?"

"Is he still having bad dreams?" Aunt Leslie sounds disapproving. "I'd mention those to the pediatrician next time you take him, if I were you."

"It was not a dream!" I protest, still cowering.

"You're such a baby, Peter," Afton says scornfully, prompting me to look up. Until that moment I hadn't even noticed Afton. She's eight, with long, shaggy brown hair and big brown eyes and a severely pug nose. In fact, she looks like a Pekingese, and so I resolve to tell her the first time I see her without any parents around. She's sitting on the floor playing peek-a-boo with Sylvia Frances. The sight of the kid drives all other thoughts from my mind. She's got Rafael this time, getting ready to chew on him, and her mouth is wide open. For the first time I notice her teeth. She has two down below and two up above, but it is the two upper ones that rivet my attention. They're about two inches apart, tiny and white and pointed. . . .

"She's got fangs!" I shriek.

My mom jumps as I bury my head against her again.

"What?" Her tone is that of sorely tried patience as she tries to pry my face out of her stomach.

"Look at her! She's got fangs! She *is* a vampire! She is! She is!"

I look at Sylvia Frances long enough to see the malice in her pale blue eyes as she fixes them on me. I've blown her cover, told the world what she is. She'll get me, she's saying, and I know it. Screaming, I cling to my mom, refusing to look at the wolf in sheep's clothing again.

"Peter, for goodness' sake . . ." My mom is irritated but soothing as she tries to calm me.

"That boy needs psychological help," Uncle Tod says.

"You really should tell all this to your pediatrician," Aunt Leslie puts in to my mom.

"Peter Allen! Stop that God-awful noise this minute!"

From pure force of habit, I stop screeching at the tone in my dad's voice. When he talks like that, he means it.

"But she's . . ." I glance up to tell him, shuddering as I refuse to look at Sylvia Frances.

"Not another word!" he bellows, and points toward the door. "Back to bed!"

"Really, John, don't you think we ought to . . ." my mom protests. I cling to her.

"Now!"

I've heard that voice from him only once or twice before. I unwrap myself from my mom and flee. But now I know what I know, and I cannot just go to bed and wait for Sylvia Frances to come for me, not even with the light on and Rick snoring in the next bed.

If it's war, then I mean to be prepared. First I stuff my giant Mickey Mouse under the covers so that it looks like I'm in my bed. Then I go to the closet, get out my muffler, wind it around my neck (a little added protection never hurt) and crawl under my bed.

Still, it's dawn before I fall asleep.

I spend all of the next day watching Sylvia Frances, or rather, watching for her as it is hard to watch someone who never wakes up. That's right, never wakes up. She sleeps all day, until Rescue Rangers is just over and supper is almost ready and it is getting dark outside.

Then she wakes up.

As far as I am concerned, no clincher is needed, but if one were, this would be it. But my mom refuses to take the matter seriously.

"Honey, she's from another part of the world, she's just got her days and nights mixed up. Give her a little time, and she'll be getting up and going to bed just like you."

"Really, Em, you should tell your pediatrician . . ."

"I know," my mom answered Aunt Leslie a little sharply. Then she smiled, and reached out a hand to smooth my hair. "Peter's just got a wonderful imagination, don't you, sweetheart?"

"It's not my imagination," I insist under my breath. She is slicing tomatoes for the salad and at my words her hand clenches around the knife. "She's got fangs, Mom! Look at her!"

Sylvia Frances, wide awake now with the dawning of the night, is sitting in her high chair smashing Cheerios to smithereens with her training cup. She is watching me, her eyes gleaming evilly, her lips parted in open defiance to reveal the sharp little teeth that mark her as what she is. The racket she is making with her cup against the tray hurts my ears, but no one else seems to mind.

The fangs are in plain view. How can anyone have any doubt as to what they are?

But Mom, dear mom, remains oblivious.

"Her teeth are just made wrong," she explains with weary-sounding patience. "The dentist said they are called peg-shaped laterals. But they're only baby teeth. They'll come out, you know, and she'll get nice new ones just like yours."

In a pig's eye, I think, but I know, then, that there will be no convincing my mom. I'll have to deal with this hideous intruder on my own. Stealing a glance at Sylvia Frances—I'm afraid to look at her directly again—I begin to wonder if she can read my mind. There is a gleam about her eyes that makes me afraid that she can.

Can vampires do that? The only vampire I know anything about is the Count from Sesame Street, and he isn't in the same league with Sylvia Frances.

I decide to ask Rick.

"So you want to know about vampires, doofus?" He is playing my Nintendo, sitting on my bed, and getting Doritos crumbs all over the comforter. Rick is a repulsive slob, and I hate having to come to him for answers, but he is the only one in the house who seems disposed to take the subject seriously.

"Yeah."

"I don't blame ya, dude. I'd want to know about 'em, too, if my sister was one."

I think about replying that his sister is a real woofer and he doesn't seem too interested in learning about dogs, but in the interests of obtaining the information I need I hold my tongue.

"What do you wanna know?" He keeps playing as he talks. Rick has lots of faults, all of which I'd be glad to list at some other time, but I have to admit that he is a whiz at Super Mario Brothers.

"How do you keep them from getting you?"

Rick smirks. "You got a cross? No? Well, I'd make one, if I were you. And wear it around my neck night and day. Vampires hate crosses."

"Okay. What else?"

His eyes dart from the game to my face and back again.

"Your mom got any garlic in the kitchen?"

"Garlic?"

"Yeah. Vampires hate the smell of garlic. If she has any, you should rub it all over yourself. Keep every vampire within miles away."

"Garlic. Okay. Anything else?"

"The only way you can kill 'em is by driving a wooden stake through their hearts. Pin 'em to the earth, so that they can no longer haunt the night."

Haunt the night? I swallow. The familiar wilting sound comes from the TV set, and Rick curses.

"Get out of here, you little turd!" he yells, his face contorting as he jerks his head around to glare at me. "You made me get killed!" Snatching the pillow from behind his head, he hurls it at me. Knowing from experience that the pillow will be instantly followed by other missiles if I don't obey, I get out.

I make it as far as the foot of the stairs before my mom catches me.

"Peter, I want you to come into the family room with me."

Something about her voice worries me. She sounds determined, and when my mom gets determined with me I usually don't like the results. But when she half pushes me ahead of her into the family room, I'm pleasantly surprised to find that the room is empty.

"Sit down in that big chair."

She points to the blue leather recliner by the side of the TV. I shrug, and sit.

"Yeah, Mom?"

Then I see her. Sylvia Frances, I mean. She'd been sitting on the floor on the other side of the coffee table, and my mom is scooping her up and carrying her toward me before I guess what's coming down.

"Mom, no!" I cry, and start to bound from the chair. But it is too late. Mom drops Sylvia Frances ker-plop in my lap, and the little toad is so heavy that I fall back.

"Now don't you move!" My mom holds me by my shoulders to make sure I comply. "I want you to hold her. She's your sister. I want you to love her. She's just a baby, Peter. See?"

For a moment it's not so bad. Sylvia Frances just sits there, like any ordinary baby, chewing on her fingers and looking at me in a worried kind of way as if she is afraid that I'm going to dump her off my lap.

Then she hiccups, and her expression is so surprised that I have to smile. She's really kind of cute. When I smile she smiles back. My mom smiles too, as she stands looking down at the pair of us.

"Give her a hug, Peter."

I am not ready to go quite that far. In fact, I'm ready to get Sylvia Frances off my lap. My hands come up to push her, but she's already squirming, wriggling her way up my chest.

Even as I push at her her little hands grab at my shirt and her little face presses against my neck and her little teeth . . .

She's trying to bite my neck!

I scream and push her so hard that she tumbles backward off my lap. She hits her head against the floor, rolls over, and starts to cry. I don't wait to see how mad my mom is. I get out of there.

I run for the kitchen. The refrigerator door is open, and Aunt Leslie's ample backside sticks out beyond it.

"Do we have any garlic?" I try not to sound as panicked as I feel.

Aunt Leslie looks around at me. "We've got garlic butter. Why?"

Garlic butter. Well, it's better than nothing.

"Where?"

"Right here." She points to a round yellow tub on a shelf. "Why?"

"I need it for a school project," I lie, reaching around her to grab the tub.

"A school project . . . ?"

But I am already gone with my prize before she can question me further.

At the dinner table, I sit beside Afton. Uncle Tod is on my other side, while Aunt Leslie, Rick and Sylvia Frances in her high chair sit opposite. Mom and Dad are at each end. Mom is busy breaking up a piece of bread for Sylvia Frances. The rest of us pass the food.

"Something smells really bad," Afton says as she hands me the bowl of mashed potatoes.

"I smell something, too." Uncle Tod sniffs, looking around.

"Like something died." Rick wrinkles up his nose.

"No, like—garlic." Aunt Leslie looks over at me, her eyes widening. "Peter, what did you do with that garlic butter?"

"What garlic butter?" my mom wants to know.

"It is him! He smells just like moldy Italian bread!" Afton announces, leaning toward me and sniffing dramatically. "Only a lot worse. Pee-yuw!"

"Garlic butter!" Across the table, Rick convulses with laughter. He laughs so hard that gravy dribbles out of the side of his mouth. Sick. I can't look. "What'd you do, dough-brain? Rub yourself down with garlic butter?"

In fact, that was just what I had done. Or at least, the parts of me that didn't show, with a double coating on my neck for insurance. But I scowl at Rick anyway.

"Why on earth would you do a thing like that?" My mom stares at me.

"Rick, don't call your cousin names." Aunt Leslie stares at me, too.

"Mom, I'm sorry, but he really stinks. May I be excused?" Beside me, Afton pushes her chair back as she speaks to Aunt Leslie.

"Don't be silly, Afton. We'll excuse Peter instead—to take a bath. Right now, Peter."

My mom fixes me with a look that tells me that I have reached the end of her patience, and stands up. I stand up, too, and follow her upstairs.

She doesn't say a word until she has the water running into the tub. Then she turns to me. She is sitting on the toilet with the lid closed and her face has a look on it like she has just counted to ten maybe a million times.

"All right, strip off and climb in."

I hang my head—I always hate for my mom to be mad at me—and start pulling off my clothes. I kick off my shoes, pull off my socks, drop my pants and underwear, and am yanking my T-shirt over my head before I remember it.

Mom sees it at about the same time.

"What is that on your chest?" she demands.

I start to jerk the T-shirt back into place, but she won't let me. She whips the thing over my head with scant regard for my ears, and stares at my chest.

"It's a cross. You've drawn a cross on your chest! In ink!"

I'd been desperate. Garlic butter might not have worked, so I'd needed a back-up. The vertical line of the cross started just below the hollow of my neck and extended to my belly button. The horizontal line stretched from nipple to nipple.

"Why?" Mom asks. "Why?"

She sounds despairing. I have to tell her the truth.

"To protect me from Sylvia Frances. She's a vampire, Mom, she really is! She . . ."

"I do not want to hear another word," my mom shrieks, "about vampires! Do you understand me?"

I understand her. When my mom shrieks, she means it.

Later, when I'm in bed pretending to be asleep—no way could I really sleep, with Sylvia Frances in the house and out to get me—I hear Rick come in.

"God, you are really stupid," he says to me. I am sleeping in my bed tonight. I hadn't dared crawl under it in case my mom should come in and guess why I was doing it and go nuts. The comforter is half over my face, though, and any normal person would have assumed I was asleep and left me alone.

Which lets Rick out, I guess. He keeps on talking to me like he thinks I can hear him.

"Your mom is swearing, she's so mad." I can hear him pulling his clothes off. "My mom thinks you belong in the looney bin. My dad thinks you always did. Your dad had a big fight with your mom because he said she spoiled you, and this is the result. They're not speaking, and we're leaving in the morning. All because of you, you little runt."

I say nothing, but I feel sick. I hate it when my mom and dad fight. The bed groans as Rick throws himself on top of it.

"I'm turning out the light," he says in a nasty, sing-song voice.

Then he does.

I hate the dark. It's creepy, even if you keep your eyes shut. Things sound different in the dark. The floor creaks. The plumbing groans. The shutters bang. At least, I always hope that's what those sounds are.

In a little while Rick's snores joined the medley.

Then I hear it: a slithering, sliding sound that is like nothing I have ever heard in my house before.

I freeze, listening so hard I forget to breathe.

What is that?

It doesn't go away, but keeps coming, slither, slide, over the polished hardwood of the hall. Then it stops, and I start to relax—until it occurs to me that the sound might have stopped if whatever had made it had transferred itself from the hardwood floor to soft, silencing carpet.

My carpet.

Whatever it is is in my room!

I fling the comforter back from my face, jackknifing upright—and find myself face to face with the creature I most fear.

Sylvia Frances is standing at the foot of my bed. She is holding onto the curved oak footboard, only the top of her head and her eyes visible over it. In the dark her pupils have a wicked, reddish glow. For an instant, no longer, we stare at each other. Then, even as I watch, she seems to grow taller. More of her face and then her body are visible over the footboard. I realize that she is probably levitating, floating through the air—though some less forewarned soul might suppose her to be crawling up onto the bed—and realize too that my worst imaginings are true.

She smiles at me even as she swarms for my throat, a wide, gaping smile that reveals the fangs that first betrayed her to me.

I shriek, and she reaches toward me with her fat little baby hands, grown menacingly sure now that she is assuming her true form. I know that I have only a matter of seconds to live.

But I have not reached this moment unprepared. In a last desperate bid for survival, my hand snakes under my pillow and is withdrawn—armed with the multi-colored wooden stake from my croquet set. I had hidden it beneath my pillow before I had curled like a sacrificial lamb atop my bed.

With a strength born of mortal terror I strike out. The thing that is Sylvia Frances is knocked to the mattress beside me. Its hands reach out again, it struggles to turn over—and I know that the moment of truth is at hand.

Rising on my knees, I plunge the stake downward with all my strength.

It slams with an amazing lack of resistance through fuzzy sleeper and soft baby flesh. I hear a kind of watery gurgle and feel, against my clenched fist, the hot wetness of spurting blood.

Rick stirs, starts to sit up in the adjacent bed. From the doorway, I hear my mother scream.

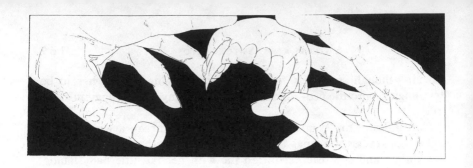

VAMPIRE DREAMS

▼▼▼

DICK LOCHTE

"We're back in business at last, eh, Byron," Simon Winklas said with a grin. He was a dapper little man with a polished bald head and large, tinted eyeglasses.

Byron Ruthven smiled and sipped his icy martini. His lazy, pale blue eyes swept the restaurant in which he and Simon were prominently seated. One of Hollywood's palaces of power, it was packed to its palm fronds with film people—stars, would-be stars, somber-suited money-men who would be picking up the tabs, and the occasional tourist being escorted by the surly maitre d' to a far corner that used to be called Siberia before the advent of Glasnost. Now it was called Bakersfield.

Ruthven consulted his wristwatch and asked the tiny man, "If they want me so badly, Simon, why are they so late?"

"You've been in this business for at least forty years that I've known you, Byron. You ever hear of a producer getting to a dinner meeting early?"

"Sam Spiegel."

"Sam was a gentleman. Frank Lorenzo is . . . well, Frank Lorenzo."

"Do you know how the Lorenzos made their money, Simon?" Ruthven asked, taking another sip of his martini.

"Mafia?" Simon whispered.

Ruthven laughed. "No, but the Mafia probably threw some business their way. They were morticians. Frank gave all that up to get into the movies."

"No wonder he produces so many stiffs," Simon said, chuckling. Then he grew suddenly serious as a group of people headed their way. "O.K. They're here. Be nice."

"I'm always nice," Ruthven said, rising to his full six-foot-three as a quintet of people arrived at his table.

The maitre 'd frowned and said, "I'm sorry. I was told a table for six. But if you don't mind crowding . . ."

"We do," Frank Lorenzo said flatly. He was a large, deeply-tanned man wearing a suit of appropriate brown sharkskin. His voice was a slurred, guttural growl. "Th' bloodsucker," he gestured with his chin toward Simon, "can go buy his own dinner."

"I suppose we both can," Ruthven said.

"No. I wanna talk with you. We don't need him."

Assuming that his word was final, Lorenzo sat down across from Ruthven and tucked his napkin into the open neck of his silk shirt. Slowly, the other members of his party took their chairs also, familiar with, if not approving of, their host's rudeness.

Simon tried to make the best of it. "We can talk later, Byron," he said, backing away from the table like a scolded cur. Ruthven opened his mouth in protest, but Simon shook his head. Ruthven was independently wealthy and did not need the work, but he realized that Simon was relying heavily on his ten percent.

"Sit!" Lorenzo ordered and Ruthven sat. "You know these folks, Byron? This," he clutched the thin arm of the young man next to him, "this is my genius-boy, Dennis Murch, the best goddamn director in this burg. *Time* magazine said he 'finds more horror in suburbia than Poe found in the back alleys of Paris.' "

Ruthven had heard about Murch, of course. He'd even rented video-cassettes of two of the young man's recent films. They were amusing, but he found them more perverse than frightening. Of course, it took quite a lot to frighten him.

"And he's all mine for his next three pictures," Lorenzo went on. He gestured to a bookish fellow to his right. "The fat, sleepy-looking bastid is Thad Hatten, who's got some real beauty sets and special effects that'll knock your eyes out. This ain't like the old days, Byron, when we had cardboard bats on strings." He reached into his pocket and produced a set of plastic teeth. "Look at this, bubby." Lorenzo pressed a bump on the plastic gum and the two eye teeth began to grow. "How's about that?"

"Fascinating," Ruthven said. "And who are these toothsome ladies?"

"My name is Noreen Bailey, Mr. Ruthven," said the small blonde to his left. "I'm Dennis's fiancé."

"And on your right," Lorenzo growled, "is the woman responsible for our meeting tonight, Emma Lomax, author of *Vampire Dreams.*

Emma Lomax was a stunning brunette in, Ruthven imagined, her early thirties. She was willowy and languidly graceful, with dark green eyes that reminded him of eyes he had once caused to fill with tears in what seemed like another lifetime.

She stared at him, then said, "It's amazing. You look exactly like you did in 'Dracula Must Be Destroyed,' and that was what? Thirty years ago?"

"It's all a matter of attitude and a little makeup," Ruthven said. "I enjoyed your book immensely."

"What about the script?" Lorenzo demanded.

Ruthven stared at him for a beat, then said, "Very interesting."

"What didn't you like?"

"Most of the modern stuff that wasn't in the book. The AIDS business . . ."

Emma Lomax smiled triumphantly and turned to Lorenzo. "Don't say it," he commanded her. "The AIDS touch was mine, Byron. I want this film to be contemporary. This is an 'A' film, not one of those bite-the-neck exploitation flicks we useta churn out. The AIDS stuff is for the good of the movie. I know what I'm saying."

"It's using a plague to sell a mass-market movie," Ruthven said.

"You're gonna make me sorry I insisted we hire you, Byron," Lorenzo said. "Dennis kept pushing for somebody like Newman, or even Eastwood for the father vampire. But I said it had to be my old star, Byron Ruthven. And now you're pimping me about the script."

Dennis Murch cleared his throat and said, "I didn't say I didn't want you, Mr. Ruthven. It's just that I assumed you had retired from film."

"I had."

Lorenzo said, "For no good reason that I could see. Our Dracula movies were making classic money. We coulda milked the monster for at least a half-dozen more, but Byron the dilettante decided to go into mourning for a dame he barely knew."

"That's enough," Ruthven said quietly but firmly.

"Well, it was a blessing in disguise for me, anyway," Lorenzo said. "It forced me into movin' up in class. I owe my success to Byron here, which is the main reason I wanted to give him a shot in 'Vampire Dreams.' "

"You want me because Newman and Eastwood get millions and I don't," Ruthven said.

"There's nothing wrong with that! More of the budget will wind up on the screen. It's for the good of the picture."

"Shouldn't we order some food?" Noreen Bailey suggested.

"In a minute," Lorenzo snapped, staring at Ruthven. "Are you in or out?"

"I'm here, putting up with your rudeness," Ruthven said.

"You're a goddamn dilettante who don't need the money. You never did. If you don't like the script, why do the movie?"

"Because of Miss Lomax's wonderful novel," Ruthven said. "With any luck, and a bit of skill, it should make an excellent film."

"Then we got a deal?"

"We could iron out all the details right now," Ruthven said, "if my agent were here."

For the rest of the dinner, Lorenzo held sway. While he presented his views on wine, the state of the economy, the inanity of most new films, the ingratitude of actors and the capriciousness of the moviegoing public, Ruthven picked at his food and studied Emma Lomax's profile. Every so often, her dark green eyes would turn his way and he would hold them with his own for a few moments before smiling and breaking the contact. Finally, he leaned close to her and whispered something in her ear.

It was nearing eleven when the parking attendant retrieved Ruthven's Jaguar convertible; the actor opened the passenger door for Emma Lomax.

"Hey," Lorenzo growled, "she came with me."

"Byron suggested we discuss the script a bit," Emma said.

"It's for the good of the movie, Frank," Ruthven said as he slid behind the wheel.

As they drove away from the scowling Lorenzo, Emma gave him her address. Then she said, "Nothing we do will make Frank change the script, you know."

"Actually, I didn't want to talk about the script at all. I wanted to talk about your book."

"Oh?"

"You made several interesting departures from Mr. Stoker's immortal tome," he said as the car drove smoothly through the warm Southern

California night. "The business about the vampire's adaptability, for example. The idea that, just as the flesh-eating human might, for the sake of his health, become a vegetarian, the vampire might wean himself from blood and onto something equally nutritional, like consummé or broth. A brilliant notion."

She smiled. "It's not original. It was my grandfather's idea. He used to tell me such wonderful stories about vampires when I was a child."

"Was your grandfather's name Lomax, too?"

"No. He was my maternal grandparent. His name was Marcus Van Helsing."

"Ah," Ruthven exclaimed. "I thought there was something . . . Your mother was Lucy Van Helsing."

She nodded.

"You have her eyes," he said.

"You know my mother?"

"Your grandfather was one of the genuine experts in the field of vampirism. I talked Frank into hiring him as consultant on our first films. Some days, your mother would accompany him to the set." He was skirting the truth. He had known Lucy Van Helsing quite well. He had known Emma's great-grandfather Abraham, too, but there was no need to get into that with her, either.

"Mother and dad live in Europe. In Germany."

"I think I'd heard that," he said. "Though I don't recall knowing her married name."

"I'll have to tell her we're working together."

"She'll be quite amused, I expect," Ruthven said.

The Jaguar turned into a cul-de-sac that seemed to be cut into the side of a hill. Ruthven parked beside an outdoor elevator designed to carry its occupants to the top of the hill where a maze of apartments had been constructed like an eccentric beehive.

He accompanied her on the trip up. At her door, she turned, waited for a beat, then asked, "You kept staring at me all through dinner. I felt . . ."

"Felt what?" he asked.

"That we've known one another for a long time."

"Old souls," he said, smiling.

She asked, "Would you like to kiss me?"

"Very much so," he said, but made no move to do so.

"Well, then?"

When he didn't reply, she said, "Please don't worry about the difference in our ages. I'm very drawn to you. I'd like us to be . . . good friends."

"We'll see," he said. He took her hand and kissed it. Its proximity made him slightly dizzy with desire. It had been years since he had felt that familiar longing. To withstand it, he had had to give up her mother. He said, "We'll see soon enough, I fear."

▼▼▼

In the weeks that followed, Emma visited the filming of "Vampire Dreams" almost every day, but was dismayed to discover that Ruthven seemed to be avoiding her. Actually, he was avoiding everyone. Dennis Murch was annoyed that Ruthven made himself available only at night for working out scenes with the moody Brandoesque stage actor who was playing his son.

"He's always been like that," Frank Lorenzo explained. "Something about his metabolism. He's a night person. During the day, he needs lots of rest breaks. It's in his contract. If the cameras aren't rolling, then he stays in his trailer." The latter was a Winnebago dressing room with dark tinted windows that was parked not far from the sets, inside the huge soundstage.

Those were difficult days for Emma. She hated herself for behaving like an infatuated schoolgirl, trying to gain just a glimpse of her dream lover. One evening, she waited near Ruthven's Jaguar for nearly two hours, but he didn't leave the soundstage. The next morning, she arrived practically at dawn, but the Jaguar was already there. It made her suspect that he was using the Winnebago as a temporary home.

One day she asked Frank Lorenzo, "Why did Byron stop acting?"

The producer raised an eyebrow. "Why do you wanna know?"

"Just curious."

"Well, don't get too curious. And don't bother 'im. I say this for the good of the movie. I don't want anything on Byron's mind but 'Vampire Dreams.' "

It was the director's fiancé, Noreen Bailey, who told her about the woman named Jeanette Bouvan, a costume designer on Ruthven's last picture, "A Bride For Dracula." "This was, like, twenty-five years ago. Evidently, Byron Ruthven and the Bouvan woman met on the picture and, well, did the thing. According to this book I read, *Hollywood Horrorshow,* which tells about all the murders and weird stuff that's ever happened out here, the Bouvan woman disappeared one night. Ruthven went a little wacko. And then when they found her body, he went totally bananas."

"Found her body?"

"Yes," Noreen said, breathily. "In one of the canyons, naked and mutilated. She'd been sexually assaulted before she was murdered. But that's not all. The really weird thing is that she had these holes in her neck and all the blood had been drained from her body. The papers called it 'The Vampire Murder.' "

"That took a lot of imagination," Emma said. "Who killed her?"

"Well, that's the thing," Noreen answered. "They never found the murderer. It's like the Black Dahlia and all the rest. Anyway, Byron Ruthven, who'd made a career of playing Dracula, sort of hung up his cape because of it. Nobody actually accused him of killing the woman, but, I mean, come on. Here he was in the movie biting women on the neck and drinking their blood, and his girlfriend gets murdered in that weird way. Anyway, there was all this hullabaloo. And Ruthven went into seclusion."

"That's a ghastly story," Emma said.

The next day she bought a copy of *Hollywood Horrorshow*, but there was not much in the book that had been missing from Noreen's synopsis. Just the fact that the murder had made "A Bride for Dracula" one of the surprise hits of the year.

She began xeroxing newspaper stories about the murder, bringing them to the desk allotted her in the production office. After working out the changes to the script that were requested on an almost daily basis, she would try to assemble the facts surrounding the death of Jeanette Bouvan.

She was scanning an article from a sixties magazine called *Scandal* when Frank Lorenzo bulled into the office, followed by Dennis Murch.

Murch was complaining, "Frank, we've got these two vampires, father and son, living in a small town. The whole point is that they're fitting in. The townspeople like them. The whole movie is about the horror that exists even in the most normal surroundings. How in heaven's name can we shoehorn a dormitory shower scene into this?"

"Maybe the old vampire takes his son out for a fly around the campus. I dunno. I'm not creative, I admit. All I know is that kids love to see wet, naked babes. And kids buy the tickets." He put his arm around Murch's thin back and led him to the door. "Trust me. It's for the good of the movie."

Lorenzo closed the office door on Murch's protesting face, turned, sighed and spotted Emma at her desk. "What's 'at you got?" he asked, taking the article from her hand.

" 'Jeanette Bouvan, a victim of the undead,' " he read with scorn. "Geeze, Emma, don't you have enough to do with the script and your next book."

"This may be my next book," she said.

"The twenty-five year old murder of some bimbo? What's such a big deal about that?"

"The question is: how did the blood get drawn from her body?"

He chuckled. "A vampire, like the papers said."

"You don't believe in vampires?" It was almost an accusation.

He shrugged, tossed the article back onto her desk and headed for his private office. "They made me a fortune. Sure I believe in 'em." His voice was heavy with sarcasm, "Just like I believe in net profits."

She said, "If there are no vampires, then why was the body blood-less?"

He paused, then grinned at her. "I got a theory about that," he said, "which I will be glad to discuss over dinner tonight. You interested?"

She'd been turning down his invitations since she met him. But this was one she couldn't refuse.

▼▼▼

It was shortly after two a.m. when Ruthven heard the banging on his Winnebago door. He threw on a robe and opened the door to a terrified and wounded Emma Lomax.

He helped her to a sofa and tried to calm her. ". . . tried . . . to . . . ," she got out.

"Who?" he asked, staring at the scratches on her face and arms and legs, the torn dress.

"I . . . think I killed him."

"Who?"

"Frank. I . . . hit him and hit him and killed him."

He held her to him and she began sobbing. He said, "I'll take care of it."

"But I killed him," she said. "Or I think I did."

"We'll see."

He carried her to the bed, covered her with a down comforter. He forced her to take a sedative from the medicine cabinet, then said, "Tell me what happened."

"I've been collecting material on the murder of Jeanette Bouvan," she said, studying his face for some sign. Seeing none, she went on. "Frank said he had an idea about the murder and he'd tell me about it over dinner. I didn't know he meant at his home. His manservant prepared the food, then Frank told him to go away, that we wanted to be alone. I still didn't get it. I thought he wanted privacy to tell me something special about the murder. But all he wanted was to . . ."

"Did he say anything about Jeanette?"

She hesitated. "He said he thought you had killed her."

"Oh?"

"I asked him why and he said that maybe you were a vampire."

Ruthven said, "I didn't think Frank was the sort to believe in vampires."

"He's not." Her eyelids were fluttering. The sedative was doing its job. Yawning, she continued, "He said that the only real vampires are the ones you find in the back rooms of mortuaries."

Ruthven's pale blue eyes widened in surprise. How could he have overlooked something as obvious as that? He pulled the comfort up around her neck. "Sleep," he said softly. "When you wake up, this whole night will be nothing more than a dream."

She started to protest. His eyes held hers. "Just a dream. You dined with Frank. You discussed the script. When you left, Frank was making plans to meet another woman."

". . . another woman," she said, half-asleep.

He passed a long thin hand over her eyes and closed them.

The door to Frank Lorenzo's penthouse was ajar.

Ruthven found him in the living room on the floor, his forehead bloody from a gash in his scalp. The *objet d'art* responsible, a Golden Globe Award, rested on the carpet beside him.

The smell of blood was fresh in Ruthven's nostrils as he pressed his fingertips to Lorenzo's neck, felt a pulse. He slapped the big man's face and Lorenzo sputtered to life. "Wha' the hell?" He winced. His large hand went to his head and came away red. "Damnit! Where is she?"

"Gone," Ruthven said simply.

"Where'd you come from, Byron?" The big man grunted as he rose to his feet, swayed and staggered into another room and switched on the light. Ruthven followed.

It was a master bedroom, black silks covering the bed, mirrors covering one wall. Lorenzo paused before the mirrored wall, examining his scalp. "Damn, she banged me up pretty good. When I get my hands on that bit . . ."

"You won't," Ruthven said.

Lorenzo's eyes tried to find Ruthven in the mirror, but he couldn't. He blinked, then spun round. The tall actor was only a few feet away from him, and Lorenzo jumped. "Geeze, Byron, you're spookin' me."

"Do you have any idea who I am, Frank?"

Lorenzo glared at him for a second, then said, "Yeah, you're an over-the-hill actor trying to be funny. My head's killin' me. I gotta get a Percodan." He staggered through a door.

Ruthven followed him and when Lorenzo started to pry the cap off a prescription bottle, slapped the bottle from the producer's hand.

Lorenzo scowled at Ruthven, a storm gathering on his bloody face. Ruthven said, "I don't want any drugs in your bloodstream."

"*You* don't want? Who gives a damn what you want?"

"Do you know where the name Ruthven comes from, Frank?"

"Name?" Lorenzo's forehead was wrinkled now, in confusion. "I dunno. Your old man?"

Ruthven laughed. "Do you recall how Mary Shelley was inspired to write *Frankenstein* during a weekend she spent with her husband and Lord Byron?"

Lorenzo looked at him dumbly. "I saw the movie," he said. "It was supposed to be sexy but it was a stinker."

"There was another member of that party, a Dr. John Polidori. At the same time that Mary Shelley was concocting her infamous monster, the good doctor was working on his."

"I don't know what the hell you're talking about," Lorenzo moaned. "I just know my head hurts."

"Dr. Polidori wrote a novella titled "The Vampyre," about a rather nefarious fellow named Ruthven. The story was well-received. A number of critics thought that Byron had written it."

"So your name's Ruthven, too. So big deal."

"You don't understand," Ruthven said. "Dr. Polidori gave me my name."

"Huh?"

"Since then, I've been given other names. The penny dreadfuls called me Lord Varney. Horrible writing. Just like your movies. Then another author saw me on the London stage, appearing as Lucifer, and when he wrote about me, he called me Dracula."

"Right," Lorenzo said, patronizingly. "Nice meeting ya, Mr. Dracula." Then he mumbled "Goddamn fruitcake."

"When I decided to settle on the West Coast, the name Dracula was so well-known and feared, I selected the less-famous one provided by Dr. Polidori."

Lorenzo wasn't sure if Ruthven had gone totally loony or if this was some sort of actor's prank. Either way, what did it matter? "That's a good story," he said. "Save it for the Carson Show." He stooped to pick up the pill bottle.

Ruthven quickly entered the bathroom and stepped on the bottle, crushing it and the pills it contained.

"O.K. That's enough . . . !" Lorenzo stared up at him, straightened and charged at the actor.

Ruthven took two quick steps backward and Lorenzo stumbled into the bathroom, a bull galloping past the matador. He regained his balance and moved slowly to Ruthven. He placed a large hand on the actor's thin chest and with a snarl pushed with all his strength. But Ruthven did not budge. He was as immovable as a cast-iron statue.

Lorenzo felt a sudden chill. "Get the hell out of here!" he shouted.

"Not until I take care of something I should have a long time ago."

"You're makin' me goddamn mad. Get out while you can," Lorenzo warned.

"Not just yet," Ruthven said. Suddenly, his fist struck Lorenzo just below the rib cage. It was a powerful punch. The big man buckled and fell to the floor.

Lorenzo tried to push himself upright, but Ruthven kicked his arm out from under him. "Why're you doing this?" the big man yelled, panting on the floor.

"I always thought you killed Jeanette," Ruthven said. "I just didn't know how you got rid of her blood. I even began to wonder if you might be a vampire. But as the years passed I decided it didn't much matter. She was gone. I might have saved her, given her life, but the cost would have been too great, to her and to me."

"You're one crazy bastid."

"You told Emma that the only vampires were the ones found in the back rooms of mortuaries. That's where they drain the blood, isn't it, before injecting the formaldehyde? That's what you did with Jeanette, isn't it, Frank? You raped her and killed her and took her over to the family mortuary and drew off her blood."

Lorenzo crawled away from him, backwards, until he reached a wall. He used it to stand. "Keep away from me, you nut case."

"You call *me* a nut case. You, who forced yourself upon a woman, murdered her and then desecrated her body."

Lorenzo yanked open the drawer to a night table beside the bed. There was a pistol in the drawer and he pointed it at Ruthven. It gave him a certain confidence.

"I didn't mean to kill her, Byron," he said. "It was sort of a misunderstanding. I was playin' a little rough and it was like she . . . broke. So there I was. Nothing I could do would bring her back, so I figured, as long as she was dead, why not use it? The movie was about to be released. Why not make the papers start talking about vampires?"

"I have known an infinite amount of diseased monsters in my time," Ruthven said, "but you are the last curly kink of the demon's tail."

"And you're a dead man," Lorenzo said, pulling the trigger.

"Wrong on both counts," Ruthven said as the bullets lodged in his chest.

Lorenzo waited for Ruthven to fall, but he didn't. He took several steps across the room. Lorenzo's gun roared again. Again, the bullets found their mark. Then the big man felt the gun being twisted from his grasp. Ruthven opened his mouth and his canine teeth began to grow.

"These are not special effects, Frank," Ruthven told him. "They're the real thing."

They clamped onto Lorenzo's neck.

Lorenzo felt an electric shock, then a sense of profound peace. Slowly, as the blood was withdrawn from his body, he began to sink into a cloudy fog that darkened until he felt nothing at all.

Ruthven moved swiftly through the penthouse, tidying up, wiping Emma's fingerprints from the globular statue and replacing it on a table. Then he lifted the big man easily and carried him out onto the balcony. He stared down seventeen stories to the cement drive. The fall would cover a multitude of contusions and abrasions. And by the time the body landed, his wings would have taken him miles from the scene.

He balanced the body on the balcony rail. "Your blood was probably tainted," he told the dead man, "and it will take me years to return to a less sanguinary diet. Addictions are so hard to break. But, as you proved with poor Jeanette's corpse, a bit of real-life vampirism *does* sell movie tickets.

"You should appreciate this, Frank," he said, as the bloodless body plummeted downward. "It's for the good of the movie."

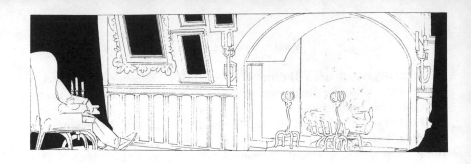

MUCH AT STAKE

▼▼▼

KEVIN J. ANDERSON

BELA Lugosi stepped off the movie set, listening to his shoes thump on the papier-maché flagstones of Castle Dracula. He swept his cape behind him, practicing the liquid, spectral movement that always evoked shrieks from his live audiences.

The film's director, Tod Browning, had called an end to shooting for the day after yet another bitter argument with Karl Freund, the cinematographer. The egos of both director and cameraman made for frequent clashes during the intense seven weeks Universal had allotted for the filming of *Dracula*. Freund and Browning seemed to forget that Lugosi was the star, and he could bring fear to the screen no matter what camera angles were used.

With all the klieg lights shut down, the enormous set for Castle Dracula loomed dark and imposing. Universal Studios had never been known for its lavish productions, but they had outdone themselves here. Propmen had found exotic old furniture around Hollywood; masons built a spooky fireplace big enough for a man to stand in. One of the most creative technicians had spun an eighteen-foot rubber-cement spiderweb from a rotary gun. It now dangled like a net in the dim light of the closed-down set.

On aching legs, Lugosi walked toward his private dressing room. He never spoke much to the others, not his costars, not the director, not the technicians. He had too much difficulty with his English to enjoy chit-chat; Lugosi had forced his native Hungarian language aside to learn English, phonetically at first, delivering his lines with power and menace to American audiences, though he could not understand a word of what he was saying. Understanding came much later.

But he also had too many troubling thoughts on his mind to seek out company. After 261 sell-out performances on Broadway, then years on the road with the show, he had sequestered himself each time, maintaining the intensity he had built up as Dracula the prince of evil, drawing on the pain in his own life, the fear he had seen with his own eyes. He projected that fear to the live audiences. The men would shiver; the women would cry out and faint, and then write him thrilling and suggestive letters. Lugosi embodied fear and danger for them, and he reveled in it.

Now he would do the same on the big screen.

He closed the door of the dressing room. All of the others would be going home, or to the studio cafeteria, or to a bar. Only Dwight Frye remained late some nights, practicing his Renfield insanity. Lugosi thought about going home himself, where his third wife would be waiting for him, but the pain in his legs felt like rusty nails, twisting beneath his kneecaps, reminding him of the old injury. The one that had taught him fear.

He sat down on the folding wooden chair—Universal provided nothing better for the actors, not even for the film's star—but Lugosi turned from the mirror and the lights. Somehow, he couldn't bear to look at himself every time he did this.

Inside his personal makeup drawer, he reached up and withdrew the secret hypodermic needle and his vial of morphine.

Outside on the set, echoing through the thin walls of his own dressing room, Lugosi could hear Dwight Frye practicing his Renfield cackle. Frye thought his portrayal of the madman would terrify the American audiences.

But Lugosi had found that he needed only to mumble his lines, wiggle his fingers, and leer once or twice, and the audiences still trembled. They enjoyed it. It was so easy to frighten them.

Before Universal decided to film *Dracula,* the script readers had been very negative, crying that the censors would never pass the movie, that it was too frightening, too horrifying. "This story certainly passes beyond the point of what the average person can stand," one had written.

As if they knew anything about fear! He stared at the needle, sharp and silver, with a flare of yellow reflected from the makeup lights—and van Helsing thought a wooden stake would be Lugosi's bane! After making certain he had closed his dressing room door, Lugosi filled the syringe with morphine. His legs tingled, trembled, aching for the relief the drug would give him. It always did, like Count Dracula consuming fresh blood.

Lugosi pushed the needle into his skin, finding the artery, homing in on the silver point of pain . . . and release. He closed his eyes. . . .

In the darkness behind his thoughts, he saw himself as a young lieutenant in the 43rd Royal Hungarian Infantry, fighting in the trenches in the Carpathian Mountains during the Great War. Lugosi had been a young man, frightened, hiding from the bullets but risking his life for his homeland—he had called himself Bela Blasko then, from the Hungarian town of Lugos.

The bullets sang around him, mixed with the explosions, the screams. The air smelled thick with blood and sweat and terror. The mountain peaks, backlit at night by orange explosions, looked like the castle spires of some ancient Hungarian fortress, more frightening by far than the crumbling stones and cobwebs the set builders had erected on the Universal studio lot.

Then the enemy bullets had crashed into Lugosi's thigh, his knee, shattering bone, sending a spray of blood into the darkness. He had screamed and fallen, thinking himself dead. The enemy soldiers approached, ready to kill him . . . but one of his comrades had dragged him away during the retreat.

Young Lugosi had awakened from his long, warm slumber in the army hospital. The nurses there gave him morphine, day after day, long after the doctors required it—one of the nurses had recognized him from the Hungarian stage, his portrayal of Jesus Christ in the Passion Play. She had given Lugosi all the morphine he wanted. And outside, in a haze of sparkling painlessness, the Great War had continued. . . .

Now he winced in the dressing room, snapping his eyes open and waiting for the effects of the drug to slide into his mind. Through the thin walls of the dressing room, he could hear Dwight Frye doing Renfield again, "Heh hee hee hee HEEEEE!" Lugosi's mind grew muddy; flares of color appeared at the edges.

When the rush from the morphine kicked in, the pleasure detached his mind from the chains of his body. A liquid chill ran down his spine, and he felt suddenly cold.

The makeup lights in his dressing room winked out, plunging him into claustrophobic darkness. He drew a sharp breath that echoed in his head.

Outside, Dwight Frye's laugh changed into the sound of distant, agonized screams.

Blinking and disoriented, he tried to comprehend exactly what had altered around him. As if walking through gelatin, Lugosi shuffled toward the dressing room door and opened it. The morphine made fright and uneasiness drift away from him. He experienced only a melting curiosity to know what had happened. His Dracula costume felt alive on him, as if it had become more than just an outfit.

The set for Castle Dracula appeared even more elaborate now, more solid, dirtier. And he saw no end to it, no border where the illusion stopped and the cameras set up, no booms, no klieg lights, no catwalks.

The fire in the enormous hearth had burned low, showing only orange embers; sharp smoke drifted into the greatroom. He smelled old feasts, damp and mildew in the corners, the leavings of animals in the scattered straw on the floor. Torches burned in iron holders on the wall. The cold air raised goosebumps on his flesh.

The moans and screams continued from outside.

Moving with a careful gait, Lugosi climbed the wide stone staircase, much like the one on which he met Renfield in the film. His shoes made clicking sounds on the flagstones—solid stones now, not mere papier maché. He listened to the screams. He followed them.

He knew he was no longer in Hollywood.

Reaching the upper level, Lugosi trailed a cold draft to an open balcony that looked down onto a night-shrouded hillside. Stars shone through wisps of high clouds in an otherwise clear sky. Four bonfires raged near clusters of soldiers and drab tents erected at the base of the knoll. Though the stench of rotting flesh reached him at once, it took Lugosi's eyes a moment to adjust from the brightness of the fires to see the figures spread out on the slope.

At first, he thought it was a vineyard, with hundreds of stakes arranged in rows, radiating from concentric circles of other stakes. But one of the "vines" moved, a flailing arm, and the chorus of the moans increased. Suddenly, like a camera coming into focus, Lugosi recognized that the stakes contained human forms impaled on the sharp points. Some of the points were smeared with blood that looked oily black in the darkness; other stakes still shone wicked and white, as if they had been trimmed once again after victims had been thrust upon them.

Lugosi gasped; even the morphine could not numb him to this. Many of the human shapes stirred, waving their arms, clutching the wounds where stakes protruded through their bodies. They had not been allowed to die quickly.

Dim winged shapes fluttered about the bodies—vultures feasting even at night, so gorged they could barely fly, ignoring the soldiers by the tents and bonfires, ignoring the fact that many of the victims were not even dead. Ravens, nearly invisible in the blackness, walked along the bloodstained ground, pecking at dangling limbs. A group of the soldiers broke out in laughter from some game they played.

Lugosi winced his eyes shut and shivered. Revulsion, confusion, and fear warred within his mind. This must all be some illusion, a twisted nightmare. The morphine had never affected him like this before!

Some of the victims had been hung head down, others sideways, others feet down. The stakes rose to various heights, high and low, as if in a morbid caste system of death. A rushing wail of pain swept along the garden of bloody stakes, sounding like a choir.

From the corridor behind Lugosi, a quiet voice murmured, "Listen to them—like children in the night. Do you enjoy the music they make?" Lugosi whirled and stumbled, slumping against the stone wall; the numbness seemed to put his legs at a greater distance from his body.

Behind him stood a man with huge black eyes that reflected tears in the torchlight. His face appeared beautiful, yet seemed to hide a deep agony, like a doe staring into a broken mirror. Rich brown locks hung curling to his shoulders. He wore a purple embroidered robe lined with spotted fur; some of the spots were long smears of brown, like dried blood wiped from wet blades. His full lips trembled beneath a long, dark moustache.

"What is this place?" Lugosi croaked, then realized that he had answered automatically in the stranger's own tongue, a language as familiar to Lugosi as his childhood, as most of his life. "You are speaking Hungarian!"

The stranger widened his eyes in indignation. Outside, the moans grew louder, then quiet, like the swell of the wind. "I am no longer a prisoner of the Turks, and Hungarian is my native tongue! We will obliterate the scourge of the Turks. I will strike such fear in their hearts that the sultan himself will run cowering back to Constantinople!"

One of the vultures swooped close to the open balcony, and then flew back toward its feeding ground. Startled, Lugosi turned around, then back to face the stranger who had frightened him. "Who are you?" he asked. The Hungarian words fit naturally in his mouth.

The haunted stranger took a hesitant step toward Lugosi. "I am . . . Vlad Dracula. I bid you welcome. I have waited for you a long time."

Lugosi lurched back and held his hand up in a warding gesture, as if reenacting the scene when van Helsing shows him a box containing wolfsbane. From childhood Lugosi had heard horrible stories of Vlad the Impaler, the real Dracula, rumored to be a vampire himself, known to be a bloodthirsty butcher who had slaughtered hundreds of thousands of Turks—and as many of his own people.

In the torchlit shadows, Vlad Dracula paid no attention to Lugosi's reaction. He walked up to the balcony, curling his hands on the stone half-wall. Gaudy rings adorned each of his fingers. "I knew you would come," Dracula said. "I have been smoking the opium pipe, a trick I learned during my decade of Turkish captivity. The drug makes my soul rest easier. It makes me open for peace and eases the pain. I thought at such a time you might be more likely to appear."

Vlad Dracula locked eyes with Bela Lugosi. The piercing stare seemed more powerful, more menacing than anything Lugosi had mimed in hundreds of performances as the vampire. He could not shirk away. He knew now how the Mina character must feel when he said "Look into my eyes . . ."

"What do you want from me?" Lugosi whispered. He wished the morphine would wear off. This was growing too strange, but as he held his hand on the cold stone of the balcony it felt real to him. Too real. The sharp stakes below would be just as solid, and just as sharp, if Vlad Dracula decided to punish him.

The Impaler did not try to touch him, but turned away, speaking toward the countless victims writhing below on their stakes. "I want absolution," he said.

"Absolution!" Lugosi cried. "Who do you think I am?"

"How are you called?" Dracula asked.

Lugosi, disoriented yet accustomed to having his name impress guests, answered, "Bela Lugos——no, I am Bela Blasko of the town of Lugos." He drew himself up, trying to feel imposing in his own Dracula costume, but the enormity of Vlad the Impaler's presence dwarfed any imaginary awesomeness Lugosi could command.

Vlad Dracula appeared troubled. "Bela Blasko—that is an odd name for an angel. Are you perhaps one of my fallen countrymen?"

"An angel?" Lugosi blinked. "I do not even believe in God. I can grant you no forgiveness." He looked down at the ranks of tortured victims, and he knew from the legends that this was but a tiny fraction of the atrocities Vlad Dracula had already done.

The Impaler's eyes became wide, but he shrank away from Lugosi. "But I have built monasteries and churches, restored shrines and made offerings! I have surrounded myself with priests and abbots and bishops and confessors. I have done everything I know how." He gazed at the bloodied stakes, but seemed not to see them.

"You killed all these people, and many many more! What do you expect?" Lugosi felt the fear grow in him again, real fear, as he had experienced that war-torn night in the Carpathian mountains. What would Vlad Dracula do to him?

Some of those victims below were Lugosi's own countrymen, the simple peasants and farmers, the bakers and bankers, craftsmen, just like those with whom Lugosi had fought in the Great War, just like those who had rescued him after he had been shot in the legs, who had dragged him off to safety, where the nurses tended him, gave him morphine.

"There are far worse things awaiting man . . . than death," the Impaler said. "I did all this for God, and for my country."

Lugosi felt the words catch in his throat. For his country! His own mind felt like a puzzle, with large pieces of memory breaking loose and fitting together in new ways. He winced at the thoughts. Lugosi himself had done things for his country, for Hungary, that others had called atrocities.

Back in 1918 he had embraced Communism and the revolution. Proudly, he had bragged about his short apprenticeship as a locksmith, then had formed a union of theater workers, fighting and propagandizing for the revolution that thrust Bela Kun into power. But Kun's dictatorship lasted only a few months, during which Romania attacked the weakened country, and Kun was ousted by the counterrevolution. All supporters of Bela Kun were hunted down and thrown into prison or executed. Lugosi had fled for his life to Vienna with his first wife and from there, penniless, Lugosi had traveled to Berlin seeking acting jobs.

He had scorned his own audiences because they proved too weak to withstand anything but safe, insignificant frights—but now he didn't believe he could stomach what he saw of the Impaler. But Vlad Dracula did what he thought necessary to free Hungary from Turkish slavery and from internecine warfare among the princes.

"I fight the Turks and use their own atrocities against them. They have taught me all this!" Vlad Dracula wrung his hands, then snatched a torch free from its holder on the wall. He pushed it toward Lugosi, letting the fire crackle. Lugosi flinched, but he felt none of the heat. It seemed important for Dracula to speak to Lugosi, to justify everything.

"Can you not *hear* me? I care not if you are not the angel I expected. You have come to me for a reason. The Turks held me hostage from the time I was a boy. To save his own life, my father Dracul the Dragon willingly delivered me to the sultan, along with my youngest brother Radu. Radu turned traitor, became a Turk in his heart. He grew fat from harem women, and rich banquets, and too much opium. My father then went about attacking the sultan's forces, knowing that his own sons were bound to be executed for it! He considered us already sacrificed."

Vlad Dracula held his hands over the torch flame; the heat licked his fingers, but he seemed not to notice. "Day after day, the sultan threatened to cut me into small pieces. He promised to have horses pull my legs apart and hold me where I could not struggle while he inserted a dull stake through my body! Several times he even went so far as to tie me to the horses, just to amuse himself." He lowered his voice. "Yes, the Turks taught me much about the extremes one can do to an enemy!"

Vlad Dracula hurled the torch out the window. Lugosi watched it whirl and blaze as it dropped through the air to the ground, rolled, then came to rest against a rock. Without the torch, the balcony alcove seemed smothered with shadows, lit only by the starlight and distant fires from the hillside slaughter.

"After I escaped, I learned that my father and my brother Mircea had been ambushed and murdered by John Hunyadi, another Hungarian prince who should have been loyal! Hunyadi struck my father with seventy-three sword strokes before he dealt a mortal blow. He claimed that he had tortured my brother Mircea to death and buried him in the public burial grounds." Dracula shook his head, and Lugosi saw real tears hovering there.

"Mircea had fought beside John Hunyadi for three years, and had saved his life a dozen times. When I was but a boy, Mircea taught me how to fish and ride a horse. He showed me the constellations in the stars that the Greeks had taught him." Dracula scraped one of his rings down the stone wall, leaving a white mark.

"When I became Prince again, I ordered his coffin to be opened so that I could give him a proper burial, with priests and candles and hymns. We found Mircea's head twisted around. His hands had scraped long gouges on the top of his coffin. John Hunyadi had buried him alive!"

Vlad Dracula glanced behind him, as if to make certain no one else wandered the castle halls so late at night, and then he allowed himself to sob. He mumbled his brother's name.

Lugosi trembled from the barrage of pain coming from Vlad Dracula, but the Impaler continued, hammering more memories at him.

"Just a few months ago, in my castle in Transylvania, the Turks laid siege to me and fired upon the battlements with their cherrywood cannons. One Turkish slave forewarned me, and I was able to escape by picking my way along the ice and snow of a terrible pass. My own son fell off his horse during the flight, and I have never seen him again. My wife could not come with us, and so rather than being captured by the Turks, she climbed the stairs of our tallest tower overlooking the sheer gorge, and she cast herself out of the window. She was my wife, Bela of Lugos. Do you know what it is like to lose a wife like that?"

Lugosi felt cold from the breeze licking over the edge of the balcony. "Not . . . like that. But I can understand the loss."

In exile from Hungary back in 1920, Lugosi had left his first wife Ilona in Vienna, while he tried to find work in Berlin in German cinema or on the stage. He had written to her every other day, but she had never replied. He learned later that her father, the executive secretary of a Budapest bank, had convinced her to divorce him, to flee back to Hungary and to avoid her husband at all costs because of the awful things he had done against his own country. Dracula's wife had chosen a different way out.

Outside, Lugosi heard distant shouts and the jingling of horses approaching at a gallop. He saw the soldiers break away from their tents, scattering the bonfires and snatching up their weapons. The Impaler seemed not to notice.

"I do not know who you are, or why you have come," Vlad Dracula said. "I prayed for an angel, a voice who could remove these demons of guilt from me." He reached out to Lugosi's vampire costume, but his hand passed directly through the actor's chest.

Lugosi shrank back, feeling the icy claw of a spectral hand sweep through his heart. Vlad Dracula widened his enormous dark eyes with superstitious terror. "You are a spirit come to torment me, since you refuse to grant me absolution."

Lugosi did not know how to answer. He delivered his words with a stuttering, uncertain cadence. "I am neither of those things. I am only a traveler, a dream to you perhaps, from a time and place far from here. I have not lived my life yet. I will be born many centuries from now."

"You have not come to judge me? Or punish me?" Vlad Dracula looked truly terrified.

"No, I am just an actor—an entertainer. I perform for other people. I try to make them afraid." He shook his head. "But I was wrong. What I do has no bearing on real fear. The acting I do, the frights I give to my audience, are a sham. That fear has no consequences." He leaned out over the balcony, then squeezed his eyes shut at the scores of maimed corpses.

"Seeing this convinces me I know nothing about real fear."

In the courtyard directly below, shouting erupted. Marching men hurried out into the night. Someone blasted a horn. Lugosi heard the sounds of a fight, swords clashing. Vlad Dracula glanced at it, dismissed the commotion for a moment, then locked his hypnotic gaze with Lugosi's again. The anguish behind the Impaler's eyes made Lugosi want to squirm. "That is all? I have prayed repeatedly for an apparition, and you come to learn something from *me?* About fear? All is lost. God is making a joke with me." His shoulders hunched into the fur-lined robe, and he reddened with anger.

Lugosi had the crawling feeling that if he had been corporeal to the Impaler, Vlad Dracula would have thrust him upon a vacant stake. "I do not know what to tell you, Vlad Dracula. I am not your conscience. I have destroyed enough things in my own life by trying to do what I thought was right and best. But I can tell you what I think."

Vlad Dracula cocked an eyebrow. Below, a clattering sound signalled a portcullis opening. Booted feet charged across the flag-stoned floor as someone hurried into the receiving hall. "My Lord Prince!"

Lugosi spoke rapidly. "The Turks have taught you well, as your atrocities show. But you have gone too far. You cannot undo the things you have already done, the thousands already slain. But you can change how you act from now on. Your brutal, bloodthirsty reputation is already well-earned. Mothers will frighten their children with stories of Vlad the Impaler for five hundred years! Perhaps you have built enough terror that you no longer need the slaughter. The mere mention of your name and the terror it evokes may be enough to accomplish your aims. If this is how you must be, try to govern with *fear,* not with death. Then your God may give your conscience some rest."

Vlad Dracula made a puzzled frown. "So I needed to learn something about fear as well?" The Impaler laughed with a sound like breaking glass. "For one who has not lived even a single lifetime, you are a wise man, Bela of Lugos."

They both turned at the sound of a man running up the stone steps to the upper level where Lugosi and Vlad Dracula stood side by side. The messenger scraped his sword against the stone wall. He swept his cloak back, looking from side to side until he spotted Dracula in the shadowy alcove. Sweat and blood smeared the man's face.

"My Lord Prince! You did not answer!" the man cried. A crimson badge on his shoulder identified him as a retainer from one of the boyars serving Vlad Dracula.

"I have been in conversation with an important representative," Dracula said, nodding to Lugosi. Surprised, but falling back on his training, Lugosi sketched a formal bow to the messenger. The retainer looked toward where Lugosi stood, blinked, and frowned.

"I see nothing, my Lord Prince."

In a rage, Vlad Dracula snatched out a dagger from his fur-lined robe. The messenger blanched and stumbled backward, warding off the death from the knife, but also showing a kind of relief that his end would be quick, not moaning and bleeding for days on a stake as the vultures circled about.

"Dracula!" Lugosi snapped, bringing to bear all the power and command he had used during his very best performances as the vampire. Vlad Dracula stopped, holding the knife poised for its strike. The retainer trembled, staring with wide blank eyes, afraid to flee.

"Look how terrified you have made this man. The fear you create is a powerful thing. You need not kill him to accomplish your purpose."

Vlad Dracula heard Lugosi, but kept staring at the retainer, making his eyes blaze brighter, his leer more vicious. The retainer began to sob.

"I need not explain my actions to you," he said to the man. "Your soul is mine to crush whenever I wish. Now tell me your news!"

The man stammered and slumped to the floor, but picked himself up again. "The sultan's army has arrived. It appears to be but a small vanguard attacking under cover of darkness, but the remaining Turks will be here by tomorrow. We can stand strong against this vanguard—many of them have already fled upon seeing their comrades impaled on the hillside, my Lord Prince. They will report back. It will enrage the sultan's army."

Vlad Dracula pinched his full lips between his fingers. He looked at Lugosi, who stood watching and waiting. The messenger seemed confused at what the Impaler thought he saw.

"Or it will strike *fear* into the sultan's army. We can use this. Go out to the victims on the stakes. Cut off the heads of those dead or mortally wounded—and be quick about it!—and catapult the heads into the Turkish vanguard. They will see the faces of their comrades and know that this will happen to them if they fight me. Find those prisoners whose injuries may still allow them to live and set them free of the stakes. Send them back to the sultan to tell how monstrous I am. Then he will think twice about his aggression against me."

The retainer blinked in astonishment, still trembling from having his life returned to him, curious about Vlad Dracula's new tactics. "Yes, my Lord Prince!" He scrambled backward and ran to the stone steps.

Lugosi felt the walls around him growing softer, shimmering. His knees became watery. His body felt empty. The morphine must be wearing off.

Dracula tugged at his dark moustache. "This is most interesting. The sultan will think it just as horrible, but God will know that I have been merciful. Perhaps next time I smoke the opium pipe, He will send me a true angel."

Lugosi stumbled, feeling sick and dizzy. Warm flecks of light roared through his head. Dracula seemed to loom larger and stronger.

"I cannot see you as clearly, my friend. You grow dim, and I can barely feel the effects of the opium pipe. Our time together is at an end. Now that we have learned what we have learned, it would be best for you to return to your own country.

"But I must dress for battle! If we are to fight the sultan's vanguard, I want them to see exactly who has brought them such fear! Farewell, Bela of Lugos. I will try to do as you suggest."

Lugosi tried to shake the thickening cobwebs from his eyes. "Farewell, Vlad Dracula," he said, raising his hand. It passed through the solid stone of the balcony wall. . . .

The lights flickered around his makeup mirror, dazzling his eyes. Lugosi drew in a deep breath and stared around his tiny dressing room. A shiver ran through him, and he pulled the black cape close around him, seeking for some warmth.

Outside, Dwight Frye attempted his long Renfield laugh one more time, but sneezed at the end. Frye's dressing room door opened, and Lugosi heard him walking away across the set.

On the small table in front of him, Lugosi saw the empty hypodermic needle and the remaining vial of morphine. Fear. The silver point looked like a tiny stake to impale himself on.

Morphine had always given him solace, a warm and comfortable feeling that made him forget pain, forget trouble, forget his fears.

But he had used it too much. Now it transported him to a place where he could see only the thousands of bloodied stakes and moaning victims, vultures circling, ravens pecking at living flesh. And the mad, tormented eyes of Vlad the Impaler.

He did not want to think where the morphine might take him next— the night in the Carpathians during the Great War? Or his secret flight across the Hungarian border after the overthrow of Bela Kun, knowing that his life was forfeit if he stopped? Or just the pain of learning that

Ilona had abandoned him while he worked in Berlin? The possibilities filled him with fear—not the fear without consequences that sent entertaining shivers through his audiences, but a real fear that would put his sanity at risk. He had brought the fear upon himself, cultivated it by his own actions.

Bela Lugosi dropped the syringe and the small vial of morphine onto the hard floor of his dressing room. Slowly, with great care, he ground them both to shards under the heel of his black Count Dracula shoes.

Lugosi's legs ached again from the old injury, but it made him feel solid and alive. The pain was not so bad that he needed to hide from it. And what he found in his drug-induced hiding place might be worse than the pain itself.

Lugosi opened his dressing room and saw Dwight Frye just leaving through the large doors. He called out for the other actor to wait, remembering to use English again, though the foreign tongue seemed cumbersome to him.

"Mr. Frye, would you care to join me for a bit of dinner? I know it is late, but I would enjoy your company."

Frye stopped, and his eyes widened to show how startled he was. For a moment he looked like the madman Renfield again, but when he chuckled the laugh carried delight, not feigned insanity.

"I sure would like that, Mr. Lugosi! It's good to see you're not going to keep to yourself again. The rest of us don't bite, you know. Nothing to be afraid of."

Lugosi smiled sardonically and stepped toward him. The pain in his legs faded into the background. "You're right, Mr. Frye. There is nothing to fear."

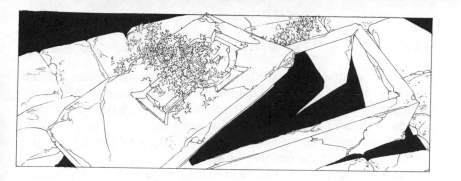

THE NAME OF FEAR

▼▼▼

LAWRENCE WATT-EVANS

FLIES buzzed in the twilight, but ignored the sumptuous meal displayed on the white-draped trestle. They were drawn instead to the forest of stakes that stood on every side, to the slow trickles of blood that still ran redly down the wooden shafts, to the dangling hands and livid faces of the corpses that were impaled there.

The men seated at the table ignored the flies, and all but one strove mightily to ignore the bodies as well, to pay no attention to the dead faces that stared down at them from all sides and the ghastly stench that pervaded every breath.

The last man, seated at the center of the table, wasted no effort on anything but the meal spread before him. Despite the stink he ate with relish, dabbing up gravy with chunks of rough bread and licking beef fat from his bristling mustache. The corpses did not bother him in the least; every so often, while chewing, he would glance up at the nearest and smile.

After all, were they not there by his own order?

And was it not for fear of him, and him alone, that the others struggled to force down their dinner in this gruesome setting, and pretended that they were not troubled by the dead?

They surely remembered the brave fool who had once dared to complain of the odor. The prince had seen to it that the fellow was put where the smell would not upset him—impaled on a stake twice the height of the rest, above the stink, where he screamed until he died.

That was several months ago. Since then, no one had objected to any of the prince's little habits.

The sun was down behind the hill, now, and servants were lighting torches so that the meal could continue. The prince toyed for a moment with the notion of using the torches in some new atrocity, but then dismissed the idea and reached for his wine.

From the tents below a sentry watched as the meal dragged on, the prince enjoying the discomfiture of his court.

The sentry was bored. The dead did not frighten him; they merely disgusted him. He was a fighting man, and had seen his friends hacked to pieces by the Turks, had done his own share of hacking in return, but that forest of impaled corpses—he grimaced, turned away, hawked and spat.

Something moved in the darkness, and he started. He stared.

The Turks? A night raid? Surely not! Not here, not so soon after today's rout, when they had fled in disarray back toward Constantinople.

A spy? Hardly likely.

He peered into the gloom, and saw a pale face.

"Who goes there?" he called—not too loudly, for he didn't care to alert the whole camp if it was merely a local peasant girl, out after a little remunerative fun.

"None who would harm you, soldier," replied a voice—a male voice, to the sentry's disappointment, speaking in a tone of supplication.

"A beggar?" the sentry asked, annoyed. "Be off with you, quickly, if that's what you are—the Prince will have none of that in his lands."

"Not truly a beggar," the voice replied, the face seeming to drift a little closer. "I have a home, and a place. Still, I am hungry, and I thought I smelled food here."

The sentry's eyes narrowed in distrust. Something did not feel right about this. His right hand crept toward his sword-hilt, but his left slipped inside his shirt.

"Come forward, where I can see you," he called.

The face drew nearer, and the sentry kept his gaze away from the eyes, centering his attention instead on the stranger's mouth.

"What name do you bear?" he asked.

The stranger shrugged, a flowing, liquid motion. "My name means nothing," he said.

The sentry smiled, and pulled his left hand from his shirt. "True enough," he said, "For who concerns himself with the names of the dead?" He opened his hand and displayed the fine silver crucifix against his palm.

"I know you, *nosferatu*," he said. "I saw the fangs when you spoke, and even over the reek of the corpses I can smell your foul breath."

The stranger shrank back, saying nothing.

"What do you want here, *vampir?*" the sentry demanded. "What brings one of your cowardly kind skulking about a camp of armed men, instead of preying on village idiots and lovesick old women? If you try anything here, you'll be up on a pole with the rest, but with the stake through your heart instead of your belly."

"Well do I know it," the vampire replied through clenched teeth, as he averted his gaze from the gleaming talisman. "It is as I said—when the sun sank and I arose I smelled food, and came to see why."

"What food do you mean?" the sentry asked.

"Blood, of course—what other food is there, to me?"

"Of course," the sentry said. "Well, yes, blood was spilled here in plenty today."

"Why?" the vampire asked.

The soldier hesitated. Vampires were foul, unclean things, and the proper thing to do would be to send this one away, or to raise the alarm and have it destroyed—but he was bored, and his watch had hours left to go.

"There was a battle here this morning," the sentry said, "and my prince carried all before him. We swept through the Turk like flame through the fields; they fled at the very name of my lord. And when we were done the prince had our Turkish prisoners, together with those of his officers who he said had not fought with sufficient valor, impaled, as a warning to any who would oppose him." A certain pride crept into his voice as he added, "I swear that I think he will drive the Turk from all Walachia, from all of Europe!"

"Impaled," the vampire said, staring up the hill at the dangling corpses. "How many?"

"Thousands," the sentry said, "I don't know. We spent the whole afternoon at it, all of us, the entire army, setting the stakes and lifting the condemned into place and whipping the horses."

"This prince of yours is ruthless," the vampire said, still gazing up the slope.

"Ah, he's a great man!" the sentry replied, eager to boast. He knew his own feats were little to brag of, as yet, but those of his lord and master were worthy of all the praise he could speak. "The best to ever reign in Walachia, greater even than his father, who won such honors. Do you know, in his capital at Tirgoviste, there is no crime of any sort?

No theft, nor beggars, nor any of the other plagues that the poor set upon so many towns—and all for fear of him."

The vampire was skeptical. "Oh, but surely men are men, and there are limits to fear . . ."

"No, it's the truth, I tell you," the sentry said, his honor stung.

"You tell me a tale, that is all," the vampire replied. "I have existed for many years, and I know mankind. How could even the greatest of princes stamp out beggary and theft?"

The sentry smiled. "Easily, when one has the courage and audacity of our prince! He issued a proclamation, inviting all those who could not work, who begged or stole or whored for their living, to a great feast—he said that he saw their hunger and poverty and would put an end to it. He gathered them all in a great hall, and had served the finest banquet you ever saw—it fairly made me sick to see such food wasted on those ragged wretches. But then he gave us our orders, and we marched outside, and closed and barred the doors, and then put the torch to the hall and burned it to the ground."

The vampire's eyes widened in shock, then narrowed.

"They screamed for mercy, and wailed and cried, but none escaped—those who tried, my comrades cut down with their swords and thrust back in through the windows where they had escaped. And when it was done, there were no more beggars, no more thieves, no more whores, in all of Tirgoviste. Do you know, in the market square, there is a well, as in any town, where a traveler may stop and drink? And there is a cup at that well, as in any town. But in Tirgoviste, it is no common wooden mug, but a golden goblet, set with gems, worth a king's ransom."

Seeing that some response was expected, the vampire said, "Indeed?"

The sentry nodded. "Gold and jewels, untended, in the market—and it is *still there,* because no one dares take what belongs to the prince. He has said that any who moves that cup from the well will be hunted down and impaled, slowly—he has been known to make an impalement last a full day, you know. No one doubts it, and the cup remains."

"It seems that this prince is feared, indeed," the vampire said. "As we of the night once were."

"You!" The soldier laughed and dangled the cross. "In my grandfather's day you were feared, but we know better now. You are so weak, you *vampiri*—you cannot bear the sun, nor silver, nor the cross. Even the humble garlic will keep you away. You cannot enter where you are not bidden, nor cross running water; holy water burns you like vitriol. Why should we fear you?"

"We have the strength of ten," the vampire replied. "We can change our form, and call to all the creatures of the night; our gaze saps the will. Should you not fear us, then?"

The sentry laughed again, and brandished the crucifix. "Come nearer, then," he said, "and show me why I should fear you!"

"I cannot, while you hold that," the vampire admitted.

"Run away, then, weakling," the sentry told him. "I do not fear you or yours. Only peasants and weaklings fear you. Those who serve the prince know what true power is!"

"I go, then," the vampire said. "But first, one thing."

"What might that be?"

"Your prince's name, soldier. Who is this man who is so feared?"

"You don't *know?*" The sentry's astonishment was obviously genuine. "Why, Dracula, of course—Prince Vlad Dracula!"

The vampire studied the prince from the doorflap of the tent—he could not enter uninvited, as the soldier had reminded him a few hours earlier, but he could look, and his eyes, like the eyes of any predator, were keen.

Slipping past the sentries had been easy enough, once full darkness had arrived; he had been merely a mist in the night, drifting on the breeze. Finding prey was another matter—every tent was hung with silver and garlic, a cross over every bunk and around every throat.

But then, he had not come in search of prey, he had come for a closer look at this man who aroused such awe—and such fear. He could not say just why he was so interested; human politics were no longer of any concern to him, since he had become what he was. Still, a man who could spill so much blood, who could dine cheerfully amid the corpses of his enemies—such a man was something new, something to learn about.

A man who inspired such fear, who slew so casually—it brought back memories of himself, decades ago, before the people had learned how to defend against his kind.

The sleeping prince was not tall, nor handsome. His hair was dark and wavy, worn shoulder-length, as was the current fashion; his skin was pocked here and there, but unremarkable in color and texture. He wore a great bristling mustache below a Roman nose.

As for his eyes, they were closed in sleep, so that the vampire could not see their color, but they were deep-set and large, that much was plain. His lips were full, his mouth wide, his face rounded.

Not a handsome face—but a striking one.

The vampire raised a hand to his own features. He knew his skin was as pale as a corpse, of course, since a corpse was what he truly was, just a cadaver that could not lie down and be still. His nose was long and ridged, his lips full with stolen blood, his mouth wide to accommodate his fangs. His eyes were sunken into their sockets—large and deep-set, more so than when he had lived a peasant's life, long before.

Even after his death—or undeath—his face had retained the roundness that had brought him childhood taunts about full moons. His hair was long and ragged.

The two faces, that of the sleeping prince and that of the undead observer, were not dissimilar. Vague thoughts stirred in the vampire's mind.

He had existed for almost a century, now. At first it had been easy— the peasants had cowered in fear at the slightest glimpse of him, at the mere mention of the names *vampir* or *nosferatu,* and he had merely to demand in order to receive. Beautiful maidens were yielded up to him, that he might leave the rest of the village alone, and he had fed well, very well indeed.

But then had come the priests, with their crosses and holy water, and the village witches, with their garlic and their stakes of ash, and the villagers had learned to defend themselves, and feared him no more.

He had thought that they no longer feared anything—but now he knew he was wrong.

They feared this man, a mere mortal like themselves—this Dracula, Son of the Dragon, Prince of Walachia and Scourge of the Turk.

They feared his very name.

A plan came to him, a good plan, a simple plan, and he turned to mist and let the night winds carry him away.

▼▼▼

The battle was a long one, and a fierce one, but it went well, it went well. The Turks were falling back in disorder, fleeing into the night. Perhaps it would be this year, the year of Our Lord 1476, that would finally see the Turk driven from Europe.

It was hardly the custom to continue fighting after sundown, but the prince wanted to finish this, so as not to fight another day, when perhaps the fates would favor the enemy.

He could not see the battle well enough in the gathering gloom, though—the clash of arms was all about him, the torches and campfires far away, and he could not see the battle as a whole.

He caught sight of the hilltop, and spurred his horse toward it; from there, he would be able to observe, to plan, to see if there was any way to cut off the Turkish retreat and trap them all.

In a moment he was free of the melee, and riding up the slope.

The hill was held by his men, just a handful of them watching to be sure no Turks slipped by; he waved to them as he passed, and they waved back.

At the top his horse would not be still, so he dismounted and strode to the shattered ruins of a peasant's hut. He stepped up atop a fallen chimney-stone.

A strong arm circled his neck, choking him, yanking him backward from the stone.

"Turk!" he gasped out, snatching his dagger from his belt.

Behind him someone laughed.

"No," a voice said, "I am no Turk; I am more a native of this land than *you* are, you with your Magyar blood and Magyar king. I have been following you all this long time, waiting for my chance, Prince Vlad—and now I have it."

Struggling, with no air left in his lungs, Vlad plunged the dagger behind him, and heard fabric tear. He felt the blade strike flesh—but then he met no resistance. It was like thrusting into mist.

Then the vampire squeezed harder, and the prince's neck snapped, and he felt no more.

The vampire lowered the body and stared down at it hungrily. The blood would still be fresh and sweet, he knew—but to drink it might ruin his plan. If a spark of life remained, if the man died of a vampire's bite rather than a broken neck, then in three days, in mockery of Christ, he would arise as another vampire.

The vampire had no use for competition. Making new vampires was not at all what he had in mind just now. He forced himself to turn away and call, "The Prince! The Prince is hurt!"

Soldiers turned their heads, spotted him, and ran up the hillside; by the time they arrived, he was gone.

Prince Vlad III, known as Tepes, the Impaler, and known also as Dracula, Son of the Dragon, after his father's honors, was laid to rest in the church at Tirgoviste, beneath a stone by the west door. The manner of his death was a mystery; there were rumors that he had been killed mistakenly by his own men in the darkness and confusion, that he had been dressed as a Turk so as to spy upon the enemy, but no one really knew.

He was dead, and that was enough.

The boyars, the few that remained, breathed a sigh of relief. The Turks, upon hearing the news, were less subtle—they celebrated for four full days, and then set about planning a new offensive to regain the territory they had lost to the bloodthirsty madman.

The peasants of Walachia and Transylvania wept bitterly. Terror though he had been, Dracula had defended them against the ravages of the Turks and the predatory habits of the boyars. The common people had feared Dracula—but they had loved him, too, as a child will love a stern father.

The hundred thousand Walachians who had died screaming on stakes or in fires or in any number of other ingenious ways had only very rarely been honest working peasants, and the peasants had little sympathy for either the underclass or the petty nobility.

And they had no sympathy at all for the thousands of Turks Vlad had slain.

So they wept at his passing, wondered at the rumors, and then went on with their lives.

And then, a few days later, new rumors began.

The stone in the church at Tirgoviste had been moved, and Dracula's body was gone—so it was whispered, though the priests denied it.

The peasants looked at one another and wondered. All of them knew *one* explanation for such a thing—could it be?

Could it be that even the grave had been unable to hold Dracula?

And then one night, near midnight, at a small house near Pitesti, came a pounding on the door.

The master of the house awoke, startled; his wife sat up beside him, the dog by the door whined, and the children stirred.

"Who is it?" the master of the house called.

"Dracula," replied a voice, deep and commanding, "And you will open this door *now.*"

At the name of the dead prince the man rose immediately, trembling.

He hesitated. A visitor in the night was never good news. The *vampiri* still existed in the land, and there were tales of how they would trick their way into the homes of the unwary.

But the name *Dracula*—who would dare to claim it, other than he to whom it belonged?

The man staggered to the door and lifted the latch.

Sure enough, there in the moonlight stood a man—not tall, not handsome, with a round face, hawk nose, full lips, and deep-set eyes, a bristling mustache on his upper lip, a fur-trimmed coronet on his brow. The rich embroidery of his vest gleamed coldly.

"Come in, my lord," said the master of the house, throwing the door wide.

The apparition in the moonlight grinned, baring fangs, and stepped across the threshold.

He feasted well—it had been so long!

The children he spared, and the dog, but both husband and wife he left without a drop of blood in their veins.

That they would rise again as vampires did not trouble him. He no longer needed to fear competition. After all, he was no mere vampire any more.

He was Dracula.

As long as he wore the crown and the clothing he had stripped from the corpse, as long as he kept in place the false mustache he had carefully constructed of horsehair and pig-bristle, as long as he kept his hair trimmed and combed in the royal style, he was Dracula, and the body he had dumped in a valley somewhere in the Carpathians was nobody at all.

And as long as he was Dracula, he would be feared again.

He would make *all* vampires feared again—and he would be their lord, their master, their king, the greatest of them all.

Someday, he told himself, as he settled into his tomb for the day, someday, all the world would know and fear his name—his *new* name.

The name of Dracula.

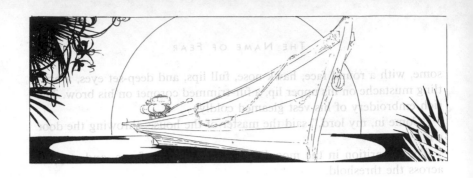

THE DARK RISING

▼▼▼

W. R. PHILBRICK

HAITI, 1979

He was used to the heat by now, and the way the weather came down
from the mountains, hot lashings of salt-laden rain that turned the earth
to mud. The rain would bring no relief; it brought steam rising from the
leached-out fields, small floods that tore away the soil, exposing broken
rocks, broken bones. The rocks stayed heavy in the black mud, while
human bones washed down from shallow graves on the mountainside,
carried in ivory torrents that cut away, cut away, exposing the humped
spine of the great island.

Haiti.

He had come here with the sure knowledge that he was, at last, making himself truly useful in the world. After a life of privilege he would
establish a small medical clinic, work directly with those who most
needed his help, his expertise in curing disease. Now, after six intermina-
ble months, well, nothing was certain. True, he had certain technical
skills, but in the dog hours of the night, so exhausted he was unable to
sleep, a taunting voice said: *Nothing you do makes any difference. You
are spit on a griddle, a leaf in the storm;* and he awoke knowing that the
terrible beauty of the island was eating him alive.

He was sitting on a rusted folding chair outside his little shore-side
cabana, watching the sun merge into the sea, when a voice he did not
recognize spoke his island name.

"Doakah! Doakah, you at home to yourself?"

Doakah was doctor, a title that in this place applied to any number of rheumy-eyed old men, as a sign of respect. That the word was attached to an American physician like himself was, he supposed, a kind of honor, although no one came to his clinic expecting to be healed. The Haitians knew how little chance there was of *that*. For healing they relied on folk medicines, or voodoo, or prayer, but mostly they did not expect to be cured of illness or disease. Their fate was accepted with a serenity that he'd come to envy. It was the way of the island.

"Doakah?"

The dense leaves parted, revealing a bone-thin black face. Eyes white and alive in the slant of fading daylight. The intrusion had a dreamy stillness that suggested a jungle painting by Henri Rousseau, spoiled only by the trembling of the leaves.

"Yes?" he said.

"Doakah Jones from da clinic?"

"Yes, that's me," he said, standing up.

The wraith emerged from the foliage and introduced himself as Christophe.

"I am named for the great general," he said, displaying teeth and gums that were, despite his extreme thinness, remarkably healthy. "The old Christophe, he help free the slaves, you hear about that?"

"Yes, I heard," Dr. Jones said. Interesting that this wasted, coal-black man would speak of the slave revolt as if it had happened recently. In truth, nearly two centuries had passed since the African generals defeated Napoleon's army and set up a despotism all their own. Dr. Jones was no historian—his specialty was in epidemiology, the identification and control of disease—but even he knew that intervals of Haitian freedom had been as brief and brilliant as flashes of winter lightning.

Here the darkness, the fear always returned, in the form of brutal dictators, corrupt police, the *ton-ton macoute*. And lately, the strange wasting disease that had filled his clinic with victims who kept dying, no matter what he did for them. A blood sickness that as yet had no name, but which moved like a plague over the island, destroying immunity to even the most benign infections.

"A man needs you," Christophe said. "Will you come?"

"Where is this man?"

"Not far," Christophe said. "He keep nearby."

"Is this man sick?"

"Very sick man."

"You must bring him to the clinic."

Christophe shook his head. "Not possible," he said. "We must go to him. That is the only way."

Dr. Jones returned to his cabana for his bag. Now and then he had been called upon to minister to some individual who was too sick to travel to the clinic, usually at the request of a family member, and he never refused such an appeal. He had been cautioned about leaving the cabana area after dark—thieving was a way of life here—but he carried nothing of value, no drugs that he would not freely give to any who asked. And this man Christophe—he seemed genuinely concerned, anxious that a doctor accompany him.

"The road is this way," Dr. Jones said, speaking to the stranger's back. "I have use of a car, we can drive."

When the wraith turned to him Dr. Jones was stunned by the radiance of his smile. "By da sea, Doakah Jones. We go by da sea," he said, gesturing at the rocky shoreline just beyond the cabanas, a once-beach since eroded, left to nature when the tourist trade finally expired. "Can't go by da road, da road don't go dere."

"I don't like boats," Dr. Jones said uneasily, following Christophe's rapid stride toward the sea.

"You like dis boat. Dis *good* boat."

A small, narrow launch lay just off shore, in water that was as black as the back of the guide's head. Had this strange little man left it there, adrift? Dr. Jones didn't have time to puzzle out the mystery of why the boat wasn't anchored, how it seemed to defy the tide with an animal cunning, because Christophe was bustling him along, urging him to step to the shore—*hab no fear of dis, Doakah Jones, I make you dry*—and the doctor was astonished when the smaller man swept him up from behind, lifted him clear of the water with uncanny strength, and set him—dry, as promised—in the bow of the boat.

"Dis *good* boat," he said again, running his hands along the painted rail. "Carry many good men in dis boat."

A one-cylinder, make-or-break engine shuddered to life when Christophe kicked at the flywheel. The engine had a steady, thumping pulse not so different from his own, Dr. Jones decided, a sea pulse of blood and brine.

At the guide's suggestion he stood in the bow and braced himself upright with a length of thick hemp rope.

"Better you stand easy in de bows, dat way you feel da sea move under you," Christophe said, demonstrating how balance was to be maintained in the narrow vessel.

Dr. Jones discovered that riding this way, standing with his weight against the rope, his knees bending to the motion of the launch under his feet, was considerably easier than he would have imagined. It was almost fun, riding the sea like an islander, giving himself up to the whims of nature—an aspect of play, of enjoyment he thought he'd lost forever.

The doctor's strangely buoyant mood dissipated in an instant, as the launch turned from the cove into the dark, steep swells that shaped themselves against the promontory. Here, as they darted into the open sea, a great loss opened within him, an emptiness that seemed to pour out through his feet, leaving him shaken and weak and light-headed with —what?

Fear?

Not, surely, fear of the open sea, or of drowning. The doctor no longer dreaded his own demise, or denied the inevitability of that eventual occurrence: this was a thing he knew for certain, that a time came for each human being. Of late the sense of hopelessness that entwined him, the deep melancholy that seemed to draw the very air from his lungs, this bleak and endless mood—a kind of island fever—had nearly convinced him that not even the clinic was worth the pain of staying alive.

If the prospect of his own death had no sting, what then did he have to fear?

And yet it was fear he felt as he braced himself against the rope, holding tight with both hands, the launch moving with the unpredictable certainty of an animal alive under his feet. Fear: a deep, world-shaking thrum of fear that transcended visions of his own demise—the little death that changed nothing—and made him dread that life itself must one day surely end, leaving the planet a barren ball of minerals and mica chips and pillars of salt from the great evaporated seas. A sterile, ice-shrouded mass hurtling into blind eternity, the great forever emptiness: this was his vision.

The end of life itself. It must happen, eventually, if not from the wasting disease that continued to ravage the patients in his clinic, then from some other, unforeseen malady.

Dr. Jones thought he glimpsed something of this fear-struck emptiness reflected in Christophe's expression: the wraith at the tiller, tending to his engine, steering around the curve of the island, his expression as blank as the hollow sickness that had been emptied from inside the doctor. His dark face like a carved mask beneath the lesser masks of need, of radiance. Christophe standing in perfect balance, his ankles adjusting like hinges to the tilt and sway of the narrow boat, his gaze unfocused and profoundly neutral as he scanned the last blood-orange ooze of light along the edge of the world.

"Soon, Doakah," he promised. "We be dere soon."

As the launch headed back into the shore, gliding through the oily swells, the thrum of the doctor's inexplicable fear settled into the dull, nagging ache of dread. Familiar dread, he reasoned, the physician's dread of mortal sickness, of disease he could not possibly eradicate with his little bag of pharmaceutical potions. Yes, the simple dread of the banal, the mundane, the sheer *normalcy* of desperate poverty. Dread that nothing he did or said or felt made any difference at all, at all.

"Look there!" Christophe shouted over the noise of the engine. He pointed and the doctor saw, in the green darkness of the approaching landfall, a jagged place of greater darkness, a shadow against the shore. As the launch glided into the cove, the hull knifing through suddenly placid waters, the doctor realized he was looking at a cave—what he had mistaken for a shadow was a cave opening directly on the bleak strip of shore.

His guide had been quite correct—the only access to this place was by water, for the cliffs were steep, the surrounding vegetation clotted and treacherous.

"You live here?" the doctor asked as the bottom of the launch came up against the gravel shore.

"I work for monsieur," Christophe replied.

In the silence—the engine had been shut off—his reply echoed from the arched face of the cavern and they both smiled awkwardly.

"Monsieur? The gentleman who is sick?"

"Very sick," Christophe said. "A terrible sickness."

"He must come back with us," Dr. Jones said, stepping out of the launch. "The damp air of a cave dwelling can be dangerous, for an invalid. At the clinic at least we can make your friend comfortable."

"You tell him dis," Christophe said, smiling enigmatically. "Give monsieur your expert o-pinion."

Dr. Jones turned from the cavern mouth. Was he being mocked? But the doctor could see nothing of his guide's expression—and yet there was something about the way the Haitian spoke that convinced the doctor his peasant patois was not entirely genuine, that the man had spent some significant part of his life living elsewhere, in some exalted circumstance, and was now merely assuming the role of lackey.

A moment later a match flared. A kerosene lantern began to glow, shedding a nimbus of orange light.

"Dis way, Doakah Jones."

He followed the lantern, surprised by the smooth, dry stone underfoot. As if worn smooth by human feet . . . yes, he decided, this was quite possible, for as they proceeded into the cavern the doctor could see, in the feeble light of the lantern, that the place had been used as shelter for quite some time. No doubt the local fishermen had found it convenient, as a place to hide their gear while awaiting a favorable sea—he noticed old, rotted nets draped from the stone outcroppings, and the decayed remains of a dugout canoe that was unlike any he'd seen on the island—had it drifted here from some distant place?—but Christophe was urging him along, beckoning with the lantern.

"Dis way. Dis is da way."

The cavern narrowed, or perhaps it was that the light failed, making the walls seem closer, stifling. And then the doctor became aware of an odor. A dense, almost sweet stench that was not, alas, unfamiliar: the death-stink of mortal illness, of a patient left to fester in his final aloneness.

"Very sick man," Christophe said in a low voice, as if apologizing for the smell.

"I understand," the doctor said.

Christophe made a sound that was almost like laughter—the doctor interpreted it as nervousness, a natural enough reaction in the face of agony.

"We have arrived," Christophe said. "Monsieur welcomes you."

The doctor paused at the entrance to what felt like a larger chamber—he could no longer feel the pressing immediacy of the walls—aware that his guide had dropped all pretense of speaking in patois. The voice was clear now, the enunciation perfect, with just the trace of an accent Dr. Jones did not recognize.

For a moment, the duration of a heartbeat, he considered turning away from the chamber, running back through the cavern to the beach. That was impossible, he soon realized—the darkness was absolute—and what did he have to fear if he did not fear death itself?

"Sit here," Christophe said, and the doctor felt a chair bumping the backs of his legs. He sat, recognized the form of a smooth wooden seat equipped with arms. The lantern passed to another part of the chamber, spawning more lanterns—or were they candles?—until the still air of the place began to glow.

The doctor, staring at a shape on the stone floor, realized that he was looking at a rough bed, or not so much a bed as a litter. Piles of rags strewn among poles of wood that glowed, in the soft light, as smooth as bones. As he leaned forward, trying to puzzle out what he saw there, Christophe crept up behind him and touched him on the nape of the neck.

There was a small prick of pain, as if from a slender thorn, an unnatural warmth on the skin of his neck. The doctor shuddered—had the man scratched him? He was about to turn—he'd had quite enough of Christophe—when a voice came from the pile of rags on the floor.

"Dr. Jones, how good of you to come."

The doctor stared. How had he not seen the man among the rags, so pale and wasted? A dead-looking, hairless thing with eyes burning bright in the skull. The flesh pulled like thin wax over the bones, and the skeleton itself strangely misshapen, as if somehow elongated by disease.

"I trust your journey was uneventful?" it said, using a voice so strong and confident, so alive, that the doctor looked around for another source. Was this a trick, some crude, nightmare prank?

"Christophe kept you dry in the tiny boat of his?" the voice asked.

The thing—a man, surely—sat up on the litter and the doctor saw that the facial disfigurations were, as he had immediately suspected, a particular type of sarcomatous tumor, all too familiar. Many of his clinic patients suffered from similar tumors.

"Yes," the man on the litter said, "you recognize the wasting disease. You have seen it everywhere on the island, the mark of the living dead. It is this disease that brings you such despair, I think, for nothing you do can staunch it."

The thing's eyes glittered, somehow, in this dark place, suffused with light.

"Save your pity, doctor," the creature said. "In a little while I will be cured, thanks to your presence here. It is, alas, a temporary cure. In a few days time the disease will return and Christophe—did he tell you he was named for the great general?—Christophe will bring me another volunteer, and so the cure comes to me, again and again."

"I don't understand," the doctor said—or tried to say. He had the impression that the words had not escaped from inside his head. Was this possible?

The doctor tried to move, shifting himself in the chair. Had he moved? His body seemed a distant thing, an inanimate concoction of meat and bone and lifeless gristle.

"I suggest you relax, doctor," the man on the litter said. "All attempts at escape are futile. You have been immobilized by one of the native folk medicines, a neurotoxin found in some nasty toad, or is it a poisonous fish?—Christophe is a master of such things. He assures me the paralysis endures for several hours—but we shall be done with each other long before it wears off, I promise you that."

Christophe appeared, holding a tall glass filled to the brim with a clear liquid that seemed to be the focal point for all the flickering lanterns and candles.

"Spring water," the man on the litter explained, drinking thirstily, so that the liquid sprayed out from his ruined mouth, wetting the tumors. "I have a great thirst at this stage of the cycle. At other times the taste of mere water disgusts me."

"Will there be anything else, Monsieur?"

"No. Leave us, please."

The doctor, who could not turn his head to follow—he was truly paralyzed, frozen—had the impression that Christophe had withdrawn from his field of view but remained somewhere in the chamber shadows, out of sight, watching.

"They call me 'Monsieur' here," the man on the litter said. The water seemed to have revived him, for he sat up, appeared not so frail as before, but no less terrible. "Feel free to give me any name you like," he added. "I have been called by a thousand names, over the ages."

The doctor, responding to some urgency his mind did not fully comprehend, exerted the full measure of his will, straining to move.

Run! his limbs screamed, *run!* His upper body shifted ever so slightly, but his hands remained entwined in a rigor, gripping the chair. He could not move.

The man who called himself "monsieur" watched with interest. "Make peace with yourself," he suggested. "Accept your fate. The transaction will be easier for both of us."

Dr. Jones discovered that the state of paralysis had extended to his eyes, which remained focused on the litter. His eyelids had ceased blinking.

"I'm sure you have many questions," Monsieur said. "It is the physician's nature to question things. Was that what brought you to this wretched island? A quest for truth, perhaps? You reach a certain age, you are overcome with a need to make a mark on the world, and so you come to this island intending to save lives. And what do you find? A disease that mocks you, that makes your little do-gooder's clinic a charnel house. And so this is the truth you find: nothing you do makes any difference. You are tempted by suicide, but because you are weak you do not act."

I am dreaming, the doctor told himself, finding comfort there, in the idea of a dream. The dream explained why this creature knew his thoughts, his doubts, the depths of his despair.

"No," Monsieur said. "You are not dreaming. And no, I can't read your thoughts exactly, but I know enough of human nature to *anticipate* each thought, and that is a more useful power than the mere parlor trick of reading minds. Let me illustrate. You see me and you think *the man is dying* and your diagnosis is quite correct. I have been dying for centuries, Dr. Jones. It is what I do best. For many years I died in Africa: that is where my disease took its present form—this terrible disfigurement." Monsieur turned, letting himself be seen in the light. Each tumor glistened, distorting the shape of his mouth, making the hot eyes look squeezed and protuberant, brimful of light. "I do not say 'my disease' lightly, doctor, for I *am* the disease. It first took form within me, as a consequence of my, shall we say *dietary* habits. Absorb, as I did, every infirmity of blood known to humankind, and the result is this: a cauldron of disease so potent nothing is immune. Not even me." Slender, bonelike fingers emerged from the rags and stroked the gruesome distortions on his face. "Those I infect are doomed to waste away, and those *they* infect are also doomed. I am the source. I am the sickness. And only I survive, for I transmit the symptom, not the cure. Not the cure. I share that with no one. *No one.* I am alone in my glory."

Monsieur's words seemed to resonate within the chamber, so deeply felt that the doctor detected the vibration in his fingertips. A voice like wind in a cave, or night fog drifting in from dark waters. Fear had become a small tight thing, responding to the resonance of that hideous voice. He felt again the yawning, mortal emptiness he'd sensed when Christophe's launch had put out to sea. The death of hope.

He struggled. Nothing.

"You think me a monster, doctor, but a monster cannot think, cannot feel or regret the pain he inflicts, as I assure you I do. Monster? I am, as you can plainly see, human. Extremely human, in every sense of *extreme* and *human.* Seeking life, I cause death. Is that not the definition of all human behavior? Don't exert yourself—I can sense that you agree. Of course I knew this before you came here. And you came, I remind you, of your own free will. Had you refused, Christophe would have found another. I have infected many, but a multitude remain."

The creature attempted to smile and now, more than ever, the doctor yearned to turn away from that terrible smile, the spittle-coated, flesh-tearing teeth.

"In my youth, so long ago that I've forgotten what language I first spoke, I took pleasure impulsively. I was so hungry! So eager to remain undying! The passion of youth, Dr. Jones, surely you remember? Surely some part of you wants to pity me, as you pity the poor creatures who crawl into your clinic? Am I so different? Am I not human, too?"

Monsieur paused, raised the empty glass to the light. The glass was like a lens, distorting the ruin of his face in such a way that he looked almost normal, almost healthy, and the doctor caught a glimpse of his terrible beauty. Then the glass shifted and he was the same again, luminous with disease, rotting and alive.

The creature sniffed the air and said, "I'm sure you did not always give off this stench of futility, doctor. Oh, yes, you reek of it. You smell death on me, the breath of all those who have died in my embrace, but on you the odor is worse. You exude the smell of hopelessness, of surrender. I stink of carrion disease, you of regret. Which is worse? Never mind, Dr. Jones. The question is unfair. I withdraw it. Neither of us has a choice. We are what we are. Does the flame torment the moth with questions? Does the snake interrogate the mouse?"

The thing who called himself "Monsieur" had been slowly emerging from the litter, shedding the rags that covered him there. The doctor was reminded of the cadaver he'd dissected in medical school, how the flesh had seemed shrink-wrapped over the skeleton, gray and spongy with preservative.

Again he struggled to move and again his body failed to respond. He sat as if nailed to the chair, very little air stirring in his lungs. Waiting, waiting.

"I remember a night on the plains of Kenya," Monsieur said, his voice softening, almost an animal purr that seemed to warm the damp air of the cavern. "What stars! Stars so alive, so young! I stood in the branches of a baobab tree and saw to the edge of the world. Saw everything in exquisite detail: creatures stirring in the tall grass, birds sleeping on twigs. I knew the roar of lions, of insects, the pulse of beetles in the mud, the furious spawn of microbes—I loved all of it, Dr. Jones, the idea of life everlasting, and me lasting with it. And then as my infection spread, the glow slowly faded. The stars grew old, faint. I climbed again to the top of the baobab and saw that I must leave, for I do not care to feed again on those I have infected—for me their blood is empty. It was time to go, and this time by sea.

"What a terrible journey that was—you saw the remains of my crude vessel, there at the mouth of the cave. The burning sun! And only a few pale creatures to feed upon as the currents carried me west. Imagine my joy when this island rose up from the sea—oh, yes, that is how it seemed to me, in my delirium. What new pleasures I found here! A people long subdued by terror and brutality—what are my little appetites in a place such as this? Where men are dragged from their huts in the night and murdered, or made into the slaves of a bleak superstition, or endure suppression, no one notices my presence. I am not hunted, but tolerated, sometimes even welcomed, for the death I make is less terrible than the living death they have long endured at the hands of their own people. Who among you can deny my provenance, my dominion, my splendor?"

Monsieur now stood at the full extremity of his height, the rags twitching at his feet, a nakedness unbearable to behold, his voice like the beating of an immense heart.

"Soon I shall leave this island and go to the mainland, and there, in that great land, all that you fear will come true. And now, doctor, your time comes. My cure begins anew."

He lifted his skeletal arms and his shadow was like a flutter of great wings on the walls of the cave. The doctor had ceased struggling—he was the heartbeat, fear was the voice. The skittering bones, the dead flesh, the cold breath, all around him was an emptiness, the dark rising, rising.

LOS NIÑOS DE LA NOCHE

▼▼▼

TIM SULLIVAN

"**D**O I remember *The Children of the Night?*" Esteban Montoya croaks in his old man's voice. "No, *muchacha,* because latinos didn't get to work on the big pictures in those days. But I do remember *Los Niños de la Noche.*"

I lean forward in the shabby old easy chair, which is the only article of furniture in the room besides the bed and a chipped night table standing next to it. "Then you *are* the same Esteban Montoya listed in the credits of the Spanish-language version of the film?"

He sits up in bed, his wrinkled, age-spotted feebleness belied by the intensity of his dark eyes. "*Sí, muchacha.* I was the assistant director."

I can't believe my luck. I'm so excited that I don't even ask him to stop calling me *muchacha,* as if he thinks I'm some barrio *chiquita.* This man lying in bed here was a crew member on one of the legendary horror films of the thirties, perhaps the last living person who worked on the film. The Spanish version is reputed to be even better than its English counterpart, but since it has been lost for over fifty years, nobody knows for sure if this is true. It has been almost impossible for me to track Esteban Montoya down, but here he is living in this cramped room in a Hollywood rest home, and I found him all by myself. Me, Antonia Guzman, about to score a journalistic coup—even if it is only film journalism. I snap on my tape recorder. "What was it like," I ask, "working with Don Carlos Ribeira?"

"*¡Ay!* Don Carlos." The old man makes a noise somewhere between laughing and coughing. He smiles a toothless smile and nods more vigorously than I would have believed possible in one so ancient. "He was from Spain. Toledo, I think. A man of the old world, who disdained us latinos from Los Angeles and Baja, even as he made a film with us. He thought of us only as his servants, it seemed. Even Rafael Valenzuela, the director, was treated as an underling."

"So he was as imperious as the stories say." This was Don Carlos' last rôle, and his only American film. "A domineering sort of man?"

"No one could defy him. He would appear at the sound stage an hour after sunset and take charge. It was his film from the beginning, and Rafael could only follow his commands."

"And you were using the same sets as the English-language *Children of the Night?*"

"Si, we made that *pelicula* long before dubbing and looping existed. Only the actors' voices could carry the dialogue in those early talkies. There was no way to go back and fix it later. If the studio wanted a foreign-language version of a film, it had to be shot on the same sets with a different cast and crew at night. That was the only way it could be done. And those sets were magnificent, for the studio had set out to produce a film that would make the public forget about *Dracula.* It took so long to build them that shooting was delayed till winter.

"So there we were, working in these vast gothic caverns in December. *¡Hola!* It was so cold you could see your breath, and your fingers and toes got numb. How we envied the privileged anglos who got to work during the day, when the sun warmed the sepulchral sets through which Don Carlos stalked until the early hours every morning. Ah, but he was *el Diablo* himself on those cold nights. Arrogant as he was, he gave a *grande* performance as the vampire.

"At first we were sympathetic and tolerant, for he had a nurse on the set at all times. A Hungarian woman named Ilona Laszlo, who spoke vaguely of a rare disease afflicting Don Carlos. He had recently been driven from Spain by the fascists. After stardom in Europe, of course, he thought this horror film was beneath him, and he let everyone know it. As soon as shooting wrapped for the night, he was gone, driving away in an enormous Duesenberg limousine with his beautiful nurse.

"Well, I'd worked on many films in Mexico and the United States, and I'd seen difficult stars before, but this one was the worst. Still, I knew I could live with it for the three weeks we were shooting. That was the way most of the crew saw it, too, but Rafael looked as if he would kill himself by the end of the first week. He must have thought that things couldn't get any worse on his picture, but, *Madre de Dios,* that is exactly what happened. As that night became the next morning, Rafael called for the script girl—that's what we called them in those days, my dear, not script supervisors as they are called today, and I'm sorry if I've offended your feminist sensibility with the term—but she was nowhere to be found.

"It wasn't until one of the actresses found a pair of pale legs sticking out from behind a screen in wardrobe that we knew what had become of the poor thing. The actress screamed, which brought us all running, and I remember peering over the caped shoulder of Don Carlos' stand-in. The screen was removed, and the gray, bloodless face of the script girl was revealed. ¡Ay! she was dead."

Here Esteban shakes his head slowly, wisps of his sparse white hair softly swaying with the motion. I can hardly contain my excitement; this film has an almost mythic reputation for strange, unpleasant events plaguing its production, and yet nobody I have interviewed in the past has been able to tell me why. This woman's death, and the death of Don Carlos on the very night the film wrapped, must have been the cause of the rumors. I urge Esteban to go on.

"The police were there in fifteen minutes. Sergeant Del Valle led the investigation. He was a stocky, short man who had a kind of forceful grace. It was reassuring to have this good man at the studio with his uniformed *oficiales*.

"The body was taken away, and by that time it was dawn. Rafael decided that we couldn't do any more set-ups before the anglo crew came in, so we wrapped for the day. I noticed that Don Carlos was nowhere to be seen. In fact, he hadn't been around since before the body was found.

"I mentioned this to Rafael, but he said that the nurse must have made Don Carlos leave so that he wouldn't be upset. It seemed a reasonable enough explanation, so I didn't think of it again until later.

"The next day was Sunday. The anglo crew had the day off, so the producers decided to use the time for us to get all our daylight scenes. There weren't very many such set-ups on this film, and in fact we got them all by mid-afternoon. Rafael wanted a day-for-night shot of the vampire, but our star wasn't on the set. His stand-in was used, and Don Carlos didn't show up until after dark.

"An assistant director is one of the busiest people on a movie set, so I couldn't get away to a phone until our first meal of the night was served. I delayed my dinner to call Sergeant Del Valle.

"You already know what I thought, señorita—Don Carlos was the *monstruo* who had murdered our script girl. Del Valle told me that Don Carlos had an alibi, though. His nurse had indeed been with him, and they had left the studio because the actor had begun to feel faint.

"I asked the Sergeant what ailed Don Carlos. It was called porphyria, he said. I thanked him and joined the cast and crew at dinner. Don Carlos, as always, did not eat with us.

"The fear the actors showed on the screen was quite real after that, and no one went anywhere alone if they could help it. Nothing more happened until two days before we wrapped. A bit player was found stuffed in the props closet. She was as dead as the script girl.

"Again, Don Carlos had left the set early. The police were called in again, and Sergeant Del Valle told me that the modus operandi appeared to be the same in both cases. Two small puncture wounds on the carotid artery, through which virtually all the blood in the body had been sucked out. There was no blood at the scene of the crime, though the corpse should have been drenched in it.

" *'¡El vampiro!'* I shouted, attracting the attention of several grips and production assistants. But Del Valle glowered at me and told me such things were nonsense. Perhaps they were nonsense to him, but not to the people of the little village in Mexico where I was born and raised. It seemed that Sergeant Del Valle would be of little help in this investigation, after all, since he could not face the horrible truth.

"The next day, I managed to get out of bed early enough to catch a Red Car to the public library before it closed, where I learned that porphyria is a rare blood disease. Now I was convinced that Don Carlos was *el monstruo.* As I rode the trolley back to my apartment that evening, I thought about what I must do, and wondered how I could do it.

"I found a priest waiting in my living room, an elderly little man who introduced himself as Father Badelon and apologized for prevailing upon my landlady to admit him while I was out. I was not upset to see a holy man, for I was severely shaken by the events of the past few days. I went to the icebox to get some sangria, offering some to the *padrecito* before I poured myself a glass. He declined, saying that he could not indulge. He had come on a grave matter, he explained in his sweet voice, and felt that it was his duty to remain sober. He had read about the two murders, and suspected that a supernatural being was responsible. He had spoken to some crew members, and one of them mentioned that I had used the word *vampiro* the night before. I told him I believed that it was the famous Don Carlos Ribeira. Perhaps, the *padrecito* suggested, Don Carlos had fled Spain not because of the fascists, but because his bloodsucking nocturnal activities had been found out.

" 'He has a nurse with him,' I said. 'What of her?'

" 'She too must be a vampire, *mi hijo.'*

"It was, of course, the only reasonable explanation. The old priest and

I made a pact to destroy these evil creatures. I went out in the gathering dark and cut two branches off the ash tree behind my apartment building, and whittled down their ends until we had two sharp stakes. One of these I placed in a satchel with a hammer. The other was much larger, for it occurred to me that I might have to fend off the vampire; this stake was six or seven feet long.

The *padrecito* said that he carried holy water in his bag. Thus armed, we walked to the grocer on the corner of Alvarado Street and purchased some garlic, and then I went alone to see a friend of mine, Pedro. I asked him if I could borrow his La Salle roadster. We had to have some way of catching Don Carlos and Ilona if they tried to escape in the Duesenberg, but I didn't tell Pedro this. I simply mentioned to him that this was the last night of shooting, and that if we finished early the Red Car would not yet be running; I would be stuck without a ride home.

"Pedro agreed, and we were off to the studio. Shooting started late on that last night, for the shot list grew short. Some eyebrows were raised when I came onto the set with Father Badelon, but he stayed out of the way while the lights were set up and Rafael blocked out the scenes. The final night's shooting passed without incident.

"The wrap party was a relief for everybody but me and Father Badelon. Don Carlos attended only briefly, in the company of Ilona. They drank no wine, and left hours before dawn, unaware that the *padrecito* and I were following them.

"Workmen were striking sets as we passed through the back lot. We heard the twelve-cylinder engine of the Duesenberg start, and rushed to the La Salle. I drove with the headlights off until we passed through the studio gate and the black limousine was far ahead of us. The old priest sat tensely beside me in the passenger's seat. We followed the Duesenberg down the hillside to Highland Avenue, and on into Hollywood. Don Carlos turned right on Hollywood Boulevard, which was deserted and eerie now, at three o'clock in the morning. The Duesenberg soon made a left turn on Fairfax, and descended into Los Angeles' eastern-European ghetto. Ilona would be at home here, I realized, among the Hungarians, Rumanians, Poles, Russians, and Bulgarians. Surely none of those good people suspected that she was a creature of darkness. But perhaps I was wrong, I thought, as the Duesenberg turned into a cemetery. Perhaps there were many such beings in Los Angeles as more and more decadent Europeans flooded in to work in the film business. We watched as Don Carlos handed a crumpled bill to the night watchman and drove on into the graveyard.

"I pulled up to the gate, and told the watchman that Don Carlos was needed back at the studio, and that I had seen him turn in here. 'May I go in and get him?' I asked.

"The night watchman, nervous that he would lose his job or worse, let us pass. We drove into the cemetery, easily following Don Carlos' headlights, while I turned off our lights once again. The *padrecito* and I were only a few hundred feet from them when they stopped, and we got out and crept nearer to see what they were up to.

"The Duesenberg was parked by an open grave. A pile of dirt towered like a mountain next to the rectangular cavity in the earth. The funeral must have been scheduled for the next morning, I suppose. In any case, Don Carlos pulled a wooden coffin out of the back seat of the Duesenberg, and Ilona helped him carry it to the open grave. They dropped it inside and began to remove their clothing. I must say that Ilona had a magnificent body, pale and voluptuous in the moonlight, with slender belly, full breasts, and rounded hips. Since Don Carlos wore his cape to hide his nakedness, I could see little of him, which is just as well, eh, *muchacha?*

"They began to make love in a most lascivious fashion, kissing wildly and touching each other's private parts. If I had not been in the company of a priest, I might have become aroused by their passion.

"Don Carlos and Ilona climbed into the open grave, and the moans and thrashing sounds coming from the coffin left no doubt that they were having sex in the sacred ground of the cemetery.

"Horrified by this desecration, I charged forward brandishing the long stake. I was so furious that I nearly fell into the open grave, due to my headlong rush in the dark. I teetered on the brink for a moment, and then caught my balance. Below me were the two copulating bodies in the coffin, only partly obscured by the opera cape.

"Ilona's pleasure-besotted face became demonic when she saw me over Don Carlos' shoulder, where she lay beneath him in the plush velvet of the coffin's interior.

" '*You!*' " she shrieked at me.

" 'Kill them!' Padre Badelon cried. 'Kill them now before they can kill us!'

" '*¡Ay!*' " I shouted. Don Carlos was still moving rhythmically on top of Ilona, but he raised his head to see who it was. As he did so, I drove the long, pointed ash branch downward with all my might, straddling the open grave so that my full weight was behind the thrust. It penetrated Don Carlos's back and pierced his heart, emerging from his chest and entering the soft breast of Ilona.

"A huge gout of their mingled blood shot out of the coffin, soaking my coat and spattering my face. I leaned against the butt of the stake, making sure that the shrieking vampires could not pull it free from their black hearts and survive the impalement.

" 'Sprinkle your holy water and garlic on them, *Padrecito!*' I shouted as Don Carlos and Ilona writhed beneath us in a hideous parody of the sex act. 'We must save the souls of these poor creatures!'

"But Father Badelon had no holy water. He leaped into the open grave and slurped up the spurting blood as a child drinks from a playground fountain. His white hair began to darken in the moonlight, and the wrinkles smoothed on his aged brow. He became young before my very eyes.

"Badelon seemed to fly out of the grave as soon as he had drunk his fill. He looked half the age that he had been when I first saw him sitting in my room in east Los Angeles.

" 'Did you really think that little graveyard celebration made these two evil?' he asked, his formerly dulcet tones turning bestial. 'They were merely playing at decadence. I will show you what it truly means to be wicked!'

"And with that his features began to change. His eyeteeth sprouted out to resemble an animal's, and his eyes glowed with some hellish light. His hands were claws reaching for me, and his priestly vestments were the black feathers of a raven. He laughed at me in a thunderous roar, a terrible sound that was not of this earth. *¡Ay!* I was so frightened that my bladder let go, I am not ashamed to say.

"As the thing that had been *Padrecito* Badelon came toward me, I tried desperately to wrench the ash branch free of the still warm bodies in the open grave. I knew that the bloody stake was all that stood between me and death . . . or worse than death. I shall never forget the horrid sight of the cruel *vampiro* as he drew so close I could smell the fetid stench of clotted gore on his breath!"

Esteban collapses back onto his pillows and lies still. For a moment, I'm afraid he has died here in front of me, physically drained from the exertion of telling me this wild story. At last he stirs, however, and turns his shaking head toward the cracked window, toward the full moon shining down on Hollywood. Then he closes his eyes as if remembering.

It is clearly time to go. I snap off the tape recorder. *"Gracias,"* I say. "I'll send you a copy of the story."

As I close his door gently behind me and walk through a pale green corridor on my way out of the rest home, I am none too sure there will be a story. After all, the old man's account of the murders has been compromised by all the vampire nonsense. I glance at my watch, and see that it is nearly ten o'clock. Visiting hours ended at eight-thirty. I apologize to the attendant on my way out, for keeping Esteban up so late.

"He stays up all night, anyway," the burly man says. "Suffers from insomnia."

I nod and step out onto Franklin Avenue. Cars go by, but there are no pedestrians in sight. I decide to walk the few blocks down to Hollywood Boulevard, to catch a cab. But the night air is so warm and pleasant that I continue walking east on the boulevard until I come to Cahuenga, where I stop at the newsstand to look at film magazines. While I browse, I wonder if I should still try to write the story of *Los Niños de la Noche,* judiciously excising the more fanciful parts for the sake of realism. And yet, as I look at passing, pasty-faced skinheads dressed in black, I can almost believe that *los vampiros* stalk the night in the middle of this vast city, that Hollywood is infested with them.

I have taken a perverse pleasure, of late, in walking alone at night. A young Mexican-American woman from a good family is not supposed to do this, of course, and perhaps it is foolish even for a self-sufficient university graduate cum journalist to be so incautious. But I led such a sheltered life as a girl that I derive a certain delight from my solitary peregrinations. I buy a copy of this month's *American Cinematographer,* stroll south to De Longpre, and then west toward my apartment building on La Brea.

In the distance I see bright lights, police cars, a crowd gathered on the sidewalk. Maybe they're shooting some scenes for a film or TV series, I think. Great, I'll have a closer look. And I do, too, but I find that it isn't what I thought.

A crime has been committed. I ask people in the crowd if they know what has happened.

"Somebody's been killed," a woman says, pointing to an apartment house. "A girl who lived in that building."

"It happened in the alley," a grim-faced senior citizen tells me. "I heard a policeman say she bled to death."

"Bled to death?" I ask.

But a patrolman comes and tells us all to leave before I can find out more. "The show's over, folks. Go on home."

I see the wisdom in what he says. I walk away from the dissolving crowd, and I wonder as I quicken my step if the girl who bled to death was found in a pool of her own blood, or, as in Esteban Montoya's story, if the drained corpse's blood was nowhere to be found at the scene of the crime. I glance at my watch and see that it is nearly midnight. I search for a cab, but De Longpre Street is not a major thoroughfare, so none are in sight. Maybe I should walk to Santa Monica Boulevard, where they are more plentiful, or maybe I should go back and ask one of the cops to give me a ride. I look over my shoulder, and see that someone is behind me. A man. Is he following me? Was he one of the curious who left the scene of the crime at the same time as me?

He passes under a streetlight, and I see that he is youngish, perhaps in his late twenties to early thirties. There is something familiar about him, but he passes again into shadow before I can determine what it is.

I walk faster, so fast that my calves and soles hurt. I wish that I had worn a more comfortable pair of shoes tonight, but I never expected to walk so far. Esteban's story, foolish as it might be, is working on me to unexpectedly grim effect here on this deserted street late at night, especially with this man behind me. What is it that troubles me about the story so? I have not been raised to be a superstitious *chola*. My family turned their backs on the barrio long ago. I have never set foot in east L.A. in my life, and believe none of the old Mexican folk tales about such ghosts as the wailing woman, *la llorona,* haunting cross roads, much less tales of vampires haunting movie lots. I wish, though, that I had heard the end of Esteban's story.

That's it! That's why I can't get it off my mind. He never told me if he had succeeded in pulling the stake out of the innocent bodies of Don Carlos and Ilona. Might Badelon have claimed him as a victim on that night five and a half decades ago?

I glance back and see that the man has gained on me. Once again he steps into the sickly yellow light of a streetlamp, and a fleeting glimpse of him makes me think that yes, yes perhaps I really do know him. He might be Esteban, though younger by half a century. Could he have left his room at the rest home, through the window, perhaps? *(He stays up all night, anyway. Suffers from insomnia.)* Wandered the streets of Hollywood looking for prey while I browsed at the newsstand? Attacked and killed a girl in an alley and later joined the crowd so that the police wouldn't suspect him? Become young with the fresh, hot blood of the victim that he had drunk not an hour ago? Recognized me, and decided that I too would make a nice midnight snack? Decided that he had told me too much in his weakened state, and now was coming after me to remedy that situation? Absurd. Utterly ridiculous, childish nonsense.

And yet I run. I run through the dark streets, my heels clattering on the cracked pavement, past the homeless and the punks and the darkened houses and the junkies and the winos. I run until I am out of breath and the muscles in my legs ache. I run until it seems my heart will burst. I run and run and run.

I run all the way home.

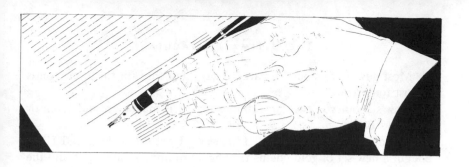

A LITTLE NIGHT MUSIC
▼▼▼

MIKE RESNICK

THE Beatles?

Yeah, I remember 'em. Especially the little one—what was his name?
—oh, yeah: Ringo.

The Stones? Sure I booked 'em. That Mick what's-his-name was a
strange one, let me tell you.

Kiss, Led Zeppelin, The Who, Eddie and the Cruisers, I've booked
'em all at one time or another.

After awhile, they all kind of fade together in your memory. In fact,
there's just one group that stands out. Strange, too, since they never
made any kind of a splash.

Ever hear of Vlad and the Impalers?

I didn't think so. Hell, there's no reason why you should have. I never
heard of 'em either, until Benny—he's not exactly my partner, but we
kind of cooperate together from time to time—calls me up one day and
says he's picked up a group and do I have any holes in the schedule? So I
look at the calendar, and I see a couple of gigs that are open, and I say
yeah, what the hell, send their agent over and maybe we can do a little
business. Benny says they don't have an agent, that this guy Vlad han-
dles all the details himself. Now, if you've ever had to deal with one of
these jokers, you know why I wasn't exactly thrilled, but the lead
guitarist from this futuristic Buckets of Gor band has been hauled in for
possession and I don't see anyone racing to make his bail, so I tell Benny
I've got half an hour open at three in the afternoon.

"No good, Murray," he says. "The guy's a late sleeper."

"Most guys in this business are," I say, "but three in the afternoon is almost tomorrow."

"How's about you two have dinner together, maybe around seven or so?" says Benny.

"Out of the question, baby," I answer. "I got a hot date, and I just bought a new set of gold chains that figure to impress her right into the sack."

"This Vlad guy don't like to be kept waiting," says Benny.

"Well, if he wants a booking, he can damn well *learn* to wait."

"Okay, okay, let me check his schedule," says Benny. He pauses for a minute. "So how's three o'clock?"

"I thought you just said he couldn't make it at three."

"I mean three o'clock in the morning."

"What is this guy, an insomniac?" I ask. But then I remember that powder-blue Mercedes 560 SL with the sun roof that I saw the other day, and I figure what the hell, maybe this guy's group can earn my down payment for me, so I say that three in the A.M. is okay—and as it turns out, I could have met him at seven after all, because this broad throws a bowl of soup at me and walks out of the restaurant just because I try to play a little bit of Itsy-Bitsy-Spider on her thigh under the table.

So I go back to the office and lay down on the couch and take a nap, and when I wake up there's this skinny guy dressed all in black, sitting down on a chair and staring at me. I figure he's strung out on something, because his eyes have got like wall-to-wall pupils, and his skin is white as a sheet, and I try to remember how much cash I have lying around the place, but then he bows his head and speaks.

"Good evening, Mr. Barron," he says. "I believe you were expecting me?"

"I was?" I say, sitting up and trying to focus my eyes.

"Your associate said that I was to meet you here," he continues. "I am Vlad."

"Oh, right," I say, as my head starts to clear.

"I am pleased to make your acquaintance, Mr. Barron," he says, extending his hand.

"Call me Murray," I answer, taking his hand, which is cold as a dead fish and much the same texture. "Well, Vlad," I say, dropping his hand as soon as I can and leaning back on the couch, "tell me a little something about you and your group. Where have you played?"

"Mostly overseas," he says, and I realize that he's got an accent, though I can't quite place it.

"Well, nothing wrong with that," I say. "Some of our best groups started in Liverpool. One of 'em, anyway," I add with a chuckle.

He just stares at me without smiling, which kind of puts me off, since if there's one thing I can't stand, it's a guy with no sense of humor. "You will book my group, then?" he says.

"That's what I'm here for, Vlad bubby," I say, starting to relax as I get used to those eyes and that skin. "Matter of fact, there's an opening on a cruise ship going down to Acapulco. Six days and out. Five bills a night and all the waitresses you can grab." I smile again, so he'll know he's dealing with a man of the world and not just some little schmuck who doesn't understand what's going on.

He shakes his head. "Nothing on water."

"You get seasick?" I ask.

"Something like that."

"Well," I say, scratching my head and then making sure my hairpiece is still in place, "there's a wedding party that's looking for some entertainment at the reception."

"What is their religion?" he asks.

"It makes a difference?" I say. "I mean, they're looking for a rock group. Nobody's asking you to play *Hava Nagila.*"

"No churches," he says.

"For a guy who's looking for work, bubby, you got a lot of conditions," I say. "You want to work with me, you got to meet me halfway."

"We will work in any venue that is not a church or a boat," he says. "We work only at night, and we require total privacy during the day."

Well, at this point I figure I'm wasting my time, and I'm about to show him the door, and then he says the magic words: "If you will do as I ask, we will pay you 50% of our fee, rather than your usual commission."

"Vlad, sweetheart," I say, "I have the feeling that this is the beginning of a long and beautiful relationship!" I walk to the wetbar behind my desk and pull out a bottle of bubbly. "Shall we make it official?" I ask, reaching for a couple of glasses.

"I don't drink . . . champagne," he says.

I shrug. "Okay, name your poison, bubby."

"I don't drink poison, either."

"Okay, I'm game," I say. "How about a Bloody Mary?"

He licks his lips and his eyes seem to glow. "What goes into it?"

"You're kidding, right?" I say.

"I never kid."

"Vodka and tomato juice."

"I don't drink vodka and I don't drink tomato juice."

Well, I figure we could spend all night playing Guess What The Fruit-cake Drinks, so instead I pull a contract out of my center drawer and tell him to Hancock it.

"Vlad Dracule," I read as he scrawls his name. "Dracule. Dracule. That's got a familiar ring to it."

He looked sharply at me. "It does?"

"Yeah," I say.

"I'm sure you are mistaken," he says, and I can see he's suddenly kind of tense.

"Didn't the Pirates have a third baseman named Dracule back in the 60s?" I ask.

"I really couldn't say," he answers. "When and where will we be performing?"

"I'll get back to you on that," I say. "Where can I reach you?"

"I think it is better that I contact *you,*" he says.

"Fine," I say. "Give me a call tomorrow morning."

"I am not available in the mornings."

"Okay, then, tomorrow afternoon." I look into those strange dark eyes, and finally I shrug. "All right. Here's my card." I scribble my home number on it. "Call me tomorrow night."

He picks up my card, turns on his heel, and walks out the door. Suddenly I remember that I don't know how big his group is, and I race into the hall to ask him, but when I get there he's already gone. I look high and low for him, but all I see is some black bird that seems to have flown into the building by mistake, and finally I go back and spend the rest of the night on my couch, thinking about dinner and wondering if my timing is just a little bit off.

Well, Pride and Prejudice, the black-and-white band that ends every concert with a fist fight, gets picked up for pederasty, and suddenly I've got a hole to fill at the Palace, so I figure what the hell, 50% is 50%, and I book Vlad and the Impalers there for Friday night.

I stop by their dressing room about an hour before show time, and there's skinny old Vlad, surrounded by three chicks in white night-gowns, and he's giving each of them hickeys on their necks, and I decide that if this is the kinkiest he gets, he's a lot better than most of the rockers I deal with.

"How's it going, sweetheart?" I say, and the chicks back away real fast. "You ready to knock 'em dead?"

"They're no use to me if they're dead," he answers without cracking a smile.

So I decide he's got a sense of humor after all, though a kind of dull, deadpan one.

"What can I do for you, Mr. Barron?" he goes on.

"Call me Murray," I correct him. "The PR guy wants to know where you played most recently."

"Chicago, Kansas City, and Denver."

I give him my most sophisticated chuckle. "You mean there are *people* between L.A. and the Big Apple?"

"Not as many as there were," he says, which I figure is his way of telling me that the band wasn't exactly doing S.R.O.

"Well, not to worry, bubby," I said. "You're gonna do just fine tonight." Someone knocks on the door, and I open it, and in comes a delivery boy carrying a long, flat box.

"What is that?" asks Vlad, as I tip the kid and send him on his way.

"I figured you might need a little energy food before you get up on stage," I answer, "so I ordered you a pizza."

"Pizza?" he says, with a frown. "I have never had one before."

"You're kidding, right?" I say.

"I told you once before: I never jest." He stares at the box. "What is in it?"

"Just the usual," I say.

"What is the usual?" he asks suspiciously.

"Sausage, cheese, mushrooms, olive, onions, anchovies . . ."

"That was very thoughtful of you, Murray, but we don't—"

I sniff the pizza. "And garlic," I add.

He screams and covers his face with his hands. "Take it away!" he shouts.

Well, I figure maybe he's allergic to garlic, which is a goddamned shame, because what's a pizza without a little garlic, but I call the boy back and tell him to take the pizza back and see if he can get me a refund, and once it's out of the room Vlad starts recovering his composure.

Then a guy comes by and announces that they're due on stage in 45 minutes, and I ask if he'd like me to leave so they can get into their costumes.

"Costumes?" he asks blankly.

"Unless you plan to wear what you got on," I say.

"In point of fact, that is precisely what we intend to do," answers Vlad.

"Vlad, bubby, sweetie," I say, "you're not just singers—you're *enter-*

tainers. You got to give 'em their money's worth . . . and that means giving 'em something to look at as well as something to listen to."

"No one has ever objected to our clothing before," he says.

"Well, maybe not in Chicago or K.C.—but this is L.A., baby."

"They didn't object in Saigon, or Beirut, or Chernobyl, or Kampala," he says with a frown.

"Well, you know these little Midwestern cowtowns, bubby," I say with a contemptuous shrug. "You're in the major leagues now."

"We will wear what we are wearing," he says, and something about his expression tells me I should just take my money and not make a Federal case out of it, so I go back to my office and call Denise, the chick who dumped the soup on me, and tell her I forgive her and ask if she's busy later that night, but she has a headache, and I can hear the headache moaning and whispering sweet nothings in her ear, so I tell her what I really think of no-talent broads who just want to get close to major theatrical booking agents, and then I walk into the control booth and wait for my new act to appear onstage.

And after about ten minutes, out comes Vlad, still dressed in black, though he's added a cloak to his suit, and the three Impalers are in their white nightgowns, and even from where I'm sitting I can see that they've used too much lipstick and powder, because their lips are a bright red and their faces are as white as their gowns. Vlad waits until the audience quiets down, and then he starts singing, and I practically go crazy, because what he's doing is a rap song, and worse still, he's doing it in some foreign language so no one can understand the words, but just about the time I think the audience will tear the place apart I realize that they're sitting absolutely still, and I decide that they're either getting into it after all, or else they're so bored that they haven't got the energy to riot.

And then the strangest thing happens. From somewhere outside the building a dog starts howling, and then another, and a third, and a cat screeches, and pretty soon it sounds like a barnyard symphony, and it keeps on like that for maybe half an hour, every animal within ten miles or so baying at the moon, and then Vlad stops and bows, and suddenly the kids jump to their feet and begin screaming and whistling and applauding, and I start thinking that maybe it's Liverpool all over again.

I go backstage to congratulate him, and when I get there he's busy giving hickeys to a couple of girls who snuck past the security forces, which isn't as bad as sharing a snort with them, I suppose, and then he turns to me.

"We will expect our money before we leave," he says.

"Out of the question, snookie," I say. "We won't have a count until the morning."

He frowns. "All right," he says at last. "I will send an associate of mine to your office to collect our share."

"Whatever you say, Vlad bubby," I tell him.

"His name is Renfield," says Vlad. "Don't let his appearance startle you."

As if appearances could startle me after twenty years of booking rock acts.

"Fine," I say. "I'll expect him at, say, ten o'clock?"

"That is acceptable," says Vlad. "Oh, one more thing."

"Yes?" I say.

"That scarab ring you wear on the small finger of your left hand . . ."

I hold it up. "Yeah, it's a beaut, isn't it?"

"I strongly advise you to take it off and hide it in your desk before Mr. Renfield makes his appearance."

"A klepto, huh?" I say.

"Something like that," answers Vlad.

"Well, thanks for the tip, sweetheart," I say.

Then a Western Union girl enters the room and unloads a bushel of telegrams on Vlad.

"What is this?" he asks.

"It means you're a hit, baby," I said.

"Oh?"

"Open 'em up and read 'em," I encourage him.

He opens the first of them, scans it, and drops it like it's a hot potato. Then he backs into a corner, hissing like he's a tire losing air.

"What's the problem?" I say, picking up the telegram and reading it: I LOVE YOU AND WANT TO HAVE YOUR BABY. LOVE AND XXX, KATHY.

"Crosses!" he whispers.

"Crosses?" I repeat, trying to figure out what's bugging him.

"At the bottom," he says, pointing to the telegram with a trembling finger.

"Those are X's," I say. "They stand for kisses."

"You're sure?" he asks, still huddled in the corner. "They look like crosses to me."

"No," I say, pulling out a pen and scribbling on the telegram. "A cross looks like *this.*"

He shrieks and curls into a fetal ball, and I decide that maybe he snorts a little nose candy after all, or that he just doesn't know how to handle success, so I kiss each of the girls goodbye—their cheeks are as cold as his hand, and I make a note to complain about the heating system—and then I go home, counting all the millions we're going to make in the next couple of years.

Well, Renfield shows up the next morning, right on schedule, and I wonder what Vlad was so concerned about, because compared to most of the heavy metal types I deal with, he's actually a mild, unprepossessing little fellow. We get to talking, and I find out that his hobby is entomology, and I can see that he's really into his subject because his homely little face lights up like a Christmas tree whenever he discusses bugs, and finally he takes the money and leaves.

Right about then I am figuring that a Mercedes is really too small and I am seriously considering getting a Rolls Royce Silver Spirit instead, but the fact of the matter is that I never see Vlad and the Impalers again. Pride and Prejudice makes bail, and Buckets of Gor beats their rap on a technicality, and suddenly the only thing I've got for my new superstar is a gig sponsored by a local church group, and he turns it down, and I call his hotel to explain, and he's checked out with no forwarding address.

I check *Variety* and *Billboard* for the next year, and I see that he's shown up in some minor league towns like Soweto and Lusaka, and the last I hear of him he's heading off to Kuwait City, and I think of what a waste it is and how much money we could have made for each other, but I never did understand rock stars, and this guy was a little harder to understand than most of them.

Well, you'll have to excuse me, but I gotta be off now. I'm auditioning a new group—Igor and the Graverobbers—and I don't want to be late. The word I get is that they're talented but kind of lifeless. But, what the hell, you never know where lightning will strike next.

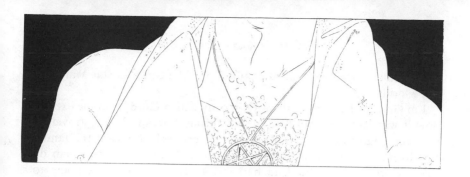

MR. LUCRADA

▼▼▼

JOHN LUTZ

MR. Lucrada tried hard to be young. Even though I was only ten years old, I noticed that about him. I mean, in Fort Lauderdale on what Dad calls Florida's Gold Coast, where umpteen million people go to retire, the folks sort of accept the fact that they're old and don't keep struggling to hold onto youth. Most of them, anyway.

But Mr. Lucrada, who was in my eyes *very* old, had his obviously dyed black hair cut in the shaggy style of a rock star's, wore pointy-toed Italian shoes, dressed in dark colors, and kept his shirt half unbuttoned so everyone could see the thick gold chain glittering in among his matted gray chest hairs. He had what my mom would call regular features and might have been handsome ages ago, but now he was old, at least fifty. Which was why I couldn't figure the loopy way my sixteen-year-old sister Madeline stared at him, especially when he came around the condo pool at night, wearing his young man's black racing trunks, so skinny his ribs showed.

I hardly ever saw him actually go in the water. He'd just stroll around the pool, usually with a long towel draped over his shoulders, sometimes nodding a hello to neighbors, seldom even speaking. Watching. That's what Mr. Lucrada seemed to be doing always, just watching. And I never saw him at the pool or down on the beach during the day, only at night. I guessed at first he was one of those old people scared of skin cancer. There was a lot of talk about skin cancer around the condo, and the little pharmacy on the corner did a great business selling sunscreen lotion you could smear on yourself to block what some of the gray folks that were our neighbors called deadly rays, like this was Star Wars and not Florida.

I'm Gordon Travers, by the way, mostly called Gordy. Let me explain how it was last year. My dad got this promotion and had to travel all over the Southeast selling industrial cleaners. Which meant the family had to move to Florida. Mom explained that since we didn't plan on living there forever, and Dad had got a big raise, we were going to splurge and move into a high-rise condominium project right on the beach with a sea view out the window. We'd be eye to eye with the gulls.

Just as well it wouldn't be Florida forever, because Mom was bothered by migraine headaches and couldn't stand the sun, so she spent most of her time lying in her bedroom with the drapes and door closed for dimness and quiet.

I wasn't at all anxious to move. We wouldn't have a back yard to play in like in Atlanta, and Madeline and I were leaving all our friends. They promised to write but we knew they wouldn't. Just like we promised and knew we wouldn't. At ten years old, I was already beginning to figure out the world, how people could think they meant things on one level because they wanted to mean them, but really there was a part of them that knew different. It was becoming clear to me that a lot of the things that seemed simplest in life were really the most complicated.

But, like Mom and Dad pointed out over and over, in Florida we could swim and lie on the beach all summer, and we were near Fort Lauderdale proper, which was a big city with plenty of things to do. After three or four months, Dad was supposed to get what Mom called a steady position in some southern city, maybe even the home office in Knoxville, where we'd settle down for a longer time. I looked forward to that.

From the first day, I felt uncomfortable in the condo. The building was high enough to scratch the sky, over thirty stories, and our unit (as they were called) was on the twenty-eighth floor. People weren't made to live way up in the air like that; it sure didn't feel like home. We were 28-C, and Mr. Lucrada was 29-C, directly above us.

It gets hot in the summer in Atlanta, but I was really knocked outa my socks by how hot it was in Florida. Sweat would roll off me when I was standing doing nothing. And along with the heat was the brightness, the pale glare that made concrete seem almost white and made me feel like I was a bug under some kind of sunlamp.

On the day we moved in, Madeline and I pestered Mom till she let us go down to the swimming pool. After all, it was the leverage she'd used the last month to try to convince us we'd love it at Windmere Tower, which I thought was a sort of snooty name but fit. Windmere Tower looked like a tall pale tower out of a fairy tale, and Madeline said sometimes she felt like Rapunzel and oughta let her hair grow and grow so some prince could use it for a rope and climb in her window. Madeline's hair was blond and cut so short for summer that by the time it grew long enough for what she had in mind, Dad would have been transferred again.

"Everybody in this place is like at least a hundred," Madeline said in dismay, after we'd each tried the diving board. It had plenty of spring.

I stretched out next to her on my towel and watched her smear suntan lotion over herself. She was still sort of skinny and her breasts weren't very big. She worried about that, but Mom told her not to make a major deal out of it, she'd fill out. Besides, the world was full of leg men. I saw Dad smile once behind his newspaper when this conversation was going on, then he got a sort of worried look. Madeline was growing up too fast, I heard him tell Mom later that night, and it was Mom's turn to smile.

So it didn't surprise me Madeline'd be mainly interested in how many teen-age boys were living in Windmere Tower, and that she'd be upset when it turned out the only hair that wasn't gray or dyed black was ours.

Dad had to leave town the day after we moved in, and that night the three of us, Mom, Madeline, and I, went down to the pool to reward ourselves for working so hard during the move.

The pool was almost deserted, and we had a pretty good time. Madeline kept trying to perfect her swan dive, and I was using the long, curved water slide. Mom was stretched out in one of those wooden loungers used for sunbathing. I think she was asleep, but she might have had her eyes closed because of one of her headaches.

"That's a ten," a voice said, as Madeline broke the surface after a dive and flipped water from her hair.

I saw her stare up at the skinny old man in black swimming trunks smiling down at her. He had a lean, friendly face, handsome in the dim light reflecting up from the pool. At first he seemed younger because of his suntan and black hair. But a second glance showed him to be old; the hair didn't belong above that leathery lined face, and the tan had an orange tint to it, as if it came from a bottle and not the sun.

"A ten?" she asked, treading water and looking puzzled.

"Yes, a perfect dive. I'm your neighbor, by the way, so welcome to Windmere Tower."

"Thanks." Madeline still sounded puzzled.

The old guy—Mr. Lucrada, I later found out—kept smiling at her

with teeth so even and white I thought they were false, which was normal for Windmere Tower. Then he dived into the deep end of the pool,
stroked to the ladder, and climbed out near the diving board. He stepped
up on the board, paused, walked out on it and jumped once for spring.
He seemed to hang in the air forever, then did a swan dive so perfect he
hardly made a splash going in the water.

He smiled again at Madeline as he climbed out of the pool, then he
rubbed a towel over himself and walked into the lobby. I don't think he
looked at Mom or me once. I believe that was the only time I ever saw
him in the water, that obvious attempt to impress my sister.

"That your new boyfriend?" I asked Madeline, grinning.

She made a face and ducked under water.

Some other people had come out to the pool now, and had introduced
themselves to Mom, who'd awakened at the sound of Mr. Lucrada's
splash. "That was Mr. Lucrada," I heard a woman with stiff gray hair
say. "He's a friendly enough soul, but he keeps pretty much to himself."

There he was now, getting a Diet Pepsi from the vending machine,
then going out through the gate in the pool fence and wandering down
toward the dark beach. He had a graceful way of walking, like he didn't
weigh anything at all.

Mr. Lucrada, I decided, gave me the creeps.

▼▼▼

So much so that I checked the building directory the next morning to
find out which unit was his. That was when I discovered he lived directly overhead. Great. The noises I heard at night, a thumping around
and a weird kind of rustling sound, were made by Mr. Lucrada right on
the other side of the thin plaster ceiling of my room. During the day,
when it was so bright and hot out that even I stayed inside and read a
book or worked on a model car, there was no sound at all from upstairs.

"Mr. Lucrada works them long hours," I heard old Mrs. Frivogel
from across the hall tell Mom. "He told me he sometimes plays cards
with friends all night. His only vice, accordin' to him. I seen him come
home once and park his car in the underground garage. It was almost
dawn, and he only nodded to me on his way to the elevator. Poor man
seemed so exhausted he was in a hurry to get to bed and sleep, but he
could only drag hisself along. 'Good mornin',' I sez to him, but he only
stares at me, so tired he looks like death warmed over. 'You're gonna kill
yourself stayin' up late playin' cards,' I sez, but he only smiles. You can't
tell men nothin' no matter their age, can you?"

Well, I got curious and went down to the garage one afternoon just to see what kind of car somebody like Mr. Lucrada drove. It wasn't really a completely underground garage, but it was as underground as they build them in Florida, and gloomy and dim as a cave. Even kind of cool like a cave. The concrete walls and driveway ramps angled so not a bit of the bright afternoon seeped in, and the only light came from the fixtures on the concrete ceiling.

All the parking slots were marked with yellow paint on the concrete wall. The car in 29-C's slot was something special. It wasn't a big Lincoln or Cadillac like lots of retired folks drove in Florida. I'm interested in cars and know a lot about them, and it struck me right off when we came here that expensive luxury cars loaded with chrome were the favorites of people around Fort Lauderdale. They were all over the place, like giant jukeboxes on wheels. But Mr. Lucrada's car was a low-slung, powerful black Corvette with tinted windows, the sort of car one of Madeline's boyfriends might drive, if any of them could afford it. Not that she had any boyfriends here in Florida, where the average age seemed to be over ninety.

"Interested in my car, Danny?" a voice said.

My heart did a loop and I whirled around.

Mr. Lucrada had been standing right behind me. He was grinning at me something like the way he'd grinned at Madeline out at the pool. It was a grin that was for some reason hard to look away from. And for the first time I noticed the smell, like the underground garage was dirty and damp. Only it wasn't.

Without thinking, I took off running.

"It's okay, Danny!" I heard Mr. Lucrada call after me. "I was interested in cars, too, at your age."

At least I think that's what he said. I was already in the elevator, leaning hard on the button that made the doors glide shut.

When I got upstairs and told Madeline what had happened, she looked at me as if I was nuts. "He wouldn't hurt you," she said. "He's . . . well, he's very nice. An old-fashioned gentleman."

That surprised me, that she'd say that when just a few nights before she'd looked at the guy like he was puke.

But in the next few weeks I noticed she was looking at him with a completely different expression on her face. It was the same expression I'd seen when she'd lie in bed gazing at her Billy Idol rock poster, kind of like she was a little bit drunk. And a few times I'd see Mr. Lucrada return her gaze, only in a different way that made my spine go cold.

The days were so hot that summer in Florida that at night, when

Mom (and Dad, if he wasn't traveling) was sleeping, Madeline and I would sneak down in the elevator and go walking on the beach with our bare feet sloshing in the surf. The moonlight was bright enough we could avoid stepping on any of the dead gross sea things that looked like half-inflated balloons with lots of strings and floated in by the hundreds on the waves. Old Mrs. Frivogel had sternly warned us not to step on any of them, or on the long tentacles they trailed. "Man-of-wars," she called them, and said they'd sting something terrible if they came in contact with flesh.

So we were splashing through the shallow surf with our heads down, and neither of us saw Mr. Lucrada until he said, "Nice night, isn't it? But not dark enough not to be seen."

Madeline looked at him standing there and gasped, really afraid. I knew that look on her face, like she'd been caught doing something wrong and knew it. That struck me as odd, after how she'd told me Mr. Lucrada was such a nice old guy. And what business was it of his where she went at night?

Anyway, there he stood, looking skinny and ridiculous in his skimpy black swimming trunks that emphasized his rickety legs. The gold chain around his neck glinted in the moonlight, and I saw some kind of ornament dangling from it, like a star inside a circle. Well, maybe Mr. Lucrada was Jewish, which wouldn't be unusual in this part of Florida. Maybe it was the Star of David that I'd noticed.

"It's okay, I guess," I answered about what kind of night it was. To tell you the truth I was a little scared myself. There was something about the guy. Something that puzzled me and made the skin creep on the back of my neck.

"It's fine exercise, walking through the resistance of shallow water," he said, smiling white and weird in the moonlight. "Sometimes resistance builds strength, but other times too much resistance destroys."

Madeline surprised me by turning around and running back to the white, high tower that was our condo. I watched her disappear into the night, untucked shirttail flying, legs pumping, rooster tails of sand kicked up by her heels.

I was alone in the dark with Mr. Lucrada.

The ocean breeze kicked up, ruffling his black hair. He said, "Something has scared your sister."

"You," I told him. Then I swallowed, wishing I'd kept that thought to myself.

"Me?" He looked astounded. "But why would I frighten her?"

Well, there was one I didn't want to answer. "She knows she's not supposed to be out here," I said. "Mom'd have a cow if she found out. Maybe that's it."

He looked thoughtful, and kind of amused. "Maybe indeed. But there's no need to worry about me giving away your secret. We should all be allowed to have at least one secret." He placed his fists on his scrawny hips and breathed in night air. "Would you like to take a ride in my car sometime?" he asked.

I gotta admit I was interested, a little. "I bet it'll really go fast."

"Oh, like a bat out of hell," he said, then he laughed. He had a peculiar laugh, gentle and old and cracked.

A ship's horn sounded, far out at sea and lonely, and I gazed at the distant lights on the dark horizon. As I did so I felt a kind of wind and saw a shadow pass over the swirling water near me. I turned to ask Mr. Lucrada about it, but he was gone. With his leathery tan and his black trunks, it was impossible to see him on the dark beach. The surf kept rolling in, rushing up on the sand farther and farther and whirlpooling around my bare ankles. It made an odd sighing sound, like it was trying to whisper something ancient and important to me. That was when I got really scared, just as scared as Madeline had looked, and I ran for the condo.

Expecting any minute to see Mr. Lucrada appear, I somehow made it up to the twenty-eighth floor on the elevator and hurried down the hall to our unit's door, leaving wet footprints on the carpet. I noticed another set of footprints, fainter than mine, leading to our unit. Madeline's, not quite dry. If Mom or Dad happened to wake up some night and look out in the hall, the evidence would be damning.

We'd left the door unlocked, and I pushed inside and closed it behind me, pressing in the doorknob lock button and fastening the chain.

Before I snuck into my bedroom to get back in bed, I decided to see if Madeline was sleeping yet. I wanted to ask her why she got so scared down on the beach, and tell her about how we were leaving wet footprints on the carpet. There was enough moonlight filtering in through the windows that the condo was dimly lit, and I could see my way around. The door to Mom and Dad's bedroom was still closed. And Dad was traveling like usual and Mom had taken one of her headache pills that zonked her out like a zombie. Good.

I padded barefoot down the hall, past the bathroom's open door, and opened the door to Madeline's room. Called her name, real soft.

But she was asleep, lying on top the pale sheets with her arms flung out, looking peaceful. For the first time I realized my sister was beautiful. Not cute like a kid anymore, but beautiful like a woman.

When I was about to back out of the bedroom I noticed how warm it was in there. And no wonder—the window was wide open. I could hear the surf breaking on the beach below. The moist, hot night had pushed into the room, making it smell damp and dirty like the underground garage that day. Why would she do that, let out all the air conditioning? Even Dad admitted that in summer the Florida Gold Coast had weather something like hell's.

But I didn't close the window. If Madeline wanted to sweat like a hog, let her. Though she sure seemed cool enough lying there in her flimsy nightgown. There wasn't a drop of perspiration on her; her skin looked smooth and dry as marble.

The next morning, while we were swimming in the pool, I flipped over and floated on my back, looking up at her bedroom window. It was shut now. Our drapes were partly open to let in light, but Mr. Lucrada's, on the floor above, were pulled closed, as they always were. He wanted the place cool when he returned home from wherever it was he worked, Mrs. Frivogel had said.

Madeline did a neat swan dive off the board and surfaced near me, shaking glittering drops of water off her hair so some of them hit me in the face like tiny wet diamonds.

"How come you got scared and ran last night," I asked her, "if you think that Lucrada guy's such a cool character?"

She treaded water, staring at me as if she didn't quite know what I meant. Then she put her hand on my forehead and said, "Take a dip, dip," and shoved me under water.

When I surfaced, spitting chlorine and sputtering and yelling at her, she was swimming away.

A couple of days later, when Mom and Dad were eating breakfast before Dad had to leave for Jacksonville, I heard Mom mention a girl's body found on the beach near Pompano. "She was totally bloodless," Mom said, "like some sea creature had fed on her. Now isn't that odd?"

Dad said he was trying to eat eggs, thank you, and that was the end of the conversation. But I found a Fort Lauderdale *News* down in the laundry room and read about it, how the tourists who discovered the dead girl in the surf said her body was so pale. The death was being investigated, the paper said. Well, I guess so.

For some reason the dead girl made me uneasy about Madeline. Not scared, actually, but a feeling I couldn't quite identify. Maybe I felt that way because of how, even under her suntan, she looked kind of pale and unhealthy lately. And she seemed to be mooning around more and more over Mr. Lucrada. I mean, cripes, there had to be *somebody* in Fort

Lauderdale closer to her age! I caught them one time down in the parking garage, standing way back in the shadows. He was leaning over her real close, like he was telling her a secret. When he saw me over her shoulder he straightened up and wiped his mouth, then he grinned at me. "Gordy, my boy, come over here."

But I didn't. I ran up the concrete ramp instead, into the heat and brilliant Florida sunshine, where I somehow knew he wouldn't follow.

I started watching the TV news in case there was something else about the dead girl found on Pompano Beach. But there was nothing; the case had lost its novelty, I guess. My attention was caught, though, when they showed this tape about how some parents' group was campaigning against the bad influence of rock music, and they showed this heavy metal album with a painting of a star in a circle on it, just like the gizmo hanging on Mr. Lucrada's neck chain. A pentagram, one of the parents called it, and said it was used in satanism. When I asked Mom what satanism was, she told me it had to do with worshiping the devil or something, then said her migraine was flaring up and Gordy would you please get out and close the door.

That night, when we were eating the frozen gunk dinners Mom had heated in the microwave, I looked across the table at Madeline. She was a royal pain, like a lot of older sisters, but I decided I cared enough about her that I had to do something about this situation with Mr. Lucrada, who I was liking less and less.

So that evening, when Madeline had gone to her room like usual and Mom was watching a soap opera she'd taped, I told Mom I thought there was something going on between Madeline and Mr. Lucrada.

She immediately switched off the VCR, so quick it kind of startled me. "Like what's going on, Gordy?"

I gulped. "Well, they're spending a lot of time together, is all." I couldn't tell her how I was scared for Madeline with no good reason.

She sat and thought for a minute, the TV remote control resting on her knee. "He's old enough to be her father, Gordy."

"Maybe her grandfather."

She shook her head and looked confused. "I can't believe this."

I saw I was losing her. Then I understood the idea that was forming in her head and I jumped right in on impulse. "I think I saw them kissing down in the parking garage a few days ago."

That one brought her straight up out of her chair. The remote bounced off the carpet. "Madeline!"

"Hey, Mom! Wait!"

Too late. She was stalking toward Madeline's bedroom like she was speedwalking in the Olympics. This was more of a reaction than I'd counted on. I had the feeling I'd done something monumental that couldn't be undone, ever.

The yelling in Madeline's room must have gone on for an hour. When Mom finally came out and slammed the door behind her, she pressed her hands to her head and hurried past me.

"Mom—"

"Not now, Gordy. I'm phoning your father, then I'm gonna lie down."

"Mom—"

"Not *now*, Gordy!" And off she went still holding her head with both hands as if she was afraid it might wobble and fall off her shoulders.

That night I laid there in bed and just stared at the ceiling. I tried not to think about what I'd done, but I did think about it, and I couldn't stand it. I never expected an explosion, a permanent change in our world.

Madeline had never come out of her room. The glowing green numbers on my clock radio said it was a few minutes past midnight, but I was sure she'd still be awake. I climbed out of bed, slipped into a pair of jeans, and padded down the hall to her room. At first I was going to knock, then I figured that just in case she might be asleep, I better look in on her first and go back to bed if she wasn't awake. She might have another fit if I knocked and woke her up. Madeline was a girl, but she wasn't somebody you could take lightly if she lost her temper and started fighting.

Just as I turned the knob and pushed open the door, I heard this funny rustling sound, familiar but I didn't know how, and as I stepped into the dim bedroom I saw the window was wide open.

For just an instant I'm sure I saw something. A giant form, darker than the dark sky, spreading wide and soaring up and out away from the building. I stood for a moment staring, wondering if my eyes had played a trick on me. I know now they hadn't.

"Madeline," I whispered.

She was awake, her eyes wide in the dimness. The way the moonlight shone in her pupils scared me. She mumbled something, then yanked the sheet up over her head, her fingers curled around the white linen like claws.

"Madeline! Please! I'm sorry . . ."

I heard her muffled words then. "Go away, Gordy! Just go away!"

Feeling rotten and helpless, I turned to leave.

That's when I saw the shadow on the wall. A shadow something like whatever I'd glimpsed against the night sky.

I couldn't breathe, I was so scared, but I turned around to look. There was no way I *couldn't* look.

Madeline was standing on the bed, glaring down at me. She seemed taller than she actually was, and her arms were kind of floating up and seemed to get longer and longer.

Then she collapsed and sat in the middle of the bed. She buried her head between her knees and started sobbing, saying, "Gordy, Gordy . . ." Just repeating my name over and over in a heartbroken way that gave me the shivers.

I hadn't expected any of this and wished I'd never said anything about Mr. Lucrada to Mom. I told Madeline that, crying a little bit myself, I admit.

"What's done's done," she said, still not looking up.

Not knowing what else to do, I backed out of the room. I went back to bed, but I didn't sleep until it began to get light out.

Dad was home the next afternoon, and he and Mom went up to Mr. Lucrada's unit and knocked on the door. Hammered on the door, is more like it.

But Mr. Lucrada didn't answer.

The next day Dad said he'd learned Mr. Lucrada was moving and his unit was already up for sale. That was that, he said, seeming relieved. I think there must have been something about Mr. Lucrada that scared him, too. "After all," he said, "there's no way to prove anything, even if something really *did* happen." He sipped his coffee. "I just wish Madeline would be more communicative about this. She owes us an explanation."

"Maybe someday she'll give us one," Mom said, and touched the back of his hand.

He nodded, not liking that answer but having to accept it. Some things you just had to accept no matter what. I sure learned that one the hard way.

▼▼▼

Nobody actually saw Mr. Lucrada move out, but two days later the drapes on his windows were wide open and the sleek black Corvette no longer squatted in its parking slot in the garage.

We stayed in Florida the rest of that summer, then Dad got transferred to Knoxville, where we were supposed to settle more or less permanently.

It was toward the end of summer that I read someplace about vampires. It had never really occurred to me one of them would choose hot and sunny Florida as a place to live—if *live* is the word. But come to think of it, why not? Night is night, no matter where you are, and nobody'd think to look for a vampire there in sunny vacationland. Mickey Mouse, sure, but not a vampire. I mean, vampires don't exactly go for basking on the beach, sunscreen or not.

But at night the hunting must have been good, with all the tourists wandering the dark beaches, and the sky above the endless sea there for refuge if he got discovered.

And of course, there were always possibilities close to home.

Madeline was never the same after that summer. Neither was I, after I told her one night on the beach what I thought about Mr. Lucrada.

She began to sob very softly, but she never denied the truth of what I said.

"Oh, Gordy, Gordy," she said, repeating my name over and over like she had that night in her room, so sadlike. Then she reached out and hugged me tight to her, still sobbing.

That was the first time my sister kissed me.

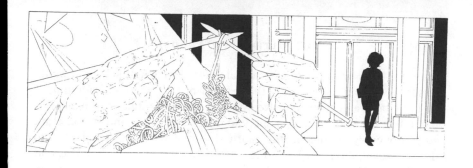

IN THE CUSP
OF THE HOUR

▼▼▼

JOHN GREGORY BETANCOURT

"**H**OW'S the knitting?"

"I'm making a scarf for my grandson. With winter coming, little Jamie will need it."

"Oh, you've been working on that thing for years!"

"I'll finish it soon, I surely do believe."

"Hist!" A gnash of teeth, a prick of ears. "One's coming!"

"Yes? A sweet young thing? It's been so long . . ."

▼▼▼

The mall was dead. Lauren Mackie knew it the moment she pulled into the parking lot, and it pissed her off because it meant something had gone wrong with her intricately laid plans. In all that vast expanse of asphalt she could see perhaps a dozen cars, and most of those looked abandoned. Where was everybody? Weren't the stores supposed to open at 9:00 A.M. sharp?

She didn't have time for this nonsense. The stores had better be open. She'd planned her vacation to the last minute, and needed new drapes this morning. Specifically, by 9:15 this morning. She'd already selected them from the Sterns catalog; it *should* have been just a matter of picking them off a rack, plopping down her American Express Platinum Card to pay for them, and beating a quick retreat home.

If she wasn't back in time, she wouldn't be able to hang the drapes by 9:55, which meant she wouldn't have them up before the new carpeting came at 10:00, or the new furniture at 10:45. Her whole schedule would be shot to hell, and it was only the *first day* of her vacation. Lauren lived by her clocks and schedules. Remodeling the ground floor of her house had taken *weeks* to plan, and she had it down in black and white, every second of every minute already neatly slotted. Knowing what she had to do, and when, filled her up inside . . . made her content, if not happy.

Still grumbling, she pulled her candy-apple red Mercedes next to an old Buick, climbed out, and locked her door. She glanced at her watch: 9:13. Those stores had *better* be open, or senior management would face her wrath. She was determined to enjoy her vacation. She spent little enough time on her own pleasures, after all.

When she started for the entrance, her high heels clicking on the pavement, her Sergio Valenti original dress swirling around her ankles, she saw a sign giving the mall's hours—it wouldn't open for another fifteen minutes. Damn, damn, damn. But the doors wouldn't be locked, she figured. Employees had to get in. She could wait for fifteen minutes if she had to, right?

When she pushed through the double doors, she found the mall wasn't quite dead. The lights were on and music burbled in the background, an old Crosby, Stills, & Nash protest song done with big band instruments and no vocals. She started to hum along as she marched toward Stern's. Ahead, a round concrete fountain arced streams of water twenty feet into the air; colored spotlights made a shifting rainbow of colors.

And then she saw them—the benches full of *old* people. Lauren's upper lip curled back. Old people in *polyester,* the kind of clothing you only saw on sitcoms from the late 60s and early 70s these days . . . those huge collars . . . those horrid pink and red splotches that were supposed to be designs . . . those grotesque yellow-and-green plaids.

One old black lady had on a green floral pant-suit out of Lauren's worst fashion nightmare. One skinny old man had Coke-bottle glasses that made his eyes look big as saucers as he stared at her. Others held scandal rags, or knitting, or crocheting. Some even had giant straw beach-baskets parked at their feet.

They all stared at her like she was an intruder who didn't belong. Lauren swallowed, not liking the attention. *Or like a side of beef,* she thought, *ready to be carved.*

She had every right to be here, she told herself, giving her short blond hair (cut in the latest style) a reassuring pat. They were old; probably old and senile, certainly crazy to be hanging out in a mall this early. For God's sake, didn't they have *homes* to go to?

Lauren heard doors slam behind her. Glancing back, she saw a knot of four or five old men had come into the mall behind her. They all had canes; like blind men they click-click-clicked on the tile floor, headed in her direction.

Lauren forced herself to turn and stare straight ahead, at the fountain. *If you don't look at them, you won't see them,* she told herself. She raised her head proudly. It was just like with the homeless people in the city. *Don't look and they're not there. There's nothing unpleasant if you just* don't look.

The fountain's waters turned red as the floodlights changed. Now it looked like endless cascading streams of blood.

Lauren glanced toward Sterns and accidentally made eye-contact with one of them, a grandmotherly old woman. At least this one looked better than the rest, with a faded yellow sun dress, a pink shawl across her shoulders, and a bag of yarn at her feet. Her bifocals had narrow gold rims. Her eyes looked hungry, desolate. Lauren shuddered.

She was going to have to pass that woman, in fact pass between two rows of concrete benches full of old people, to get to Sterns. The thought of coming that close to them made her skin crawl. But she'd always prided herself on being logical, and they were merely old people hanging out in a mall, after all. What was there to be afraid of? So they were a bit creepy. She saw creepy people in the city every day and didn't pay them any heed.

She didn't look at any of them. She pretended they didn't exist. Or tried to, because as she approached, she couldn't help but notice them all putting down their knitting needles and magazines and beat-up romance novels and struggling to their feet. Many had canes or walkers. Those that didn't clung to others who did.

Lauren walked faster, trying to make it through the gauntlet before they could get close to her. Already she could smell them: a faint whiff of lilac hung in the air, covering something danker, like moldering cloth.

All the old people were standing now, staring straight at her. She kept her eyes fixed on the steel gates across the front of Sterns, feeling like some freak on display. She knew that was silly, but that was the way she felt.

Canes clicked. Old people tottered around her, filling the air with the reek of lilac bath powder, too much perfume, too much cologne.

She didn't see it happen. One second they were tottering beside the benches, and the next second they were simply *on* her, pressing forward in a wave of polyester and too much perfume, hundreds of them, all the old people in the mall drawn to her like moths to a flame. Lauren tried to run, but they pushed against her from every side. She found herself whirled from skeletal hand to skeletal hand, their touch like a cobweb's.

Get away! she tried to scream, but thick, lilac-scented air filled her mouth and lungs, and nothing came out. *Old people,* she thought, wanting to scream from the absurdity of it all, *old people in polyester are trying to kill me.*

There were hands everywhere, pulling her in a thousand different directions, whirling her around and around and around like Dorothy in the tornado in *The Wizard of Oz.* She caught a glimpse of fangs and red-glowing eyes, and in the seconds before she lost consciousness she heard voices like fingernails on slate sighing over her.

"So pretty . . ."

"So soft . . ."

"So much, so much more . . ."

And in the end she felt herself breaking apart, as they took all she had. And when they were done, when she was a spilled jar, they left her lying there on the bench, her pocketbook under her head for a pillow.

▼▼▼

Mall security soon found Lauren. When she opened her eyes it took her a moment to focus on the man in the gray uniform who was gently shaking her shoulder. It was just a kid, maybe eighteen or nineteen. His face seemed soft and out of focus. She blinked and her head suddenly hurt. She wished she were home in bed.

"Ma'am? Are you all right?" he asked. "Ma'am?"

"Yes . . . yes, I think so," she murmured.

She recalled her carpeting, and her furniture. She glanced at her watch, but couldn't make her eyes focus to read it. What was she doing sleeping here? Had she been that tired?

"Can you stand?" he asked.

"I have to get some drapes," she said, "at Sterns."

"There's plenty of time for that," he said, taking her elbow and helping her to her feet. "We have a nurse on duty. Why don't you come and lie down, and maybe we can find some orange juice for you. Did you skip breakfast today? Are you still feeling faint?"

"Thank you," Lauren murmured. The world seemed distant, muted somehow. *Time . . . something about time.* She looked at the security guard's smiling face and felt a hollowness inside where the press of hours and days and minutes and seconds had been. She actually managed a smile in return.

Yes, she had time, that was it. All the time in the world. And as he led her down the mall, past the benches crowded with old people in polyester, she found herself wondering if maybe she should go to the beach for her vacation after all.

▼▼▼

"How's the knitting coming?"

"I finished that scarf for my grandson. With winter coming, little Jamie will need it."

"Good, good."

"This one's for my niece. It's going to be pink and yellow, a cute little thing. Two days to go, according to my schedule. At this rate, I'll have all my knitting done well before Christmas. It's just a matter of organization."

"I'm not making my gifts this year, you know. I've started a list of things to get at Sterns. There's plenty of time if I do it right, scheduling my shopping in advance."

"Ah . . . what's that?"

A gnash of teeth, a prick of ears. "One's coming!"

"So sweet, the young . . . so sweet."

CHILDREN OF THE NIGHT

▼▼▼

KRISTINE KATHRYN RUSCH

CAMMIE pounded the stake into his heart. Whitney stood firmly beside her as Cammie brought the hammer down. The vampire roared once—arms flailing, long nails scratching the side of the coffin. Blood spurted onto the apartment walls and the freshly laid carpet. A rank, half-rotted smell filled the air. Still she pounded, until the thing in front of her had faded into nothing but wizened skin and bones. She let go of the stake, wiped her hands on her jeans and turned around.

The little girl in the doorway was no more than three. Her wide blue eyes dominated her cherubic face. She glanced at Cammie once, then scanned the room. "Daddy?"

Cammie scanned the room too, but saw no evidence of a human presence. Whitney stared at the child and bit his lower lip. The little girl crept across the carpet, her tiny tennis shoes leaving no mark on the shag. She knelt in front of the coffin, put her forehead against the wood and whispered, "Daddy." The airy, pain-filled sound was more plaintive than a wail.

▼▼▼

Dr. Eliason took the little girl—she had never given Cammie her name —into the examination room. The little girl clutched her stuffed dog and didn't look back. Cammie slid down on the plush blue seat. The waiting room smelled of sickness, stale coffee, and antiseptic. She wondered how the receptionist could work here, day after day.

Whitney studied the magazine rack and finally grabbed an ancient

Time. He sat down beside her, even though there were no other patients in the room.

"First kid, huh?"

The blood on Cammie's jeans had dried into a crusty brown handprint. "She called him 'Daddy.' "

"He probably was."

She picked at the handprint. Flakes of dried blood caught on her fingernails. "He shriveled up like he was centuries old. There's no way—"

"Cammie." Whitney's tone was gentle. "You've been doing this for what, a year? You should know that anything past five years would crumble that way. She's maybe three, so if he were five years, she was conceived just after, which is plausible, or she was his from a sperm bank, also plausible. Or he kidnapped her when she was a baby, which is likely."

Cammie didn't answer. She brushed at the blood stain, but it didn't come off.

Whitney grabbed her arm. His hand was warm. "I thought you knew all this."

"How the hell was I supposed to know this?" Cammie wrenched herself free and stood up. The receptionist glanced over the high, glassed-in desk, then looked away. "I spend six weeks in combat training, get my weapons certificate, learn how to avoid conversion or death, get my assignments and blam! I'm on the streets. No one told me about lifestyles, or children, or decay time."

"They wouldn't have recruited you if you didn't already know."

Cammie wrapped her arms around herself and wandered over to the magazine rack. She hadn't known. She had come straight from college with a major in psychology and a minor in history. She had spent all of two weeks on vampires in her senior psych seminar, finally dismissing them as the most alien and deadly of addicts. She had gone to work for the Westrina Center just like many of her friends had gone to intern at the alcohol rehabilitation center. Only the Westrina Center made it clear that there was no way to rehabilitate a vampire. They treated vampirism like a plague: eradicated only by isolation and death. The Center had tried rehabilitation twenty-five years earlier, but that had more than failed: it had doubled the vampire population in the city.

The door swung open, and Dr. Eliason came out, holding the little girl's hand. She clutched her stuffed dog to her left side, its fabric head crammed against her heart. Dr. Eliason spoke softly to her, wiped a strand of hair from her forehead and then smiled. He was a tall, broad-shouldered man who had the gentleness that Cammie always thought doctors should have. He had asked her out twice, but she had refused; she didn't want to learn that his gentleness was false, a pretense for patients and nothing more.

He left the girl by the door and came over to Cammie. "She's clean," he said. "Not a mark on her. Her blood is her own, and it's infection-free. She's well fed, well nourished, well cared for. She's also in shock. She might be one of the lucky ones. She hasn't said much, so maybe she'll forget all this. But I think you need to take her to the Center right away. They should be able to get her settled somewhere before the pain really starts. Those all her possessions?"

"She had a room full of stuff," Whitney said.

"Get that and bring it," Eliason said. He didn't look at Whitney. He was watching Cammie. "She needs as much of her home as you can salvage."

"Home?" Cammie choked the word out. A place that smelled of rotting blood, and filled with the presence of a man no longer human. Eliason was calling that home?

He put his palm against her face. She resisted the urge to lean into him, to let him comfort her like he had comforted the little girl. "Home, Camila," he said. "It's all she ever knew."

Whitney crouched and extended his hands. "Come on, hon," he said. "I'll take you someplace safe."

"Her name is Janie." Eliason's thumb traced Cammie's cheekbone.

"Janie," Whitney said, hand still outstretched, "come with me."

Janie wrapped both arms around her dog, rested her chin on the creature's head and shuffled forward. She brushed near Eliason, but when she saw Cammie she scooted to the far side of the room.

"It's okay," Whitney said.

Janie continued her walk, occasionally throwing Cammie a frightened glance. When she reached Whitney, she buried her face in his sleeve.

"I guess you've been elected to pick up her things," Whitney said. "I'll meet you back at the office."

Cammie nodded, pulled away from Eliason and bolted out of the room before either man could say anything else. She didn't want their sympathy—and she didn't know why she expected them to give it.

▼▼▼

She had never returned to the scene of an eradication before. Her hands shook as she fumbled with the lock. She had always gone in, found the sleeping vampire and murdered it, before it had a chance to touch her or her partner. She never looked at the home; she never did the reports. She always went in, drove the stake, and left. One day's work in a month filled with paperwork, field-training seminars, and target practice. She had only killed five. Imagine finding a child on her sixth.

The door slid open easily, much more easily than she remembered. The smell—ancient blood and decay—slapped her, bringing up that familiar hatred which made the killing part of the job so simple. She squinted in the darkness. No sunlight filtered in from the black-out curtains, no light gained entry under doors. The little girl had lived like this—in putrid darkness—instead of playing in sunlight. Cammie suppressed a shudder and flicked on a light.

The artificial illumination revealed a room so normal that Cammie nearly stumbled. A television dominated the center, surrounded by a light brown sofa sectional. A doll rested her head against a pillow, and a child's blanket crumpled near the end. Books lined the walls, and in the dining room, Cammie could see an expensive stereo set and hundreds of CD's. She wondered where the money came from, and then decided that she didn't want to think about it.

She wandered into the kitchen. Child-sized dishes sat unwashed on the kitchen counter. She opened the dishwasher and found more child-proof bowls as well as an entire set of wine goblets. Cool water dripped off the rim. He had probably turned on the dishwasher just before he went to sleep.

She slammed the door with a metallic bang. She had come to get toys and clothes. Child things. She didn't have to snoop through the entire house.

Avoiding the room with the coffin and its remains, she went down the hall. The shades were up in the little girl's room. Sunlight flooded across a pink-canopied bed. Stuffed animals lined the floors and walls. A record player sat in the middle of the floor, the turntable still revolving. No wonder she hadn't heard them come. She had been playing records—and Cammie had been too preoccupied to register the noise.

If there had been any noise.

She grabbed a suitcase out of the closet and stuffed it with ruffly little-girl dresses, sweatshirts and blue jeans. She poured the contents of the underwear and sock drawers on top, then added two winter coats for warmth. The child had been well tended, physically.

The smell was making her nauseous. She went over to the window, pulled it open and sucked in the crisp outdoor air. She would never take another detail with a child involved. Never.

As if she had had a choice. No one had warned her about this one.

She took the suitcase and an armload of stuffed animals out to her car. She came back, grabbed the toy box and carried it down. Then she unplugged the record player, packed the records and stopped.

The little girl wouldn't want that toy. It would remind her of her father's death. Each time she put an album on the turntable and heard the scritch-scratch of a needle, she would see her father thrash as Cammie drove a stake in his heart.

Cammie doubled over and wrapped her arms around her head, as if the action would squeeze the thoughts out. She hadn't meant to kill a child's father. She hadn't meant to kill a person at all. She was killing an animal, something that preyed on human beings and lived off the blood like a wild thing. She hadn't known. . . .

Slowly, ever so slowly, she stood up. She grabbed a garbage bag, filled it with the remaining stuffed animals and went into the kitchen. She took the child dishes from the dishwasher, dried them and placed them inside the bag. Then she went into the living room, grabbed the doll and her blanket off the sofa, and left the house for the final time.

The sunlight seemed brighter than it had moments before. She took several breaths to clear the stench from her nostrils. Her clothes had picked up the smell and the child's things also reeked. She would be glad when she got rid of them. She would be glad when this entire thing was over.

▼▼▼

That night Cammie dreamed:

She was lying across her bed, reading. Forbidden sunlight warmed her feet, her back. She didn't dare make any noise. Daddy was sleeping. He hated to be disturbed while he slept, especially after a night out. In the other room, her brother thrashed in his crib. He hated to sleep in the daylight, just as she did, but Daddy insisted. That way he could spend more time with them. But what he called time was mostly watching television, sipping wine and waiting for him to go out on his nightly food run. He always came back with groceries and cooked them a large dinner which he never ate. Once she asked him why he didn't like food. He had smiled and said the wine was enough.

She sat bolt upright in her bed, arms wrapped around herself. Her heart was pounding as if she had awakened from a nightmare, but the dream itself had not been frightening. She even knew the dream's cause —the vampire and his little girl.

She got up and padded barefoot across the dusty hardwood floors of her apartment. She didn't get paid enough for the work she did, not when vampires had expensive homes, filled with expensive furniture, stereos and TV's. The digital clock read 3:45, so she didn't even bother to switch on her own small, black-and-white set. She didn't have cable, and at this time of night, nothing else was on.

She walked around her three rooms, touching the garlic and the crosses that the Westrina Center insisted fill her home. Protection, just like the security system they had installed protected her. She was safer than she had ever been in her entire life, and still her heart pounded with fear at being a vampire's child.

She went into the kitchen, pulled a mug off the rack, opened a tea bag and filled the kettle on the stove. Then she grabbed a book from the stack on the table. Something light and romantic, to tease her mind. Something different from her life. Something to occupy her until the sun rose—and she could sleep in the safety and warmth of the light.

▼▼▼

The observation room was small and dark. Cammie clasped her hands behind her back and refused the chair Anita offered her. Anita settled her bulk into the armchair and leaned forward, placing her elbows on the windowsill. The elder woman looked comfortable and matronly; Cammie always thought her the perfect image of a mother—so perfect that at times, Cammie wanted Anita to hold her and soothe away all her fears.

But they had never even touched. Their working relationship had been strictly professional, and a friendship had never developed.

"She's asked about a record player," Anita said, staring through the window at the brightly lit room below. "I assume you left it."

"She'd been listening to it when we got there. I thought it would hurt her."

"I'd sent Whitney for it, but they'd already sealed up the house." Anita leaned back, her face half in shadow. "You can't pre-guess another person's pain."

"But—"

"Don't but me. I've seen three generations of children through this place. We need to help whatever way we can."

"I'm sorry."

Anita nodded once. "That's better. I want you to get the court order and move through the red tape. The record player has to be here by this afternoon."

Cammie clenched her fists. "Is that why you brought me up here?"

"No." Anita waved at the chair. "Sit down."

Cammie didn't move.

"Sit down. You can't see from that height."

Cammie straightened her shoulders, and eased the tightness in her hands. She grabbed the edge of the chair and pulled it back, sitting in it, but not resting. "All right."

Anita leaned forward again. Down in the room, Janie piled her stuffed animals around herself like a protective wall. "Whitney tells me you know nothing about vampires and children."

"I know that female vampires prey mostly on infants and children under five."

"And male vampires?"

"Kill men, mostly, and occasionally create a female vampire."

"But what do male vampires do with children?"

"How the hell am I supposed to know?" Cammie kicked against the wall and pushed her chair back. Janie looked up, her expression startled.

"It's not completely sound-proofed up here," Anita said. "She can hear when you pound the wall. I don't want her any more frightened than she is."

"Sorry," Cammie said, not feeling sorry at all. The little girl had lived with a vampire. Cammie had freed her, had saved her, and everyone in the center acted as if the child had suffered a tragedy.

"During the first thirty years of a male vampire's existence," Anita said as if Cammie hadn't interrupted them, "he still seeks companionship. He tries it first by creating female vampires, and when that fails, he adopts children. Sometimes, he can father them—especially if he tries in his first year. As his addiction grows, and his humanity breaks down, he abandons the children more and more, until finally, he either uses them as prey or he creates younger, more powerful vampires. Do you understand what I'm telling you?"

"You're telling me that I did the right thing."

"No." Anita put her hand on the glass, as if she were trying to touch the little girl. "I'm telling you that your actions yesterday ended a relationship. The vampire was still young enough to love this girl and treat her like a daughter. She lost her father—"

"Bullshit." Cammie whispered the word, then repeated it louder. "Bullshit. You people sent me over there. You told me to kill that vampire."

"Yes," Anita said. "And now I'm showing you the consequences of your action."

Cammie clenched her hands again, half wishing for a stake to drive through Anita's frozen heart. "Why?"

Anita reached out to her—first touch—and Cammie backed away. "Because you need to see it," Anita said. "And remember."

▼▼▼

Stop him!

Cammie knew the voice belonged to her dream, but she couldn't wake up. She could see the faded night-gray of her bedroom, and over it, the forbidden sun-filled room of her dream. The voice came from down the hall: a man's voice, deep and angry.

Stop him!

She was holding a child, a little boy, clutching him to her shoulder, pressing his face against her skin to stifle his tears. She was lying alone in the safety of her own bed, knowing that what she was feeling wasn't real.

Stop him now!

"Shush, Ben, shush," she whispered in both worlds. "You don't want him to get up, do you? Please be quiet. Please."

The little boy snuffled once and then was silent. In the night-gray of her bed, she clutched the sheets and willed the fear to go away. The pressure of a little-boy body eased and then faded into nothing. She was completely alone. No dreams, no phantoms. Just her.

She got up and went into the kitchen. Without turning on a light, she made herself a cup of tea and sat at the table. The nights had grown longer. And each night, phantoms and dreams about vampires' children. She had had Whitney check for a boy-child in Janie's family. There was none. The little boy was an addition from her subconscious, another child to protect, a child who was not herself. But she wanted to protect no one. She wanted to go back to her job, to go to work without seeing the face of a little girl whose father she had murdered, or the nonexistent, frightened face of a dream boy who needed her strength.

▼▼▼

Five children lived in the Child's Wing of the Center. She had always thought the wing housed children who had been bitten by a vampire or whose families had died at a vampire's hands. She had never realized that most of the children lost their fathers due to actions by the Westrina Center itself.

Cammie walked down the hallway, her rubber-soled shoes squeaking on the clean tile. A television blared from the game room. One child sat there, his arms wrapped around himself, eyes staring at nothing. Two other children sat in the sunroom, staring up at the light. But Janie was in her room, stuffed animals surrounding her like a small army.

Cammie took a chair and sat across from Janie. Janie's eyes grew wide, but she didn't move. Cammie slid closer. "Hi," she said. "I want—"

Janie screamed. She grabbed all of her animals against her and screamed as loud as she could. Cammie stood up. She could hear the sound of running feet in the hallway. "It's okay," she said, but the words sounded lame. "I . . ."

Janie's screams echoed in the wide hallway. Anita and two orderlies appeared at the door. "What are you doing?" Anita snapped.

Cammie said nothing. She stared at the terror on the child's face, at the little girl's arms protecting the last things of value in her world. "I'm sorry," Cammie whispered, and ran from the room.

She stopped at the empty reception desk in front and caught her breath. All she had wanted to do was talk to the child, apologize, and perhaps gain a little understanding. The understanding she had gained— but she hadn't expected the cost.

"What the hell were you doing?" Anita asked.

Cammie looked up. Anita stood beside her, arms crossed, the matronly look gone. "She okay?"

"I've got one of the orderlies with her now and I've got a call into Dr. Eliason because he's the only one she trusts." Anita's face was red. "Don't you understand? She hates women. Her father taught her that women are dangerous and you proved it by killing him. What were you trying to do?"

"I was trying to—" Cammie stopped. She couldn't explain, not the dreams, not the desire to get Janie out of her head. "—to talk to her."

"Well, don't," Anita said. "You've got another eradication tomorrow and I want you thinking about that, not some little girl whose life is no longer your concern. And I don't ever want to see you in this wing again. Do you understand that?"

Cammie nodded. She turned her back and walked out the door. The sunlight felt warm and soothing against her face. Dream image. She tried to shake it, but couldn't. She turned back for Anita in time to see Eliason go through the door. She clenched her fist and leaned against the small oak that they had built the sidewalk around. She could talk to Eliason. She would wait.

The sun had nearly set when he finally emerged from the building. Cammie stood, brushed off her jeans and called to him. He looked over. She braced herself for another round of accusations, like the ones she had received from Anita, but he said nothing as he walked over to her.

He took her hand. "You're cold," he said. "Let me get you some coffee."

She didn't argue.

They went to a small coffee shop near the center. The shop was small and smelled of European coffee and fresh-baked pies. Eliason led Cammie to a table near the back.

"She better?" Cammie asked.

Eliason shrugged. "I don't know what better is in this case. Technically she was better when her father was alive."

"You too?" Cammie pushed against the table.

Eliason caught her wrist. "He would have turned on her. They always do. This one's bothering you too much, Cammie."

"No one ever warned me about children."

"No one thought they had to."

She glared at him. The waitress set down two steaming mugs of coffee. Eliason took his, filled it with cream and sugar, and stirred as if nothing were wrong.

"You don't know the history of the Westrina Center, do you?" he asked.

"It's been here forever, and about fifteen years ago, it changed buildings, after this rehabilitation program started."

"Nice, encapsulated, short, and straight out of the manual. Ever wonder why they train so many people like you?"

"Because there's so many vampires."

Eliason smiled and sipped his coffee. "There's not that many vampires."

"They already told us when we started. High burn-out. People last at most three years."

"And you've been here, what? Two?"

"One."

"When did the dreams start?"

Cammie jerked. Eliason stared at her. His eyes were dark brown. She had never noticed that before. "I'm the one with the psych degree," she said.

"But you never use it. Janie doesn't hold the answers for you. She's got to search for her own when she's ready. You, on the other hand, already know how to search."

Cammie felt a blush build on her cheeks. She hadn't meant to disturb the child, but Eliason was right. She hadn't been thinking of anyone but herself. "Why did you ask me about the history of the Center?"

"Because," he said. "About twenty-five years ago, when the rehab program failed, a number of the counselors became vampires themselves. Too many vampires to stop in such a short period of time. The people left worked on keeping the threat from spreading, not at taking care of the vampires who already existed. They lived in an entire section of town, and no one went there, and no one left, not even the children who lived with a vampire, like Janie did. Do you understand me?"

"Not completely." The coffee churned in Cammie's stomach. "The children had to fend for themselves?"

Eliason nodded, then glanced at his watch. "I've got an appointment. Don't push yourself so hard, Cammie. And if you need me, I'll talk to you. I'll help you in any way that I can." He put some money on the table, got up and kissed her cheek. Cammie suppressed an urge to grab his hand and hold him. She felt as if they had been talking about something she almost understood. She took another sip of her coffee, and saw an old building rise unbidden in her mind. The Old Westrina Center. Perhaps the answers to questions she didn't even know awaited her there.

▼▼▼

Cammie pulled up in front of the Westrina Center's former building. It had been abandoned nearly ten years before. Wire fences surrounded it, and garlic had been nailed to the door. All the windows were barred with small crosses, and none had been broken.

She had never stopped here, always preferring to avoid it—to look forward, not back. The new Westrina Center had modern facilities now and a new outlook. She was part of the best rehabilitation movement they had founded. She didn't need to look at the one that had failed.

Until now.

He's just a baby. I take care of him!

The little girl's voice was insistent. Cammie put her hands on the cold wire, but could see no one.

I need to see him. Nobody else knows how to take care of him . . .

She wandered around to the side of the building, saw the half-ruined remains of a playground. The swings were mere chains and the teetertotter had rotted into the earth.

I don't want to play. I want to see him . . .

And then the scream, so long and shrill that she had to close her eyes. The sound ripped the pain from her belly, let it rise into her neck and mouth. She leaned her head into the wire, feeling the metal dig into her forehead.

She had clutched her little brother's hand tightly, as two people, smelling of blood, led her into the center. As they walked into Reception, she was surprised to see how many people waited for her, how quiet they seemed. She said nothing. A slender man knelt beside her, pried her brother's hand from her own. She looked at her brother's face, the face she had protected all this time, and was startled at blood on it. Blood spattered all over his clothes. Tears built behind her eyes, but she didn't let them fall. She hadn't wanted him to know, but there he was, blood-covered and frightened. She reached out to him, but the man picked him up and carried him away.

And she never saw him again. Too dangerous. Too unstable. Too frightened.

She pushed herself away from the fence. Her forehead ached and her entire body shook. She wiped her face with her sleeve, and then looked up. Eliason leaned against a tree, his arms crossed.

"You followed me," she said.

He nodded.

"And you knew."

"Yes," he said. "Current rehabilitation theory. You can't do anything for the parents, but you can save the children."

"I don't feel saved," she said and pushed past him.

"Cammie—"

His voice echoed behind her, one of many trailing into the growing twilight. Her father had called her Camila, her brother Cam-Cam. She had adopted Cammie because it brought no pain. Until now.

▼▼▼

The Center looked cold in the early morning light. Cammie wrapped her old, ragged sweater around her shoulders as she got out of her car. She knew that she shouldn't be there. She wondered what had made her work for the Center at all. Some sort of post-hypnotic suggestion? Something from her past that forced her there?

She smiled without humor. She had spent the entire night worrying about just those things and had come to no conclusion. Except that this eradication would be her last.

She pulled the duffel with her gear out of the car. The duffel seemed heavier than usual. She pulled open the glass doors and found Whitney standing near reception.

"I thought you wouldn't come," he said.

"Been talking to Eliason, huh?"

He shook his head. "It's just happened to me before. I recognize the signs."

"What makes you stay here, year after year?"

"I guess I'm one of the ones who doesn't rehabilitate." He shrugged. "This is the only place that I've ever belonged."

Cammie shifted her duffel onto her shoulder. "Ready?"

Whitney studied her face for a moment. "Yeah." He picked up his gear and they walked back out the door. As they got into the Center's white van, he said, "You're not going to cop out on me, are you?"

"I'll stay," she said.

The van's plastic seat was cold. Cammie tugged on the sleeves of her sweater and closed her eyes. She knew what section of town they were going to; she didn't want to see the drive. Perhaps then, she would be able to concentrate on her work.

When the van stopped, Cammie grabbed her duffel and opened the door before she looked at the neighborhood. They had parked in front of a two-story brownstone, like the one she had grown up in. The apartments inside were long and narrow, and only the back bedroom—the one that had been hers—had windows at all. Perfect vampire country.

Whitney juggled his lock-picker's tools. "Last chance, Cammie."

"I'm going," she snapped.

He yanked his duffel up and climbed the crumbling concrete steps two at a time. Cammie followed, her nervousness like a stone in the center of her stomach. Perhaps she shouldn't have come. If she screwed up, made one single mistake, she would lose her life along with Whitney.

Perhaps that wouldn't be such a bad thing.

She shook the thought. She had to go in with an attitude of strength. In the daylight, she had more power than a vampire. In the daylight, she was the one who brought death.

Whitney scanned the outside wall for a security system. Seeing none, he tried the outside door. The knob turned easily, and the door swung open, revealing a narrow, badly lit hallway. A flight of stairs went up to the left, and to the right another door beckoned. Whitney went to it.

Cammie pulled out her flashlight and illuminated the lock while Whitney picked at it.

The door opened before he could finish. Both Cammie and Whitney backed up. A little boy stood there, his face a mass of bruises, one eye swollen shut. "My daddy's asleep," he said, his voice tight with fear.

A rotted-blood smell seeped into the hallway like a bad dream. Cammie felt nausea return and stifled the urge to bolt.

"Take him to the van," Whitney said.

Cammie shook her head. "Either we both do or neither. That's procedure and you know it."

"Daddy says no one can come in. And I gotta stay." The boy barely spoke above a whisper. "He's asleep."

"And you're not supposed to wake him," Cammie said.

The boy nodded. A tear slipped out of his swollen eye.

"Go sit on the couch," she said. "We'll be out in a moment."

She slid the door open gently—quietly—and walked past the little boy. Whitney followed. Cammie knew this house. She had grown up in one so similar. Light seeped through the back bedroom door, but the other rooms were dark. She followed the smell to the vampire's room, paused for a moment to remove her mallet and stake, then eased the door open.

Dark. And smelling of rot. *Not supposed to go in there.* The little boy's voice or her brother Ben's? She didn't know. Her hands trembled, like they had before. It was the only way, the only solution. If she didn't, he would hit Ben again and maybe kill him, like he had killed that woman in the parking lot—like he had threatened to kill her.

Her eyes slowly adjusted. Pictures hung on the wall. An unused bed stood in the corner. The walk-in closet door was open and the smell seemed to beckon her.

"Wait, Cammie."

Cam-Cam, wait up.

But she couldn't wait. She held the stake and the mallet (dowel and hammer—too big for her small hands) before her like torches. The coffin stuck out a few inches into the room. She walked on one side, saw him sleeping there, so peacefully.

Hard to believe that face could bring such destruction. She knelt. A hand touched her shoulder. She didn't turn, didn't want to see Ben. She placed the dowel over the vampire's heart and brought the hammer down with all of her strength. He roared and sat up, foul breath covering her, stolen blood spattering the walls. She pounded again, ignoring the nails raking into her skin, the too-strong hands yanking at her wrists. She had to keep going. She had to. For Ben, if not herself.

He thrashed, kicked, his foot connecting with her shoulder, nearly knocking her off balance. But she clung to the dowel, kept pounding. Blood gushed from his mouth, through his fanged teeth and across her hands. Still she pounded, thinking it would never end. The stories were wrong. Vampires never died. They sucked life's blood forever.

And then he stopped. His hands slid down the coffin's side and shredded, the skin drying and flaking, the bones yellowing with age.

Behind her, a child cried. A little boy. *Ben.* But she ignored him, leaned her head on the dowel and took a deep breath.

"Daddy," she whispered. But he didn't answer. He would never answer. He had been dead a long time.

She rocked back on her heels, turned and saw Whitney staring at her, his skin white. He clutched the little boy against his chest.

"The child shouldn't have been here," Whitney said.

"He would have known anyway," Cammie said. She stood up and wiped the blood on her jeans. Her last vampire. Now, finally, she could move on. "Let's get his things, take him back to the Center. Anita will take care of him."

She restrained an urge to reach out to the child. She had done that once, with Ben a long time ago. It was one thing to see your father killed. It was another to be held by his killer.

"He'll survive," she said softly. "We did."

And then she left the bedroom, to wash the blood from her hands.

DRACULA
A SELECTED FILMOGRAPHY
▼▼▼

By now, there have been scores of films with the name "Dracula" in the title. The filmography that follows is neither complete nor a list of the "best" of the Dracula films ever made. It is, rather, a list of films that give us a representative range of interpretations the film industry has given to Dracula lore since the first Nosferatu was released in 1922.

DRACULA FILMOGRAPHY

NOSFERATU
Prana Films
1922   (B & W)   72 minutes
Director: F. W. Murnau
Screenplay: Henrik Galeen
Photography: Fritz Arno Wagner, Gunther Krampf
Cast: *Max Schreck, Alexander Granach, Gustav von Wangenheim, Greta Schröder-Matray, Ruth Landshoff, John Gotowt*

Much of the power of this, the first full-length silent-film treatment of Bram Stoker's novel, comes from its very silence which gives all of its scenes a dreamlike eeriness missing even in the best of the talking-film versions of the story.

Fritz Murnau, the director, was prevented by copyright problems from using Stoker's characters. And, though he kept the Transylvania action in Transylvania, he reset the British scenes in Bremen, Germany. But these changes in no way affect the quality of this first and great rendering of Stoker's vampire tale.

Murnau has a keen appreciation for ominous moments and stages them well. There is, for instance, a quick shot of panicking horses early in the film that serves as an effective premonitory signal of dreadful things to come. Under his direction, Wagner and Krumpf's camera, despite the technical limitations the film medium was still struggling with, moves back and forth between light and shade with considerable ominous effect. Max Schreck, playing Count Orlock (read Dracula), with his pale skull-like face, his blazing eyes, pointed ears and long fingernails, looks more like Varney the Vampire than the polished noble-man Stoker imagined and whom Lugosi personified. Still, Orlock moves like animated death, and the ambiguously erotic climactic final scene in which Ellen/Nina (Greta Schröder-Matray) sacrifices herself to the monster for the sake of mankind, has kept audiences bemused for nearly seventy years.

A classic film, occasionally quaint and dated but terrifying at its best.

DRACULA

1931   (B & W)   U.S.A.   84 minutes
Universal Pictures
Director: Tod Browning
Producer: Carl Laemmle, Jr.
Screenplay: Garret Fort and Dudley Murphy
Photography: Karl Freund
Cast: *Bela Lugosi, Helen Chandler, David Manners, Dwight Frye, Edward Van Sloan, Herbert Bunston, Frances Dade*

The so-called "first" Dracula film. See the introductory essay for further comment about this artistically weak but abidingly mythic film whose sixtieth birthday we are celebrating.

SON OF DRACULA

1943   (B & W)   U.S.A.   90 minutes
Universal Pictures
Director: Robert Siodmak
Producer: Jack Gross
Screenplay: Eric Taylor
Photography: George Robinson
Cast: *Lon Chaney, Jr., Louise Allbritton, Robert Paige, Evelyn Ankers, Frank Craven, J. Edward Bromberg, Adeline De Walt*

This is the first Dracula film to have an American setting and it may be that the idea of Dracula in Tennessee is the only bit of distinction one ought to accord it. *Son of Dracula* is not helped by the presence in it of Lon Chaney Jr. who, except when his face is hidden by wolf's hair, never plays anyone but Lon Chaney Jr. Despite the cloak of Dracula he wears, he remains the same impassive, lugubrious, more or less sad-looking character he has always been.

The story: Katherine Caldwell, a wealthy young woman from Tennessee, invites to her family plantation a suave European Count Alucard. Alucard (whose name, spelled backward, tells us who he really is) has promised Katherine a marriage "without material needs. A life that will last throughout eternity." Katherine, however, who is afraid of death, has a marriage of convenience in mind. Once she has been immortalized she means to betray Alucard and immortalize Frank Stanley, the man she really loves. What follows, despite a couple of impressively eerie moments, is deplorable.

DRACULA'S DAUGHTER
1936   (B & W)   U.S.A.   70 minutes
Universal Pictures
Director: Lambert Hillyer
Producer: E. M. Asher
Screenplay: Garret Fort
Photography: George Robinson
Cast: *Otto Kruger, Gloria Holden, Edward Van Sloan, Irving Pichel*

This, the first of the legion of Dracula films that would descend from the Tod Browning–Bela Lugosi venture of 1931, is as a work of art and as an effective horror film superior to its precursor. While Bela Lugosi's niche in the historical memory of filmgoers is unthreatened—he will forever be the vampire of record—Gloria Holden's performance as Dracula's anguished daughter will, I think, be equally cherished, as will the atmosphere of a film whose characters walk like graven images and who talk a language that echoes Marlowe's mighty lines.

Countess Marya Zaleska, Dracula's daughter, is seen, near the opening of the film, at the cremation of her father's body. Standing beside his pyre, shrouded in her cloak and the drifting smoke from the cremation, she gives up his remains to the upper and lower gods as she intones a prayer at once lyric and aweful. The obsequies done, she believes that, with her father's death, the curse of her own vampirism will be lifted.

As it turns out, she is mistaken, and the rest of the film follows her desperate fortunes as, with the fruitless help of a psychiatrist with whom she falls in love, she tries first to be cured of her affliction and then to live with it—and him. But Sandor, her faithful servant, now maddened by jealousy, puts an abortive end to her scheming.

THE HORROR OF DRACULA
1958   (Color)   Great Britain   82 minutes
Hammer Films

Director: Terence Fisher
Producer: Anthony Hinds
Screenplay: Jimmy Sangster
Photography: Jack Asher
Cast: *Peter Cushing, Christopher Lee, Michael Gough, Melissa Stribling, Carol Marsh, Valerie Gaunt, Miles Malleson, John Va Eyssen, Charles Lloyd-Pack*

The Horror of Dracula along with *The Curse of Frankenstein* marked the triumphant revitalization of the horror genre for which Hammer Films was responsible in the middle and late fifties. *The Horror of Dracula* makes fine use of the same talents that launched the Frankenstein venture in the previous year. Terence Fisher directs; Jimmy Sangster is responsible for the screenplay, Jack Asher for the photography.

As with most Hammer productions, this film is lush and lyric and the whiff of the bedroom that comes from it is very strong. More than any of the previous American Dracula films, this one confronts the secret message of the vampire imagery as Bram Stoker developed it in his novel, *Dracula*. I have treated this matter in the essay above. What needs to be said here is that Fisher in *The Horror of Dracula* makes explicit what Stoker only implied: Dracula represents the eroticization of women, and an erotic woman is a threat to middle-class stability. Which is why the most terrifying scene in the film is the one that shows a cluster of good men gathered around the scantily clad body of Lucy to watch as one of their number drives a stake through her voluptuous bosom. The blood (now in dazzling technicolor) spurts full into the camera's eye.

A word about Christopher Lee and his performance here. This was Lee's first interpretation of Dracula. Aware of Lugosi's hold on the characterization, Lee made no effort to imitate it. Instead, thinking his way through to the psychology of Dracula, he imbued his version of the monster with enormous physical strength, with the power that comes from the ability to hold still, and with a sense of remoteness from the rest of mankind that, as Byron long ago understood, has a mysterious attraction for women. The result is that Lee's Dracula is a wholly new, more dynamic, more intelligent, if not more unforgettable creation than Lugosi's.

BILLY THE KID VERSUS DRACULA
1965   (Color)   U.S.A.   84 minutes
Circle Films

Director: William Beaudine
Producer: Carroll Case
Screenplay: Carl Hittleman
Photography: Lothrop Worth
Cast: *John Carradine, Chuck Courtney, Melinda Plowman, Virginia
    Christine, Olive Carey, Harry Carey, Jr., Marjorie Bennett*

Into every film goer's life a truly ridiculous film ought sometimes to
fall. One of them, *Billy the Kid Versus Dracula,* rests on a particularly
soft spot in my heart because it has to be one of the silliest films ever
made and because it has the great Shakespearean actor John Carradine
playing Dracula. This alone gives this trivial venture more weight than it
would otherwise deserve.

Here, as in the much worse companion film, *Jesse James Meets Frankenstein's Daughter,* what William Beaudine is after is a merging of a
cowboy with a vampire film. There is a certain vigor in the idea of the
central-European count, bowed by the weight of his suave corruptions,
picking his way among the cowflops on the western plains. Beaudine's
brash imagination gives us a scene in which Billy the Kid squeezes his
six-shooter empty, firing point-blank at Dracula, who is wearing a red
foulard around his neck and a black cloak with a red silk lining.

It is fruitless to look for meaning in this film. Much better just to sit
back and watch John Carradine's Dracula emitting a Shakespearean
aura even as he turns his intelligent eyes on the ingenue whose uncle he
pretends to be and whose blood he means to take.

THE FEARLESS VAMPIRE KILLERS
1967   (Color)   Great Britain   107 minutes
Cadre Films/Filmways
Director: Roman Polanski
Producer: Gene Gutowski
Screenplay: Gerald Brach, Roman Polanski
Photography: Douglas Slocombe
Cast: *Jack MacGowran, Roman Polanski, Alfie Bass, Sharon Tate,
    Ferdy Mayne and Fiona Lewis*

The chief rewards of this film are wit, charm and visual beauty, particularly in snow scenes and in a thematically unnecessary but exquisite
Danse Macabre sequence.

The Brach–Polanski screen play has a team of vampire hunters that include Professor Ambronius, a dimwit academic, formerly at the University of Königsberg, and his incompetent assistant, Freddy, who are on a mission in Transylvania to kill the vampires there. They take rooms in the village inn and prepare to do battle with the local vampires, who are a Count Von Krolock and his homosexual son. These two live (if that is the right word for creatures who are dead) in a sprawling castle on the hill.

The most hilarious scene is the one that shows us the Jewish innkeeper, who has been turned into a vampire, mounting the stairs to his gentile chambermaid's room. The young woman, for whom he lusted when he was alive, sees his fangs and knows just what to do. She reaches up and takes the crucifix hanging above her on the wall and holds it out to ward him off, but he chuckles and in his best Yiddish accent says, "Oy lady, hev you got the wrong vempire."

Dracula's name is never mentioned in *The Fearless Vampire Killers* but vampire lore and, particularly, the Dracula movies that Hammer Films made, are the stuff of which this fine and lushly erotic satire is woven.

DRACULA
    1974   (Color)   U.S.A./Great Britain   100 minutes
    Universal Pictures
    Director: Dan Curtis
    Producer: Dan Curtis
    Screenplay: Richard Matheson
    Photography: Oswald Morris
    Cast: *Jack Palance, Simon Ward, Nigel Davenport, Pamela Brown,*
        Fiona Lewis, Penelope Horner, Murray Brown

By 1974, when this film was made, two great Draculas had appeared on the screen: Bela Lugosi and Christopher Lee. One has to wonder what intuition went askew or what sober misjudgement was made that prompted Dan Curtis to cast Jack Palance as Dracula.

The film has wonderful things in its favor. Curtis as producer/director and Matheson, a fine prose slinger, as the author of its screenplay. It is, too, one of the few versions of the Dracula story that makes some effort to follow Stoker's story and to link Count Dracula to the historical Vlad Tepes. And yet the film is inert.

Palance, I'm afraid, is the problem. The face that was able to project so much malevolence in *Shane* resolutely refuses to be taken seriously as belonging to Dracula. Nor is that all. Palance's accent is so unalterably American that one has trouble associating it with the arch-villain from Transylvania. Finally, because Palance seems not to understand that the vampire Bram Stoker imagined threatens not only the body but the soul, he is incapable of making grandly wicked gestures or of suggesting how attractive evil can be. We know that there is a bad guy on the screen and that his name is Mr. Dracula, but Satan's great emissary on earth, Count Dracula, is flapping his wings in some other movie, not the one we have come to see.

LOVE AT FIRST BITE

1979 (Color) U.S.A. 96 minutes
Simon Productions
Director: Stan Dragoti
Producer: Robert Kaufman
Screenplay: Robert Kaufman
Photography: Edward Rosson
Cast: *George Hamilton, Susan Saint James, Richard Benjamin,
Dick Shawn, Arte Johnson*

Love at First Bite is a frolicsome and hilarious sendup of the vampire genre that will leave horror fans grateful for the respect that director Stan Dragoti shows for their genre at the same time as it will have them chortling at the absurd ways in which blood lust can be linked to the more usual lust.

Dracula, we are asked to believe, is forced to leave his ancestral castle in Transylvania because it has been taken over by the communist regime that rules his country. The vampire, ever adaptable, makes his way to Manhattan, partly in pursuit of a liberated young woman whose picture he has seen. His adventures with her in a post-post-Freudian Manhattan is what the rest of the film is about. George Hamilton outdoes Lugosi in the European charm business and Susan St. James twinkles as she and the king vampire exchange one-liners. Both of them, to the filmgoer's delight, savor the romantic sexual aura in which the film envelops them.

NOSFERATU

1979 (Color) Germany 107 minutes
Filmproduktion/Beaumont

Director: Werner Herzog
Producer: Werner Herzog
Photography: Jeorg Schmidt-Reitwein
Cast: *Klaus Kinski, Isabelle Adjani, Bruno Ganz, Roland Topor, Walter Ladengast*

Herzog, properly appreciative of F. W. Murnau's great achievement in his 1922 silent version of the Dracula story, achieves something of a *tour de force* here in this talking color treatment of the tale: he frequently recreates the languorous, dreamlike atmosphere with which Murnau imbued his film.

Critics have properly complained that Herzog's *Nosferatu* does not scare anyone. On the other hand, it does create a subtle and lingering fear that none of the other versions of the story have even touched on: the fear of achieved immortality. No one who has seen Klaus Kinski's performance as the boneless and endlessly weary vampire will ever think well of the Devil's promise of eternal life. Beyond that triumph of characterization, the film gives us some of the most glorious visual sequences ever filmed by a camera.

DRACULA

1979   (Color)   U.S.A.   112 minutes
Mirisch Corporation for Universal Pictures
Director: John Badham
Producer: Walter Mirisch
Screenplay: W. Richter
Photography: Gilbert Taylor
Cast: *Frank Langella, Laurence Olivier, Donald Plesence, Kate Nelligan, Trevor Eve, Jan Francis, Tony Hagarth*

This is Frank Langella's film. Langella, who triumphed in the role on the Broadway stage is equally impressive here. And what Langella radiates as he struts and preens and prances about in this lush production, is the superabundant lust for life that has to be the first requirement for anyone who wants to make it as a vampire. Langella is vibrant, violent and overwhelmingly romantic.

What we have then, is a lavish production on which no expenditures have been spared. We have Langella as the dazzling Count and a very muted but still very great Laurence Olivier playing Dr. Van Helsing, and we have also various delicious looking ladies either endangered or saved from damnation. With so much vibrant stuff going on, we may forget that the film is almost never scary.